T0209215

# RETRIBUTION
# TIMES
## TWO

PAUL MARK TAG

# RETRIBUTION TIMES TWO

*iUniverse books may be ordered through booksellers or by contacting:*

*iUniverse*
*1663 Liberty Drive*
*Bloomington, IN 47403*
*www.iuniverse.com*
*844-349-9409*

*Because of the dynamic nature of the Internet, any web addresses or links contained in this book may have changed since publication and may no longer be valid. The views expressed in this work are solely those of the author and do not necessarily reflect the views of the publisher, and the publisher hereby disclaims any responsibility for them.*

*Any people depicted in stock imagery provided by Getty Images are models, and such images are being used for illustrative purposes only. Certain stock imagery © Getty Images.*

*Flag art by Archelle Wolst*

*ISBN: 978-1-6632-2226-8 (sc)*
*ISBN: 978-1-6632-2254-1 (hc)*
*ISBN: 978-1-6632-2225-1 (e)*

*Library of Congress Control Number: 2022912116*

*Print information available on the last page.*

*iUniverse rev. date: 06/14/2021*

To Robin Brody,

who has read and critiqued, one chapter at a time,
every word of fiction I've written over the past twenty years.

I thank him for his keen eye for detail and
his insistence that I get it right.
Most of all, I thank him for being my friend.

# ACKNOWLEDGMENTS

I am indebted to many others who made the completion of this book possible. Foremost on the list is my wife, Becky, who gave me both emotional support and critical guidance for the three-plus years that it took to develop, research, and write this story. Besides Becky, my enduring thanks go to my primary reader, Robin Brody who, week after week, met me for lunch to review each of the fifty-nine chapters as I wrote them. As I've often said, Robin knows my books as well as I do.

Once I completed the first draft, I turned the manuscript over to ten readers who were the first to read the entire story. They made numerous corrections and suggestions for improvement. In alphabetical order, they were: Doug Basham, Bud Booth, Leonard Dickstein, Peggy Dold, Dan Duryea, Michael Guy, Jeff Hawkins, Kris Hoffman, Fran Morris, and Ann Schrader. Of these, I offer special thanks to Michael Guy, who not only provided editorial review but was always available when I needed editorial advice. His ability to "turn a phrase" is unsurpassed.

In terms of specific areas of expertise, I single out four of the reviewers above. In addition to their contributions in general, Leonard Dickstein made vital weapons' selection recommendations; Doug Basham critiqued the aviation aspects of the manuscript; and Bud Booth and Jeff Hawkins reviewed the satellite references.

I thank artist Archelle Wolst for designing the flag art for the cover and for her patience in bringing to life the concept I had in mind.

Finally, I thank my story editor, Bill Thompson. He provided much-needed encouragement as well as critical recommendations for improving the storyline.

Everyone referenced above provided accurate and relevant information and advice. If you discover errors in the book and are looking for someone to blame, look no further than the author whose name appears on the cover.

# AUTHOR'S NOTE

*Retribution Times Two* is a work of fiction. All characters, names, incidents, organizations, and dialogue in this novel are either the product of the author's imagination or are used fictitiously. I have attempted to create an interesting story within realistic scientific, theoretical, temporal, and geographic boundaries. But before you begin readiing, please take note of what I have to say below.

In my thrillers, I have personally scouted many of the geographic locations and documented the GPS coordinates. You can go to my website, www.paulmarktag.com, where I have posted satellite images for all chapters. Alternatively, the reader can visualize all locations cited in this book using Google Earth software to view earth locations using satellite imagery. Type into your computer browser "Google Earth" and follow the directions for loading the software. Then insert the chapter GPS locations to see where the action unfolds. For example, from Prologue Number 1, type in 50° 5' 35"N 14° 26' 22"E, and you will find yourself looking at the Hotel Hilton in Prague, Czech Republic. Do the same for Prologue Number 2: 23° 6' 34"N 82° 26' 33"W. This time, you will arrive at the Hotel Melia in Havana, Cuba. My wife, Becky, and I have stayed at both locations and have imagined the action occurring there.

As well as location, please note the date and time at the beginning of each chapter, particularly early on. Except for the two Prologues and two Epilogues, all action takes place in late March and early April of 2018. All chapters and scenes move forward either simultaneously or sequentially in time. The story evolves across three time zones:

PDT, Pacific Daylight Time; EDT, Eastern Daylight Time; and MSK, Moscow Standard Time. Remember that Russia does not observe daylight saving time.

IMPORTANT NOTE: The level of detail available at the beginning of all chapters (location, date, and time) is not meant to intimidate the reader. As I wrote the book, I needed that degree of spatial and temporal detail to ensure that the story was both feasible and logical. As you will see, there are times when multiple actions (scenes) evolve very quickly, sometimes within seconds or minutes of each other. My goal as a writer, as always, is for the reader to have a good time and to enjoy the story. Please use only what information seems to be important to you and ignore the rest.

As hard as I have tried, I am sure that mistakes remain in the manuscript. *Retribution Times Two* is a complex thriller with many moving parts, written from multiple points of view. If you find a *significant* error, and you are the first to notify me of that error, I will give you the choice of one of my earlier novels for free. Please go easy on me. If I am off by three minutes on one of my chapter timings, that doesn't count. Don't forget that this is a work of fiction, and I can bend the rules.

Finally, please note the Cast of Characters section at the beginning of the book and the Glossary section at the end. The information there may assist the reader as the action unfolds.

# CAST OF CHARACTERS

Baxter, John—Chairman of the Joint Chiefs of Staff

Brickman, Judy—Raymond Brickman's wife

Brickman, Raymond Charles III—co-antagonist, responsible for threatening to destroy U.S. weather satellites

Bristow, Navy LCDR John—NCDE employee who assists Silverstein

Brody, Dr. Eli—neurologist from the Stanford University School of Medicine, hired by the CIA for Dmitri Smirnov

Bryan, Jeremy—NSOF satellite code expert, employed by Lopez to decipher Brickman's typing

Cadillac, Susan—veteran CNN journalist and broadcaster

Craver, John—on-call night editor for *The Washington Post* on March 29, 2018

Duringham, Bob—TSA chief at the San Francisco airport

Erickson, Kathy Ann; AKA, Viktoriya Ratimirovna Popova—co-antagonist, holds Russia responsible for killing her family in Afghanistan

Flanagan, Jim—NSOF employee working the night shift on Thursday, March 29, 2018

Gomez, Juan Francisco—alleged hitman for Joaquin Guzman, otherwise known as El Chapo

Guzman, Joaquin—AKA El Chapo, Mexican drug king-pin extradited to the U.S. in 2017

Ham, Rachel—*The Washington Post* employee who answers the call from Brickman on March 29, 2018

Hammer, Major Rick—Air Force pilot for the Pave Hawk helicopter

Hancock, Major General Winfield—commander of the Union's Army of the Potomac's II Corps, against General Lee's assault on the Union line at Cemetery Ridge, known as Pickett's Charge, July 3, 1863

Hancock, Steve—head of NSOF

Henderson, Rick—pilot for Kipling's aircraft from San Jose to Pittsburgh

Hermosa, Julie—CIA agent tasked with photographing Judy Brickman in Charlottesville, North Carolina

Ivanov, Artur—Directorate I agent enlisted by Popov to track down his niece

Jackson, Calvin Emmett—Silverstein's alias in confronting Brickman at his house in Silver Spring

Jimenez, Tech Sergeant Albert—loadmaster for the Pave Hawk helicopter

Jones, Howard Edward—great-great-great-grandfather of Brickman, fought under General Lee and died at the Battle of Gettysburg

Kandronich, Olexi—Russian Prime Minister, second in command to Vladimir Putin

Kipling, Dr. Linda Ann—co-protagonist, scientist at the Naval Research Laboratory in Monterey, California; works for Silverstein

Longway, Henry—replacement head of NSOF after the murder of Hancock

Lopez, Hector Rodriguez—senior counterintelligence agent for the CIA

MacDonald, Skip—copilot for Kipling's aircraft flying from San Jose to Pittsburgh

Manchester, Colonel Mylene—Army surgeon at the Walter Reed National Military Medical Center in Bethesda, Maryland

Marshall, Jimmy—low-level staffer for *The Washington Post* on March 29, 2018

Martell, Sue—co-owner of the tech company, Preemptive Computer Resolutions

McElroy, Tom—editor-in-chief of *The Washington Post*

McFadden, Alexandria Jane—Director of the CIA

Medvedev, Dmitry—President of the Russian Federation from 2008 to 2012

Miller, Marc—Hector Lopez's assistant at the CIA

Mutinoff, Alexander—Russian ambassador to the United States

Newhower, Robert—American ambassador to the Russian Federation

Obama, Barack—President of the United States from 2009 to 2017

Orlov, Major Yuri—watch commander at the Main Centre for Missile Attack Warning in Russia

Petrov, Nikola—Soviet agent who in 1980 developed a nation-wide DNA repository for the Soviet Union; received Hero of Labor of the Russian Federation award for development of that system

Popov, Alexei—younger brother to Viktoriya; killed in a bombing in Afghanistan in 1979

Popova, Viktoriya Ratimirovna, AKA Kathy Ann Erickson—one of two principal antagonists, holds Russia responsible for killing her family in Afghanistan

Popov, Oleg Vladimirovich—Deputy Director, SVR Directorate X, Science and Technology, Russian Federation

Popov, Ratimir Vladimirovich—Brother to Oleg Popov, father to Viktoriya Popova and Alexei Popov

Putin, Vladimir Vladimirovich—President of the Russian Federation from 2000 to 2008, and again from 2012 to the present

Robinson, Jim—U.S. Secretary of Defense

Smith, Captain Henry—Air Force copilot for the Pave Hawk helicopter

Stepanov, Igor—Deputy Director of SVR Directorate I, Computer Science, Russian Federation

Silverstein, Dr. Victor Mark—co-protagonist, senior scientist, Naval Research Laboratory, Monterey, California

Smirnov, Dmitri—Russian spy for the SVR (Foreign Intelligence Service)

Thomas, Mike—local reporter for KFKA, CBS affiliate for the Fort Collins-Greeley, Colorado area

Trump, Donald John—President of the United States in 2018

Ulrich, Henry—co-owner of the company, Preemptive Computer Resolutions

West, Clark—on-air announcer for radio station KCBS in San Francisco, California

Wilkinson, Major Frederick—CIA McFadden's communication interface in the White House Situation Room

Wilson, Dan—CNN Pentagon reporter

# PROLOGUE NUMBER 1

## ATHENA

*Hotel Hilton, Prague, Czech Republic*
*50° 5' 35"N Latitude, 14° 26' 22"E Longitude*
*Thursday, April 8, 2010, 10:25 AM*

The START I treaty represented the most complicated and ambitious arms control agreement ever enacted between two world powers. The acronym START stood for *Strategic Arms Reduction Treaty*. It was created to reduce the proliferation of nuclear weapons, which had advanced to the point where both the U.S. and Russia could destroy each other many times over. Initially proposed by President Ronald Reagan, the agreement took nearly a decade to complete, beginning in May 1982. President George H. W. Bush and Soviet General Secretary Mikhail Gorbachev signed it on July 31, 1991, four months before the collapse of the Soviet Union.

START I expired on December 5, 2009, and was significant in reducing by some 80% the number of strategic nuclear weapons.

Recognizing that a follow-up agreement to START I would be in both countries' interests, work continued on both a START II and START III treaty. Neither came to fruition. But on May 24,

2002, Presidents Vladimir Putin and George W. Bush signed a new agreement in Moscow, SORT, which stood for *Strategic Offensive Reductions Treaty*, otherwise known as the Treaty of Moscow. Unlike START, SORT addressed limitations to warheads in the field deployed operationally, in contrast to START's emphasis on limiting warheads according to their delivery method. This new treaty was set to expire in December 2012.

So as not to lose momentum, and recognizing the impending endings for START I and SORT, both countries struggled to create a new agreement. It was called New Start, officially named the *Treaty between the United States of America and the Russian Federation on Measures for the Further Reduction and Limitation of Strategic Offensive Arms*—or, in Russian, where U.S. and Russian country names were reversed, Договор между Российской Федерацией и Соединёнными Штатами Америки о мерах по дальнейшему сокращению и ограничению стратегических наступательных вооружений.

The idea this time was to reduce strategic nuclear launch platforms by half. Presidents Barack Obama of the United States and Dmitry Medvedev of Russia, both relative newcomers to their positions, signed that agreement on April 8, 2010.

Following that signing, something unusual occurred. To Obama's surprise, because it had not been part of the schedule, Medvedev invited him to an adjoining room on the Hotel Hilton's top floor. Obama learned immediately that Medvedev had a good command of English. Accordingly, the meeting proceeded unnoticed by both the press and either president's handlers.

Obama was also amazed at Medvedev's sudden change of tone, more informal, differing significantly from the game face he had projected during the signing. Pacing back and forth, he railed over the insanity of nuclear weapons and the reality that neither side could, in practice, use them.

"They're useless," said Medvedev, emotionally. "Worse than useless because they cost our countries a fortune to maintain." What worried him most was the possibility of an accidental launch, one that could instantly lead to World War III. He said that he was amazed that there had been no such incident so far.

Obama knew perfectly well the risks involved. His advisors had briefed him on several terrifying incidents that had occurred over the decades, involving both American and Russian launch vehicles.

As if they had been friends for decades, Medvedev took a seat next to Obama. "What I'm going to propose to you now is so controversial that if my government knew what I was doing, I would be on my way to Siberia." He paused before making his next point. "I've been watching you, and I think that we have been cut from similar cloth, that you would not be averse to a solution to this problem."

Obama, who understood that skepticism was an essential human asset, wondered if this might be some sort of trick. Still, judging from the sweat forming on Medvedev's brow, Obama felt obliged to listen. Without thinking, he glanced about the room, looking for potential surveillance equipment.

Medvedev replied reassuringly. "There are no bugs, Mr. President. I can promise you that."

Still on the alert, Obama chose to keep his powder dry. "No one would argue with you about the danger of an accidental launch."

Medvedev chose his words carefully, speaking slowly. "I want you and me to agree on the creation of a safety valve, a way to stop an accidental launch if it should happen, before it triggers a retaliation. One of my scientists—whom I trust completely—has told me how the concept would work and how we could install this system covertly on a nuclear missile using software alone. He says that his design will work on both U.S. and Russian missiles."

His interest peaked, Obama leaned toward Medvedev, who continued. "I am willing to share this technology with you, but we need to be very careful. I recommend that only one person on each side be involved in the primary interactions. Beyond him, there can only be a handful of people who would do the actual implementation. I'm confident that I can make this happen on my end. I'm here to ask you if you think you can do the same."

Obama recognized the one colossal weakness to Medvedev's proposal. "The downside is obvious. How confidant are you that someone couldn't hack into our systems and make all of our nuclear missiles useless?"

Medvedev shot to his feet. "You're a smart man, Mr. President. That is precisely the question I posed. My scientist tells me that this cannot happen with his design. This code is *physically and mechanically fenced*—that's the way he puts it—from the Internet. Only the country to whom the missile belonged could activate the procedure.

Medvedev held up his finger. "But your point is well taken. My generals and yours as well will *never* accept that this failsafe mechanism could not be compromised. That is why, if either of us tried to promote the idea on our own, we'd face extreme opposition. That is why I suggest that the technical discussions involve just one person from each side. For us, I have someone in mind; he's a member of our foreign intelligence division. I've known him for twenty-five—."

Medvedev cut himself off. "Please! Tell me what you think about what I'm proposing."

Obama was intrigued. That this idea had come directly from the president of the Russian Federation was remarkable. "I'm trying to imagine what your reaction would be if our roles were reversed, if I had presented this idea to you. Surely you would be suspicious too."

Medvedev exploded with passion. "Goddammit, Mr. President! Work with me here! What can I do to convince you that I am sincere?"

Obama thought it over, considering the risks. "You've made a persuasive argument. You must understand that I won't commit until I'm convinced that what you say is true."

Medvedev nodded. "Of course! I would expect nothing less. Do you have anyone in mind to act as your representative?"

Obama remembered meeting a very capable scientist who worked for the Naval Research Laboratory in Monterey, California. Only a month or two after taking office, Obama had attended a secret Central Intelligence Agency (CIA) function where this individual had received a distinguished award for *unselfishly committing himself to the greater good of human society.* "I do," Obama said. "He is one of our Navy civilian scientists, probably the most brilliant person I've ever met. And I'm confident I can trust him."

"выдающийся! Outstanding! I propose that these two meet secretly, maybe back here in Prague." Medvedev reached for a decanter of liquid that Obama assumed was vodka. He poured two glasses, and the two toasted the potential agreement that had arisen between them.

Medvedev seemed pleased and had calmed down. "If you will permit me the honor, Mr. President, I propose that we give our project a secret code name. What would you say to calling it Project Athena, after the Greek goddess?"

Obama's first thought was that Athena made no sense. "Wasn't she the goddess of war?"

Medvedev smiled and nodded. "Very astute, Mr. President. You are correct. But she is also the goddess of reason and wisdom. And that is what I'd like to think you and I are, in our own small way, contributing to the realities of modern warfare. Without those two qualities, one of these days we *will* have war. That, my friend, I am sure of."

# PROLOGUE NUMBER 2

## ON ASSIGNMENT

*Hotel Melia, Havana, Cuba*
*23° 6' 34"N Latitude, 82° 26' 33"W Longitude*
*Saturday, October 21, 2017, 7:20 PM*

Dr. Victor Mark Silverstein wasn't expecting much to come of this assignment. On the positive side, he was adapting to his new role as a spy, at the same time acknowledging that his old disposition as the gruff, know-it-all scientist would be hard to change. He needed to wrap his brain around a different, more flexible persona, one that could adapt to situations quickly.

His partner in crime, Dr. Linda Ann Kipling, had left him at the banquet table to fend for himself, claiming an upset stomach. The dinner at the Melia Habana Hotel in Havana had progressed from the shrimp appetizer to the salad. To Silverstein's left sat Dmitri Smirnov, the principal Soviet representative to the conference.

Silverstein had known Smirnov for years, back when Silverstein earned 100% of his keep as the Navy's preeminent scientist. But now, NRL's lead scientist would, on occasion, serve the *greater good*. One Hector Rodriquez Lopez at the CIA had convinced him and Kipling that their "unique talents and skills" could be put to better use at a higher level within the government. Silverstein and Kipling kept their government positions as research scientists but were essentially *on call* to the CIA. When that happened, their official positions remained as cover.

Smirnov would not have known about Silverstein's change in status. Only one person outside of the CIA, the superintendent of the Naval Research Laboratory in Monterey, knew of his and Kipling's dual role. In both national and international circles, he remained Dr. Victor Mark Silverstein, meteorologist/overall scientist extraordinaire. Kipling's position description read similarly. On the other hand, Silverstein had long known that Smirnov was a Russian agent.

This international conference on climate change—roughly the thirteenth since the first in 2008—was sponsored by Russia. Hence, the Cuban location. It was no secret that Putin wanted to stick it to President Trump, who had declared his opposition to the Paris Climate Accord. Having signed on to the Iran nuclear deal, Russia was also taken aback by Trump's threat to leave that agreement. Silverstein had concluded that if Putin had interfered with the 2016 Presidential election, he had long since kicked himself in the ass for backing the wrong horse.

Alternatively, Silverstein could imagine Putin's delight at making the United States look weak when it came to environmental compliance, even though Russia was decades behind the rest of the Western world in mitigating the effects of fossil fuels.

At the same time Silverstein felt the vibration in his pants pocket, Smirnov attempted conversation with his old friend. Although Silverstein spoke a little Russian, Smirnov's English was far better. "When will your government come to its senses?" he asked. "For the life of me, I cannot understand how you, of anyone from the Western world, could oppose doing something about climate change. No?

"Does no one in your state of Florida read the newspapers? It won't be long before they're wearing rubber boots if sea levels continue to rise." Smirnov had drunk too much vodka, which perhaps was why he was making perfect sense. "Over the past decades, you've continually painted us as the bad guys, and sometimes I've had to agree with you…."

Silverstein pretended to listen but had tuned out his colleague's diatribe. He took a sneak peek at Kipling's text on his phone. She offered no encouragement.

This assignment had to do with the recent U.S. Embassy's partial exodus from Cuba. Staff members had mysteriously taken ill, and a few had serious complaints, including loss of hearing. News reports suggested that Cuba had employed ultrasonic devices to either spy on or harass the embassy staff. Cuban officials had vigorously denied these claims. Nothing about this mystery made sense.

For openers, President Obama's inroads into establishing diplomatic ties with Cuba had produced nothing but positives for the Cuban economy. Yankee tourists were visiting the island in droves and leaving behind their greenbacks. Why would Raoul Castro do anything to cause visitors to have second thoughts about a Cuban vacation?

Second, physical complaints like those from U.S. embassy personnel had also come from the Canadian embassy. Everyone knew that Canada and Cuba were on good terms.

Third, U.S. scientists, including Silverstein, had offered up a few significant realities, namely that it was virtually impossible to cause much havoc using ultrasonic frequencies. Ultrasonic waves did not penetrate walls, for example.

And fourth, if Cuba was involved, why had they invited U.S investigators to visit and research the issue.

Some suspected Russia instead. Not particularly happy that Washington was making nice with one of its usual allies—scarcely one hundred miles from Key West, the southern-most point of Florida—might Russia be behind this mischief?

And so it was that Silverstein and Kipling, as part of the U.S. contingent to the conference, had been sent to investigate. As Silverstein ate dinner, Kipling was making her rounds playing the tourist. In addition to her exceptional observational skills, inside her backpack were miniaturized electronics to detect and isolate both infrasound (a more practical frequency with which to cause trouble) and ultrasound transmissions. In her phone text, Kipling reported that she had discovered nothing—not unexpected since there had been no further reports of problems from embassy personnel since the previous spring.

While Kipling played itinerant spy, Silverstein tread carefully with Smirnov, attempting to secure a perspective from within a country that many would consider America's primary antagonist.

"Dmitri, I hear you. Don't you think I agree? More Americans than not are unhappy for pulling out of Paris."

Silverstein hoped to take advantage of Dmitri's impaired mental condition. "Maybe you should tell your leader to be more careful next time. Trump said during his campaign that he thought global warming was a hoax. We have a saying in America: *Be careful what you wish for.*"

The fog that Silverstein had noticed in Dmitri's eyes evaporated, and they locked eyes. "You Americans want to blame us for everything." But then, he caught Silverstein off guard. After turning his head side to side, looking about the room, Smirnov leaned closer. "Comrade Victor. We have known each other for thirty-some years now. We can trust each other, can we not? No?"

Silverstein's response was sincere and truthful. "I would never betray you, Dmitri. Never!"

———◆———

There was good reason for Silverstein's candid reply. It was perhaps an exaggeration to suggest that Smirnov had saved Silverstein's life. But not by much! They had first met in 1984, well before the fall of the German wall in 1989 and the breakup of the Soviet Union in 1991. They were attending the 9th International Cloud Physics Conference in Tallinn, Estonia, both young scientists at the time.

Fittingly, Silverstein and Smirnov met at a session on nuclear winter, the prolonged period of cooling expected after a nuclear war threw up soot that blocked the sun. Silverstein remembered the eerie quiet in the hall where the U.S. and U.S.S.R.—two adversaries who had the potential to create such an event—sat adjacent to each other pondering the unthinkable. On the positive side, these two scientists became friends.

The incident that linked their lives forever occurred three years later in South America. It had been another international conference, and the two had opted to have dinner in town. On their stroll back to the hotel, several thugs attacked them. The situation quickly became ugly. When the local toughs proceeded to pull knives, Silverstein feared for his life.

Both he and Smirnov did themselves proud. But had not another group of conference-goers happened along, yelling and screaming, they might both have been hacked to death. As it happened, after Smirnov had successfully neutralized one of the attackers, he turned to help Silverstein, and that was when he suffered a knife wound to his side.

An ambulance arrived, and Silverstein accompanied his now-to-be lifelong friend to the hospital. The wound was serious, but Smirnov recovered.

————◆◆◆————

Silverstein watched as the glaze returned to Smirnov's eyes. "I tell you the truth, Victor." Again, he looked around the room. "I have no way of knowing whether someone tried to make mischief with your election. Like you, I am just a lowly government scientist. What can you tell me?" The preceding month Lopez had shown Silverstein proof that Russia had hacked the Democratic computer servers.

"You've heard the same reports as I have, from our security services who say they have proof." Silverstein held up his hands to bolster his upcoming fib. "Who should I believe? My computer friends tell me that with Internet transmissions bouncing off servers around the world, it's impossible to trace the origins of a hack."

Silverstein chose to press his actual agenda, all the while making it seem to be an aside. "What do you think is happening here in Cuba?"

Smirnov's expression stiffened. "You're referring to the ultrasonic sounds that are supposedly making your people sick? No?"

Silverstein nodded. "From what I've read, the attacks started about a year ago and ended last April."

Smirnov shifted nervously in his seat. "I suppose you think we're to blame for that too?"

"Is that so far-fetched? Putin seems to take pleasure in sowing discontent between us and those who might become our friends."

Smirnov protested. "Now that is not fair, my dear Victor. What about our recent support in the UN, where we voted for the North Korean sanctions as you asked?" Smirnov leaned closer. "You want to talk about disruptions? Look no further than your president. Now he's going after the Iran nuclear agreement that Obama worked so hard for. *No one*, including us, wants *that deal* to fall apart." Smirnov pointed his finger. "And who in their right mind would taunt Kim Jong Un the way Trump is doing? Out of respect for you, my friend, I will not repeat some of the adjectives I've heard describing your president."

After a pause, Smirnov sighed and continued. "I wish I could give you more information, but just because you and I work for our governments doesn't mean we know anything. At least I don't." Smirnov smiled. "Unless you've been holding out on me."

Silverstein added, mostly as a private joke to himself, "I doubt either of us would make very good spies."

From Silverstein's viewpoint, the conversation was going nowhere. He was anxious to compare notes with Kipling.

———◆◆———

On his way out of the banquet hall, Dmitri Smirnov reflected on his conversation with Silverstein. Yes, they were friends. Although they were adversaries as well, he felt almost guilty about his deception. But such was the nature of spying.

For openers, Smirnov knew that Russia had meddled with a few Democratic computer servers during the 2016 U.S. presidential election. *Why* had they done it? Because absolutely *no one* in the Russian hierarchy thought that Trump had a snowball's chance in hell of winning the election! Trump had come across as an egotistical, immature, man-child bully that Smirnov would have bet his last ruble that American voters would reject. The American psyche was unfathomable.

Smirnov couldn't help but smile to himself. The irony of it all! *It had all been an afterthought*: Putin had casually suggested that his cyber interference team "play around" and see what kind of havoc they could create in the American election. Never in his wildest imagination did he expect anything to come of it. When Trump won the election, and Democrats started looking for a scapegoat, they stumbled across the Russian hacks. Because of pending retaliatory sanctions and general ill will from the Americans, Russia had come out on the losing end of this affair. Already, within Russian security channels, this debacle was becoming known as the Russian Fiasco of 2016.

Concerning Cuba, Smirnov knew that his government had nothing to do with the strange occurrences at the U.S. embassy. Russia's SVR (Foreign Intelligence Service) had contacted Cuban security services and had received assurance that they were innocent as well. So, what was going on?

After months of study, the SVR concluded that this was another example of mass hysteria, a psychologically induced effect transmitted among individuals. Smirnov knew that such an effect could be behavioral or medical. He remembered the 2009 event in Afghanistan. Schoolgirls started reporting dizziness with fainting. Many citizens suspected poisoning by the Taliban. Several organizations, including the United Nations and the World Health Organization, went to investigate. After testing blood, urine, and water samples, no toxins were ever found.

Smirnov had googled "mass hysteria" and had learned of other similar incidents throughout history. American historians had long ago concluded that the effects attributed to "witches" during the late 1600s in the United States were caused by mass hysteria.

Having come to this deduction regarding American embassy personnel, the SVR had discreetly contacted their counterparts at the CIA to offer their assessment. Smirnov wondered if they had even listened. Certainly, Silverstein had not brought up this theory. And so, from Smirnov's perspective, the evening with Silverstein had been of little consequence.

# 1

## RETRIBUTION ONE

*Silver Spring, Maryland*
*39° 3' 42"N Latitude, 76° 59' 38"W Longitude*
*Sunday, March 18, 2018, 9:30 PM (EDT)*

Raymond Charles Brickman III considered himself a proud Southerner. His great-great-grandfather, Howard Edward Jones, had fought under General Lee and died at Gettysburg. Jones had been part of Lee's final desperate assault on the Union line at Cemetery Ridge, where more than 12,000 of Lee's infantry made one final attempt to turn the tide. Their goal had been to attack the center of the Union's Army of the Potomac's II Corps, commanded by Major General Winfield Hancock.

The Confederates failed, forcing Lee's retreat south to Virginia. That costly battle, known as Picket's Charge, took place on the 3rd of July in 1863. Hancock had been famously heroic during these battles, charging into the fight alongside his men. Even after being severely wounded on that day, he refused to move to the rear. Brickman cursed his foolish risk-taking and considered him personally responsible for Jones's demise. That Hancock would later become the Democratic nominee for President in 1880 added salt to the wound.

The Battle of Gettysburg resulted in more than 51,000 casualties, with 7,000 dead, the highest number for a single battle in the Civil War. With Gettysburg considered by historians to represent the turning point of the war, Brickman cursed the shameful reality that not one person in his circle of southern relatives even remembered such important historical details. But *he* remembered.

On April 9, 1865, General Lee surrendered to General Grant at the Appomattox Courthouse in Virginia. For Brickman, that disgrace—and the accompanying social ramifications—cried out for retribution. Jones had been a prosperous plantation owner outside of Atlanta, Georgia, with no fewer than twenty slaves shouldering the backbreaking work required to keep the nation supplied with cotton.

Six months before Pickett's Charge, on January 1st, President Lincoln had signed the Emancipation Proclamation, which heralded the end of slavery. The Proclamation stated that a slave could claim freedom either by escaping from the Confederate South or as the result of the advance of the Union's army. That Proclamation was the reason that Jones joined the Confederate army. Unless the South could win the war, he knew that his days as a wealthy Southern aristocrat were ending.

Although Brickman, over the years, had reluctantly acknowledged that those of African descent had had a few legitimate grievances, he still considered them complicit in the North's subjugation of the South. To this day, he couldn't help but remember that fact every time he saw someone with African blood.

After the war, Jones's widow, Winifred, Brickman's great-great-grandmother, could not accept the surrender of what she considered her birthright. Having lost her husband, slaves, income source, and social status, she chose to end her life by drinking a quart of dissolved household lye. That happened on the 26th of March in 1866. Her children found her on the floor, gagging and writhing in pain. Thirty minutes later, when she drew her last breath, each swore never to forget the reasons why their mother saw no joy in continuing her earthly life. As the years went by, most *did* forget.

———◆◆◆———

Brickman had been counting the years for tomorrow to arrive. Unofficially, he'd retire then, but because he had unused vacation leave available, he wouldn't do so *officially* until precisely twenty-one days later. He had been nothing if not patient in his pursuit of justice. For good reason: the survivor's benefit from his federal pension! If something happened to him, his wife, Judy, would need that for herself and to provide support for a troubled son who lived out of state. When questioned, she could honestly say that she had known nothing of her husband's plans.

If asked, Brickman would have argued that his difficult life as a child and teenager had nothing to do with shaping his personality. To be sure, nature had not been kind to him. His creator had ignored the rules that define the usual spacings between the mouth, nose, and eyes—and not in a good way. Incessantly teased through middle school, by eleventh grade he had developed a personality that could usually overcome the split-second reaction that his looks invariably generated.

Brickman's vocational journey had taken a convoluted path. After a short stint in the Army, followed by a Bachelor of Arts degree from Georgia College in 1988, he skipped from job to job, eventually realizing that his degree hadn't prepared him for much. He found his calling when, on a lark, he signed up for night school to learn computer coding.

About this time, the government was offering training positions for those with computer skills, and Brickman found himself employed at the Suitland Federal Center in Maryland. He became a specialist in meteorological satellites, specifically command and control, for over five billion dollars' worth of equipment traversing the globe 24/7. His employer, NSOF, the NOAA Satellite Operations Facility, moved into its new, state-of-the-art building in 2007. NOAA stood for National Oceanic and Atmospheric Administration.

Brickman's favorites were the geostationary satellites, the GOES, which maintained continuous vigil over a single area of the globe. GOES stood for Geostationary Operational Environmental Satellite. Most weather satellites were polar-orbiting, which provided two pictures daily of every spot on the globe. Most of the public had no idea that some 85% of the data fed to modern weather prediction models came from satellites. It was no small statement to say that much of today's improved weather forecasting was attributable to that satellite data.

From the moment Brickman turned in his security identification card, he knew there would be no turning back. He had duplicated all relevant software on his home computer. All this preparation had been remarkably easy. NSOF wasn't the CIA or the National Security Agency (NSA). Brickman had repeatedly walked out of the building with tiny flash drives containing gigabytes of source code.

Ironically, Brickman's plans would come to fruition at a period in history when the country showed signs of coming to its senses. Brickman never felt so proud as when the Commander-in-Chief, President Donald John Trump, refused to denounce the legitimate protests at Charlottesville the previous August. The "Unite the Right" movement had been protesting the removal of a statue of General Lee. To Brickman, those peaceful citizens were simply exercising their constitutional rights. In his opinion, the press ignored the fact that the liberal nut jobs were responsible for the violence that caused the one fatality.

Acknowledging that the worst could happen, Brickman had no intention of surrendering without a fight. A fierce advocate of the Second Amendment and the National Rifle Association, Brickman had weapons aplenty, consisting mostly of his two favorite handguns, one of which was the Ruger LCP II, a lightweight, compact, .380 caliber with a six-round magazine, ideal for close-in action. For heavier, outdoor duty and target practice, he preferred the Ruger GP100 357 Magnum Revolver with a six-inch barrel. Three copies of the former, each accompanied by its loaded magazine, lay ready for action at strategic locations about the house, much to the chagrin of his wife, who had grudgingly come to accept her husband's eccentricities. When leaving the house, Brickman left carrying, usually with the LCP II.

———————◆◆◆———————

Brickman's plan consisted of two phases. He would take particular delight in Phase I, in which he would come face to face with one man who would take the full measure of his wrath. Why? Because that person had biological roots in the North's assault at Gettysburg. Brickman marveled at the ridiculous coincidence that his very own boss was culpable—and that his surname, Hancock, had transited the decades intact. Brickman's research confirmed the genealogy. In casual conversations, Henry Adam Hancock acknowledged his Southern roots.

Brickman knew where his boss lived and the usual time he left for work. A drive-by shooting was an ideal assignment for the 357. More accurate than the LCP, the 357 revolver was also less prone to jamming and, importantly, left behind no traceable, ejected brass. Brickman's Army job with the Military Police had left him with weapon skills that he had refined at his local gun club.

Taking the life of his boss, one deserving Union descendant, was a personal, symbolic gift to himself. No one would suspect why anyone would want him dead. Brickman would wait a few days to initiate the next phase, which would be much more than symbolic. Brickman had no similar compunction about hiding his reasons for Phase II. In fact, his plan hinged on the outcry that his demands would foster—and the support that he'd garner from like-minded Southerners.

To broadcast his intentions, Brickman chose *The Washington Post*. Nothing if not a perfectionist, his ultimatums had taken months to craft, making sure that all punctuation and grammar were perfect. Before long, the world would know them all.

# – 2 –

## RETRIBUTION TWO

Kathy Ann Erickson busied herself with routine duties at her computer in Silicon Valley. She typed with both hands but had developed a special technique for using her left. To anyone who asked, she explained the childhood incident that had caused her to lose her pinky. As her American colleagues would have said: *If I had a nickel for every time I explained that a poisonous spider bit my finger, forcing an amputation, I'd be a rich woman.* Other than the missing finger, her looks were ordinary—verging on dowdy. At five foot seven, her larger than normal frame featured hefty breasts that some men would call sexy. On the negative side, her substantial figure was offset by a face too easily forgotten—a perfect complement for her mission in life.

The company for which Erickson worked, Preemptive Computer Resolutions (PCR), was a mid-level player in software development. The two owners, Henry Ulrich and Sue Martell, had joined forces even though their interests were dissimilar. Henry was a computer gamer; their bestseller, *Ultimate Conflict*, provided 60% of PCR's annual profit. Sue's specialty, Internet security, revolved around

*Martellin*, a virus-protection software package for protecting home and business computers.

Although she could have worked anywhere within the company, Erickson chose Martell's side of the house because of the intrinsic access she had to the outside world via the Internet. Gamers, for the most part, needed no such connection. The joke was that you could toss them all into a locked room with no link to the outside world (save for regular pizza deliveries), and they'd still get their job done.

Besides making what they considered to be bulletproof anti-virus software, Martell's group employed a handful of employees who had what many considered to be the company's most interesting jobs. Erickson was one of them. These talented programmers broke into, or hacked, other companies' computer systems—legally, of course. Their job was to isolate software vulnerabilities before those out to harm their clients discovered them first. Erickson was the brightest of the bunch.

When someone asked Erickson *how* she hacked a computer system, she explained it in simple terms. "Imagine an office building with one door but thousands of windows. The easiest way to get inside is to trick someone into letting me in through the door. Ninety-nine times out of one hundred, that works. If it doesn't, it gets harder," she'd say. "I have to look for a window that someone forgot to close and lock."

Erickson's background was unique—and secret! She had spent the past fifteen years in a carefully orchestrated progression to arrive at her present position. Before emigrating to the U.S. with a green card in 2007, she had spent four years in Mexico preparing. Once she became a permanent U.S. resident, she obeyed all laws and did her best to stay beneath everyone's radar. Five years later, she became a citizen.

It had been a carefully executed plan to launder her past, to blend into American society where no one could trace her Afghani or Soviet roots. Although she could still speak Russian, she had studiously honed her English-speaking skills.

———◆◆◆———

Erickson was born in Moscow in 1968. Her Soviet father, while attending college at Moscow State University, had fallen for a dark-haired beauty named Ghazal, who hailed from Afghanistan and also attended Moscow State.

Ghazal's presence at any institution of higher learning was no less than a miracle. Afghanistan was 99% Muslim, and within an ultra-conservative society in which women's education was considered not only unnecessary but against Allah's tenets, girls had little chance for advancement.

Ghazal's family was wealthy, which gave them some leeway in their personal lives. Although legally listed as Muslim—practically a government mandate—the family were apostates; they had secretly adopted Christianity and practiced it covertly. Because of the family's means, and because both parents considered education important, Ghazal was homeschooled, albeit with private male tutors—who well understood never to reveal to anyone the source of their additional income.

The name her parents had chosen for Ghazal was prophetic, translating from the Arabic as Gazelle. Tall and willowy, she stood a fraction of an inch above six feet. Although shorter and not as physically imposing, Erickson's father made up for his stature with two other qualities, perseverance and common sense. His name was Ratimir Vladimirovich Popov. Erickson's birth name was Viktoriya Ratimirovna Popova, owing to the convention of honoring both the first and last name of the father. Raised as an atheist in the Soviet Union, Ratimir was rather proud of his flexibility, having widened his perspective to where he considered himself an agnostic. The fact that his wife was Christian didn't affect him one way or the other.

As the 1970s evolved, the Soviet Politburo became increasingly concerned about Afghanistan, related to a complex combination of factors, including national security, the Cold War with the Americans, and historical relations. During that period, Afghanistan had remained neutral, having reasonable ties with both the Soviet Union and the United States. From her home in Moscow, Ghazal kept up with news from her homeland. Her family still lived there.

In April of 1978, the Democratic Republic of Afghanistan (DRA) came into power, a Soviet-backed movement that promulgated atheism and various progressive ideas that flew in the face of the conservative Muslim population. DRA President, Nur Taraki, worried that the Muslim majority—with various segments collectively known as the *Mujahideen*—would overwhelm his Marxist group.

For example, Muslims resented the communists who had the gall to suggest that women have educational opportunities comparable to men. Accordingly, Taraki repeatedly asked Moscow for help. Even though Soviet advisors had occupied Afghanistan for years, Taraki feared that his situation could spiral out of control.

Into this international complexity and intrigue arrived the Popov family. Ratimir's college degree came by way of his obligation to the military, and as a result, he began his military career right out of school. It wasn't long into the 1970s before he *became* one of those military advisors sent to Afghanistan, accompanied by his family, including Viktoriya and Alexei, her baby brother born in 1972. Ghazal was thrilled with the opportunity to return to her native country, if not her hometown. Then in the spring of 1977, fate granted another wish. Ratimir transferred to the city of Herat. After a dozen years, Ghazal once again lived among parents and relatives.

By March of 1979, the local Muslim population in Herat had had enough. On Thursday, the 15th, an armed and angry group marched on the city, destroying many examples of communism along the way. They set fire to government buildings and harassed anyone who did not wear appropriate Muslim garb. They arrived at the provincial Governor's office and killed him straightaway, along with other party officials. They also murdered several Russian advisors and their families. For upwards of a week, the city roiled with anarchy.

The Popov family, aided by family and friends, bided their time. Afterward, they rejoiced and thanked God for sparing their lives.

Infuriated that they had lost a major city to a group of ragtag locals, the DRA reacted forcefully and destructively with an aerial bombardment. It didn't escape anyone's notice that Soviet planes did the bombing, and even if Afghani pilots flew them, the Soviets had trained them. The Popov family again faced death.

Following this period of incredible vengeance, the DRA once again gained control of the city. By the end of the year, with increasing unrest and the murder of Taraki in September, Moscow invaded. Later to be known as the Soviet Union's "Viet Nam," the Soviet Union pulled out in 1989.

The DRA bombing raids in 1979 took a heavy toll. Erickson remembered with absolute clarity the instant her life changed forever. She had been playing hide and seek with seven-year-old Alexei, their parents watching television from a sofa in the adjacent room. It was her turn to hide, and she slid under the bed in her parent's bedroom.

"I bet I know where you are," Alexei yelled out. It would be the last time she would hear his voice.

Viktoriya was eleven years old when the bomb struck their house. The blast was so severe that she lost her hearing for weeks. Dazed and suffering from shock, Viktoriya crawled from beneath the bed, scarcely able to breathe, coughing, struggling to see anything through a cloud of white dust. The air tasted pungent, her nostrils burning from the gaseous effects of an explosion and fire, the scent searing itself into her memory. She hadn't gone but a step or two when her toe stubbed something soft. Shaking with fear, she dropped to her knees.

"Alexei! Alexei!" Viktoriya screamed into her brother's ear. She instinctively ran her hands along his body and extremities to locate any wounds. Finding nothing that felt like blood, she held out hope when she observed movement in his upper body. She rested her hand on his chest and felt an irregular vibration.

"Mom! Dad! It's Alexei. Help! We need to take him to the hospital!" The hope behind those words vaporized into the dust. At once, the pulsation stopped. Both hands now spasmodically searched for any form of movement in his upper torso. When the reality of what had just occurred hit Viktoriya, she fell to her brother's side and lost consciousness.

Viktoriya did not know whether it had been seconds, minutes, or hours before she came to. The dust had cleared to the extent that she could see across what used to be her parents' bedroom. *Where are the walls? Where is the ceiling?* She willed herself to her feet and yelled out again, confused by realizing that she couldn't hear her own voice. Everything in sight was obliterated. What used to be the kitchen was no longer identifiable as such. Everything was gray and white—except for the enormous red stain in the location where her parents had been sitting.

Following the catastrophe, Ghazal's sister, Anna, and her husband, Andrei, took Viktoriya into their home. For almost two years, she refused to speak. Her Herat relatives tried to break through, with no success. The family doctor gave his analysis: the trauma of losing her family was the cause. From his limited knowledge of psychology, he diagnosed *elective mutism*. He said that she had either chosen not to or was unable to speak to her family. He suggested that they be patient and observe her carefully, to see if she talked to anyone else—or even to herself.

It was at that time in 1981 when IBM introduced the Personal Computer to the public. Desperate to try anything that might stimulate Viktoriya's mind, the family bought one. The results were phenomenal. Interaction with an inanimate object (that could respond in its own special way) changed her demeanor almost overnight.

One evening, as Anna passed Viktoriya's closed door, she heard her speak as if talking to herself. Anna wisely chose not to interrupt, nor to bring it up later. Over the next month, Viktoriya opened up, and with Anna and Andrei's gentle encouragement, began speaking once more. They wisely avoided any discussion of her parents or brother.

A side benefit of this change in her life was Viktoriya's complete absorption with this new computer technology. Anna and Andrei had known that their niece was smart, and although they knew nothing about computing, it soon became apparent *how* smart. She became the go-to person for computing advice, even for her tutors who consulted her frequently.

Assaults on Herat continued into the 1980s; staying alive became a challenge. In 1984, when Viktoriya turned sixteen, Anna decided to do what she knew her sister Ghazal would have wanted—smuggle her out of the country, back to Moscow, to live with Ratimir's younger brother, Oleg. He had been among those encouraging Anna and Andrei to move his niece to a safer location.

Upon arriving in Moscow, memories from Viktoriya's early life there came flooding back. She had been six years old when her father had departed Moscow, when he had taken his first assignment as a military advisor, and the family left for Afghanistan. As she stepped from the train, she realized this was the god-awful place where those weapons of destruction had come from, those murderous instruments of death that had destroyed her family.

It took Viktoriya six years to devise her plan before she left her uncle, aunt, and Moscow city. When she did, she made sure that there was no trail to follow. If those looking followed the breadcrumbs she had painstakingly left behind, they would conclude that she'd gotten no farther than the edge of the city. She regretted the pain that she knew it would cause her family, both in Moscow and Afghanistan. But to initiate her plan of revenge, she had had no choice.

━━━━•◆•━━━━

Erickson shuddered as her mind boomeranged back to the present. As she had done countless times before, she cursed her creator. For the past thirty-nine years, the crushing memory of that unspeakable tragedy in Herat flooded her mind daily. She missed her brother terribly and prayed for his soul.

She had read about the five stages of grief: denial, anger, bargaining, depression, and acceptance. She understood the concept but realized that they didn't apply to her. She had negated two of the five and reordered the remaining three. Only denial, depression, and anger remained from the original steps—in that order. To those three, she added a fourth: revenge.

Until the day arrived when revenge took center stage in her life, depression and anger would dominate Erickson's waking hours. Further, she feared the possibility of capture before she had the opportunity to unleash her fury. Although she had been meticulous in her journey to become the phantom she had morphed into, as Murphy's Law attested, *if something can go wrong, it will.*

Accordingly, Erickson purchased a *safe house* to which she could retreat in case the unthinkable happened. Within driving distance of several airports, she chose a small resort town less than two hours' drive from Washington, D.C., three hours from Philadelphia, and two and a half from Pittsburgh. Berkeley Springs, located in the state of West Virginia, was a sleepy resort town famous for mineral baths that had drawn Washington elite for centuries.

Registered to a pseudonym and managed by a local real estate company, the well-supplied stone cabin stood ready to escape to should it become necessary. Erickson had stocked it with food and water, as well as a small cache of weapons, all purchased legally. Together with some fifty acres of old-growth forest, the cabin sat securely hidden one mile off the well-traveled Route 522—on a dirt road fronted by a metal gate with a sign that read *Keep Out!*

In the three years since its purchase, there had been no intrusions or vandalism. Erickson knew this to be true because the seven cameras, connected to the Internet, monitored the cabin's surroundings with video surveillance 24/7. That same Internet connection would prove useful should she need to continue her operations on the run.

Regrettably, the downside of Erickson's background and paranoia was that she had no friends and had turned into a virtual recluse. She had managed to buy a house on the outskirts of San Jose and made a point of not interacting with her neighbors. She owned a car, but mostly it sat in the garage. Starting several years earlier, she had given up driving to work, instead enjoying the convenience of Uber and Lyft.

Aside from the occasional pizza or Chinese delivered to the house, she cooked her own meals. Entertainment revolved around television, preferably 50's and 60's detective serials. Her coworkers at PCR accepted her as the extreme introvert she had become. But so long as she did her job, no one cared.

The Soviet Union lost much of its status in 1989 when the Berlin Wall came down and later, in 1991, with the breakup of the Union. Erickson intended to finish the job in 2018. Using the United States as a foil, she would bring Russia to its knees. Erickson had spent her entire adult life waiting and planning for this moment. She recalled the Christian saying: Vengeance is mine, sayeth the Lord. *Not this time*, she vowed. *Not this time!*

# — 3 —

## TROUBLE IN THREES

*Naval Research Laboratory (NRL), Monterey, California, U.S.A.*
*36° 35' 34"N Latitude, 121° 51' 17"W Longitude*
*Monday, March 26, 2018, 8:00 AM*

Dr. Victor Mark Silverstein returned the phone to its cradle, stretched back in his office chair, and pondered the news. He'd often heard that bad news arrived in threes; this was the third installment and by far the worst. First, last week, one of his bicycling partners had a mishap. Down with a broken hip.

The second of the trifecta involved their superintendent, whose mother had passed away unexpectedly. He'd be out of the office for at least a week.

Not one to wax superstitious, nonetheless Silverstein had been subconsciously waiting for the third proverbial ax to fall.

---

Although now fifty-nine years old and occasionally feeling his age, Silverstein could still keep up with the staff's younger hotshots. Two years earlier, his doctor had issued an edict: *Watch* your calories, *drop* twenty-five pounds, and *start* exercising! Silverstein got the message and achieved all three goals. In addition to working out at a health club thrice weekly, of the sports options that seemed reasonable at his age, he chose bicycling. He voted against jogging when he noticed how many of his colleagues were lining up for knee replacements.

In addition to his doctor's advice, and after finally accepting the reality that his hair showed significant graying, Silverstein took one more personal step as a concession to his vanity. After congratulating himself for dropping to a svelte one hundred ninety-five—perfect for his six-foot-two-frame—he shaved his head. He was surprised at the reactions, overwhelmingly positive, from his colleagues. He still smiled when he recalled Kipling's amused response: "Who gave my boss's job to Samuel L. Jackson?"

Although he knew that co-workers were just being kind, he appreciated their encouragement: "I swear, you look ten years younger." Never one to suffer fools, he found it remarkable that some even suggested that his demeanor had softened.

Looking back on his career, Silverstein had made his mark on the Navy and meteorology, laying claim to be being one of the Navy's preeminent scientists. He had been one of several student prodigies who had attended Pennsylvania State University in the late 1970s. In 1975, he had enrolled there in meteorology at the age of sixteen. Three and a half years later he received his BS diploma, in another year his MS, and two and a half years later his PhD.

As word of Silverstein's brilliance spread, numerous government and commercial activities competed for his talents. Silverstein ended up choosing a small research facility in Monterey, California, far removed from Penn State and his native Atlanta.

The Monterey division (numerically known as Code 7500) lay organizationally within the larger NRL in Washington, D.C. The division title, Marine Meteorology, was deceptive. Research ranged from developing sophisticated computer models that predict the weather on both regional and global scales, to producing scores of satellite-derived weather products, to applying Artificial Intelligence

(AI) techniques to weather problems—with a variety of projects in between, some classified.

His thoughts interrupted by a noise behind him, he swiveled around in time to greet his colleague Linda Kipling. Silverstein tried to look upset. "Don't you ever knock?"

"Why would I knock?" Kipling fired back, sending along both a wink and smile.

———————◆◆◆◆———————

Linda Kipling accepted the nature of their relationship, which had evolved over the years. Kipling didn't quite have the scientific pedigree of Silverstein but came close. Coming off a sad divorce in 1998, she welcomed the move to California and NRL from Boulder, Colorado, where she had worked at the National Center for Atmospheric Research (NCAR), another of the country's foremost meteorological research facilities. Over time, she had migrated to Silverstein's work circle and never left.

Over the years, whether by fate or just chance, the dynamic duo had gotten themselves involved in more than one incident that involved not only mayhem and death but also international intrigue— such that the U.S. government had classified as top secret even the mention of those events. The most recent, involving Kipling's discovery that former Nazis planned to create an environmental catastrophe, entailed such intrigue that Kipling often envisioned the caper culminating as a movie screenplay. *Well, at least a novel,* thought Kipling. That would never happen, she knew. *National security always takes precedence!*

The resourcefulness, cunning, and skill with which Kipling and Silverstein had handled the South American escapade did not go unnoticed by higher-ups at the CIA. Kipling's association with the CIA came by way of Silverstein, a friend of one Hector Rodriquez Lopez, a senior intelligence agent. Over the years, she had come to realize that Silverstein possessed security clearances that stretched above the typical Top Secret—a level often referred to as Sensitive Compartmented Information (SCI).

Owing to their acknowledged contributions to the cause, the CIA had made the two an offer that they found hard to refuse: to remain on retainer to assist the CIA should the need arise. *Who wouldn't want to be a spy?* Kipling remembered herself thinking.

And so, they had agreed. That said, Kipling regretted the notable detail that, except for Lopez, Lopez's superior, and their boss in Monterey, not one other person knew of this arrangement. No bragging rights! Except for a trip to Cuba the previous fall, nothing exciting had come from their undercover assignments. Kipling had hoped for more.

———◆———

"Sit down." Silverstein didn't waste any time. He knew that what he had to say would hit Kipling hard. She and Hancock had worked together at NCAR years earlier. Because of cooperative research over the years and NRL's interest in all things satellite, she also knew many of the people who worked at NSOF.

Silverstein chose not to pull any punches. "Steve Hancock was shot and killed yesterday morning! Outside his house! On his way to work!"

Silverstein watched as Kipling's composure crumbled—faster than it took him to make his sixteen-word statement.

# — 4 —

# HOT LINE

*Preemptive Computer Resolutions, San Jose, California*
*37° 24' 38.26"N Latitude, 121° 57' 45"W Longitude*
*Monday, March 26, 2018, 9:10 AM*

Most people called it the Moscow-Washington Hotline. They envisioned two red telephones, beside which sits someone with some sense of responsibility (and the ability to speak both Russian and English), who would pick up the receiver should it ring, listen to the message, and forward the information to superiors.

In fact, a telephone was never involved. A Teletype represented the first implementation of the hotline. It became operational in August of 1963, before the Kennedy assassination that fall. Further, the term "superiors" had a limited connotation: The system design dictated that only the U.S. President and Soviet Premier could communicate—for emergencies only. A Memorandum of Understanding set forth the details. Proving that absolutely anything can be mangled politically, the Republican platform in election year 1964 criticized the hotline, claiming that the U.S. had favored a potential enemy with this convenient tool, rather than a proven friend. Great Britain, for example.

More than one political leader had previously suggested such a hotline between the Pentagon and the Kremlin. The 1962 Cuban Missile Crisis gave the idea more impetus. During that daunting diplomatic situation, the reason became obvious: Messages sent by normal diplomatic channels took upwards of six hours to deliver—hardly enough time to react in a nuclear weapon-driven crisis.

From the beginning, the architects of the design chose text as the medium for outgoing messages, using Russian in Moscow and English at the Pentagon. Translators would be available at either end. It was apparent to everyone that voice recordings were unacceptable. Nuances in the spoken language could too easily be misinterpreted.

Erickson knew all of this—and much more. She knew that the system had taken on upgrades over the years, transitioning first from Teletype to facsimile. In its current form, the system was a secure e-mail connection conducted over two satellite links, with a backup fiber-optic landline.

Every hour on the hour, test messages flew back and forth, alternately. The messages were purposely mundane, noncontroversial passages from books a popular choice. The only deviations occurred on two dates: August 30 and January 1, when good-will greetings were permitted. August 30 represented the anniversary when the hotline became operational.

Over the years, both sides had used the hotline sporadically, usually because of various international crises: the "Six-Day War" in 1967, the 1971 Indo-Pakistani War, and the Arab-Israeli War of 1973, among others. More recently, President Obama warned Russia not to interfere with the 2016 U.S. presidential election.

———◆———

The part of Erickson's job at PCR that involved breaking into business computer systems was both challenging and satisfying—and vital to her plan! She had never yet found a computer system that she could not hack. Even after a client's budget had been exhausted, and PCR certified that their system was secure, Erickson knew that, given more time, she could find other weaknesses, other points of entry. It was only a matter of *when*, not *if*.

Although Erickson felt loyalty to PCR and her boss, she reminded herself daily of her sole purpose in life. Hatred for Russia consumed every waking moment. Accordingly, her plan to seek retribution had evolved since she first departed Moscow. Notably, Erickson had decided that using America as her base for operations was the best option—a bonus being that she might possibly survive the Armageddon she intended to create. Her convoluted journey to the United States was part of her subterfuge. In America, she reasoned, there'd be little chance that anyone would detect or question her Internet activities. Case in point: For about a quarter of the one hundred and twenty-one companies for whom PCR had, to date, given their gold-star certification of invincibility, Erickson had installed a secret *back door*. On her own time, often at night when the office was empty, she had identified, hacked into, and installed similar entrances for an equivalent number of Russian companies.

To the uninitiated, a back door was what it sounded like, a clandestine entry point, one that bypassed normal security software. Because only Erickson knew the locations of these clandestine entry points, the odds of anyone finding and unlocking her hidden pathways were virtually nonexistent.

Erickson's ingenious plot to bring Russia to its knees would begin soon—because the last piece to the puzzle was finally in place. It was only six weeks earlier when she achieved her astounding feat. Even with her impressive computer skills (she fancied herself on a par with Stieg Larsson's fictional computer genius, Lisbeth Salander, from *The Girl with the Dragon Tattoo*), it had taken years.

She had finally hacked the Moscow-Washington Hot Line and installed the back door! Not only could she monitor the hourly messages, but she could change them at will. As a brazen display of her considerable hubris, she had already replaced several of them with her own innocuous substitutions—in both directions! For the Russian transmissions to the Americans, Erickson had written in Russian using the Cyrillic alphabet; because that communication

35

necessitated the use of a Cyrillic keyboard, she composed those messages at home.

Erickson's hack was nothing short of brilliant. Once she initiated her master plan, the only messages that would traverse the hotline would be hers. All others would be intercepted and discarded.

All technical components lay in place. Not only did Erickson control the Hot Line, but she also had access to forty-one U.S. electric, gas, and water utilities, sixteen banking institutions, thirty-eight hospitals, and numerous transportation control systems. She made sure that she had equivalent Russian companies representing those same categories of modern everyday life. She hadn't yet decided which ones she would use. That decision would come soon.

Kathy Ann Erickson had in place more than enough computer firepower to start World War III. She would begin soon.

# — 5 —

## SVR RF

*SVR Headquarters, Moscow, Russian Federation*
*55° 35' 2"N Latitude, 37° 31' 1"E Longitude*
*Tuesday, March 27, 2018, 2:30 PM (MSK)*

Dmitri Smirnov was more than an insignificant cog in the Russian Federation's bureaucratic web of security service operations. He reported directly to the Deputy Director of Directorate X who, together with the deputies from seven other directorates, reported to the Director of the SVR RF, the Foreign Intelligence Service of the Russian Federation. A few old-timers longed for the days when SVR's predecessor reported to the famous KGB.

From Smirnov's perspective, the directorates had more than enough authority and flexibility to handle Russia's intelligence needs in the modern era. Russia's President, Vladimir Vladimirovich Putin, a former KGB intelligence officer himself until 1991, wouldn't allow his intelligence service to degrade, even if it meant depriving other governmental departments of the funds needed.

Directorate X represented Science and Technology and was a perfect match for Smirnov's skill set. He had graduated from the prestigious Moscow Institute of Physics and Technology with three degrees, all of which gave him an appreciation of the hard sciences like physics and chemistry. Interestingly, Smirnov also found himself drawn to computer programming, networking, and the infinite possibilities available in the world of the Internet. Accordingly, he spent some of his time interacting with Directorate I, which represented Computer Science.

Compared to his co-workers, Smirnov's position within the Directorate allowed him a certain degree of autonomy. He did what he wanted, within reason. With Smirnov's high level of intelligence (he had consistently maxed out his test scores) and his successes with previous assignments, the Deputy Director of X recognized that Smirnov could best serve the Federation by allowing him free rein.

But with that natural ability came negatives. His life was his career, and his career his life. Smirnov lamented his situation and the sad fact that, at the age of forty-six, he had no one to go home to or even sleep with. Often, his sole companion inside his apartment at night was a stiff shot of vodka or a bottle of wine, either one sufficient to dull his loneliness and catapult him into dreamland. Being a spy allowed him little time to cultivate luxuries such as a family and home. He had a handful of spy friends who had successfully developed a relationship that made it to the altar; without exception, all ended in divorce.

To make up for this shortage of emotional connection, other agents bragged about their foreign escapades, the affairs they were having for the sake of mother Russia. Smirnov had no idea how much of that was fantasy, bravado intended to elevate their inflated perception of themselves. His own involvement in like situations came by way of dreamland. Upon waking, he had often asked himself whether he could ever use sex to deceive another human being. He certainly had the looks to do the job: More than one colleague had referred to him as 007, the Russian version of Sean Connery, the real James Bond. There was a fleeting physical resemblance, Smirnov had to admit.

As he pondered this abstraction, Smirnov heard a knock at his office door. He recognized the distinctive pattern of his Deputy Director.

———————◆———————

The Deputy Director (DD) of X, Oleg Vladimirovich Popov, was physically striking only from his eyelids upward. Shorter than most, and sufficiently rotund as the Russian elite tended to become, it was the hair that dominated his physical appearance: a shock of incredibly dense gray that gave the impression of having never been combed since birth. Sixty-two years old, he had been in his position for some twelve years.

The DD had spent his entire career within the framework of the SVR. He had graduated from the same Moscow Institute as Smirnov. Not having Smirnov's intellectual gifts, Popov had advanced to his elevated position the old-fashioned way—through hard work and perseverance. He had done his share of time in the field, most recently in Ukraine. Earlier assignments included Western Europe. He spoke German, French, and English fluently.

In the early years of his career, Popov's devotion to work had arisen primarily as a defense, a virtual shield that isolated his mind from the misfortunes that had ravaged his own family. His only sibling, a brother, Ratimir, had served and perished—along with his wife and son—during the Soviet Union's Afghanistan fiasco of the 1970s and 80s.

It hadn't ended there! Following this tragedy, and because he and his wife, Natasha, were childless, they had happily accepted responsibility for raising Ratimir's orphaned daughter, Viktoriya, who had survived the incident that killed her family.

The years that followed Viktoriya's return were not easy for the Popov family. She had returned to Moscow a broken teenager. There was no mystery behind the reasons for her erratic, sometimes violent, behavior. Accordingly, Oleg and Natasha spent a small fortune on counseling. Nonetheless, they saw no improvement in Viktoriya's disposition or her outlook for the future.

And then, six years after she joined her Moscow family, Popov's bad luck struck again: On a warm Saturday afternoon, Viktoriya left the house—and seemingly vanished from the face of the earth.

Beside himself with grief and overwhelming feelings of inadequacy in his failed responsibility to his brother and to solve the mystery of his niece's disappearance, Popov used every resource available to him from his intelligence position at the time. The official conclusion by the authorities: Viktoriya had been murdered and her body disposed of.

Popov considered that conclusion premature. The only evidence they had was meager indeed: a severed finger, complete with an identifiable tattoo. He did not question that the finger was Viktoriya's. Years later, DNA matching confirmed the identification. *But a single finger is not a body!* His working theory was that someone had kidnapped his niece and left the finger to suggest a more sinister crime.

Popov marveled over the fact that the DNA the police used to match the finger was still available. The capability to match DNA samples had arisen because, since 1980, anyone who had either been born in or had immigrated to Russia had his or her DNA taken and stored for future reference. A relatively insignificant agent named Nikola Petrov had convinced his superiors to put into practice this federal program—well before DNA matching became widely available in the mid-1980s. He was forward-thinking indeed. President Putin certainly thought so when, in 2014, in a ceremony within the SVR, he presented him with the prestigious Hero of Labor of the Russian Federation award. For obvious reasons, the public knew nothing of this database.

Never accepting—refusing, actually—the reality that his niece was dead, Popov had surreptitiously continued his search. Until recently, data sources for such discovery were meager, mostly from HUMINT, human intelligence. But the Internet had changed *everything*. Putin's idea to interfere with the American election was a prime example. Aside from such nefarious use of the Internet, Popov's purpose was benign indeed. All he wanted was to find his brother's daughter.

Within the past five years, Directorate I had made significant progress in its application of facial recognition. Not with the recognition algorithms themselves—which worked remarkably well—but with obtaining image data on which the algorithms operate. That's where the recent breakthroughs had come from. Directorate I stated that, conservatively, they had hacked into some 90% of the world's traffic and street cameras. Compared to Internet connectivity for systems like the military and most civilian organizations dealing with sensitive data, security protocols for traffic and street cameras were almost nonexistent.

In fact, this new technology allowed Putin to locate a few Russian spies who had made the mistake of switching sides. Putin had a long memory for such betrayals.

To initiate the search process, it was only a matter of providing a photograph of Viktoriya—except for the significant complication that Popov had no current picture. The one that he did have was some twenty-eight years old; if alive, Viktoriya would be fifty. However, there was a solution.

*Aging* software had the remarkable capability to provide an updated facial depiction of someone years into the future. A PhD student at a prominent American university had developed the technique. She had demonstrated that a person's primary facial features evolved predictably over time. As a bonus, her data indicated that aging software worked reliably until the age of sixty!

Very few who worked for the SVR had the clout to command the resources necessary to conduct such a search. But, as of one year earlier, two supercomputers began running searches 24/7, looking for a visual match to one Viktoriya Ratimirovna Popova. Unless she *was* dead, Popov was confident he'd find his niece.

———————◆◆———————

Smirnov liked his boss. Popov had always treated his underlings fairly and with respect. Smirnov knew only the basics of Popov's life history but had heard bits and pieces that alluded to some tragedy involving his niece. He watched as Popov chose the more comfortable of the two chairs available to guests in Smirnov's spartan government-issue office.

Popov initiated the conversation. "Tell me what you know about this Trump fiasco. I seem to recall that you met up with your American friend Silverstein last fall?" Popov knew that Smirnov kept his ear to the ground concerning Directorate I, the folks who'd been in charge of the disinformation campaign against Hillary Clinton.

"I think that—"

The DD couldn't help himself. "We've been caught at our own game," he lamented. "The Americans have revealed some pretty damning evidence." He paused to shake his head. "And all because *my friend* and *our President* made the unfortunate suggestion that we meddle in their presidential election. Once a spy, always a spy, I guess."

It was common knowledge that, in his earlier career, Popov had worked with Putin—before the latter chose to enter politics. They still knew each other, Popov had admitted to Smirnov during a private Vodka-fueled dinner one night. But he also said that they had not communicated in some time. He conceded that Putin was smart enough, but in a moment of mental lapse, confessed that "Vladimir" tended to get stuck in political ruts, with little flexibility to think long-term. "Still, you don't skid when you're in a rut," Popov had joked.

Smirnov made a point of sitting up straight, not knowing how to respond. It was all water under the bridge. "Obviously, our comrade president can't admit any of this is true. These things blow over, you know. They always do."

Popov snorted in response. "If so, why is it taking such a damn long spell to do that? That election was, what, some seventeen months ago? I swear! Those Americans get themselves so easily confounded over the most minor of incidents. It's a wonder their society functions at all."

For the next half hour, Popov and Smirnov discussed other hotspots that impacted Russian interests. As big as the ensuing mess that accompanied the American election interference, there was something even more worrisome: Syria. Moscow had no choice but to continue supporting Assad in controlling the rebel insurgency. In return, Syria was bleeding Russian rubles and giving its patron little to show for it.

Apart from Syria, they discussed North Korea. Between Kim Jung Un and Donald Trump, neither spy could decide who was the more dangerous leader.

On the plus side, oil prices were finally edging up, somewhere around $60 per barrel. With Russia's considerable dependence on oil revenue, that was about the only good news of the day.

It looked as if the DD had said all he wanted to say. He stood and turned to go, but then pivoted back. "Somehow, we need to stay on top of this election interference issue. Put your mind to it. You might consider getting a little closer to your friend Silverstein. He and his sidekick, Linda Kipling. From what you've told me, their jobs seem to make them quite knowledgeable about what's going on in their government."

"It does seem so," Smirnov agreed.

Popov added. "Do you think you could turn him? It's been a while since we've run a double agent who's done us any good."

The question took Smirnov by surprise. "I think you know the answer to that. He'd be the last person in America who'd turn. There's absolutely nothing we could offer him that he wants. He has his own money, you know. His parents left him a fortune. I'm surprised that he even continues to work."

The DD thought some more. "Kipling?"

"It's not going to happen. With due respect, comrade deputy director, that's impossible." Realizing that his reply had been a little too emphatic, Smirnov paused and pretended to think. "Still, you make a point. Between the two of them, Kipling would be the better target."

The Deputy Director of the X Directorate nodded and turned to go. Before he closed the door, he offered one final comment. "Still, it wouldn't hurt to stay close to both. Don't you think?"

With that off-handed remark, Smirnov had his marching orders. If the Deputy Director of the X Directorate thought "it wouldn't hurt," it was, by definition, so. He, like the Roman Catholic Pope in Vatican City, was recognized to be infallible by all who worked beneath him.

Smirnov glanced at the wall clock, subtracted ten hours, and realized that Silverstein was likely fast asleep in California. He'd go home and return to work at midnight Moscow time when he'd make the call. He'd have until then to fabricate an excuse to visit his friend at the Naval Research Laboratory—in the town of Monterey, in the state of California, in the United States of America.

With that thought, Smirnov smiled to himself, his outlook on life suddenly brightening. He snapped to his feet, grabbed his coat, closed the door, and walked sprightly down the hall. *Kipling. Dr. Linda Ann Kipling. Silverstein's loyal assistant.* He had met her twice. The stories Victor had told him about her were nothing short of amazing. *What I wouldn't give to get to know a woman like that!*

# − 6 −

# THE UNFORESEEN

*Naval Research Laboratory (NRL), Monterey, California*
*36° 35' 34"N Latitude, 121° 51' 17"W Longitude*
*Wednesday, March 28, 2018, 9:00 AM*

"The weather's half decent. Want to go for a walk?" Silverstein asked without even so much as a friendly "good morning." Both had been in foul moods since Monday's news about the murder of Steve Hancock at NSOF.

Kipling understood instantly what was going on, but revealed her surprise with only a raised eyebrow. "Sure."

They had learned in spy school that they should never discuss CIA business within a confined space such as an office, or at home. Some of the rules seemed silly, but both had seen enough spy movies to know that the bad guys had ingenious ways to eavesdrop. Even the out of doors wasn't always safe. *Loose Lips Sink Ships* remained as true today as during World War II.

They exited their building into the adjacent Spark's Park, a grassy area named after an earlier facility manager, Bob Sparks. They made the perimeter walk around the flagpole before settling on a bench beneath a tree.

"You haven't called me out here since Cuba last fall. What's up?" Kipling rubbed her hands together. The air was cool, with a slight breeze, and the sun was low on the horizon.

"Dmitri Smirnov called me yesterday afternoon," offered Silverstein.

"Really?"

"Yeah. He wants to come visit. And that's going to be awkward! We've known all along that he works for the SVR."

"What's he want?"

"He was vague, almost purposely so. Says he wants to talk about more scientific cooperation, particularly regarding the earth sciences. I've known all along that he works part-time at the Hydrometeorological Centre of Russia."

"I've heard you mention that before."

"Besides earth science, that's where they make their operational weather forecasts."

Silverstein continued. "So, I suppose we shouldn't look a gift horse in the mouth. Any cooperation between our countries couldn't help but lead to better relations."

The two quietly pondered the reality of a Russian spy on their home turf. Kipling broke the silence. "What's Lopez think? Did you call him?"

"First thing I did."

"Yeah?"

"You know Lopez. There's nothing that goes on that he isn't suspicious about. Smirnov was up to something, he said."

"Has Lopez ever met him?

Silverstein shook his head. "Don't think so."

Kipling bent forward and stared at the ground. "I agree with Lopez. I think it's time we put on our CIA hats. We're not on his payroll to forecast the weather. We need to think creatively. Think about it." Kipling straightened herself. "Smirnov might be our private conduit into the mind of the Kremlin."

Silverstein nodded in response.

She continued. "I think that if we're going to make something of this visit, we need more information than you have from your casual friendship over the years. The CIA must know more than we do."

"I'm ahead of you there. That's what I told Lopez last night, and he said he'd get back to me."

"By the way, you didn't say. When does Smirnov want to come?"

"Today's Wednesday. He's flying into San Francisco the day after tomorrow. I told him we'd give him a tour of the area on Saturday."

Kipling snapped to attention. "Seriously? That sure doesn't give us much time to prepare."

Before Silverstein could respond, he both heard and felt the vibration of his cell phone in his pocket. As he noted that it was an incoming satellite call, he nodded toward Kipling. "Speak of the Devil."

Even though Silverstein's iPhone 7 looked normal enough to the casual observer, it was hardly so. In addition to the electronics common to every other iPhone on the market, his phone sported satellite communication software and voice encryption.

Per protocol, for security purposes, Silverstein entered a 3-digit key that changed on a preset schedule. "Hello."

Lopez asked if this was a good time to talk.

"Your timing's good, Hector. I'm outside with Linda; nobody's around," Silverstein reassured his CIA boss.

———◆———

Kipling watched as Silverstein listened, his demeanor changing before her eyes. He began to fidget and jumped to his feet, turning his back to Kipling.

"I don't know about that, Hector. Are you sure, sir? Don't you think there's a better way—." Lopez had obviously cut him off. The one-sided conversation continued. From the time Silverstein had first said hello, his body language morphed from concerned to upset to thoroughly agitated.

Silverstein rotated slowly to face Kipling, his eyes noticeably moist. He handed her the phone. "He wants to talk to you."

Kipling didn't understand her colleague's sudden transformation. Before she had a chance to ask what was wrong, he stormed back across the grass toward their offices.

Kipling took a breath to regain her composure. "Hello. You wanted to talk to me?"

# 7

## PHASE II

*Silver Spring, Maryland*
*39° 3' 42"N Latitude, 76° 59' 38"W Longitude*
*Thursday, March 29, 2018, 10:15 PM*

Brickman was ready. His wife was asleep. Blessed by genes from his mother's side of the family, he could easily function on four hours of sleep, his wife the opposite, eight being her norm. To make up for the difference, he stayed up late so that they could wake up together in the morning.

In his basement home office, it was during those extra hours that Brickman had formulated his strategy and the components necessary to implement it. He had also used that time for field trips. One of those occurred the previous night when Brickman delivered a critical piece of hardware.

Progress thus far had been as anticipated. Phase I was complete. The look on Steve Hancock's face in the instant before the bullet penetrated the geographic center of his body was priceless. Before pulling the trigger, Brickman allowed his boss the dignity of seeing his assassin—but reluctantly accepted the irony that Hancock had no idea whatsoever why he'd been targeted.

No matter! The sins of the father pass directly to the son. That was what the Bible proclaimed in Exodus 20:5: *You shall not bow down to them or serve them, for I the Lord your God am a jealous God, visiting the iniquity of the fathers on the children to the third and the fourth generation of those who hate me.* Some scholars argued that other Bible quotations absolved the descendants of their father's sins. Raymond Charles Brickman III preferred the literal interpretation.

With Phase I completed, all stood ready for Phase II. Brickman couldn't believe the good fortune afforded by the date of his retirement: Both orbiters and geostationaries were undergoing major upgrades—and the first of their series had already launched!

The previous generation of polar orbiters had been part of the National Polar-orbiting Operational Environmental Satellite System (NPOESS). Budgeted by Congress in 2011, the new Joint Polar Satellite System (JPSS) represented the latest generation of polar orbiters, the replacements. Five months earlier, on November 18th of 2017, the first of that series launched into orbit, officially named NOAA-20 (changing from its pre-launch designation, JPSS-1). JPSS-2 would launch in 2021.

Simultaneously, the geostationaries were undergoing major updates. Over the years, it had become common practice to refer to the two that covered the eastern and western portions of the United States as GOES-East and GOES-West. The specific satellites assigned to those roles were GOES-14 and GOES-15; both had become outdated since their launch in 2009 and 2010, respectively.

The first of the replacements, GOES-16, represented a significant upgrade. Launched in November of 2016, it became operational as GOES-East in December of 2017. The successor to GOES-West, GOES-17, took to space a month earlier, on March 1. GOES-14 had already powered down and moved into space storage as a backup; GOES-15 would face a similar retirement.

Brickman would be taking out the latest satellite technology. As a warning shot, he would target NOAA-20, the polar orbiter, followed by the geostationary backups, GOES-14 and 15. If there were still no response to his demands, the nation's crown jewels of weather observation from space, the latest renditions for GOES-East and GOES-West, would follow.

Brickman looked around his office, storing memories to enjoy later. Over previous weeks, he had uploaded booby-trapped software into all five satellites. Although NSOF itself had no uplink ability, it had been a simple matter to hack into that capability at the NOAA Command and Data Acquisition Station at Wallops Island, Virginia, where both orbiting and geostationary uploads were possible. A single keystroke would initiate the countdown for all satellites, except NOAA-20, which would self-destruct immediately.

With no further concern evident, he pressed *return*. After confirming that his wife was still asleep, he let himself out through the side garage door and proceeded on his planned forty-five-minute walk.

He arrived in the middle of a vacant lot and took out his *burner*. His call to Shanghai, China, would initiate what was known as a *spoofed* call. Months earlier, Brickman had purchased this unique service—available only on the dark web—to reroute his call. If the *Post* had the wherewithal to trace the call they were about to receive, they'd discover its origin: St. Petersburg, Russian Federation. Not Maryland or Shanghai.

"May I speak to the news desk?" Brickman's voice was strong and assertive.

"May I help you?"

"I have an important news story that I want to report."

"I'll transfer you, sir. One moment."

"News desk. May I help you?"

"Listen carefully. About an hour ago, I destroyed the observing capability of NOAA-20, the country's newest polar-orbiting weather satellite. Unless you meet my demands, I will incapacitate more weather satellites. You will find those demands on a red flash drive located at the Union Station Metro, near where the payphones used to exist on the platform between the two trains. Look hard, and you'll find it."

With that opening salvo, Brickman smashed the burner beneath his shoe, reflected briefly on the maelstrom he had created, and headed home. It was thirty-five minutes before midnight. He wondered how long it would take before all hell broke loose at NSOF—and within the upper echelons of the governing bodies of the United States of America.

# — 8 —

## IT STARTS

The Washington Post, *Washington, DC*
*38° 54' 10"N Latitude, 77° 1' 50"W Longitude*
*Thursday, March 29, 2018, 11:28 PM (EDT)*

Rachel Ham dialed quickly. Stories like this didn't often show up just minutes before midnight. She hoped that John Craver, the on-call editor for the night shift, hadn't gone to bed.

He answered in two rings. "What's up?"

"We might have something big!"

"Talk to me."

"We got an open call just a minute ago. I'll let you listen for yourself." Ham initiated the recorded message:

"About an hour ago, I destroyed the observing capability of NOAA-20, the country's newest polar-orbiting weather satellite. Unless you meet my demands, I will incapacitate more weather satellites. You will find those demands on a red flash drive located at the Union Station Metro, somewhere near where the payphones used to exist on the platform between the two trains. Look hard, and you'll find it."

"That's it?" Craver shot back.

"Sir, I know a little bit about weather satellites. I've done a couple of news pieces. NOAA-20 is our latest polar-orbiting weather satellite. He's got that right."

"Could be a hoax, but we can't take that chance. If he says there's a flash drive somewhere waiting for us, that is rather specific. Get someone over there. I'll hold the line."

"Yes, sir." Cupping the receiver between her hands, she yelled out for Jimmy Marshall, one of the younger night-beat writers. "Jimmy, can you come here, please?"

Marshall came running. "What's up?"

Ham stared at the wall clock. "We got a blind call regarding a threat to our nation's weather satellites. The caller's demands are on a red flash drive at the Union Station Metro, near where the payphones used to be. I need you to get there before it closes at midnight. Take a taxi and tell the driver there's an extra hundred in it for him if he gets you there before it closes. We *need* that flash drive." She thought for a second. "Can your cell phone make a hot spot?"

Marshall nodded.

"Okay, then. Take your laptop and forward the contents to my e-mail." As Marshall grabbed his coat and sprinted down the floor, Ham yelled after him. "Call me the instant you find it!"

Ham got back on the line with Craver. "I'm back. Listen! If anybody knows whether there's any truth to this, it's the people at NSOF."

"What the hell's NSOF?"

"Sorry, sir. NSOF stands for NOAA Satellite Operations Facility. It's over in Suitland. I've been there."

Craver yelled. "Make the call! I'm on my way! We may have stumbled upon the latest version of eco-terrorism!"

Ham hung up and checked the time. They were an hour away from the production run for Friday's paper.

*NOAA Satellite Operations Facility, Suitland, Maryland*
*38° 51' 7"N Latitude, 76° 56' 12"W Longitude*
*Thursday, March 29, 2018, 11:33 PM (EDT)*

Jim Flanagan answered the phone. He preferred the night shift when there was little activity. Tonight had been an anomaly. About an hour earlier, computerized alarm bells had gone off, and technicians were investigating. There appeared to be a problem with the data stream from one of the orbiters.

"NOAA Satellite Operations Facility. Flanagan. May I help you?"

A female voice came across the line. "This is Rachel Ham from *The Washington Post*. We've heard a rumor that you're having some difficulty with one of your polar orbiters, NOAA-20. Is there any truth to that?"

Flanagan was flabbergasted. "How the *hell* did you know that?"

---

The Washington Post, *Washington, DC*
*38° 54' 10"N Latitude, 77° 1' 50"W Longitude*
*Friday, March 30, 2018, 12:10 AM (EDT)*

Ham's hand shot to the phone. "Yes."

"It's me. We almost got t-boned by an SUV, but we made it. They were just shutting the gates. I had to sweet-talk a metro police officer, and it ended up costing us a year's subscription to the *Post*. But he went down with me and even let me use his flashlight. You were right. A red flash drive taped to the wall."

Ham felt relieved. "Good work, Jimmy. Where are you now?"

"I'm on the street."

"Is there somewhere you can fire up your hotspot?"

"That's where I am now, a corner between two walls. Hold on a second."

Ham felt her heart beating through her throat.

"Okay. I've opened the drive. There's only one file, a pdf. I'm opening it now." Seconds ticked by. "What the fuck? You're not going to believe this!"

"Don't keep me hanging here, Jimmy."

"Check your inbox in a few seconds. See for yourself. I'm sending it now."

———————◆◆◆———————

Ham had just finished scanning the two-page letter when she heard footsteps from behind. It was Craver.

"I've got it, John. Take a look." They stared down together at Ham's computer screen:

*To the Editor of* The Washington Post

*In a sense, I am honoring your newspaper with my announcement this Thursday, the 29th of March. At ten o'clock this evening, I initiated a software sequence that rendered one of our country's latest and most modern weather satellites, NOAA-20, inoperative. You cannot undo this sequence.*

*Perhaps to your dismay, I must inform you that this action is not an act of eco-terrorism. You may find it amusing that I am an ardent environmentalist. No! I am doing this for a cause that has long been ignored: the North's complete and utter devastation of the South and its people during and following the Civil War. Some would say that because we were wronged, we should seek revenge. I think that the more apt term is retribution. And so, I proudly share what I am doing with my Confederate brothers and sisters.*

*NOAA-20 is the first of five weather satellites that I intend to destroy. The remainder are geostationaries, and one will be made inoperable every forty-eight hours following the March 29 demise of*

*NOAA-20. For your benefit, here is the schedule (Eastern Daylight Time):*

*GOES-14—10 PM, March 31, 2018*
*GOES-15—10 PM, April 2, 2018*
*GOES-16—10 PM, April 4, 2018*
*GOES-17—10 PM, April 6, 2018*

*FYI, there is nothing you can do to stop or slow the countdown clocks inside each satellite. If you think that you can power down a satellite to avoid its destruction, think again. As soon as it is powered up again, it will immediately self-destruct.*

*But all is not hopeless from your point of view; I am offering a way out. I have included code that will allow me to stop future internal clocks before activation. Don't bother to look for my "kill" switch; you'll never find it.*

*If the conditions that I enumerate below are satisfied, I will stop all countdown sequences on any remaining satellites. I require only three concessions from the government of the United States. They are straightforward and easily satisfied:*

*The President of the United States must appear on national television and make the following announcements, the terms of which are non-negotiable:*

1. *The President will apologize to the South, conceding that its people were treated horribly and unfairly by the North prior to, during, and following the Civil War.*
2. *The President will announce that all Civil War statues and other public memorabilia that commemorate the South's participation in the Civil War will be protected forever. Any such remembrances already removed will be reinstated.*
3. *As monetary restitution, the President will authorize the payment of one trillion dollars, divided equally among the*

*eleven states of the Confederacy. In case you've forgotten, those states are Alabama, Arkansas, Florida, Georgia, Louisiana, Mississippi, North Carolina, South Carolina, Tennessee, Texas, and Virginia.*

*In conclusion, my demands are clear. Consequently, there is no need for further communication. I will await the President's national television broadcast.*

*Have a good day!*

Craver and Ham stared at each other. Craver backed off, hands behind his head. "Have a good day, he says?"

Ham asked the obvious. "Do we publish, sir?"

Realizing that this was a decision that fell above his pay grade, Craver grabbed for the phone. "We need McElroy. He'd want me to wake him up on this one."

In the seconds that Craver took to get the conversation going, it was obvious to Ham that he had awakened their editor-in-chief, Tom McElroy. For the next five minutes, she listened to Craver's side of the conversation, in which he read back Ham's phone conversation as well as the page from the flash drive. At one point, Craver stopped the conversation, held the phone at his waist, and stared down at Ham. "Are you positive your contact said they'd lost a satellite?"

"I told you what he said, sir. Do you want me to call back to confirm?"

"Under the circumstances, I'd say yes."

Ham dashed off to a phone at another desk. Two minutes later, she returned and caught Craver's eye. "Very interesting, sir. Their tune has changed. They now say 'no comment.'"

Most of the rest of the phone conversation involved Craver listening.

Ham looked up hopefully. "What does he want to do?"

Craver responded. "He's coming in, but he's going to make a call first. From my viewpoint, if we move too quickly, are we interfering with the country's response to a threat to our national security?"

Ham had already thought it through. "No, I don't think so, sir. We've got to look at this logically. The sooner we get this information out, the better the chances are that we catch this guy. If we do nothing and days from now when we've lost more of our satellites, what do we tell our readers? We admit that we knew about it beforehand but decided to say nothing? We'd lose credibility, sir."

Craver smiled. "What you just said is what McElroy implied just now. As we speak, he's calling Production. Tomorrow's delivery will be two hours late. He also recognized that time's a-wasting. The folks at your NSOF may know that they have a problem, but they don't know about this letter."

"Higher-ups need to know. FBI? CIA?"

"No. Better than that. The advantage McElroy has, he knows everybody. The President's Chief of Staff is an old service buddy. He can sound the alarm to the appropriate government agencies. But for you and me, that's irrelevant. We need to find room on the front page for our story."

---

*Silver Spring, Maryland*
*39° 3' 42"N Latitude, 76° 59' 38"W Longitude*
*Friday, March 30, 2018, 1:05 AM (EDT)*

Brickman slipped into bed, trying not to wake his wife. He couldn't be more pumped; decades of thought and preparation had come to fruition this very night. Given the short amount of time he had given them to find the flash drive, he had set the odds at fifty-fifty that they'd arrive before the Metro's closing time. But they'd done it and would now be struggling over what to do with the information on that drive.

Brickman had recognized that he needed to know when and if the flash drive was retrieved and read. After all, it would have been disappointing indeed to discover, days from now, that the duct tape and flash drive remained stuck to the wall at the Metro station. It was for that reason that more than the pdf of his demand letter resided on that drive. Opening the file activated a hidden program that sent a signal to a temporary website set up earlier. That website had done its job. The signal initiated by the flash drive arrived at eight minutes after midnight.

The only question now was whether the *Post* would choose to publish the letter. They'd have to delay the presses to do so.

Brickman couldn't sleep. Instead, he lay patiently as time ticked by on his bedside clock. Six in the morning was when he typically heard the swat of the paper on the sidewalk outside. If he heard nothing, his undertaking was afoot. And if so, he'd slip out of bed to check the digital version of the *Post*.

◆

*George Bush Center for Intelligence, McLean, Virginia*
*38° 57' 7"N Latitude, 77° 8' 46W Longitude*
*Friday, March 30, 2018, 2:45 AM (EDT)*

Along with hundreds of others, Hector Rodriquez Lopez rushed through the front doors of the CIA. The call had come in at two in the morning. What with the antics of the current Trump administration, everyone was working at breakneck speed concerning events surrounding North Korea, Iran, and Syria. Lopez was exhausted.

That phone call consisted of one word, repeated twice: "Codex." All CIA agents knew what this word told them to do: *Return, immediately, to your primary place of business.* Lopez couldn't recall the last time this had happened. It signified a dire emergency. He had rolled over in bed and kissed his wife, Barbara. "They need me, honey. Got to go." Per protocol, *Codex* told Lopez nothing, other than to get his butt to work stat!

Lopez, senior counterintelligence agent for the CIA, had spent his entire career at the CIA, starting right out of college in 1984—which meant that he could have retired at the age of fifty-five, four years earlier. But he had chosen to stay on, owing to two facts, one being that he loved his job and had no idea what he would do to amuse himself in retirement. But he couldn't deny that a significant promotion and accompanying pay raise had sweetened the pot.

His other motivation complemented reason number one. One advantage of his long tenure was that Lopez knew almost everyone. This noninconsequential fact gave him more power and influence than he had ever imagined. And then, just three months following President Trump's election, came the coup de grâce, the hiring of their new director, Dr. Alexandria Jane McFadden.

Since Trump's election in 2016, more than a few at the CIA had questioned his devotion to *draining the swamp*, as he put it. That was not the case with Dr. McFadden. About the same age as Lopez, she had advanced steadily through the ranks of the CIA. And for good reason: She was whip-smart (Ph.D. in mathematics) and known for having infallible integrity. But there was something else! McFadden had people skills. Those who had worked for her swore that, in a one-to-one conversation, the tone and cadence of her words could mesmerize anyone.

Lopez knew all this to be true because he had known McFadden back in the day, in spy school. In fact, under full disclosure, he would have to reveal that they had once gone out on a date. Nothing had come of it, but over the years, they had run into each other now and again. One day, shortly after her Senate confirmation, after Lopez had responded to a firm knock on his office door, a big smile washed over his face. Although it had been years since they had last seen each other, McFadden made it seem like yesterday.

———◆———

Marc Miller, Lopez's longtime assistant, lived closer to the office and was waiting when Lopez arrived. Although Miller was impetuous and had some annoying quirks, he had the best mind of anyone on Lopez's staff. Most annoying was his habit of drawing out an explanation, to the point when the listener had already forgotten the original thrust of the discussion.

"Okay, Marc. What's up? Are we at war? Is it Israel? Iran? Syria? Talk to me!"

"No, it's nothing like that." Miller paused to gather his thoughts. "Do you remember the Civil War?"

Lopez rolled his eyes. *Oh, God, help me! Not again!* "Yes, Marc. I do remember reading about that one in high school. That was a real bummer."

"Well, it appears that there are some people from the South who still hold grudges."

Lopez shook his head. "You're not telling me that they've decided to secede? Come on, Marc, can you please get to the point?"

Miller handed Lopez a single sheet of paper. "Read this, and you'll know as much as I do. *The Washington Post* received it some three hours ago. They're delaying their print run so that it'll make today's paper."

———◆———

*Halcyon Heights home subdivision, Monterey, California*
*36° 33' 30"N Latitude, 121° 46' 29"W Longitude*
*Thursday, March 29, 2018, 10:55 PM (PDT)*

*Monterey Image Apartments, Monterey, California*
*36° 35' 55"N Latitude, 121° 51' 7"W Longitude*
*Thursday, March 29, 2018, 10:55 PM (PDT)*

Within seconds of each other, two phones on the Monterey Peninsula awoke their owners. The recorded message was identical: Codex, repeated twice. For Victor Silverstein and Linda Kipling, it took a moment to recall the significance of this signal.

As they checked the time and climbed slowly from their beds, their responses were identical. "This has never happened before!"

———◆———

*Dulles International Airport, Gate C9, Dulles, Virginia*
*38° 56' 44"N Latitude, 77° 26' 56"W Longitude*
*Friday, March 30, 2018, 7:35 AM (EDT)*

Aeroflot Flight 65, a ten-hour nonstop from Moscow, had just landed. Dmitri Smirnoff had gotten only a few hours' shuteye in his cramped seat in economy; his SVR pay grade wouldn't allow business class. After a three-hour layover, he'd fly next to San Francisco and then take the short flight south to Monterey, where Silverstein would be waiting this afternoon.

As the plane taxied, Smirnov texted Silverstein to give him an update. He blinked in surprise when he received a quick reply, acknowledging the message's reception. *What's he doing up at this hour?* Smirnov checked the time on his phone and again subtracted three hours to make sure that he hadn't overestimated how early it was in California.

Over the years, Smirnov had been to the United States dozens of times. Except for his accent, which immediately informed anyone that he was foreign-born, he could pass as an American. As good spies do, he had built up an extraordinary sense of awareness of his immediate environment; he liked to call it *spydar*. Without such a faculty, no spy would last long in this business. He'd be more likely dead.

As Smirnov exited the Jetway, his self-defense detectors flashed red almost immediately. Something was wrong! People were acting nervously, with many chattering among themselves. Others grouped around the overhead television.

Smirnov cozied up to the TV and casually asked an older gentleman what was going on. "Someone's destroying our weather satellites. There's a letter, supposedly from some Confederate nut.

I don't believe it, I tell you. Fake news! I'll give you odds that it's the Russians again. They just won't leave us alone. It's going to lead to war."

Smirnov couldn't help but wince at the comment. *So easy to blame us again!* He listened further to the TV and soon had the gist of the satellite attack. It wasn't just any satellite. Someone had it in for America's weather satellites. Contrary to the delusional and excitable statement from an old man, the perpetrator did appear to come from the South. Smirnov knew American history well enough to understand the hatred that had arisen after President Lincoln abolished slavery.

Smirnov realized that he had enough time to exit the building and call Popov. He added seven hours to east coast time; it was mid-afternoon in Moscow. The springtime air felt crisp, gusting wind making tiny swirls from paper debris on the sidewalk. He checked his surroundings and casually walked to an open area.

Smirnov carried two phones: an ordinary unencrypted smartphone and a larger, more basic, satellite phone that allowed for encrypted voice conversations and data transmissions. He'd use the latter. Popov answered without delay. "You're in Washington?"

"Yes. Listen! Are you aware of what's going on here?"

Popov replied quickly. "Word is just coming in. The Americans seem to have a terrorist bent on destroying their weather satellites. Our analysts are on it. Keep us informed of what you see at your end, particularly regarding what Silverstein tells you."

"Yes sir, Comrade Popov."

The conversation went no further.

Pondering what few details he had learned, Smirnov returned to the terminal to pass through security. He cursed his bad luck. He had thought of this trip as being something of a vacation. He doubted that there would be time for a tour of the area come Saturday. Silverstein and Kipling, both meteorologists, would be beside themselves over any threat to their livelihood.

*San Jose, California*
*36°33'30"N Latitude, 121°46'29"W Longitude*
*Friday, March 30, 2018, 6:45 AM (PDT)*

Kathy Ann Erickson sat at her table eating breakfast, digesting the news that had expanded to become a torrent. Alerts on her iPhone had begun to pop up well before her alarm clock started blaring at six. She read with interest analyses from the various web news feeds. Facts pointed to a domestic act of terrorism that had the nation not only enthralled but anxious. This wasn't war, but to lose America's weather satellites would be a blow to the nation—and even to its security. "And was there more to come?" interviewees worried. Erickson knew the definitive answer to that question.

The news gave Erickson pause. Because this incident might well consume the nation's attention for some time, should she delay her own planned operation?

She came to an immediate conclusion. No! This random, unexpected event might work to her advantage. Why not lead the government and the public to think that the two events were linked? Might the Americans conclude that there was, in fact, *no* disgruntled rebel from the South? Might it be that Russia—not unlike their "fake news" involvement with the 2016 presidential election—was behind it all?

Erickson felt giddy as she recognized the sheer genius of this new strategy. As the old saying went: *No amount of planning or foresight can take the place of pure dumb luck!* There was no need to delay. Her assault on the infrastructure of the U.S. mainland would begin later this morning. And she had decided to start with a doozie! She'd program the start before heading off to work.

# ～ 9 ～

## ON THE JOB

*Naval Research Laboratory (NRL), Monterey, California*
*36° 35' 34"N Latitude, 121° 51' 17"W Longitude*
*Friday, March 30, 2018, 7:15 AM (PDT)*

Silverstein flinched, the squeak from his office door piercing his subconscious. It had been eight hours since the Codex call had rousted them from bed.

"Wakey, wakey! No time to be sleeping on the job." Kipling's voice was strong and fresh. "I went to McDonald's. I have two Egg McMuffins for you and a Fruit 'N Yogurt for me. Plus, two large coffees. Let's get with the program."

Silverstein straightened. "You're the best." He went straight for the coffee.

Kipling slowly spooned her yogurt. "I may appear to be calm and collected, but I'm pissed as hell. Do you know how many years I've worked on that satellite? NOAA-20 was as much my baby as anyone's."

It wasn't long after the Codex alert that Lopez called. He summarized what he knew and told them to stand by. Once the workday began back in DC, they proceeded to reach out to everyone they knew at NSOF—although they learned little more than what

Lopez had revealed. NOAA-20 was not responding to commands. Following the delayed print edition of *The Washington Post*, Silverstein and Kipling hovered over their cell phones, searching for additional details from the various news feeds.

Silverstein finished the first of his sandwiches. "Can we talk about this? Two brains are better than one."

"You start."

"First, the letter to the newspaper wants us to believe that it's just one person trying to right the wrongs he thinks were inflicted on the South because of the Civil—."

Kipling interrupted. "How much do you want to bet he's a racist? Probably laments the fact that he doesn't have any slaves to boss around anymore."

Silverstein winced at Kipling's characterization. "Second, he decides to use our weather satellites as leverage. Why not something sexier, like a spy satellite?"

Again, Kipling jumped in. "Why not a she?'

"What?" Silverstein pretended to be confused.

"You said it was a *he*. Why not a she? In case you haven't noticed, women can do anything these days."

"Terrorism?"

"Damn straight. *Hell hath no fury as a woman scorned.*"

"That's different," he responded.

"Affairs of the heart? Sure! But there are other reasons."

"Could be." Silverstein waved his hand in mock dismissal. "Listen, there's something else that's obvious to me now that my brain's functioning again." He pointed to the window. "Now that I finally see daylight!"

"Yeah?"

"Think about it. It's like writing a book. The adage is that *you write what you know.*"

Kipling stopped eating, mid-spoon. "I've thought about that. Whoever did this knows satellite code. And from what I've seen operationally, there's little physical security on the job."

"Well then, the problem's half solved, isn't it? All we have to do is gather all of the code writers together, set up an array of polygraphs, and see who's lying."

"Trouble is, we don't have time. You read the letter."

Silverstein understood. He casually leaned back in his chair, hands behind his head—only an instant before his whole body snapped forward. "Dammit!"

"What?"

"I completely forgot! You've probably forgotten, too."

"No, I haven't." Kipling made a point of catching his eye. "Do you want to talk about it?"

———◆———

Kipling knew precisely what was bothering her partner. Since Lopez's telephone call under the tree two days earlier, Silverstein had been distant, to the point of avoiding eye contact and eschewing his usual casual banter. In contrast, he had been acting normally since their meetup after midnight. Why? Kipling was certain that the satellite crisis made him forget that Dmitri Smirnov would be arriving this afternoon.

Why the dustup? Several years earlier, during the Greenland escapade, Silverstein and Kipling had hooked up romantically for one brief fling. She still became aroused when she reran that movie in her head: when she had arrived in San Francisco, beaten up and bloody, and Silverstein had given her a massage in their hotel room. Hands down, that had been the most erotic experience of her life. Afterward, worn down to the consistency of Jell-O, she had asked him to make love to her.

To be sure, they *were* in love, but it didn't last. They had come to a similar conclusion, that their careers would be better served if they disregarded the romantic part, that there were too many pitfalls that could poison the trust and admiration they had for each other. In truth, their love had evolved into a different form.

Kipling understood that she was not an unattractive female: five-foot-ten, dark blond hair that she often pulled back into a ponytail, lean, taut body, curves in all the right places. So, two days earlier when Lopez suggested that if she felt comfortable doing so, she had his blessing to use her feminine wiles on Smirnov.

That was what had Silverstein in a dither. And Kipling understood. She imagined that if the situation were reversed, she wouldn't be any too happy either.

Kipling chose to be direct. "I know you're worried about Smirnov and what Lopez was suggesting during that phone call."

Silverstein, known for his usual *take no prisoners* approach, revealed a different side. His shoulders drooped. "I don't want you to get hurt, Linda. You know how I feel about you."

He swiveled to the side and stared at the floor. "Smirnov comes across as a reasonable guy, but hell, we know he's a Russian agent. He works for the SVR, for God's sake. Directorate X. I find myself thinking fondly of him because of what he did for me in South America. Still, if push comes to shove, he'd probably throw both of us under the bus."

Kipling couldn't argue with her boss's concerns. Smirnov's file revealed sordid details—although, as with many summaries of that sort, documentation was lacking. It led one to believe that he had played a role in the Crimea debacle. Also, there *was* confirmation of him visiting Syria's President, Bashar al-Assad, as a Russian representative.

Silverstein raised his finger. "Let me get this off my chest. Smirnov's a good-looking guy and has, no doubt, seduced dozens of women for his nefarious purposes. You and I are pretend spies. He's the real thing. So please keep your wits about you and be careful." The smile that Kipling had learned to love returned. "There, I've said my piece. I'll shut up now."

Kipling blinked rapidly, trying to hide any emotion that had migrated as far as her eyes. Silverstein's honesty and—rare for him—humility had taken her by surprise. She responded sincerely. "I will, Victor. I promise."

A news ding from Kipling's phone interrupted the moment. *Breaking News* confirmed their fears. "NSOF is reporting the loss of all communication with NOAA-20."

# — 10 —

## TROUBLE IN THE SKIES

*On Approach to San Francisco International*
*Airport (SFO), California*
*37° 39' 21"N Latitude, 122° 21' 00"W Longitude*
*Friday, March 30, 2018, 1:15 PM (PDT)*

For the second time in six hours, Smirnov's spydar went on alert. This time, it wasn't a flashing red but a less ominous yellow. His plane was on approach to SFO, the San Francisco International Airport, having spent some forty-five minutes circling and making various unusual maneuvers. The plane's captain made some offhand remark regarding increased air traffic. *Increased traffic* made no sense because Smirnov knew that the job of air traffic control was to keep the movement of aircraft uniform and steady. He glanced at his watch. With luck, he'd make his connection to Monterey.

An uneventful landing put Smirnov on the Jetway into the terminal fifteen minutes later. He was anxious to catch his next flight and about to put this unusual flight experience behind him when, for the third time today, he recognized that something was odd. *Anyone* would have noticed. The reason for concern became evident when he scanned the "Departures" display. Up and down the board, it read CANCELED—including his 2:35 PM flight to Monterey.

Jumping ahead to the obvious solution, renting a car for the two-hour drive to Monterey, Smirnov took out his conventional cell phone and dialed.

"Silverstein here."

"Victor, it's me, Dmitri. I just landed in San Francisco, but my flight to Monterey's been canceled. *All* flights have been canceled. What's going on?"

Silverstein paused, just a bit longer than would have been usual. "Something's happening with our air traffic control system, Dmitri. You were lucky to make it to San Francisco. A lot of airlines are rerouting their planes, some to Canada."

"What do you want me to do?"

"We'll come get you if we have to, but a rental makes more sense." Smirnov sensed urgency in Silverstein's voice. "With what's going on, everyone else probably has the same idea." Silverstein cleared his throat. "Listen! Get yourself over to the Rental Car Center. Look for signs to the AirTrain. It's an above-ground electric trolley that'll take you there."

"I'm on my way!"

"Whether you get a car or not, call me as soon as you can. Okay?"

"Will do."

As his gait transitioned from a fast walk to a jog, Smirnov's mind raced through the possibilities. One word began to dominate his thinking. Terrorism! *Twice on the same day? Impossible! Unless they are somehow connected.*

Whether he got a rental or not, he needed to contact Popov. Did he have any further intelligence on *either* of today's events?

Smirnov began to wonder if a timely opportunity may have fallen into his lap. Although he had never directly suggested it to Popov, he had subconsciously wondered if Silverstein and Kipling had close ties to national security. A few incidental comments over the years suggested that Silverstein knew a bit more than one would expect. If so, a discussion of today's events might prove interesting—but perhaps tricky for Silverstein. How would he handle their meeting? If Silverstein and Kipling *were* CIA operatives, might they respectfully send him home? So far, nothing in their conversation had suggested that.

---

*Naval Research Laboratory (NRL), Monterey, California*
*36° 35' 34"N Latitude, 121° 51' 17"W Longitude*
*Friday, March 30, 2018, 1:45 PM (PDT)*

Silverstein stared at Kipling. She had been listening to his side of the conversation. "He's on his way."

"I gathered." Kipling scratched her forehead. "Of all times for him to come, could he have picked a worse time?"

"Nope."

More than two hours earlier, their cell phones had again repeated the cryptic message, Codex. The current crisis had begun not long before that, about the time Smirnov's plane was flying just south of Denver, Colorado. Lopez called and provided a summary: "One by one, communications from and between our Air Route Traffic Control Centers are failing, leaving about five thousand civilian and military aircraft in the lurch." Lopez called again, an hour later, to provide further guidance.

"Do you agree with him?" Kipling asked. "He's putting us in a precarious situation."

Silverstein wondered as well. "I don't know, Linda. I would have preferred to play it safe, telling Smirnov to turn around and head home. We could have told him that it was for his own safety since we have no idea what's happening."

Kipling shook her head in disgust. "So, we're supposed to babysit a *bona fide* Russian spy while two terrorist events are proceeding within our borders?"

Silverstein motioned toward the door, and as they walked outside the building, he continued. "Lopez knows, I know, and you know that Smirnov's a spy. But we're confident that he has no idea that we have connections with Washington, outside of our own Naval Research Laboratory."

Kipling stopped suddenly, grabbed Silverstein by the arm, alarm visible in her eyes. He figured that she had just arrived at the same conclusion he had. "I haven't been thinking straight," she said. "We talked about this earlier. You know what this might mean, right?"

"Yup," Silverstein said.

"That Lopez wonders if there's a Russian connection to these incidents."

Silverstein frowned. "And there's reason to consider that possibility. The satellite debacle? Lopez says that the call to the *Post* originated in St. Petersburg."

Kipling rolled her eyes. "Dammit! This makes no sense."

"I know. If Russia's involved, why would they send one of their top spies to the scene of the crime?"

Kipling seemed upset and took a seat on their bench. "This is starting to really scare me. Could he be part of an operation that has all been preordained?"

———◆———

*San Jose, California*
*37° 24' 38.26"N Latitude, 121° 57' 45"W Longitude*
*Friday, March 30, 2018, 2:45 PM (PDT)*

Airspace within the United States consists of twenty-one centers—and three hours earlier, Kathy Ann Erickson had disabled all of them, the Air Route Traffic Control Centers (ARTCC). Those centers allowed for the seamless movement of aircraft traversing the continent.

To make sure that no one even considered the possibility of a logical, accidental reason for the outage, Erickson employed some artistic license. First, she simultaneously shut down the centers farthest west and farthest east: the Anchorage Center in Alaska and the Miami Center in Florida. In between those geographic extremes, over a period of two hours she then randomly disabled the remaining centers. To be sure, she had no desire to leave any permanent damage. If someone had tasked her to locate the offending code that caused the shutdown, it would take her some three to four hours at most. Worst-case scenario, air traffic control would be back in operation by midnight. Importantly, once discovered, it would be obvious that the malware code she had inserted originated from a hack.

Erickson knew that there would be absolute panic at the Air Traffic Control System Command Center (ATCSCC), the facility to which all ARTCCs reported. If everything proceeded as she hoped, there would be no loss of life. Responsibility for returning aircraft safely to the ground would fall to the Terminal Radar Approach Control (TRACON) stations. TRACON's ability to take charge of all aircraft would be severely tested. However, once TRACON did take control of an aircraft, they'd hand it over to a specific airport tower for arrival sequencing.

Erickson's plan to start a conflagration that would destroy the country of her origins had begun. The hacks that the IT folks uncovered would point, unmistakably, toward Russia.

By late this evening, West Coast time, a mirror image of Erickson's plan would commence on the opposite side of the planet. Russia would experience a comparable retaliative response from the United States.

In the meantime, she was ready to take advantage of her manipulation of the Hot Line and send out her first message. It would speed its way to Moscow within seconds. Ultimately, it would be this provocative kind of interference that would prove critical in pushing both countries toward the abyss.

———◆———

*Silver Spring, Maryland*
*39° 3' 42"N Latitude, 76° 59' 38"W Longitude*
*Friday, March 30, 2018, 6:45 PM (EDT)*

Brickman was so furious he could spit. He sat transfixed to his TV, not believing that the culmination of his life's effort—retribution for the South—a story that would normally be consuming 110% of the national news, had dropped to second-page status.

# — 11 —

## FLYING DEBRIS

*Moscow, Russian Federation*
*55° 44' 24"N Latitude, 37° 36' 18"E Longitude*
*Saturday, March 31, 2018, 3:45 AM (MSK)*

Inside his Moscow apartment, Oleg Popov sat bleary-eyed on his sofa. It was late, and he was exhausted. The Deputy Director of Directorate X had just hung up his secure satellite telephone, after telling Smirnov what he knew, which wasn't much.

None of the directorates had picked up any chatter regarding potential terrorist attacks against the United States. Popov was worried because this was not usual. Counterintuitive to what a civilian might think, an electronic buzz usually preceded major terrorist events—discussions on open airwaves, such as telephones, the Internet, and even walkie-talkies and ham radio.

As did the United States, Russia had rooms bustling with computers dissecting and segmenting text and voice, searching for keywords common to terrorists and their activities. Often, it wasn't even individual words that gave away an operation, but a sudden uptick in cell phone or Internet traffic, particularly if concentrated in a geographic region associated with terrorist involvement. Such an increase preceded most of Al Qaeda's major attacks.

Ironically, had Directorate I noticed such an uptick, Washington would have heard about it soon enough—by way of SVR backchannels. It had become an unwritten rule among spy agencies to alert not only friends but also foreign states with which there might be diplomatic tension. Except for a few extremists in the Middle East, all nations with mature governments and infrastructure at stake recognized that terrorism was bad for business. America's 9/11 attack had changed everything.

Popov reclined on his sofa, replaying in his head the conversation with Smirnov. How could the U.S. be so unlucky as to experience two, very different, terrorist attacks so close together? First, the threat to America's weather satellites followed by a nation-wide outage in their air traffic control system? For just an instant, Popov wondered whether human error might have caused the air traffic control problem. *No matter. I'd bet a month's pay that these two events have nothing to do with each other.*

Popov struggled to relax and enjoy the spectacle. *This crisis has nothing to do with us,* he thought. *We have our own fish to fry. Let the Americans stew over this one. He and his intelligence community would watch from the sidelines.* In America, incidents like this didn't stay secret for long. Their press would soon provide blow-by-blow analysis of unfolding events. Popov preferred CNN.

Feeling superior was an emotion that Popov savored. But that emotion wasn't meant to last. His personal cell phone gave off a distinctive ring that meant only one thing.

"What the hell!" He dressed quickly and rushed to his car. Whatever emergency this was required him to be in his office at the SVR as soon as possible.

———————◆———————

*Naval Research Laboratory (NRL), Monterey, California*
*36° 35' 34"N Latitude, 121° 51' 17"W Longitude*
*Friday, March 30, 2018, 5:50 PM (PDT)*

For the third time today, Silverstein concluded a call with Lopez. Someone had hacked the FAA. The good news was that the software entry point through which the hacker had wormed had been located; further, the hacked code was obvious. With luck, the nation's air traffic control system would be back in operation later tonight, he said.

"Well, at least they found the hack, and they're fixing it." Kipling tried to be optimistic.

"Don't count your chickens, Linda. A third of the planes are still in the air." Using their smartphones, they had been alternating between reports from various national news stations. NBC had just reported the one-third figure.

Being meteorologists, the first thing they had done was to examine the national weather picture. Of concern was an area of low pressure bringing snow to the northern plains and upper Midwest. Although modern aircraft control systems essentially precluded the chance of a mid-air collision, odds were not zero. Silverstein recalled the 2002 collision between a Russian airliner and a DHL cargo aircraft over Germany. Conflicting orders from air traffic control and the onboard TCAS (Traffic Collision Avoidance System) resulted in a horrific disaster. Silverstein knew to be worried until the last plane landed safely.

Silverstein's phone chirped. He recognized the number from earlier. "Where are you, Dmitri?"

"According to my GPS, I've just turned off Highway 101. The sign says I'm headed to the Monterey Peninsula on 156. Does that make sense?"

"Yes, you're fine. You're about thirty minutes out. Linda and I will be outside waiting for you on Airport Road. See you soon."

Silverstein stared at Kipling. Lopez's instructions had been ambiguous at best. "Well, here goes nothing," Silverstein said. "We're supposed to stay sharp and focused. Don't give anything away."

Kipling gave Silverstein a wink. "You know me. I was born sharp and focused."

⬥

*Route 156 between Prunedale and Marina, California*
*36° 46' 48"N Latitude, 121° 42' 13"W Longitude*
*Friday, March 30, 2018, 5:50 PM (PDT)*

Smirnov couldn't wait to tell his comrades back home the kind of vehicle he got to drive in the United States. By the time he arrived at the Avis counter, they had only two choices left: a delivery van and a huge Ford F-150 pickup. The latter had four doors, a five-foot bed, four-wheel drive, three hundred and ninety-five horsepower, and went from zero to sixty in five-point-nine seconds.

The Avis agent had gratuitously provided all this information as Smirnov signed the forms. The vehicle was twice as big as the car he drove back in Moscow. He made what he considered to be a reasonable choice and eschewed the van. The agent boasted that this was a "man's truck." Now that he had driven it for the past two hours, he couldn't disagree. This masculine machine drove like a car and was as comfortable as a limousine. He was beginning to understand America's insane fascination with these monster vehicles. Per standard operating procedures from Moscow, Smirnov had accepted the maximum amount of insurance offered by Avis. If the worst occurred, he'd owe nothing out of pocket. *Waste of money*, he thought. *What could possibly happen to a truck this big?*

During the drive from San Francisco, Smirnov kept switching radio stations to learn as much as he could about the two separate attacks. Interestingly, the satellite debacle had migrated to second-rate news. He eventually settled on KCBS, a San Francisco news-only station. By the time he turned off Highway 101, he understood the gist of what had happened in both events. Radio announcers were starting to repeat themselves.

Then it happened! Smirnov knew that this broadcast would sear itself onto his brain forever: He would remember the exact time and what he saw through the window—just as when the Berlin Wall came down in 1989. The announcer's voice was professional but gave hints of the emotion behind his report:

"This is Clark West. We are just now receiving reports of a catastrophe unfolding over and in the city of Fort Collins, Colorado. Residents have reported a massive aerial explosion. Some say it sounded like a bomb. Flaming wreckage is being reported falling from the sky. There are casualties on the ground, we've been told."

The announcer paused. "Wait! We've made contact with Mike Thomas, a local reporter for KFKA, our CBS affiliate in the area. Mike, can you hear me?"

"I can, Clark."

"Tell us what you see and what you've been told."

"Clark, in my fifteen years of reporting, I've never seen such chaos. I'm standing in the middle of a street, with buildings burning on either side of me. Ash and other debris are falling from the sky. I'm using my handkerchief to cover my mouth and—"

The transmission turned silent. "Mike, are you still there? Are you in a safe location?"

"I'm still here, Clark. I don't—." More seconds transpired. "I'm here, Clark. I'm sorry. What I'm seeing in front of me is overwhelming. Please give me a moment." More seconds passed. "I'm going to get this out before I lose it. I'm standing right next to three airplane seats, each with a body still strapped in. There has been so much trauma to the bodies that it's difficult to determine even the sex. It looks to me like their clothing burned right off their bodies. One of them, an adult—oh, my God!—appears to have both arms wrapped around a child! Oh, my God! Oh, my God!"

Smirnov's hand snapped to the radio to turn it off. He had heard enough! He veered to the side of the highway and skidded to a stop, his hands now trembling on the steering wheel, heart racing, breathing erratic, eyes open and fixed straight ahead.

Thoughts catapulted through his mind. *This is a disaster! Images of this devastation will be traversing the globe within seconds. I hope to God that whoever did this is an American. Because, if not, there's going to be hell to pay—and war! The public will be incensed and demand retribution for whoever did this.*

Smirnov's training finally overcame the emotion of the situation. He reached for his satellite cell and made the call. He'd be waking Popov once again, but it couldn't be helped. Simultaneously, he slammed the transmission into gear and squealed onto the highway— narrowly missing an eighteen-wheeler passing by.

# — 12 —

## PICTURE PERFECT

*Epsilon Restaurant, Monterey, California*
*36° 35' 57"N Latitude, 121° 53' 37.5"W Longitude*
*Friday, March 30, 2018, 6:55 PM (PDT)*

Silverstein and Kipling sat opposite Russian spy Dmitri Smirnov at a table facing the sidewalk in downtown Monterey. From previous experience, Silverstein knew that Smirnov liked Greek food, and Epsilon was a local favorite.

When Smirnov arrived earlier, Silverstein suggested they go out to dinner. The mood in Silverstein's car had been solemn, with little conversation. Silverstein and Kipling had learned about the Colorado catastrophe only moments after speaking to Smirnov on the phone earlier.

Their food orders were in, and all three fixated on their personal thoughts and concerns. Silverstein said the obvious. "You certainly picked a fine time to come visit." He turned toward Kipling, who raised an eyebrow.

Smirnov came across as sincere. "Victor, Linda, I am so sorry for what is happening in your country. Please tell me what you know. I've only picked up bits and pieces at the airport and on the radio driving down."

Silverstein considered his response. His comments had to reveal nothing more than the public already knew. He pulled out a copy of the *Post's* story from his jacket pocket and handed it over. "This is how this all started this morning: some wacko blackmailing our government, someone who's still pissed off over the South's loss in the Civil War." He avoided revealing what else Lopez had told them, that the call to the *Post* originated in St. Petersburg, Russia.

Smirnov replied. "Yes. I recall what happened in Charlottesville last August. Something about removing a statue of a Confederate general? Wasn't someone killed? No doubt parts of your country have deep feelings even after all these years. No?"

Silverstein maintained his poker face. *Seriously? You know about Charlottesville?*

Smirnov nodded, as if coming to a conclusion. "Although the situation is a bit different, it's not unlike our Chechnya. There's deep resentment there too."

Silverstein remembered, but knew that Chechnya's history was far more complicated than America's South, its history going back centuries, long before Columbus discovered America. Its modern history came to prominence after the breakup of the Soviet Union in 1991 when Chechnya wanted its independence. To counter this revolutionary spirit, the Soviet Union invaded Chechnya twice in the 1990s. In retaliation, Chechnya orchestrated reciprocal terrorism back in Russia.

Food arrived, and conversation slowed. Knowing that alcohol was an essential staple of Russian life, Silverstein had ordered wine. One of the lessons they had learned in spy school was as old as history itself: alcohol was an acceptable and logical lubricant to conversation.

"More wine, Dmitri?" Kipling asked.

———◆◆———

Smirnov knew that he needed to slow down. He considered himself a world-class drinker—as any respectable Russian would—but knew that he was approaching his limit. He placed his hand over his wine glass. "No, thanks!" Simultaneously, he motioned to the waiter for more water.

Smirnov refocused his thoughts, dull from wine and fatigue. He massaged both eyeballs with his fingers. "As bad as the threats on your weather satellites are, what happened to your air traffic control system is worse. No? Just a minute after I talked to you on the phone, I heard on the radio what happened in your state of Colorado. Two planes collided? Is that what you understand as well?"

Silverstein responded. "It is, Dmitri."

"Could it have been a failure of the system? Although it is terrible indeed, I hope to God that was it. If it's terrorism, you'll be reliving 9/11 all over again." He gulped down several swallows of water and continued. "No matter the differences between our countries, no one at home wants anything like this to happen to you."

Kipling answered this one. "We've been wondering about the same thing—about a malfunction. If you've been listening to the radio, you know what we know."

Smirnov pondered both sides of this conversation. To be sure, this was not the time to discuss meteorological cooperation. So, would they ask him to go home, suggesting that they discuss international cooperation at a more appropriate time?

That wasn't what Popov wanted. Smirnov's job was to gain intelligence. And considering what happened today, any observations he might make would have even greater significance—especially if the Silverstein/Kipling duo had security connections. Unfortunately, nothing said so far gave any indication that they knew any more than what was on the news.

Smirnov's decision was obvious. Until Silverstein said otherwise, he'd stay.

———◆◆◆———

*Offices of the SVR, Moscow, Russian Federation*
*55° 35' 2"N Latitude, 37° 31' 1"E Longitude*
*Saturday, March 31, 2018, 5:05 AM (MSK)*

Sharp words had intermixed with more reasoned thought in the hour-plus since Oleg Popov had responded to the emergency order to return to work. The reason: The United States/Russia hotline had come alive. Instead of the usual innocuous messages received on the hour, more sinister words had arrived on the three-in-the-morning transmission. The earlier threat to U.S. satellites that had plagued the United States just hours earlier—and which had received only mild recognition among the Duma and various Russian security services—was replaced by an even more ominous event.

The Americans were now blaming Russia for the air traffic control debacle. They reported that hundreds of civilians had perished from the mid-air collision over Colorado. The hotline message warned that unless Russia took immediate and full responsibility for its actions, the U.S. would retaliate in kind. The most disturbing and puzzling comment came at the end. They had proof that the Russians did it, they said.

Popov sat quietly, listening to the hawks and doves make their position clear. The absolute irony about the situation was that this entire crisis was proceeding ahead of the facts: namely, that not one person in the government—and all were awake at this hour—knew of any Russian operation that would have resulted in this tragedy. The first person that Putin had called was the head of Directorate I, the one responsible for computer services. Igor Stepanov vociferously denied that he or his directorate had anything to do with what happened.

If Stepanov said so, it was. Contrary to the propaganda that Russia spewed following their interference in the 2016 American election—that some rogue outfit within Russia had been responsible for hacking Democratic computers—such an occurrence could *never* have happened under Putin without his knowledge. He was fanatical about control. SVR had infiltrated or taken down every single person or group intent on making mischief within Russia. Further, if operations outside of the government did exist, their goal would have been to bias Putin's Russian politics, not to cause problems in America!

As head of Directorate X, Popov had considerable assets at his disposal. *But to do what?* No doubt the resident American Ambassador in Moscow was already being summoned. Once he understood the threat and listened to the Kremlin's denial, he would be in touch with the American State Department for guidance and clarification.

Would there be time for dialogue to proceed? The Americans were in a huff, obviously propelled by the resident hawks who had recently taken control of the State Department under Trump. Months earlier, SVR had warned Putin that Trump was a loose cannon who took pleasure in rocking the boat at every opportunity. Or as an old Russian saying complemented that notion: *He found delight in seeing even his own shadow.*

Popov did appreciate that in all this chaos he did have one card to play, and that was an ace. That ace was currently, fortuitously, situated precisely where he needed to be. Nothing was more valuable than intelligence from within the soul of the enemy.

Popov had often wondered if Silverstein's job description might spread beyond his meteorological interests. Considering the situation, Popov hoped that was true. And if so, might Smirnov take advantage of it? A good start would be to answer the obvious question: How could U.S. intelligence agencies incorrectly conclude that Russia instigated the crisis? *Something is rotten in the state of Denmark!*

Popov made an immediate decision, one he knew might end his career. There was no time to go through channels to get approval. He would call Smirnov and advise him to do something that he had never told any spy under his command to do. Without new and innovative action, Popov feared that this crisis could too soon spiral out of control.

———————◆———————

*San Jose, California*
*37° 13' 18"N Latitude, 121° 53' 56"W Longitude*
*Friday, March 30, 2018, 7:45 PM (PDT)*

Kathy Ann Erickson was looking forward to this evening and had dressed up. She took a final look in the mirror before heading for the garage. She'd take her own car, which was unusual. Most of the time it sat in the garage.

Today was different. To celebrate her initial accomplishment, Erickson decided to treat herself to a fancy dinner at an expensive restaurant, this one being the renowned French eatery, *Marche Ou Crepe*. With tip, the bill came to nearly six hundred dollars, augmented substantially by a three hundred-fifty-dollar bottle of *Far Niente* Estate Bottled Cabernet Sauvignon. Erickson felt no guilt in choosing a Napa California wine over the *Bordeaux* pushed by the snooty sommelier.

Feeling a bit disoriented and trying to drive carefully on the five-mile trek back to her house, she reflected on her success thus far. The shutdown of the air route traffic control system had proceeded flawlessly. There was the matter of the mid-air collision over Colorado that she had not expected or wanted. Still, the significant loss of life played to her advantage. American ire would rise to fever pitch because Erickson, in her brilliance, had made sure that the hacks into the FAA's Command Center Control System were traced back to Russia, to a Moscow location not far from the SVR.

Erickson could imagine the chaos unfolding within the Kremlin now that they had received the hotline communication from the Americans demanding retribution. She giggled with delight, looking forward to the next phase, a sequence she planned to initiate after she arrived home. In effect, the next step would signal that the Americans had had enough, retaliating immediately, shutting down the analogous Russian air traffic control system. *Tit for tat, as they say.*

"Oops! That was a no-no," Erickson said out loud, followed by more giggling. *No one was t-boned—so no harm was done. Still, I'm drunk, and I need to be more careful. Running a red light can certainly ruin your day.*

# — 13 —

## PLAUSIBLE DENIABILITY

*Silver Spring, Maryland*
*39° 3' 42"N Latitude, 76° 59' 38"W Longitude*
*Friday, March 30, 2018, 11:55 PM (EDT)*

Brickman was beyond livid. The aircraft collision over Colorado had sucked all oxygen from the news, leaving his satellite story on life support. Correspondents from every news network in the greater Denver area had set up operations in Fort Collins, cable news networks covering the situation nonstop. Even on the Internet, his story had fallen to the bottom.

The ultimate insult to Brickman: *Not one* news network was reporting yesterday's loss of NOAA-20 or the upcoming demise of GOES-14. Equally upsetting was that, earlier in the day, he had offered his services to Longway, Hancock's temporary replacement. Longway said he appreciated the offer and would let him know if they needed him. Brickman had expected more gratitude. *All hands on deck*, that sort of thing.

One of Brickman's weaknesses was his temper. When things didn't go his way, he tended to abandon logic and accentuate the negative. *Breathe! Think! What is it you could do to bring attention back to your demands? Alternatively, why do anything? Your goal was to dispense revenge, and you are doing just that. You've killed a co-conspirator—and as of ten tomorrow evening will have destroyed a second satellite. Play it cool, and you just might survive long enough to hear the gnashing of teeth from the National Weather Service—and the simultaneous congratulatory shouts of approval from like-minded Southerners. Still, I need to do something.*

Brickman realized what it was that needed doing: apply more pressure. *Forty-eight hours between satellites are much too generous!* Accordingly, he'd write one more letter to the *Post*.

---

*Hyatt Regency Monterey Hotel, Monterey, California*
*36° 35' 30.5"N Latitude, 121° 52' 36.2"W Longitude*
*Saturday, March 31, 2018, 3:35 AM (PDT)*

The noise came across as a klaxon interrupting his dream world. It took a moment for Smirnov to regain consciousness, to realize that it was his satellite phone. He checked the green-lit numbers on the bedside clock: 3:35 AM.

The previous evening was a blur, fatigue and alcohol to blame. The conversation after dinner petered out quickly. After dropping off Kipling at NRL, and allowing Smirnov to retrieve his truck, Silverstein led him to the Hyatt, only minutes away. All agreed to meet in the morning at Silverstein's office. The bedside clock had read 8:35 PM when Smirnov collapsed into bed, having succeeded in removing only his shoes.

Smirnov willed his mind to action, stumbled across the room, and successfully pressed the receive button on the third try. "Smirnov." He knew it was Popov; no one else in Russia had Smirnov's number.

"I'm sorry," Popov said. "I know you must be sleeping. But things are going to hell." Concern was evident in his voice.

Smirnov added ten hours to the time; it was early afternoon in Moscow. "I already know about the collision over Colorado," he said. "I've even discussed it with Silverstein and Kipling. Do you know something we don't?"

Seconds passed. Smirnov's heartbeat spiked. It was Popov's turn to talk. "A lot has happened since we last talked." More silence. "It was no technical glitch, by the way. The Americans say that we were behind both terrorist events."

*Both? Maybe that's why Silverstein and Kipling seemed a bit cold.*

Popov continued. "Over the hotline, the Americans said they have proof we did this. In addition to the lost satellite, they said that hundreds of people on those two planes died. They blame us for all of it and have threatened to retaliate in kind."

Smirnov swallowed hard. *Can the situation get any worse?*

Popov went on. "And they did! Four hours ago, our own air traffic control system failed. We were more fortunate. Except for one plane skidding off the runway during a thunderstorm, we had no casualties."

Sitting on the edge of his bed, Smirnov slumped in disgust. *Is this how it begins? Will there be a nuclear war? Will we all be dead by tonight?* He had to ask the question. Was Directorate I up to its old tricks? *If so, Putin would have known! And although Putin could be impulsive—in the guise of nationalism—he was no fool.* "I have to ask, sir. Did we do any of this?"

"I don't think so. Stepanov swears that nothing like that came out of his shop. I think you'd agree with me that only his people can pull off something that complex, here in our country."

"Then China? North Korea?"

"Possibly," Popov said. "But why then are the Americans so convinced it's us? I've been at work all morning. The hawks are circling and already planning an appropriate retaliation, and they're lobbying Putin hard. We both know which side he responds to."

"What do you want me to do?" *Popov wouldn't have called me if he didn't have a plan.*

Smirnov listened to his boss for several minutes, the synapses in his brain sparking to life. He certainly hadn't expected *this*. "Sir, you know that this could put us both into the Gulag!"

"If it comes to that, blame it on me. I am giving you a direct order."

———◆◆◆———

*Naval Research Laboratory (NRL), Monterey, California*
*36° 35' 34"N Latitude, 121° 51' 17"W Longitude*
*Saturday, March 31, 2018, 4:05 AM*

After four hours of sleep, Silverstein and Kipling once again wakened to the Codex calls, at 1:10 AM. Being ordered to work in the wee hours of the morning was becoming a habit.

Back at the office, it wasn't long before they heard from Lopez. For the first time in his short career as a pretend spy, Silverstein received a significant, direct order.

"Victor, in the larger scheme of things, keeping us out of a nuclear war with Russia overrides concern over a couple of satellites. As any president would do, Trump has ordered all federal security agencies to concentrate 110% of their effort on the FAA hack.

"Which brings me to my point." Silverstein pressed the phone tighter against his ear as the volume of Lopez's voice ratcheted down a notch. "I know, and you know, how important our weather satellites are. But I'd soon be in trouble if I overtly disobeyed Trump. Fortunately, no one here pays any attention to you and Kipling."

Silverstein grimaced and rolled his eyes. "Thanks a lot, Hector."

"You know what I mean! You and Kipling can work independently. Since your livelihoods depend on these satellites, you have a personal stake."

Silverstein's muscles tightened, and he sensed his blood pressure on the rise. "So let me get this straight. The future of our meteorological satellites rests with Linda and me?

"What if we need technical support?" Silverstein added. "Any chance you could grease the skids with the FCDE? Linda and I have worked with them before."

"I'll call them right now. Anything else from me, you just ask. Deal?"

"Too bad I'm not even sure where to start."

"You do realize that it's tonight when the next satellite becomes space garbage. Unknown to nearly everyone outside the CIA are the three terrorist acts that you and Kipling personally defused. The public will never know about those, but within these hallowed walls, you two are goddamned heroes. Your country is calling on you just one more time."

Silverstein was flabbergasted at his boss's remarks and had no idea what to say, and so he said what was expected of him. "Yes, sir!"

---

Kipling had been sitting quietly, listening to Silverstein's side of the conversation. "I think I got the gist. No one's going to help us. It's up to you and me to fix the satellite problem. Right?"

"Yup. Apparently, for some obscure reason, the fate of the whole civilized world is more important."

Kipling laughed. "Imagine that."

---

Another call came in not even forty-five minutes after the first. Kipling took this one. "Kipling here."

It was Lopez. "Good! It's you. Change of plans. Russia's air traffic control system has experienced the same failure that ours did yesterday. And get this! Over the hotline, Russia claims that we did it. Their ambassador is making the same assertion! Our State Department is in a dither."

"Did we?"

"Hell no! We have retaliatory mechanisms in place in case of something like this, but no!" A pause. "And it's worse than that, Linda. You know how impulsive Trump is. He's pissed big time over yesterday's incidents, and he's ordered us to prepare for retaliation. For openers, he's told us to take out Moscow's electrical grid."

"Can we do that?"

"Of course, we can do that! But I'd like to strangle the imbecile who told Trump that we could. To him, if we have a weapon, it needs to be locked and loaded. His trouble is he goes for drama, shooting first and asking questions later."

Kipling listened with increasing dread.

Lopez continued. "If sanity doesn't soon rear its head, it won't be long before we're involved in a global nuclear war. He's already raised the military alert to DEFCON 3."

Kipling knew about the DEFCON (DEFense CONdition) system of military readiness, ranging from DEFCON 5, a normal state of readiness, all the way to DEFCON 1 when, figuratively, the pistol's cocked, and nuclear war is imminent.

"Linda, you're in a unique position, and everyone knows you're smart and resourceful. You proved that in Greenland. If Smirnov knows anything about this, you're in a prime position to get it out of him. Is it a coincidence that he just happened to arrive at the very instant both terrorist attacks began?

"I don't have to tell you that this is a time-critical situation. You have my authorization to do anything you deem necessary to figure out what's going on. As I told Victor earlier, anything you two need, just let me know! In terms of transportation, I forgot to tell him that I am positioning two CIA jets in San Jose, both within twenty minutes recall from Monterey. You know the procedure for activating them."

Kipling decided it was appropriate to repeat what she had heard at the end of Silverstein's conversation. "Yes, sir."

---

Silverstein had been listening in on the conversation. Unfortunately, there hadn't been many words on her end. And what unnerved Silverstein was that, at one point, he swore that he saw her shiver. Curious, because from experience, he knew that Kipling was fearless. "What gives, Linda? Anything you can share?"

Kipling was slow to respond. "Oh, nothing much. You and I now have different jobs. Russia's air traffic control system went down, just like ours. Russia says we did it. Trump is furious and has gone to DEFCON 3. And he may order the CIA to turn out the lights in Moscow."

Silverstein snapped to attention and closed his eyes, reeling from the implications of what he had just heard. "Is that all?"

"Pretty much. Other than that, each of us now has our own private jet at the ready if we want to go somewhere. Beats flying commercial."

———————◆———————

Following Lopez's second communication, Silverstein and Kipling strategized and came to an obvious conclusion. Lopez now wanted to divide his Monterey contingent in order to tackle *both* problems.

Silverstein realized that any advice to his partner regarding her strategy toward Smirnov had best be avoided. In terms of human interaction and coercion, Kipling's skills were superior to his, and he knew it. The aptitude tests they had taken said so.

"This is going to be odd, Linda," he said. "We've always been there for each other. I might not have you to bounce off ideas or to save my butt."

Kipling smiled. "I think you'll be just fine. But before I forget to tell you, I spotted something that might be of interest. Or it might mean nothing. Did you happen to notice anything odd about that letter in the *Post*?"

"Go on."

"You know how picky I am when it comes to grammar and syntax?"

"*Everyone* at NRL knows that! So what?"

Kipling waved her hands dramatically. "That's the point, Victor! As picky as I am, even *I* could not find one error in grammar or punctuation. That's not normal.

"To me, this definitely points to a government employee or a contractor connected to the satellite business. You need to focus there."

Exiting the haze, confusion, concern, and fatigue that had clouded his mind over the past twenty-four hours, Silverstein felt his brain beginning to function again. "Linda, you remember our visit to the FCDE after the Greenland debacle?"

"Yes. The Federal Center for Data Examination in Las Vegas. Captain Stigler invited us out to take a look-see."

Silverstein pictured what he had seen there. "Do you remember the saying on the wall that greeted us when we got off the elevator?"

"Yup! It said, 'If you believe in coincidences, you shouldn't be working here.'"

Silverstein nodded. "That phrase has stuck with me ever since."

"What are you thinking?"

"I'm wondering if it really was a coincidence that your friend Steve Hancock was murdered only four days before the letter to the *Post*. NSOF *is* ground zero for satellite operations."

"Interesting thought."

"I wonder if there are any other coincidences that might have occurred during that period." Silverstein thought for a bit. "And what you suggest is where I'll begin. I'll ask for a list of employees, government and contract, who've worked at NSOF over the past two years. That's the kind of information FCDE can pull up in a flash."

Silverstein glanced at his watch and picked up the phone. It was 4:35 AM. "I'm taking Hector at his word. He did imply unconditional support."

# — 14 —

## KINGDOM COME

The Washington Post, *Washington, DC*
*38° 54' 10"N Latitude, 77° 1'50"W Longitude*
*Saturday, March 31, 2018, 7:46 AM (EDT)*

Rachel Ham was finishing up her midnight shift when the call came in. She recognized the voice immediately. The same MO: go to the Union Station Metro and pick up the red flash drive. Truth be told, the air traffic control system's hacking had become the dominant news story since yesterday. Nevertheless, she asked Jimmy to retrieve the drive as before.

The letter was much shorter this time. It read:

*As you know, NOAA-20 is now history. Because you have not responded to my first request, I have decided to accelerate the pace of my operation. The forty-eight-hour sequencing has been accelerated to 24 hours. For your benefit, here is the new augmented schedule.*

*GOES-14—10 PM, March 31, 2018*
*GOES-15—10 PM, April 1, 2018*
*GOES-16—10 PM, April 2, 2018*
*GOES-17—10 PM, April 3, 2018*

Ham sighed. She'd let her editor know about this if an opportunity arose. Considering the tense international situation, their satellite story didn't seem all that important just now.

———◆◆———

*Naval Research Laboratory (NRL), Monterey, California, U.S.A.:*
*36° 35' 34"N Latitude, 121° 51' 17"W Longitude*
*Saturday, March 31, 2018, 4:50 AM*

Because of the ongoing international crisis, the FCDE in Las Vegas was fully staffed and 100% operational, even at this hour. Silverstein called and was pleased to hear that his boss had delivered on Silverstein's request to have access to all data and software.

Silverstein's initial wish list was simple enough: a listing of all personnel who had either worked at or been associated with NSOF over the past two years. In addition to data readily available from any personnel office, Silverstein added a few items. Navy LCDR John Bristow said he'd e-mail the results in less than two hours.

Silverstein chose to pull rank. "In less than one hour would be preferable." A stand-at-attention response quickly followed. "Yes, sir."

———◆◆———

Dmitri Smirnov pulled in from Airport Road and stopped at the Naval Research Laboratory's manned security gate. He remembered his first visit to Silverstein's place of work, back in the year 2000. Back then, there had been no overt security presence. 9/11 changed all that.

Perhaps bored by monotony and the fact that the night sky was still pitch black, the gate guard tried to make conversation. "Nice ride, man!" He leaned from his window and took in the length and breadth of Smirnov's humongous rental. "I hope to have one of these babies myself one day."

"Thanks." Smirnov now waited for the inevitable reaction to his Russian passport, as the guard checked his clipboard.

The guard's eyes went wide. "You're Russian? Damn! Have you met Putin?"

Smirnov chuckled and repeated his standard reply. "I'm afraid I'm just a lowly scientist, just like…" He pointed ahead to the figure approaching them from across the street. "…just like your Dr. Silverstein coming toward us right now."

The guard appeared surprised by Smirnov's comment. "Oh, sir, I must tell you that Dr. Silverstein is no lowly scientist. Word gets around. And from what I hear, he may be the smartest person in the entire U.S. Navy."

It was Smirnov's turn to be surprised. "You don't say?"

———◆———

Silverstein approached Smirnov's vehicle and gestured to his left, toward the empty parking lot. Since 9/11, all guests had to be escorted into any of the buildings within the compound. Silverstein had chosen to save time by personally meeting his guest outside.

After a cursory greeting, the two walked smartly into Bldg. 704, up to the second floor where Silverstein and Kipling had their offices. Silverstein recognized that it would not escape Smirnov's attention that they were the only people in the building this early in the morning.

After they repeated obligatory handshakes, Silverstein tried to lower tension by making a joke. "Look what I found skulking around the grounds outside—at five o'clock in the morning, no less. Linda, do you think I should call the police? He looks like a Russian spy to me."

Kipling reacted as expected, laughing aloud. "I don't know, Victor. He certainly does look like a shady character."

Smirnov didn't seem to appreciate the humor; in fact, he had grown pale. Silverstein glanced toward Kipling to see if she had picked up something he had missed. "Dmitri, I'm sorry. I was making a joke. I doubt any of us got much sleep last night."

"May I sit down?" Smirnov seemed a bit unsteady on his feet.

Silverstein had no idea what was going on. He had never seen Smirnov in such a subdued condition. He gestured toward his chair.

"Listen to me, please." Smirnov sat straight. "What I am about to tell you will place my life in your hands. I'm sure that you are suspicious because of the timing of my visit. I swear to you that my original intent in coming here *was* to discuss meteorological cooperation. But that has all changed.

"Two hours ago, I received a call from Moscow telling me that the situation between our countries is edging close to a crisis. Do you know this?" Smirnov looked up hopefully.

Silverstein and Kipling, like they'd been taught in spy school, gave nothing away.

Smirnov continued. "My government is convinced that your government targeted our aviation system in retaliation for us bringing down yours. I can tell you for a fact that we had nothing to do with what happened here in the United States!"

"How can you know that for sure?" Silverstein chose to take the offensive.

"What I am about to tell you must go no further than this room. Do I have your word?"

Silverstein stared at Kipling and she at him. He nodded.

Smirnov, still wearing his heavy jacket, was perspiring noticeably. "My name is Dmitri Smirnov. My boss is Oleg Popov. He is the Deputy Director of Directorate X within the SVR. Directorate X deals with science and technology. As I said, I got a call not even two hours ago. He told me that our countries are edging toward a nuclear standoff. You are already at DEFCON 3, and so we have reciprocated. Not since the Cuban missile crisis back in the 1960s have we seen a situation deteriorate so quickly. Within twenty-four hours, we could be at war." Smirnov stopped talking as if to make a point. "And you need to know that Oleg Popov—by himself, with no authority from anyone else—has authorized me to tell you this."

Smirnov hesitated and then soldiered on. "My boss and I suspect that you two are somehow connected to your foreign spy service, the CIA. At this very moment, I pray that it is so.

"Here is what I need to tell you. I am a high-level Russian spy and have been so for my entire career. Popov has ordered me to work with you to figure out what's going on." Smirnov swallowed hard. "Before we blow each other to kingdom come!"

# – 15 –

## DIGIT TWO

*Naval Research Laboratory (NRL), Monterey, California*
*36° 35' 34"N Latitude, 121° 51' 17"W Longitude*
*Saturday, March 31, 2018, 5:25 AM*

Silverstein and Kipling exchanged thoughts almost telepathically, not unusual considering the years they had worked together. Silverstein couldn't recall anything from CIA school that had prepared them for such a situation. He'd have to wing it.

Silence ensued. Smirnov, head buried in his hands, stared at the floor. Given his nature, Silverstein would normally have cracked a joke. But now was not the time to poke fun or give away any intelligence they had regarding the inner workings of the SVR. Nothing Smirnov said was news to the CIA. Both Silverstein and Kipling recognized the name Popov and knew about Directorate X; they had even seen a photo that did nothing to flatter the rotund figure of the deputy director.

Aside from these thoughts, Silverstein had to recognize what was truly significant: Smirnov seemed truly alarmed over the evolving international situation—as was Popov. Kipling's facial expression told Silverstein that he needed to say something. He remembered some advice from one of their CIA classes when the instructor recommended this axiom: Whenever you find yourself in a tense situation and don't know what to say, ask a question.

"Dmitri, you'll forgive us for being a bit stunned over what you've just told us. If you are this concerned about what is happening, then Linda and I need to be so as well. I have a question for—"

Before Silverstein could advance to the question part, Smirnov interrupted, perhaps having learned the identical axiom back in Mother Russia. "I suspect that you two are *already* concerned. Or is it normal for two research scientists to go to work this early on a Saturday? Please, no games! I've already told you that I'm putting my life on the line here."

Silverstein mentally slapped himself for already having lost this initial verbal skirmish. Smirnov was the better spy, for which years of training had prepared him. Silverstein was reminded of President Trump, who had been warned repeatedly that, in one-on-one conversations with Vladimir Putin, he would be at a disadvantage with the cagey former KGB chief.

Accordingly, Silverstein made an executive decision: Forget the rulebook! Throughout his lifetime, his *gut* had served him well, and he saw no reason to abandon it now.

Smirnov finally realized that he was awash with sweat and began to remove his jacket.

Silverstein raised his hand. "Dmitri, keep your jacket on. You have been honest with us, and you have a right to expect the same from Linda and me. We need to talk. And to do that, we need to step outside."

——◆◆◆——

*San Jose, California*
*37° 13' 18"N Latitude, 121° 53' 56"W Longitude*
*Saturday, March 31, 2018, 5:45 AM*

It was Saturday. Erickson had awoken to the sound of her alarm clock some thirty minutes earlier. The United States and Russia were on the brink of war. She had flipped to CNN to see what had transpired since the night before when she had sabotaged the entire Soviet airspace.

No surprises. Reporters from inside Russia were detailing the inconvenience and danger resulting from the shutdown of all commercial air traffic. Interviews sounded little different from those in the U.S. yesterday—ignoring, of course, the huge loss of life from the mid-air collision over Colorado.

Erickson had little interest in these "human interest" stories. She needed to know what was happening at the diplomatic level and tried to imagine the White House's reaction when they read the latest hotline transmission from Russia: *We know that you are responsible for shutting down our aviation system. You are backing us into a corner and giving us no choice other than to retaliate. We strongly suggest that you stop this foolhardiness before there is no turning back.*

Erickson checked the time and decided to proceed, confident that her timing would be optimal. All of America would be awake to follow Russia's latest act of cyber warfare. She opened her laptop. With a few keystrokes, she initiated the second in her series of hacking demonstrations—one that would target one of Franklin Delano Roosevelt's proudest achievements during the Great Depression.

———◆◆◆———

*SVR Headquarters, Moscow, Russian Federation*
*55° 35' 2"N Latitude, 37° 31' 1"E Longitude*
*Saturday, March 31, 2018, 4:03 PM (MSK)*

Oleg Popov's security apparatus had been placed on alert following the shutdown of the Russian air traffic control system. Nerves were fraying, conversations driven less by reason or thought than by emotion. What happened earlier today was what the Americans said would happen in their hotline message: They would retaliate unless Russia took responsibility for yesterday's disaster in the U.S.

Accordingly, when *tit* did follow *tat*, a new level of panic pervaded the Russian Federation's archaic bureaucracy. Not since the Cuban Missile Crisis in 1962, when Russia was still the Soviet Union, could Popov remember such a serious situation—one that could potentially override the common sense fear of *mutually assured destruction.*

The only good news was that, considering today's events, Popov felt no guilt about his earlier instructions to Smirnov. Extreme situations sometimes required extreme reactions.

Ongoing group discussions were achieving nothing, such that various dialogues had expanded into the hallway and private offices. Popov sat alone. He pondered his fate. Which would it be? Would he soon be dead from a nuclear explosion over Moscow, or would he be enjoying a train ride to Siberia to serve out his remaining days?

A young man entered Popov's doorway and waited until he had his attention. Given the situation, it took a moment for Popov to recognize Artur Ivanov, his contact in Directorate I.

Ivanov stood at attention. "We found her, sir!"

"Found who?" *What's he talking about?*

"Your niece, sir, Viktoriya." Ivanov held up a black and white photograph. "Our facial recognition software says it's 90% sure this is her. A traffic camera took this picture yesterday, in the city of San Jose, in the state of California, in the United States. You told me, sir, to let you know right away if I found her."

Popov motioned for the photograph. He stared at a head-on view of a woman inside an automobile, hands gripping the steering wheel. He looked up and nodded, admitting that it could be his niece from decades earlier. As he studied the picture in more detail, he removed his eyeglasses and brought the photograph close to his eyes.

"Are you okay, sir?" Ivanov expressed concern.

It wasn't the face that caused the sudden downward rush of blood from Popov's upper torso. It was the missing little finger on her left hand at the top of the steering wheel.

# — 16 —

## TICK TOCK

*SVR Headquarters, Moscow, Russian Federation*
*55° 35' 2"N Latitude, 37° 31' 1"E Longitude*
*Saturday, March 31, 2018, 4:13 PM (MSK)*

Popov reeled at Ivanov's discovery. To finally locate his long-lost niece after so many years of searching was almost too much to take in. But beyond that, the implications! "Is this all you have, Ivanov? Just the picture?" he blurted out.

Ivanov almost smirked. "No, sir! Of all the databases out there, this one is surprisingly easy to hack. It belongs to the Department of Motor Vehicles in the state of California. And catch this, sir. The *only* reason that we came across this picture is that your niece got caught by a red-light camera. Total fluke, sir, but one that certainly worked to our advantage."

Popov was growing impatient. "Again! Do you have more information than the picture?"

"Oh, sorry, sir. Yes! I think you will be pleased indeed. The DMV records include name, home address, and home telephone number." Ivanov handed Popov a second sheet of paper.

Popov couldn't believe that it had been that easy. Years of frustration in not knowing what had happened to his niece bubbled to the surface. "Ivanov, you can be sure that what you've done here will not go unnoticed by your superior." Despite the deteriorating international situation, Popov decided to act while he could.

"Ivanov! Could you please step out into the hall while I make a phone call? Don't leave until I say so."

Ivanov snapped to attention and marched smartly from the room.

One piece of information from the sheet was bewildering. *Who the hell is Kathy Ann Erickson? Did someone kidnap Viktoriya and force her to live under an assumed name?*

Popov considered his timing as he stared at the telephone number. Area code 408, it read. He located a keyboard and a blank computer screen and typed, "Where in the United States is area code 408?" Instantaneously came the answer: *Area code 408 includes the city of San Jose in central California.*

Next, Popov brought up a map of California, surprised to see that San Jose lay not far north from Monterey, Smirnov's position.

Popov typed in a few more keys, enough to remind him that California lay ten time zones, not eleven, to the west of Moscow: None of Russia's eleven time zones used daylight saving time. Moscow's 4:16 PM meant 6:16 AM in California. Further, it was Saturday, normally an off day for workers in America. She'd likely be sleeping.

Popov couldn't resist the pull toward instant gratification. Perhaps it was foolish to be making the call before thinking through the ramifications. No matter!

He grabbed a phone and dialed a sequence of numbers to activate spoofing software, specifying that area code 408 show on the Caller ID of the receiving party. As he waited for the software to make the adjustment, Popov visualized the electronic signal snaking its way across the globe.

Popov's heart raced as the phone began to ring. *If nothing else, the number is a valid one!* He thought he might have a heart attack when a female voice answered. "Hello."

Popov tried to contain his exhilaration but failed. In Russian, he blurted it out: "Viktoriya, is that you? This is your Uncle Oleg calling from Moscow! Do you remember me?"

———◆◆◆———

*San Jose, California*
*37° 13' 18"N Latitude, 121° 53' 56"W Longitude*
*Saturday, March 31, 2018, 6:18 AM (PDT)*

Erickson panicked and dropped the cordless phone, watching it bounce twice on the hardwood floor. In an instant, she ran to the base unit in the living room and disconnected the hard line.

It was then that she started to hyperventilate and stumbled to the sofa. *How the hell could this have happened? This changes everything!*

———◆◆◆———

*SVR Headquarters, Moscow, Russian Federation*
*55° 35' 2"N Latitude, 37° 31' 1"E Longitude*
*Saturday, March 31, 2018, 4:23 PM (MSK)*

The sequence of sounds imprinted themselves onto Popov's brain: the greeting, *Hello*, in English; a pause followed by two sharp thuds; more seconds that led to a break in the connection.

Popov redialed. Twenty, thirty rings. He threw his head backward and groaned in exasperation.

"Ivanov!" he yelled out.

The exuberant aide darted through the door. "Sir?" he responded.

"Is there any way you can determine where she works or her work phone number?"

"I'm sure we can, sir. I doubt we will even need to do any sophisticated hacking. You can learn anything on the Internet these days." He gestured toward one of the available computers.

"By all means," Popov responded. He knew that Ivanov was fluent in English and could navigate an English-language browser as well as their Russian version.

"First, I'm going to transfer to Google in America and search for the name, Kathy Ann Erickson. Like most names these days, there are dozens, if not hundreds, of duplicates. I'll limit the search by adding the state of California." Before long, "Aha!"

Popov stared at the screen over Ivanov's shoulder.

Ivanov pointed. "She works for a company called Preemptive Computer Resolutions." He Googled some more, found the company's website, and scanned the words he was seeing. "This company apparently does two things. They develop computer games. You know, the kind kids play? And it also says here that they work on Internet security for private companies."

*Internet security?* Popov recalled that his niece had taken to computers during the early days of desktop computing.

Ivanov continued reading. "It looks to me like she works on the security side of the house. And here is the company's telephone number!"

Popov mentally arranged his options. Was this an opportunity to learn something more, and should he take it?

"Ivanov!"

"Yes, sir!"

"I want you to do something for me right now that will certainly test your training." Popov knew that, although Ivanov worked mostly with computers, he was a legitimate field agent—one of the reasons he had learned English. "I want you to call this company and pretend to be an acquaintance of Erickson's. We have the advantage that it is Saturday. It's more likely you'll reach a fellow worker who might be talkative." Popov knew that those assigned to answering company phones were under orders not to provide personal information.

Popov outlined a plausible scenario to Ivanov, adding other bits of information that might prove useful. "Do you think you can do it, Artur? Remember that you have to sound like an American."

"Absolutely."

"Okay. You sit there and make the call, and I'll listen in on this headset." He pointed.

Again, using the spoofing software for area code 408, Ivanov made the call. It connected quickly. "PC Resolutions. This is Dan. May I help you?"

Popov smiled widely at what he heard next. In an American southern accent that reeked with velvety smoothness, Ivanov replied. "I'm sorry to bother you so early on this beautiful Saturday morning. My name is Jimmy Bob McKinley. I am from Tupelo, Mississippi. My wife, Jessie Kaye, and I have driven all across these here United States to visit the great American parks. Our next stop is Yosemite. Have you ever been to Yosemite, Dan?"

A hesitant Dan waited a moment to respond. "Yes, I have. But I think you have the wrong number, sir."

"I am so sorry, Dan. That's my bad." Ivanov pulled the phone away from his mouth. "Ouch! I know honey, I know." He again spoke directly into the phone. "My wife just poked me and told me to get to the point. Kathy Ann Erickson is my cousin, and in her letters she has told us she works here. I don't think I have seen her in…what's it been, Jes…ten years? Have I called the right number?"

Moments of silence. Popov recognized that the conversation had moved to a critical juncture.

"I'm not really supposed to say anything about other employees."

"Listen! I understand completely, Dan. I have a cousin, Johnny Ray? He works for the federal government in Washington, DC? He tells me that, where he works, their building is more secure than a henhouse protected by a shotgun-toting Mississippi farmer. I was just hoping—"

"Oh, what the hell. I'll help you out. Your call is coincidental. Kathy called here only minutes ago to tell me that her aunt in Kansas passed away and that she needed to take a week off."

Popov could visualize the wheels turning in Ivanov's head. Without hesitation, Ivanov responded. "Gawd daamn! I never really knew her father's side of the family. That must be Edna May, her father's sister." Again, he pulled the phone away from his head.

"Honey, Edna May's passed." Back to the phone. "Dan, did she say it was Edna May? It's got to be her."

"She didn't say—just an aunt in Kansas. That's where she said she grew up."

Ivanov reacted without pause, to take advantage of this new information. "That's right. Kansas. Kathy's mother left Mississippi to live with her husband there."

"Listen, I shouldn't do this, but I will. Here is Kathy's home number. Maybe you can reach her before she leaves."

Popov gestured to Ivanov that the number was identical to the one they'd called. Quickly, Popov pointed to his cell phone.

"Dan, is there any chance you have her cell number? With the kind of luck I've been born with, she's already on her way to the airport. At the least, maybe we could have a chat before she takes off."

"Yes, I can help you there too." Dan recited a second number, and Popov copied it.

Popov made a circular motion with his right hand, and Ivanov understood. "Dan, I can't hang up before asking you one more thing. If you do not want to answer, that is okay. How is Kathy doing?"

"How do you mean?"

"Kathy's lived a hard life, Dan."

"Well, Kathy's quiet and sort of shy. She does her job and goes home. Doesn't seem to have many friends. I've tried to get to know her, with not much luck."

"I can tell you why that is, Dan. But you've got to swear to me on a stack of Bibles you'll never let on."

"I swear."

"I know *I* wouldn't be the same if I had experienced what she did—back when she was eight years old. There was in an automobile accident, Dan. Both her parents and younger brother died in the very same car in which she was riding. It was horrible. She saw it all, Dan. Then she got shuffled between relatives and was never the same again. The way you described her just now doesn't surprise me at all."

Dan replied. "That's terrible. As they say, you can never judge a person until you've walked in their shoes."

Popov recognized that he was watching an expert at work because he had just set Dan up for the kill. Too bad they had not videotaped or recorded this conversation; his superiors could have used it in their classes to illustrate human emotional manipulation.

"And on top of all that, the way she lost her finger. Such a freak incident. Did she tell you about that, Dan?"

"About the poisonous spider? Oh, yeah! The brown recluse. That's a bad one. Eats away the flesh. That's why they had to amputate, she said."

"That really must make it hard for her to do her job, typing, I suppose. I assume that she still works in clerical?"

"Clerical!? You must be joking. Kathy's a master at computer security." Dan chuckled and couldn't help himself from boasting. The words came pouring out. "Kathy is, conservatively, one of the best hackers in California, if not the United States. We can only count our blessings that she's one of the good guys."

———◆———

Ten minutes later, Popov remained dumbfounded, reviewing in his mind the key points gleaned from Ivanov's conversation. Popov had dismissed him, asking him to search for the GPS position for Erickson's cell.

What Popov had learned was invaluable—and entirely baffling! For openers, Erickson was not leaving town because of a dead aunt. She was going—to God knows where—because of Popov's telephone call some forty-five minutes earlier.

Second, clearly, Viktoriya had wiped clean her earlier existence in the Soviet Union and had taken a new identity in the United States. Nothing in the conversation gave a clue as to why.

Third, that Erickson was described as a world-class hacker gave Popov serious pause. *Interesting. Very interesting!*

———◆———

*San Jose, California*
*37° 13' 18"N Latitude, 121° 53' 56"W Longitude*
*Saturday, March 31, 2018, 07:05 AM (PDT)*

After the initial shock of her uncle's phone call, Erickson had calmly reminded herself that what had just transpired changed nothing. She had her chess pieces positioned precisely where they should be. That said, it was time to get the hell out of Dodge!

Erickson continued her mental checklist: one suitcase packed, soon to be checked aboard this afternoon's United flight to Pittsburgh, Pennsylvania; ten thousand dollars in cash, hidden inside her carry-one, with more available in her hide-a-way back East. Also included in her carry-on were two laptops. Finally, she had several burner phones.

The ring tone on her primary cell, from the 50's TV private-eye show, *Peter Gunn*, interrupted her thoughts. That meant work and likely Dan, to whom she had earlier delivered the news about her aunt. Letting the company know that she would be away from the office for a while was an obvious ruse to avoid untoward suspicion.

Erickson answered cautiously. "Hello."

"It's me, Dan. I'm glad I caught you. Have you already left the house?"

"Yes. I'm in the taxi heading for the airport now," she lied. "Did I forget something?"

"No. We're good. I was just following up to see if you got the call from your cousin."

"My cousin?" *Cousin?*

"Jimmy Bob, your cousin from Tupelo, Mississippi? He said it had been some time since he'd seen you. Quite a talker, I can tell you. Friendly as hell."

Erickson's mind raced. There was zero doubt that this call was connected to the earlier one from her uncle. "Did he say what he wanted?"

"Just wanted to hook up with you. He and his wife, Jessie Kay, were touring the national parks and remembered you living here. I told him about your aunt, and that's when he asked if you had a cell. I'm surprised you haven't heard from him yet."

Erickson realized what Dan had done. *Goddamn you, Dan! Goddamn you! And you work for a security company?* "Thank you, Dan. I appreciate the heads-up. We're almost at the airport. You have a good week, okay?"

Erickson ran to the garage, grabbed a hammer from her toolbox, and sprinted to the rear patio. There, she smashed the hell out of her iPhone 6s. Parts went flying. She identified the battery and the SIM card and separated them from the body. Next, she swept up the remaining parts and deposited them in the kitchen trash. Best not to hang around. She imagined a team of Russian agents on their way to the GPS location that corresponded to her cell. At least now, they couldn't track her once she left the house.

Erickson did a three-sixty, allowing herself a moment of nostalgia, reflecting on her seven years in this house. One suitcase and one carry-on sat ready to go. In her hand, she held a candle stuffed securely into a sturdy candlestick. Fact was, considering all that had happened this morning, she needed to erase all traces of her existence at this address. *C'est la vie.*

It was time! First, she made sure that all windows and doors were closed and locked. Next, she carried her seven-foot stepladder into the living room from the garage, choosing a position just inside the front door. She set the candle on the top step and lit it.

Erickson's final act would begin the countdown. She headed into the kitchen and stared at the old-fashioned gas stove she had come to love. She blew out the pilot lights for the four burners on top, as well as the one for the oven.

Leaving the oven door open, Erickson rotated all five knobs to the maximum, waited a moment to make sure gas flowed freely, returned to the front door, moved her bags outside, and closed and locked the door. Before leaving, she stood on a deck chair to look through the tiny glass panes at the top of the door. She confirmed that the candle had not blown out.

All was in readiness. Erickson then walked several blocks down the street, where she called a taxi using the first of her disposable phones.

# ~ 17 ~

## DIONNE WARWICK

*Naval Research Laboratory (NRL)*
*Monterey, California, U.S.A.*
*36° 35' 34"N Latitude, 121° 51' 17"W Longitude*
*Saturday, March 31, 2018, 7:10 AM*

The conversation by the tree stretched on for over an hour before the three spies realized that their body temperatures bordered on hypothermia. The sun peaking above the horizon reminded Silverstein of how little sleep he'd had the previous night.

Two Americans and one Russian had come to an understanding, one built on mutual respect and trust, admittedly instigated by what they agreed could lead to the unraveling of civilization itself—nuclear confrontation between the world's two superpowers.

As they had earlier left the building, Silverstein decided to come clean regarding their CIA affiliation. Lopez might not have approved, but Silverstein believed that Smirnov had been serious. Considering the increasingly frightening world situation, time was of the essence.

Silverstein explained that he and Kipling had come aboard as part-time CIA employees just three years earlier, following their unexpected participation in an international escapade culminating in Greenland. That oceanic island had become a Nazi staging ground for an environmental catastrophe. Silverstein had suspected that Smirnov knew of this incident—for one good reason: It was the two nuclear reactors from a stolen Soviet submarine that had fueled that nightmare in the first place. Smirnov admitted that Soviet intelligence did know and that heads had rolled because of the embarrassing theft. He also acknowledged that he had no idea that the two of them had played a part in the resolution.

Before they headed inside, Silverstein wanted to extract one concession regarding their newfound partnership. "Dmitri, you said that your boss suggested that we team up. I'm assuming that you'll brief him on what I've just told you. With that in mind, I have to ask. Will this information go any higher than Popov?"

"I thought I made that clear. If word gets out about what I've done, Popov and I will both be going to prison."

"So, I think that you can see where I'm going with this."

"You want to bring your boss into the loop too. No?"

"Correct."

"Can you trust him?"

"Absolutely," Silverstein replied truthfully.

———◆◆◆———

The trio retreated to Silverstein's office. Typically, at this hour, other NRL employees would have been arriving. Because it was Saturday, halls remained dark.

With the complexities of their newfound relationship established, conversation flowed more smoothly.

Smirnov whispered. "Do we really have to go outside under the tree to say anything sensitive? At home, we regularly sweep for bugs."

Kipling whispered back. "The reality is that only our NRL boss here knows about us. If we swept for bugs, our cover would be blown."

"I understand," he said.

Silverstein felt his stomach growl. "Anyone up for breakfast?" After he said this, he remembered that he needed to check his e-mail. He held up a finger. "Give me a second."

FCDE had come through. He made two copies.

◆━━◆◆◆━━◆

*Denny's Restaurant, Monterey, California, U.S.A.*
*36° 35' 48"N Latitude, 121° 51' 41"W Longitude*
*Saturday, March 31, 2018, 7:45 AM*

Smirnov gobbled down his American breakfast of eggs, hash browns, bacon, sausage, toast, and cups of coffee. His newfound confederates had suggested a restaurant nearby, a place called "Denny's." They chose a corner booth, as good a place as any to speak freely.

Silverstein had finished eating before the others and was poring over the pages he had printed at the office. From what Smirnov could see, they included a list of names. Watching Silverstein study this information was like watching an automaton. He scanned each line of information, stopped, and then moved onto the next. In less than two minutes, he finished all three pages. At which point, Silverstein handed one copy each to Smirnov and Kipling. "Take a look and tell me what *you* see."

"What is this, and what do you want us to look for?" Smirnov asked.

Silverstein elaborated. "Dmitri, this concerns our satellite problem. This is a list of personnel who work at the facility responsible for our weather satellites."

Smirnov understood. "You're already down one weather satellite, with more coming. No?"

"Yes. And because Linda and I *are* meteorologists, you can understand how this one hits close to home."

Smirnov wanted to make one point clear. "I too, Victor! I too am a meteorologist! All countries depend on each other for weather data. No?" After a pause, "Any clues as to who's responsible?"

"Not yet. Unfortunately, it didn't take long before our second crisis here made the entire nation forget about weather satellites."

"I understand completely," Smirnov said. "If you want, I can tell you what my boss thinks. It was a unanimous conclusion in Directorate X."

Smirnov smiled as he watched Silverstein flinch. "Please! By all means!"

"Odds are that it was an inside job. Only someone intimately involved with the satellite code—and who had access to it—could have pulled this off. Even we couldn't have done this."

"We agree." Silverstein pointed to the copies. "And what you have here is a list of anyone—employees, contractors—anyone associated with that group over the past two years."

The near-simultaneous ringing of two cell phones at the table interrupted the conversation. Smirnov watched as his tablemates listened, neither saying anything.

Silverstein explained to Smirnov. "This is not good, Dmitri. All CIA employees are to report for duty immediately."

Following Silverstein's statement, Smirnov heard yet another ring tone at the table, different from the previous two. Silverstein glanced at his caller ID. "If you'll excuse me. It's Lopez. Hang tight. We'll soon know more."

Smirnov watched as Silverstein left the table. No sooner had he exited the building than Smirnov's own phone rang. *Dammit! This would have been my chance to be alone with Kipling.*

"I'm sorry, Linda. It's my boss, and I've got to take it. With luck, I too will have something to contribute."

With that said, he retraced Silverstein's steps to the sidewalk out front.

———————◆———————

From her position in the restaurant booth, Kipling could make out the two of them, some distance apart, talking into their phones.

Sipping her coffee, she spread the three sheets of paper and scanned the employee names.

Included in the listing of some one hundred and twenty-two names were the following pieces of information: employer or contractor; college or university (if any); degree (if any); date of birth; place of birth; residence address; work address; home phone number; initial employment date; final employment date or retirement date and whether transferred, deceased, or retired; pay grade; clerical or scientist/engineer. To these data that one might typically expect from civilian personnel were three esoteric details that only a place like FCDE could produce, including criminal records and organizations to which the person belonged.

Kipling scanned the data, looking first for documentation of the murder of NSOF's boss, her former colleague. She was pleased to see that the list was current.

Silverstein's powers of observation and deduction were legendary within both NRL and the Navy. Minutes earlier, while Kipling had been finishing her breakfast, she had casually watched Silverstein's reactions as he examined this data. At one point, she noticed that his head jerked slightly. *What did he see?*

Outside, neither Smirnov nor Silverstein had budged. She continued to study the data, arranging it into neat files inside her brain. Numerical analysis was one of her strengths, and ratios came easily.

For openers, NSOF staff consisted of 81% scientists/engineers, 19% support. All contractors worked on-site. Some 60% of the workforce, all civilians, had worked there for fifteen years or more—a respectable ratio indeed. One retirement was upcoming very soon. Except for one employee who had amassed a stack of speeding tickets, all seemed to be law-abiding citizens. Some 5% of employees belonged to the NRA, a relatively small percentage but typical of a liberal state such as Maryland.

Kipling's initial analysis told her little. *If it's really an inside job, what would the profile look like for someone who could, without remorse, destroy the very instruments they had devoted their lives to develop?*

"Any clues?" Kipling flinched as Silverstein returned to the booth unnoticed. Smirnov remained outside.

"Better yet, what did *you* find out?" she countered. Before Silverstein could reply, Smirnov came running full tilt down the aisle, startling customers along the way. He seemed agitated.

"Do you know the way to San Jose?" he said louder than he probably intended.

Silverstein and Kipling looked at each other and burst out laughing. Others in nearby booths who had heard Smirnov's words joined in the hilarity. Other customers and waitstaff soon took notice.

The look on Smirnov's face was priceless. He was obviously bewildered by the response to what he knew to be a perfectly innocent question. She imagined his thoughts: *This would never happen at home. What's with these Americans?*

# — 18 —

## VERTICAL LIFT

*Heading North on U.S. 101 near Gilroy, California, U.S.A.*
*37° 1' 3"N Latitude, 121° 33' 50"W Longitude*
*Saturday, March 31, 2018, 9:35 AM*

Smirnov found himself riding shotgun in his mammoth American pickup truck. Kipling had offered to drive, and he hadn't resisted. Perhaps that had not been such a good idea. Too often, he found his eyes drifting to his left. Silverstein had the humongous back seat all to himself and had been busy since they left Monterey, either surfing the web or on the phone talking, apparently to some governmental number-crunchers.

---

Forty-five minutes earlier, they had hit the road to the city of San Jose—a direct order from Popov. At Denny's, after the restaurant's patrons had made him look the fool, their plan had come together. *How was I to know that* Do you know the way to San Jose? *had been a pop tune by some singer called Dionne Warwick?* The incident reminded him of the hazards of being a spy. The iconic story taught in spy schools the world over occurred during World War II. German spies, who had infiltrated American positions and spoke perfect English, soon found themselves dead when they could not remember who'd won the World Series.

Once the trio had reconvened in the restaurant booth, information traded back and forth in rapid succession. Immediately relevant, Silverstein reported a second major hack attack on the U.S.—on something called the Tennessee Valley Authority, constructed during America's Great Depression in the 1930s. The TVA, Silverstein explained, supplied power to seven states in the eastern half of the U.S., with much of the electricity generated by twenty-nine hydroelectric dams. Long story short, someone had hacked the hydroelectric turbines. Electrical supplies to much of the eastern half of the U.S. had dropped by half.

Silverstein also said that Lopez had been surprised to hear of Smirnov's declaration of détente and his offer to help diffuse the ongoing situation. Even so, he had not been quite so happy when Silverstein said he had reciprocated in kind.

Next to report was Smirnov. From his conversation with Popov, he had learned some interesting details regarding Popov's missing niece, Viktoriya. To everyone's surprise, Popov had located her in San Jose. Most troubling to him, said Smirnov, was his disturbing interaction with her over the phone and the fact that she now went by the name, Kathy Erickson. Popov's orders: "Go find my niece, Dmitri!"

———◆———

Smirnov's thoughts came to an abrupt halt. "I can't listen to this anymore," Kipling ranted. "We are so close to disaster!" She flipped off the radio.

Smirnov appreciated her concern. Since leaving Monterey, they had been listening to every word. Escalating tensions between the world's superpowers dominated the broadcasts. The latest body count from Friday's air calamity had risen to two hundred and twenty-six.

Added to that were at least fourteen casualties on the ground, with eight dead and six more fighting for their lives in Denver hospital burn units.

American and Russian diplomats at the U.N. were using increasingly aggressive statements toward each other. Citizenry feared the worst. Grocery store shelves lay bare, and gun sales were up dramatically. The American stock exchange the day before had closed down some 26%. President Trump had raised the military's readiness to DEFCON 2.

Silverstein had been quiet for some time, and Smirnov turned to look. "Do *your* sources know anything about this Erickson woman?" Kipling turned her rearview mirror to gauge Silverstein's reaction.

"Here's what I know, and it's not much. She seems to have shown up some seven years ago when she applied for citizenship. Interestingly, she listed her native country as Mexico. Since then, she's kept her nose clean and paid her taxes."

*Kept her nose clean? Черт бы побрал английский язык!*

"She has no criminal record and has been working at a company called Preemptive Computer Resolutions. Plus, catch this! Except for her work affiliation, there is no record of her on the Internet. For someone who uses a computer to make a living, she's not on Facebook, Instagram, any of those. I've got to tell you, Dmitri, everything I'm hearing is 100% consistent with what your boss reported. I can see why he's worried. This is a woman who doesn't want to be noticed— or found! She's like a ghost."

Smirnov, still facing backward, did not like what he was hearing. "Which is why I have been ordered to find her. And thanks to you two, that's why we're driving to San Jose right now."

"That's not the only reason, Dmitri."

"What do you mean?"

Silverstein stated it matter-of-factly. "I know who is trying to destroy our satellites!"

Both Smirnov and Kipling reacted. Smirnov was the one to vocalize his surprise. "How do you know that?"

"I'll tell you in a minute. In the meantime, Linda, we need to head straight to the San Jose airport, where I'll leave for Washington. I just got off the phone. My jet's gassed and ready, and the crew will be there in ten minutes."

Smirnov mulled over in his mind what he had just heard. Before he asked the question, he thought it through to convince himself that he wouldn't again be humiliated. "The CIA gives you your own jet?"

Silverstein responded sincerely. "Yes, but it's only a small one."

———◆◆◆———

Kipling had previously flown out of SJC, the Mineta San Jose International Airport, and knew how to get there. To locate the CIA jet, she voiced the address into her iPhone's GPS.

With their new marching orders, Silverstein and Kipling had to split up. Dmitri Smirnov would be her new partner. Their assignment, courtesy of Moscow, was to find this Erickson woman. But why should they expend effort on something that had nothing to do with the global crisis? On the other hand, did Popov suspect a connection? Besides, why not follow this lead? There certainly weren't any other clues staring them in the face.

Kipling couldn't take it any longer. "Okay, great one! Both Dmitri and I bow at your feet. How is it that you're *so sure* you've located our satellite villain?" She caught Smirnov's eye and winked.

As usual, Silverstein couldn't help but make it a production. "Elementary, my dear Watson. I just looked at the data. If it's an inside job, then it's likely to be one or more of the one hundred and twenty-two names on our list. But what do we know beyond that? We know for sure that this guy has a deep-seated resentment to the South's loss in the Civil War. That suggests that he was born and raised in the South. From our data, there were—."

"Eighteen!" Kipling interrupted. "If you count only those from the eleven official states who'd joined the Confederacy." She sensed Smirnov snapping to attention.

"Very good, Linda. From there, though, how do we narrow it down further? All eighteen had gone to college and had at least a Bachelor's degree. Interestingly, three of those eighteen did not have a Bachelor of Science; they had a Bachelor of Arts degree."

Kipling's mind was churning. "I see where you're going with this."

Silverstein elaborated. "Part of the time I've been sitting here I've been on the phone with Vegas, doing some digging. One of those three had a college major that is particularly relevant."

"Wait! Don't tell me! He was an English major."

"Bingo, Linda. Bingo."

Smirnov's body language suggested he was not on the same page. "Could we slow down, please? What does anyone's college major have to do with *anything*?"

Silverstein explained. "We can give Linda credit for that one. She noticed that the English used in the letter to the newspaper was *too* perfect. There were *no* spelling errors, *no* grammatical errors, *no* syntax errors. This is not normal, Dmitri. Whoever wrote that letter takes pride in his writing and has the training to back it up. Someone who has a Bachelor of Arts degree in English would fit the bill.

"And there's one more thing. It's subtle, but a clue that supports that idea. Do you remember his sentence in the newspaper that goes, 'Some would say that because we were wronged, we should seek revenge?'"

"I remember. So what!?" Kipling replied.

"That sentence is a variation of a famous quotation from Shakespeare. In the *Merchant of Venice*, Act 3, Scene 1, when Shylock speaks. He says, "And if you wrong us, shall we not revenge?" Silverstein paused, waiting for a response. "Don't you see the connection, Linda?"

After a moment's delay, Kipling had had enough. She turned around briefly to face Silverstein. "Oh, I see your point, all right! Sorry! But I could've sworn that quote came from Scene 2," she said as sarcastically as possible.

In the meantime, Smirnoff seemed to be having trouble deciphering the silliness passing between his two travel mates. He continued. "Still, you are skating on thin water, my friend. If I took something like this to Popov, he'd laugh me out of the room."

*Thin water? Oh!*

Kipling knew Silverstein well enough to know there was more to come.

"Dmitri, what *you* don't know is that something else happened a couple of weeks ago. The boss of the satellite facility we're talking about, Steve Hancock, was shot and killed outside his house on his way to work. We didn't think much of it at the time. Just a random, senseless shooting that happens far too often in our country. Then I got to thinking. *Hancock, Hancock.* Why does that name ring a bell? And then it came to me. If you get a chance, type just three words into Google: *Civil War Hancock.* What will immediately pop up is a reference to Winfield Scott Hancock. He was a brilliant Army general for the North who was considered a hero at the Battle of Gettysburg."

Silverstein paused a moment to let that information sink in. "To a Southerner, he would have been despised."

Smirnov interrupted. "How do you know that your Hancock had anything to do with the Gettysburg Hancock?"

"Good question, Dmitri. That's why I've been surfing the web, looking for Steve Hancock's obituary. And I found it. There it said that his family dated back to the Civil War. Is it a coincidence that he happened to work at the satellite facility? Maybe not."

Smirnov wouldn't give up. "That's still circumstantial, as you Americans say. No?"

"Probably. But you have to admit that our circumstantials are starting to add up. I doubt you'll remember this. On those three sheets I gave you was the name of one person who is going to retire in just a few—"

Kipling jumped in. "Raymond Charles Brickman III." She then paused a tick before continuing. "But without necessarily agreeing with the Russian spy seated to my right, so what? Just because this guy's retiring, hails from the South, and happens to be an English major still isn't enough to cinch the deal, is it?" From the corner of her eye, she noticed Smirnov staring at her—again! *What's with this guy? Are there no women in the Russian Federation?*

Silverstein continued. "You two are hopeless. Okay, disbelievers, let me hit you with one final detail. Listen carefully. Brickman's scheduled retirement date is the ninth of April. That means he should still be on the job, right? I called a friend of mine who works there, Jim Haver. Jim told me that Brickman retired unofficially on the twelfth of March. He's been using up annual leave until his April ninth *official* retirement."

Silverstein appeared to pause to savor the fact that neither of his partners had any idea where he was going with this. "I think that Brickman *wanted* to retire on the ninth. Why? Because, as any Civil War historian will tell you, April 9 represents a particularly ill-fated day for the Confederacy: It was on that day that General Robert E. Lee surrendered to General Ulysses S. Grant at the Appomattox Courthouse in Virginia. Brickman's our guy! I'll bet you a month's salary."

The car turned silent as Kipling and Smirnov pondered Silverstein's logic. Before long, Kipling's iPhone's GPS signaled a turn onto a nonpublic road connected to the airport. She could see a manned gate ahead.

Silverstein unbuckled his seatbelt and pointed. "You can let me out up there, Linda."

Kipling and Smirnov, recognizing the significance of the moment, both exited the car and met on the passenger side.

Kipling felt tears in her eyes but blinked them away. "Victor, what's going to happen? Are you going to call the authorities?"

Silverstein was quick to reply. "No! We know where he lives. And if this guy's as crazy as we think he is, the fewer involved the better. We can't take the chance that he'll want to go out in a blaze of Second Amendment glory. And if that happens, our satellites are doomed." He paused. "That said, I'll need Hector's help. I've got to work fast because the second of our satellites is scheduled for ten tonight. My plan? I'll try to talk nice for openers. If that doesn't work, I'll probably torture him," he joked.

Kipling chose to send a coded message to her partner. "Promise me you won't do anything that I wouldn't do!" As they locked eyes, she understood that he remembered what had happened in Bermuda some thirteen years earlier, when she had beaten the shit out of Cameron Fitzby.

Silverstein turned next to Smirnov. "Good luck, my friend."

"I wish I could go with you, Victor. I was number one in my class in interrogation skills."

"I wish you could too. But at the end of the day, you and Linda are working a far bigger problem than mine."

Silverstein then caught Kipling unawares. He wrapped her in an embrace and told her to be careful. He then shook Smirnov's hand and hugged him as well. Before grabbing his bag and walking off, he made one final comment. "With luck, the three of us will live to see the sunrise tomorrow. Godspeed!"

———————◆◆◆———————

*Norman Y. Mineta San Jose International Airport*
*San Jose, California, U.S.A.*
*37° 21' 35"N Latitude, 121° 56' 1"W Longitude*
*Saturday, March 31, 2018, 10:10 AM*

Kipling reprogrammed her GPS with the address Smirnov had given her. "It says here that we're twenty-one minutes away."

They sped away and, for a while, were alone in their thoughts. "From what your boss told you, it doesn't sound like there is much chance she'll be home," she said.

"We can learn an awful lot from what's in her house. DNA for openers. Popov is confident that it's Viktoriya. DNA will be proof positive."

Kipling thought for a moment before putting her question into words. "Popov has DNA from Viktoriya from some thirty years ago?" She turned to sense his reaction.

"Yes." Smirnov's face was expressionless.

Perhaps it was better not to pursue this, she thought. "So, you think that we'll just break into her house, grab her toothbrush, and skedaddle?"

"Skedaddle? What does that mean? I say to you, you Americans have too many slang words in your language. Russian is so much simpler. No?"

"Sorry about that. We will run away. We will *skedaddle*."

"I'll have to remember that one. So, yes, that is about it. While we are there, we will look for other clues. Anything we learn about her would be more than we know now. Maybe we will figure out where she's headed."

"And how are we going to get inside? Break down the front door and hope no one hears us?"

From the corner of her eye, she could see Smirnov shaking his head. "What kind of spy are you if you can't even pick a lock?"

Kipling shrugged. "And I suppose you were at the top of your class in lock picking too?"

"Maybe. Why?"

"And I also suppose that you just happen to have your lock-picking tools with you right now?"

"Of course! They're always in my wallet."

Kipling rolled her eyes. *This smart ass is getting on my nerves. He certainly didn't win any awards in modesty.* She chose not to brag about the one area in spy school where she had been the best in her class: evasive driving techniques.

Kipling had been watching the GPS. "Okay, we'll be there soon." They had just turned onto the very street that Popov had given for Erickson. Interestingly, the neighborhood was not what Kipling had expected. In a city where land prices were at a premium, it was almost like being in the country, with houses far apart. The tree-lined street was tidy, houses and yards well maintained. "There it is," she pointed. "There's the house on the left. Three two six. The only house on the cul-de-sac."

Kipling made a big U-turn and pulled up to the curb, both of them surveilling the neighborhood as they undid their seatbelts. She grabbed Smirnov's arm before he could open the door. "Just a second." She reached around to the back seat to retrieve her backpack. He watched, and his eyes grew wide as she removed two Glock 23s, each with one thirteen-round clip.

"Whoa! You have come prepared. I'm impressed," he said as he instinctively checked the mag and racked the slide.

"What? Popov doesn't trust you with an actual firearm?"

Smirnov took the joke well and laughed as he watched Kipling maintain a straight face. "I'm beginning to understand your sense of humor, Comrade Linda. I like you."

"I like you too, Dmitri," Kipling replied with a definitively sarcastic slant. "And don't call me comrade!"

Before exiting the truck, they tucked their firearms into their back waistbands. Once on the sidewalk, Kipling felt as if they could let down their guard because...they were alone! The nearest house was out of eyesight, around the corner of the street they had come from. *Lots of privacy! This should be a piece of cake*, she thought.

---

*San Jose, California*
*37° 13' 18"N Latitude, 121° 53' 56"W Longitude*
*Saturday, March 31, 2018, 10:45 AM*

During his long career as a spy, Smirnov had learned that seemingly nonthreatening situations could be anything but. If what Popov said was true, mere hours ago, his niece, Viktoriya, had hung up on him from this very house. What that meant was uncertain, and Smirnov knew that ambiguity was too often a birthplace for trouble.

As they approached the house, Smirnov made verbal his concern. "We have a saying back home, Linda: *All mushrooms in Russia are edible. It is just that some are a once-in-a-lifetime experience.* We need to be careful!"

Kipling chuckled in reply, crouched down, and headed off to the right, around the structure.

Smirnov took stock of what he was looking at: an older, nondescript, gray in color, well-maintained house, probably a three-bedroom. A porch extended across the front, and a separate double-car garage stood to the right. The landscaping was mature and well maintained. A fence-like enclosure sat to the left of the house. As he took a closer look, he realized that it surrounded a propane tank. Compared to the rest of the neighborhood, Popov's niece lived modestly, he thought.

Kipling had already traversed the perimeter of the house and was returning from the left side. "Except for the garage, I couldn't see into any of the windows. Too many curtains."

Showing no fear, Kipling bounded onto the porch and did what they should have done at first: She knocked, waited, and then knocked again. She then did the obvious, trying the door handle to see if it might be open. When that failed, she waved to Smirnov. "What are you waiting for, Sherlock? Do your thing."

---

Kipling watched as Smirnov did a quick three-sixty to convince himself that no one was watching. It was about this time that she noticed the front door had several small rectangular windows at the top, too high for most to look in but enough to allow in some light. While Smirnov busied himself with the deadbolt, Kipling retrieved one of the porch chairs and placed it so that she could stand high enough to look through the windows. "Sorry, Dmitri. I might be able to see something up here."

"No problem. I just opened the deadbolt. I'll now work on the door lock."

Kipling strained to see through the small openings. She glanced back and forth, trying to get a sense of what she was looking at. This door opened into the living room. There was a sofa, a TV, a couple of easy chairs, and…. *What the hell—a stepladder? Why would anyone leave a stepladder just inside the front door?*

"I've just about got it, Linda. We'll be inside soon."

At once, Kipling noticed something else very out of place. Why would anyone leave a lit candle on top of…?

"I've got it!" Smirnov boasted. "Before we open it, I need to check for tripwires. Bombs, you know."

In less time than it took for her eyes to blink, Kipling's blood pressure soared from her normal 110/55 to a heart-attack-inducing 210/110. "Dmitri," said Kipling, in a soft tone of voice he would never have heard before. "Stop whatever you are doing right now. I am going to climb down and then say something to you. And you will do *exactly* as I say!"

Kipling slowly stepped down from the chair.

"Run!!!" And with that command, she took off at full speed, sprinting across the lawn to the truck. She ripped open the driver's side door and jumped in. Smirnov had his door closed scarcely a half-second later.

"What the hell, Linda? You scared me to death. Why would you do something like that?"

Kipling located the keyless ignition button and had her index finger poised. *We're going to make it!* she thought.

But it was too late! Before she could start the truck—and a split second before the concussion from the blast not only lifted the right side of the vehicle a full foot off the ground but pushed it several feet to the left—the air outside the windows pulsed with the brightness of a thousand suns.

# ~ 19 ~

## HELLO, MOSCOW

*San Jose, California, U.S.A.*
*37° 13' 18"N Latitude, 121° 53' 56"W Longitude*
*Saturday, March 31, 2018, 10:57 AM*

"Linda, are you hurt?" Kipling's father sounded worried. "Where are you, Linda? Yell out! I'll find you."

"I'm here, Daddy. I'm right here." She looked around, trying to see where she was. "I must have fallen into a fire. Please, Daddy, help me. It's getting hot. Daddy, I'm scared."

"Crawl, Linda! Crawl out of the fire! I'm here waiting for you. I'll grab you when I see you."

"I'm getting so sleepy, Daddy. I don't know if I can."

Suddenly, through the haze, Kipling recognized her father. "I see you, honey," he said. "Give me your hand. I'll save you!"

As he pulled, Kipling found herself slipping in and out of consciousness. She locked arms with her father. "Pull, Daddy, pull!"

At once, Kipling came to, regained her faculties, and transitioned into survival mode. Everything came flooding back: running from the house, anticipating the explosion, making it to the truck, and closing the doors.

As terrifying as Kipling's memory of the initial blast was, the raging firestorm that she could hear outside the vehicle now led to aggravated panic. Remarkably, the truck's windows were still intact, but the temperature inside was rising quickly. In a second attempt to distance herself from the inferno, Kipling reached for the start button. The engine fired but was not running well. No matter. She shifted into Drive.

"Uh oh!" Kipling recognized something important: She couldn't see out the windshield! The fire had either melted the glass or deposited a layer of soot! *It doesn't matter! I remember that the road bore off to the right.* She gingerly pressed the accelerator and could sense the vehicle moving. *Good! Need to get away from the source of the fire.* Forward progress didn't last long. The big Ford crawled to a stop.

*I need to make a run for it!* It wasn't until that instant that she remembered she was not alone. "Dmitri," she screamed, as she saw him slumped over the dashboard. "Please don't be dead!"

Kipling knew that there was scarce time for assessment. It was getting so hot that it was becoming difficult to breathe. If they didn't exit the vehicle soon, they were goners.

Her instinct was to open her door and make a run for it. There was a downside: Smirnov would die for sure. Even if she made it to his side of the truck, it would be impossible to open his door using her bare hands; the handle would be too hot. With that in mind, she improvised.

She turned around to scan the back seat. All that was left there following Silverstein's departure was her backpack. Smirnov's larger suitcase lay in the bed of the truck. She positioned her backpack so that she could grab it quickly with her right hand. If nothing else, it might prove useful as a firebreak as she exited the driver's seat.

It was time! Kipling reached behind Smirnov's body and pulled his door handle. To her relief, she felt the release of the locking mechanism. The door opened slightly. With that same hand, she then pushed the door outward as hard as she could. Although it moved only a few inches, she was relieved to see no flames lapping through the opening.

Next was *her* door. First, she rotated, grabbed the backpack with her right hand, and then pulled the handle. With her left foot, she shoved it open and catapulted herself out the door, her fall cushioned somewhat by the backpack that had swung around. She shot to her feet, realizing that it was no cooler outside than it had been inside the truck. To her relief, the Ford had moved a fair distance from the house. The structure was all aflame, but luckily there were no open fires nearby—if she ignored the unfortunate reality that all four tires on the truck were ablaze—as well as Smirnov's suitcase.

Fathoming the concept that burning truck tires in the vicinity of the gas tank was not a positive, Kipling sprang into action. Grabbing a light jacket from her backpack, she raced to the passenger side of the vehicle. Using the jacket as a glove, she pulled open the door. To her relief, Smirnov appeared to be semiconscious.

"Dmitri, you have to help me get you out of the truck!"

Smirnov looked dazed but seemed to make sense of what she'd said. He reacted by slowly moving his legs to the right. His feet slid to the ground from the high perch of the truck's seat.

Kipling ditched the jacket and shouted orders. "Give me your hands, and I'll pull you out. I need you to walk for me, Dmitri! I need you to walk! Do you understand me? I don't have the strength to carry you." He stood, and with Kipling's help, began to walk slowly down the street.

"Dmitri! You keep going. I'll be right back."

Kipling raced back to the truck, grabbed her backpack, and sprinted toward Smirnov. He was beginning to make progress on his own. She caught up. "We need to keep walking, Dmitri." She then remembered their firearms and returned both to her backpack.

Thinking ahead, she decided to implement one more precaution. "Hold up a second, Dmitri." She rummaged inside her backpack. "Good! Here it is. Lean down here." She pushed one earbud into his left ear and the other into her right. After stuffing the ends of the wires into her shirt, she felt more secure. *That should do it,* she thought. "Pretend we're a couple out for a morning walk. Here, give me your hand."

As the distance between them and the explosion increased, she heard sirens in the distance. "Dmitri, we need to walk faster. We can't be connected to anything that happened here."

That concern soon became a reality. Neighbors had heard the blast, and several were streaming onto their lawns. After all, it was Saturday.

As they continued to walk, hand in hand, Kipling tried to appear nonchalant. Soon it happened. A middle-aged couple approached from an intersecting sidewalk, and the female began to speak. Kipling made a show of not hearing and removed her earbud.

"I'm sorry. What did you say?" she feigned.

The lady repeated herself. "Did you hear the explosion? It sounded close." She pointed. "You came from that direction."

Kipling played her part. "Sorry. We've been listening to our music and must have missed it." She lifted Smirnov's hand, trying to get him moving again. "I hope it's nothing serious." She smiled submissively.

To Kipling's dismay, the couple was suspicious and continued. "Are you sure you two are all right? Your friend here doesn't look any too good." Smirnov's blank facial expression and disheveled appearance had raised concern.

Kipling had been afraid that this would happen and needed to improvise. "You are very kind, but I can assure you that we're fine. I'm afraid you misunderstand. This isn't my friend; he's my brother, Sam. I try to take him for a walk every day. He *so* looks forward to it." She lowered her voice for the next part. "You see, our mother dropped him on his head when he was a baby."

The couple, now flush with embarrassment, backed up a few steps and lowered their heads in sympathy. The male added compassionately: "May God bless you, ma'am. May God bless you."

Kipling nodded and once again pulled on Smirnov's hand. Other neighbors who had witnessed the conversation headed toward the couple to see what they had learned.

"Let's get the fuck out of here, Dmitri!" For a moment or two, they walked in silence. Another explosion to their rear made them once again pick up their pace. *Scratch either one propane tank or one Ford F-150 pickup truck. If it's the truck, I sure hope he bought insurance.*

Kipling now had more time to worry. How bad was Smirnov injured? No doubt they both had sustained concussions. It was clear that Smirnov had taken the worst of it as the truck window had slammed into the side of his head. Kipling's head had initially just impacted air but then whip-lashed back to strike her own door. The adrenaline that had masked the pain in her neck during their manic exit was starting to wear off.

---

Although Smirnov's brain was not functioning fully, he had enough sense to question his situation. He looked to his left. *Why is this woman holding my hand?* Although she looked familiar, he had no recollection of what had happened in the moments before he regained consciousness. The last thing he remembered clearly was his success at unlocking the first of the two door locks.

---

The spy duo successfully exited Erickson's neighborhood and walked west on a sidewalk along a semi-major street. Although they were worse for wear, a casual glance at them would not have caused undue notice. The good news was that they had survived a horrendous explosion. By rights—and by only a second's margin—they should be dead.

Ahead and to the left, Kipling noticed a McDonald's restaurant. "Let's go in here for a bit, okay?" They went inside and found a booth in the corner. Luckily, there were few patrons. "Stay here, Dmitri. I'm going to get us some burgers and drinks." She returned and found Smirnov still sitting upright, head in his hands.

"Dmitri, we need to eat something." She unwrapped his burger and placed it in his hands. Reluctantly, he took a bite.

Kipling could not believe the situation she found herself in. It could not have come at a worse time. She and Smirnov had an assignment: to locate a former Russian citizen named Kathy Ann Erickson—AKA Viktoriya Popova. What they had experienced at her house told them that she did not want to be found.

Kipling took stock of her own physical condition. Except for her neck, she had survived intact. All limbs seemed to function. She had obviously been knocked out but had recovered quickly. Notably, her thoughts seemed clear.

Smirnov, on the other hand, was a mess. He too seemed to be physically functional; it was his brain that Kipling worried about. *Should I call someone?* Under any other imaginable situation she could think of, she would have checked him into a hospital, and he would already be undergoing a CAT scan. To be sure, this was far from an ordinary situation. If they did that, questions would be forthcoming.

Starting her own burger and drink, Kipling realized how hungry and thirsty she was. All the while, she watched Smirnov from the corner of her eye—anxiously searching for some sign that he might return to his usual self.

Abruptly, Smirnov straightened and looked around the room. "Линда, где мы находимся?" These were the first words he had spoken since the explosion.

When she heard Smirnov say her first name in Russian, Kipling's head jerked backward. "Ouch!"

Smirnov looked Kipling in the eye while simultaneously noticing himself holding something in his hand. He became visibly upset. "Линда, почему мы здесь едят гамбургеры? Попов поручил мне найти свою племянницу."

"Dmitri, you need to speak in English! My Russian is too rusty to understand you."

In a moment of lucidity, Smirnov complied. "Linda, why are we eating hamburgers? Popov has ordered me to find his—."

Interrupting his first attempt at conversation was a phone call. Kipling recognized the ringtone from earlier at Denny's. Smirnov instinctively removed the phone from his pants pocket. "I need to answer this," he said very slowly. "It's my boss."

Kipling waited. The phone continued to ring. The next step in a phone answering sequence was not happening. She made a conscious decision to intercede and snatched the phone from Smirnov's hands. She scanned the phone's odd-looking screen and located the usual green circle.

"Hello," she answered.

Following a significant delay, a heavily accented response came back in Russian. "Кто это?" followed soon by, "Who is this?"

"This is Linda Kipling. I work with Victor Silverstein. Is this Oleg Popov?"

"Yes, but why are you answering Dmitri's phone?"

Finally, the emotion from everything that had happened over the past hour came raging to the surface, and she let it rip. "Why?? You want to know *why*?? Because your bitch of a niece damn near got both of us killed." Hyperventilating, she paused to catch her breath. "That's why…sir!"

# – 20 –

## I PROMISE

*SVR Headquarters, Moscow, Russia*
*55° 35' 2"N Latitude, 37° 31' 1"E Longitude*
*Saturday, March 31, 2018, 9:34 PM (MSK)*

Oleg Popov winced at the obscene language spewing from the mouth of Linda Kipling, Silverstein's assistant. *She has some nerve, talking to me like that,* he thought to himself.

Yet after five minutes of explanation of what had transpired at his niece's house, Popov reversed his thinking, realizing that her words had been tame. Unwittingly, his respect for this unfamiliar foreign agent increased with every word. Reading between the lines of her narrative of their escape following the explosion of Viktoriya's house—which his niece had obviously booby-trapped to erase her identity—Popov understood that Kipling had saved the life of his top agent.

Kipling concluded her testimony. "So, Mr. Popov, that's where we stand. Although Dmitri isn't 100% yet, he's improved greatly in the past hour. And, finally, I apologize for my earlier language."

Popov was a practical man by nature and suffered no fools. He responded forcefully. "No apology necessary! I've concluded that my niece is involved in something evil. And listen! With our world in danger, my name is Oleg. May I call you Linda?"

"Of course."

"And until you can assure me that Dmitri is in control of his senses, I need you to be my eyes and ears. Keep Dmitri's cell. If it rings, it's me." Popov talked her through the procedure for calling him.

"Sir, you don't think there's any chance Viktoriya is involved in what's going on internationally, do you?"

What Popov was reading from his tea leaves was not encouraging. "I know four things, Linda. First, when I knew Viktoriya, which was at the dawn of the desktop computer age, she was exceptional. My brother used to brag about her computer skills. Plus, I do not know if Dmitri told you, but we determined that she is working at a place where they test online security systems. So, could she have hacked into our air traffic control systems? I suppose it is possible.

"Second, I distinctly remember that when she moved back to Moscow to live with us, she blamed the Soviet Union for the death of her family. She was very bitter. That she would provoke a confrontation between you and us to get back at Russia is far-fetched indeed. Third, I am now convinced that, back in 1982, she staged her death to flee our country and hide her identity. And fourth, thanks to you, we know that she is involved in something so serious that death and destruction are acceptable costs for her escape. Does that add up to what is going on? I do not know, but I say that we need to assume that it does!" Popov paused. "Linda, can you help us find her?"

"Yes, sir. Here is what I can add. Back at the house, before we knew it was going to blow, I walked around the back. There was only one window I could see through, and that was a door to the garage. It was a two-car garage, and one side was filled with boxes and a riding lawnmower. On the other side was a vehicle. That tells me that she did not make her getaway in her own car. Now that may not mean anything; she could have used a rental. But my gut tells me that she's flying somewhere."

"How close is the nearest airport?"

"San Jose is very close, fifteen minutes, but there are two other major airports within forty-five minutes, San Francisco and Oakland. From these three, you can fly almost anywhere."

"Черт побери!" Popov couldn't hide his exasperation.

"Here's my idea, Oleg. If I understand Dmitri's story, the way you found your niece was from a traffic camera in San Jose. Is that correct?"

Popov cringed. If he confirmed what Kipling just said, he would be admitting that Russia conducted foreign surveillance on American soil. "That is correct."

"I think you see where I'm going with this. We have surveillance cameras at our airports. If you could send me a copy of the photograph that you used for comparison, we can look for her here." Kipling thought for a second. "Wait! Better yet! Also, send me the image of her in the car. We'll use both images. This is probably a long shot, but worth a try."

---

*McDonald's Restaurant, San Jose, California*
*37° 13' 21"N Latitude, 121° 53' 54"W Longitude*
*Saturday, March 31, 2018, 11:42 AM (PDT)*

Kipling had bent the truth—a lot. What she didn't tell Popov was that, if Erickson was traveling by air, it was more than just a long shot. She couldn't tell him because she would be revealing a secret that not even the average American knew: At any U.S. airport, when a Transportation Security Agency (TSA) representative examines your picture ID and boarding pass, to match names and faces, there is a hidden camera that takes a high-resolution photograph. That image immediately goes to the FCDE where it's compared to a list of known terror suspects. If they *did* identify Erickson, they'd also know where she was flying.

Popov responded enthusiastically. "Отлично! Excellent, Linda! Excellent! It won't take me long. Stand by for a text. Attached will be the two images. Please confirm you receive them."

Kipling suddenly realized that she had no idea how to operate Smirnov's phone. "Wait!"

After confirming that he had access to an iPhone to send the images, she gave Popov her personal cell number.

Without Smirnov noticing, Kipling slid his phone into her own pants pocket.

———————◆◆◆———————

*San Francisco International Airport (SFO), Gate 65*
*San Francisco, California, U.S.A.*
*37° 37' 9"N Latitude, 122° 23' 3"W Longitude*
*Saturday, March 31, 2018, 11:50 AM (PDT)*

Erickson had arrived at the airport at 9:14 AM, the drive north on Route 101 slowed by a three-car accident that cost her an extra half-hour. She glanced at her watch; it read 11:50. Still time for lunch before her 3:19 PM United flight to Pittsburgh. Using her good hand, she counted the hours on her fingers and concluded that her San Jose house should no longer have any market value. Gone would be all traces of her existence at the place she had called home for the past six years—all documentation bearing the name of Kathy Ann Erickson reduced to ash.

More important was the incineration of her DNA, which these days could prove more problematic than a paper trail. Before leaving work the previous afternoon, she'd made a point of wiping down any surface that could harbor biological fragments of her ancestry. She had also taken home her coffee cup. Not until this morning when her uncle called did she fathom the *fait accompli*, that she would never again grace the halls of PCR.

From her phone, Erickson had been monitoring the news, observing her progress. The TVA hydroelectric turbines had spooled down as scheduled. The world was teetering ever closer to a nuclear confrontation.

Accordingly, in the spirit of proportional response—a concept that seemed to have evolved following the bombing of Hiroshima and Nagasaki at the end of World War II—next on the agenda were the hydroelectric generators of RusHydro, Russia's largest power generating company and the world's second-largest producer of hydroelectric power. She had scheduled their shutdown for 1 PM West Coast time, a little more than an hour away. In the meantime, she had been actively manipulating the hotline conversations to inflame the situation further, making clear that neither side was willing to back down.

Erickson was nothing if not fastidious. Although it wouldn't have been a disaster if she bumped into a co-worker at the airport, it was better to remain anonymous. Once she had passed through TSA security and her face identified as a match to her California driver's license, she had hurried to a corner stall in the nearest bathroom. There, not only did she change into a different outfit and don a blond wig to hide her brown hair, she had altered her makeup.

Erickson felt immense pride at being within a virtual stone's throw of avenging her family's murder. To be sure, her uncle was of some concern; how he had found her was a mystery. Still, there was no reason for him to suspect her involvement in anything sinister, let alone an international crisis. Even if he did, nothing could change the fact that he lived half a world away.

*Somewhere over the state of Kansas, U.S.A.*
*38° 25' 3.6"N Latitude, 96° 11' 14.7"W Longitude*
*Saturday, March 31, 2018, 1:55 PM (CDT)*

Silverstein checked the time yet again: nearly noon West Coast time, three PM East Coast. They had been in the air for nearly two hours.

When Silverstein arrived at the CIA's San Jose airport hangar, he was led directly to a business-size jet. Years earlier he had had the opportunity to fly aboard a Lear 60. An aficionado of business jets, he knew immediately that what he was seeing should not exist.

"Where did this puppy come from? You've obviously taken me to the Twilight Zone," Silverstein joked as he climbed the stairs.

The pilot, waiting by the door, seemed stunned. "Headquarters told me that we would be transporting special cargo. But how the hell did you know to ask that question?"

Silverstein laughed. "Because I know that the Lear 85 was *never* produced. It went on its first test flight on April 9, 2014, but Bombardier chose not to take it into production. Too expensive, somewhere around twenty mil, as I recall. Worried over too few sales, I suppose."

As he squeezed past the pilot and headed to the rear, the pilot would not give up. "How did you know that this was an 85?"

"That's easy. You and I both know that the 85 is the only jet that uses the Pratt and Whitney PW307B turbine."

The pilot grew even more exasperated. "And *you* can recognize that particular engine? I've been a pilot for over thirty years, and I could never have done that."

"Of course!" Silverstein winked. "That and the fact that the numbers and letters are written right there on the engine."

With that said, tension evaporated, and the two shared a good laugh. The pilot told the tale. It was true that the company canceled production of the 85. All that was left of the project were two prototypes. In conjunction with another existing contract with Bombardier, the CIA convinced the company to sell the two one-offs for pennies on the dollar. The 85's 3400-mile range gave the CIA a much-needed cross-country capability in a small aircraft. Not knowing where Silverstein and Kipling might need to fly with their parallel assignments, Hector Lopez had ordered both aircraft to California.

Silverstein looked around the luxurious cabin. Besides the two pilots, he was the only passenger. Given the opportunity, he tried all eight passenger seats to find the most comfortable.

For the past two hours, Silverstein had been debating with himself his strategy for confronting Brickman. He knew his address and could drive there easily once they landed at Andrews, only fifteen minutes distant.

The pilot had just reported that they were an hour and a half from landing. Unusually high jet stream winds had helped considerably. Before they took off, Silverstein had "suggested" to the two-person crew that "pedal to the metal" was the phrase of the day, that hundreds of millions of dollars in satellites were at stake. He then gave them more precise instructions: "If we run out of fuel the instant we touch down, that would be just about right." Both pilots nodded with understanding.

Silverstein knew that he had to contact Lopez but had been putting it off. He had mixed feelings. As much as he was aware that Lopez could help, the last thing Silverstein wanted was to spook Brickman. That would mean the loss of all remaining geostationaries.

With those thoughts rattling around in his head, Silverstein dialed Lopez's cell using the aircraft's onboard communication system.

"Lopez here."

"It's me, Victor." Without going into detail, Silverstein explained that Kipling and Smirnov were chasing down a lead in the San Jose area. "But, on my side, you'll be pleased to know that I think I know who the satellite terrorist is. He lives in Silver Spring, of all places. As I speak, I'm in one of your jets hightailing it to Andrews. I think we're over Kansas."

"What the fuck? Give me the name and address, and I'll send over a swat team. That son-of-bitch will come face to face with one pissed-off Hispanic!"

Silverstein had been afraid of this. He paused, trying to formulate a diplomatic response.

Lopez again. "Victor, are you there?"

"I'm here, Hector. Listen, I'm going to have to ask you for a favor. All of America's remaining geostationaries are in jeopardy. Only he knows how to stop the countdowns for each satellite."

"Talk to me."

"I have a plan, but for it to work, I need your help. It's a tad complicated, and it needs to proceed precisely as I say." Silverstein spent the next three minutes outlining a strategy to neutralize Brickman's threats.

"That's ballsy, Victor. I'll give you that. If I were a betting man, I'd rate your chances of success somewhere south of 10%. Too much can go wrong. At the opposite end, there's a more than 90% chance you'll end up dead."

"It warms my heart to know that you have that much confidence in me. From my perspective, my success is wholly dependent on you. Can you do what I ask? To rephrase that, can you have everything in place by eight tonight?" Silverstein checked his watch. "That gives you and me some five hours."

"That's cutting it close, Victor. I'll get back to you. The first part will be easy. Not so with number two. I'll call our Director and have him try to convince Trump. If he agrees, we should have enough time. In the meantime, I'll send a tech team to the address to figure out the best approach—and confirm that your mark's at home. Does this guy have a family?"

"Sorry. Don't know."

"We'll figure that out too."

Silverstein remembered something. "One more thing, Hector. I'll need a change of clothes. I need to look the part."

"I know what you should wear. Give me your measurements, along with the particulars for this guy."

Silverstein complied.

"Hector, you've got to promise me you'll let me do it my way before you send in the cavalry. I'll text you with the script you'll need to make this happen."

"Okay, I promise." After which, Lopez chuckled and added, "And at your funeral, I also promise not to remind you that I told you so."

# – 21 –

## GOODY BAG

*McDonald's Restaurant, San Jose, California*
*37° 13' 21"N Latitude, 121° 53' 54"W Longitude*
*Saturday, March 31, 2018, 12:12 PM (PDT)*

True to his word, twenty-two minutes later, Popov came through with the digital images of Kathy Ann Erickson, AKA Viktoriya Popova. Kipling took a moment to memorize them. The photograph of Erickson behind the wheel was remarkably close to the "aged" photo from when she was a teenager. Kipling forwarded the images to the FCDE. Not knowing how early Erickson might have arrived at the airport, Kipling specified that they begin their search starting the previous midnight, but limited to the three Bay-area airports.

Kipling was worried. Smirnov remained listless, disoriented, and did not speak unless spoken to. Worse, five minutes earlier he complained of a headache. With the National Football League's recent concern over concussions, Kipling had learned a thing or two. Side effects were usually temporary. However, if the brain was bruised or swollen, repercussions could last for weeks and even lead to death.

With these realities in tow, Kipling faced a critical decision, one she had earlier convinced herself would not be necessary because, *any minute*, she expected Smirnov to "shake it off." But that was not happening! *What if he's dying even as I sit here in a McDonalds, for God's sake!* Mirroring Smirnov's profile, Kipling rested her head in her hands. *Think Linda. Think!*

There were two issues. Kipling's earlier flat-out refusal to take Smirnov to the emergency room was still in effect. Implications of an American spy taking a Russian spy to the hospital were too many to consider. But the second reality was no less important: She *needed* Smirnov. When they eventually confronted Erickson, having a Russian-speaking former compatriot by Kipling's side would be invaluable—and perhaps crucial as a liaison with Erickson's uncle.

At once, Kipling's hands pulled away from her head. There was a solution to both problems, but it required Lopez's help. She dialed.

"Lopez here."

"It's me, Linda. You said to let you know. Well, here I am. I need your help."

"Whatever you need," he said. "But, first, tell me what's happening at your end? All Victor said was that you were chasing down a lead."

"You talked to Victor?"

"He's halfway here." Kipling sensed that Lopez was in a hurry and didn't have time to discuss Silverstein's plans.

Kipling brought Lopez up to date on the past twenty-four hours: Popov's discovery that his long lost niece had surfaced in San Jose; their near-death experience when Erickson's house exploded; Dmitri's concussion; her conversation with Popov, including her request for Erickson's pictures; based on her theory that Erickson would be flying from the Bay area, Kipling's decision to upload those images to the FCDE; and, finally, Popov's inability to rule out the possibility of Erickson's involvement in the ongoing faceoff between Russia and the U.S.

Kipling then read to Lopez her list of requests.

———————◆◆◆———————

*George Bush Center for Intelligence, McLean, Virginia*
*38° 57' 7"N Latitude, 77° 8' 46"W Longitude*
*Saturday, March 31, 2018, 3:25 PM (EDT)*

Lopez listened intently to Kipling's story, eyes growing wider with each new incredible detail. "Fuck, Linda! You expect me to believe that one lone woman, who has been nursing a personal grudge for decades—ALL BY HERSELF—is capable of bringing the two most powerful nations in the world into a nuclear Armageddon!?"

"Yeah, that's it in a nutshell, Hector," she said matter-of-factly. "But if you don't like that idea, *please* tell me that you're working something better at your end?" Kipling's voice turned urgent. "And, by the way, DID YOU NOT HEAR the part about Dmitri and me nearly getting killed in the explosion?" A pause. "Besides, if Oleg is that concerned over something that involves his own flesh and blood, don't you think that we should at least check it out?"

Lopez was approaching apoplexy. "Wait, wait! Oleg? Oleg? Are you saying that you are on a first-name basis with the Deputy Director of Directorate X in the Russian SVR?"

"I suppose so. Doesn't that tell you how serious this is, him talking directly to me? Remember what I told you, how this happened. When Dmitri couldn't answer his phone, that's how we met. Please don't take offense."

"Take offense? How could I possibly take offense when a *very* junior spy establishes, on a first-name basis, contact with my Russian counterpart of whom I've only seen a *photograph*?"

Lopez recognized that it was emotion talking. "Look. I'm sorry, Linda. Forget everything I just said. We're under such pressure here to avoid World War III that we're all on tenterhooks."

"I understand, Hector. You know that I know that you still love me as much as you ever did."

With that said, the strain between them dissipated, and peace returned. What he, Silverstein, and Kipling had been through over the years had made them partners for life.

"Okay, Linda. You win. Now tell me if I've got this right. You want—"

"Hold on, Hector! Hold on. NCDE's calling!"

Lopez's line went briefly silent.

"I'm back, Hector. We've struck pay dirt. NCDE *has* identified her. She went through SFO security at nine thirty-one this morning. She's leaving on a United flight this afternoon to Pittsburgh."

"Damn good sleuthing, Linda! So, again, I want to confirm what you've asked for." Lopez read from his hand-written notes. "You want me to deliver to that hangar a portable CAT scan machine, along with a technician and neurosurgeon." Lopez thought it through. "Linda, does something like that even exist?"

"Hector, there are companies out there who have them installed in vans. You should be able to find one."

"And that should go on the plane?"

"No, no! It's not *that* small. It stays in the van. They're going to have to operate it right there in the hangar."

"And you want a neurosurgeon?"

"Yes, and a technician to operate the machine. If Dmitri needs surgery, then all bets are off, and I'll leave him in your hands. But I need him, Hector! I'm praying that his concussion isn't that serious. So if surgery isn't necessary, I want Dmitri and that doctor on my plane to Pittsburgh."

"I see where you're going with this. When you get to Pittsburgh, you'll have a pretty good idea whether Dmitri can help you with Erickson. Do you plan to head her off at the gate?"

"I'm sort of playing this by ear, Hector. We can't rule out the possibility she's meeting someone who is also involved. So as soon as I drop off Dmitri in San Jose, I'm heading to SFO. Should be enough time to grab a seat on Erickson's plane. I'll be right on her tail. What's the risk? She doesn't know me from Eve."

Lopez thought for a moment before commenting. "That's brazen, Linda. I like it. Listen. In case you need it, that will put you in an ideal situation to try out the latest version of the FC19D. They've just gone out into the field. You know what that is, right?"

"Give me a little credit, Hector. I *do* read the technical bulletins you send out."

"Okay. It's settled then. I'll call the San Jose office to get going on your requests. I'll also call the pilot. His name is Henderson. I picked him personally. I'll tell him to put together a goody bag."

"Oh, almost forgot!" Kipling said. "Could you please call ahead and grease the skids with the SFO TSA?"

# ~ 22 ~

# FORCED EXIT

*CIA Hanger, San Jose International Airport*
*San Jose, California, U.S.A*
*37° 21' 35"N Latitude, 121° 56' 1"W Longitude*
*Saturday, March 31, 2018, 1:05 PM (PDT)*

The Uber driver pulled up to the gate. Two large men in suits hurried over.

"Dmitri, we need to get out of the car now," Kipling explained in a slow, deliberate tone. Although Smirnov had remained quiet during the ride over, he seemed to be more alert and had been watching the scenery go by.

The larger of the two large men addressed Kipling. "We just got the latest from Washington. Dr. Kipling, I'm the pilot, Rick Henderson, and this is my co-pilot, Skip MacDonald."

"Call me Linda. Nice to meet you." After shaking hands, she held up her finger. "Give me a second, would you?"

Kipling handed the Uber driver a fifty. "Can you wait a little bit?"

"Yes, ma'am."

Kipling turned back to the trio, grabbed Smirnov by the shoulders, looked him in the eye, and spoke firmly. "Dmitri, listen to me! I must go find Viktoriya. These men are here to take care of you. They are friends of mine, and you can trust them. They are getting a doctor to check you out. I'll call Popov to let him know. Okay?"

To Kipling's surprise, Smirnov put together several complete sentences. "You don't have to yell, Linda. I can hear you. You need to skedaddle. Go after Viktoriya. And when you find her, give her a piece of my mind." He managed a smile.

*Thank God!* At least at this moment, Smirnov seemed to be regaining his faculties and perhaps appreciating his diminished capacity.

She watched MacDonald walk him down the side of the hanger. Her attention returned to Henderson.

Henderson was nothing if not professional. "Mr. Lopez said that you are in charge. What are my orders, ma'am?"

Kipling nodded. "So you know, we might be onto something that's connected to what's going on internationally. Who I just delivered to you is a Russian spy who's on our side. His name is Dmitri Smirnov. Believe it or not, Rick, the Russians are as scared as we are about what's going on right now."

"Lopez told me a little. What you don't know is that I speak Russian. That's why Lopez wanted me on this plane."

"Outstanding! Could be useful with Dmitri. Your orders are straightforward. Get Smirnov scanned. If he requires surgery, stand down until you hear from me. If he doesn't, have the plane gassed and ready to fly to Pittsburgh, Pennsylvania, with Smirnov and the neurosurgeon as your passengers. But—and this is important—DO NOT take off until you have verbal confirmation from me!"

"Am I to understand that you will not be flying with us?"

"Affirmative."

"Should I know how to reach you?"

Kipling read off her number and asked Henderson to call her. "Okay. You and I have each other's numbers." She checked her watch. "I need to get going!"

"Wait!" Henderson jogged over to the hangar wall and picked up a backpack. "I'm supposed to give this to you."

"Impressive." A lot of work had obviously gone into the bag's design. "I read about its special feature."

"Clever people, those Mensa folk. But inside, you'll also find the PD13, our latest portable drone; in the right situations, it can be useful. It's now standard issue in the field. You'll also find an FC19D. I'm told you're checked out on the thirteen."

"Oh, yeah! In our classes, I got pretty good at flying that baby. Night certified?"

"Yes. Fully night vision compatible."

"Any problem getting this through airport carry-on security?"

"Not at all."

Kipling snapped her fingers. "Damn! Almost forgot!" She ran back to the Uber, grabbed her backpack, and returned. With her back to the car, she discreetly removed the two Glocks and handed them over."

"*These* could have been a problem for you." Henderson chuckled. "Don't worry. They'll be waiting for you in Pittsburgh."

———◆———

*San Francisco International Airport (SFO)*
*San Francisco, California, U.S.A.*
*37° 37' 4"N Latitude, 122° 23' 12.9"W Longitude*
*Saturday, March 31, 2018, 1:44 PM (PDT)*

Kipling's ride to the San Francisco Airport was uneventful. On the way, she called Popov.

"I was just about to call you!" Compared to the professional tone projected earlier, Popov was not himself.

"Talk to me, Oleg. What's wrong?"

"You called me. You first."

"Hold on one second, please." She turned to the Uber driver and asked him to turn up the volume on the radio.

"We found her, Oleg! As I speak, she is at the San Francisco airport, ready to board a plane to the city of Pittsburgh. Pittsburgh's near our east coast, about a four-hour flight from here."

"Thank God!! Ground the plane! Have your authorities arrest her. Now!"

"Oleg, what's going on?"

"What's going *on* is that an hour ago, all of our hydroelectric generators run by RusHydro were hacked and shut down. Those generators produce more than a sixth of our electricity. On the hotline, your president told us that it was in retaliation for what we did to your TVA facility. LINDA! WE DIDN'T DO WHAT YOUR PRESIDENT SAID!! At the UN, our diplomats are shouting at your diplomats. Each side is saying that if you aren't responsible, why are you continuing to hack into our systems? First, it was air traffic control and now the hydroelectric plants. Things are falling apart, Linda! For God's sake, arrest the woman!"

Kipling took in what she was hearing and consolidated her thoughts. "Oleg. We need to think this through. About an hour ago, I spoke to my boss, Hector Lopez."

"I know the name."

"He's given me everything I've asked for. When I told him that it was your opinion that your niece might be responsible for what is happening, he almost took my head off, he thought it so ridiculous.

"And so, I ask you. What will your bosses' reaction be when you go to them and say something like this: 'Good news! Problem solved. A female American spy I happen to be working with has arrested my niece in America. I'm pretty sure that she's the one causing all these problems. So, trust me. Let's just stand down, and I'm really confident that everything will sort itself out.'

"Believe me. As much as I'd like you to do exactly that, there are two problems. First, I doubt that you are one hundred percent sure that Viktoriya is responsible. On the other hand, let's assume that you are. The first thing your superiors will say is, 'Show us the proof.'"

Popov wasn't giving up. "There has to be some evidence that she's carrying, or back at her—"

"House? House?!" Kipling interrupted. "You mean the one she blew up this morning to eliminate all physical traces of her? Or on her computer, you're suggesting? If she's as brilliant as you say, she's thought through everything."

The line went silent, and Kipling waited. Popov finally replied. "You're an inventive, intelligent woman, Linda. After all of this is over, if we're still alive, remind me to offer you a job." A pause. "So, what do you propose? What is the трещина, uh, the chink—is that how you say it in English —in her armor?"

Kipling explained her intent to board the commercial airliner on which Erickson was flying and accompany her to Pittsburgh. "I hope to sit near her. If she opens her computer, I'll try to hack in, on the fly. If I see anything that gives her away, that will be my cue to take her down. And unless she has a partner, that should do it. But from what I know of her story, it's likely she's a loner."

"God, I wish I could be on that plane with you. If I could just talk to her, I'd reason with her."

"With all due respect, Oleg, I think we're long past talking."

Kipling then summarized Smirnov's condition, his upcoming examination by a doctor, her plan to fly him separately to Pittsburgh on her own jet, and meeting him there. "By then, I'm hoping that he'll have regained his senses. I wish, too, you were here, Oleg. If I make no progress on the plane with Viktoriya, we're going to have to be more inventive once we get to Pittsburgh—and that may involve Dmitri."

"Before I hang up, a personal question, please." Popov's voice changed.

"Of course."

"They let you have your own jet?"

———◆———

Kipling's first job at the airport was to make sure she got on Erickson's flight. Instead of buying a ticket like everyone else, she used her clout as a CIA employee and went straight to TSA headquarters in Terminal 3. There she met the local TSA chief, Bob Duringham.

"This must be important. I got a call direct from headquarters."

"You have no idea."

"What can I do for you, Dr. Kipling?"

———◆———

Five minutes later, Kipling left for gate sixty-five, together with a boarding pass for seat 23D, an aisle seat one row behind and diagonally across from 22C, where Kathy Ann Erickson would be sitting. Additionally, Duringham had shown Kipling the up-to-date image of Erickson taken by TSA cameras. Kipling memorized Erickson's looks and clothing.

On the way to the gate, Kipling took note of the sullen mood pervading the terminal, passengers speaking to each other in low voices, gathered around televisions, listening to ever more dire warnings that two of the world's superpowers may soon come to a confrontation. If the people in this terminal were representative, the entire nation was facing its mortality.

Laden with the CIA-issued backpack in her left hand and her own on her back, Kipling found a corner stall in the women's restroom. There she opened the one Henderson had given her. In a protective plastic case was the FC19D. As she'd been taught, she positioned it in her right hand between the index and middle finger, between the first and second joint, facing outward.

Armed and ready to go, Kipling flushed the toilet and took a deep breath, instantly regretting the fact that she had not showered or brought a change of clothing. *Be calm, Linda. It's showtime!*

Kipling walked slowly as she departed the restroom, eyes scanning the corridors for a middle-aged, professional-looking woman with dark hair, dressed in a gray suit and white blouse. The TSA photo had been definitive. It was two thirty-five. Boarding would begin in fifteen minutes, a half hour before the plane's planned three-nineteen departure.

As she approached the gate, Kipling's eyes darted back and forth, up and down. She looked at those sitting, as well as those standing. Nowhere could she see a middle-aged woman in a gray suit. She turned around and scanned oncoming passengers. *She's probably not here yet. Calm down, Linda! There are still fifteen minutes until boarding!*

Erickson sat quietly, perusing a recent issue of *People* magazine, her carry-on bag on the floor in front of her. All seats around her were occupied. A family with a screaming two-year-old stood out. With a little luck, they'd sit nowhere near her on the plane, she thought.

She could have afforded an upgrade to First Class or Economy Comfort but had reneged. Erickson needed to blend in, to become one with the masses. That said, her Mileage Plus Visa did allow her the luxury of boarding in Group 2, ahead of most passengers.

———◆——

"We will begin general boarding shortly, ladies and gentlemen. We will board according to group number. Please identify your number on your boarding pass. If your pass does not have a number, please see me here at the gate." The gate representative read off a list of those who could board early, including families with children, active-duty military personnel, and those who might need a little extra time.

Kipling felt a tingle in her spine, originating from the neurons flashing on and off inside her brain. *This was supposed to be the easy part. Did Erickson change her mind about the flight? Unlikely.* At once, her CIA training kicked into gear, and she recognized an alternate possibility: the oldest trick in the book. Erickson had changed her appearance! *That's what I would have done. Sometime after security and before now!*

"Group 1 may now board the plane," came loudly over the speakers.

Kipling was becoming anxious. What if she couldn't identify Erickson? She'd be facing a gut-wrenching situation: stay behind and assume that Erickson was not among the passengers aboard or get on the plane and possibly fly to Pittsburgh by herself. The latter would be a disaster.

*Think, Linda! Forget her clothes, forget her hair! It's her face, stupid, her face!* In her mind's eye, Kipling concentrated on the photograph emblazoned there.

"Again, if your boarding card says Group 1, you may board now."

Kipling considered her most logical tack. If Erickson had not already boarded in Group 1—a tenuous assumption—Kipling could wait near the counter and visually scan each passenger. There was a downside to this approach. If Erickson entered the plane ahead of Kipling, there would be limited, risky opportunities to attach the FC19D inside the aircraft. But right now, that appeared to be Kipling's only option.

———◆◆◆———

"Now boarding Group 2. If your ticket says Group 2, you can board now." Erickson stayed seated, preferring not to make a show by arriving first for her boarding group. *Blend in, Viktoriya! That is your only job right now, to blend in.*

———◆◆◆———

Kipling found a good spot to stand and observe. There were perhaps fifteen to twenty men and women in line. Because all passengers queued up within ropes, and because there were more men than women, Kipling decided to walk parallel to the line, easily examining each female face. She arrived at the end with nothing to show for it. *Damn!*

———◆◆◆———

Erickson decided it was time. She stood, pulled out the handle from her rollaboard, and walked toward the line, ticket in her right hand, head slightly down.

———◆◆◆———

The instant Kipling's eyes noticed the woman who had just stood, her sixth sense took charge and told her that the woman in tennis shoes, a black coat, and a cheap blond wig was her quarry—even before Kipling saw her face. In person, Erickson came across as a much larger woman than Kipling had expected: big-boned, as her mother used to say. She stood some fifteen feet from the entry to the queue, where a few Group 2 stragglers were still entering. Once Kipling saw her face, she was sure. Simultaneously, Kipling realized that there was still time to attach the FC19D.

Kipling took off on a semi-circular clockwise route without delay, walking quickly left and then turning hard right to arrive at Erickson's rear. She arrived in time; no one had cut her off. There were two options. Number one was to stay in line behind her and wait for another opportunity that may or may not arrive. The downside was that if they separated, there might not *be* another opportunity. Two: Do it now!

At once, she chose Two. Erickson was in perfect position. Kipling decided to do it exactly as her instructors had taught her in school. She backed up a step, then stepped forward, and as she pretended to lose her balance—for the benefit of anyone watching—performed a downward swipe that impacted the top of Erickson's jacket, securely fastening the tiny GPS tracker in position.

"I'm so sorry, ma'am. I am such a klutz. Please forgive me."

Before Erickson had time to turn around and acknowledge the incident and accept the apology, Kipling had rotated quickly left.

———————◆◆◆———————

*Clumsy bitch!* Erickson was ready to give the woman behind her a stern look of disapproval. But by the time she faced in that direction, the only thing that she could see was the backside of the hit-and-run walker—a woman carrying two backpacks.

Unexpectedly, Erickson's eyes opened wide. An image of her baby brother, Alexei, flashed through her mind. Tears began to form. *Where did that come from?*

———————◆◆◆———————

Kipling circled back and watched as Erickson swiped her boarding pass across the sensor and proceeded down the Jetway. Kipling then entered the empty priority line.

"Ms. Kipling, you could have boarded earlier. You are Group 1."

"I appreciate that, but I'm in no particular hurry today."

———————◆◆◆———————

Erickson arrived at Seat 22C and found space for her carry-on directly above her seat. She still felt shaken by the fleeting image that had crossed her mind.

———————◆◆◆———————

Kipling proceeded down the Jetway into the plane, and for the first time, got a clear view of the woman who might potentially be orchestrating the start of World War III. A casual observer might think that her quarry was a middle-aged schoolteacher or a kindly next-door neighbor. Her normal dark hair and undistinguished features would have supported that assumption. On the other hand, the blond wig looked ridiculous. As she arrived at row twenty-two, Kipling fortuitously witnessed the proof that gave her confirmation: a missing pinkie on the left hand.

Noting that the next passenger behind her was a distance away, Kipling took her time, casually lifting her CIA backpack into overhead storage and then squeezing her personal backpack under the seat in front of her.

Kipling let loose a sigh of relief. She could finally relax and maybe even snag a bit of shuteye on the cross-country flight. Except for hoping that Erickson opened her laptop, there was nothing more to do. Her own computer remained at the ready on the floor in front of her. Next on the agenda was to contact Henderson. Considering her position within earshot of Erickson, she texted him instead, telling him to take off whenever he was ready; importantly, he needed to arrive in Pittsburgh before United Flight 849.

Kipling watched sleepily as passengers continued to fill the plane, realizing how exhausted she had become. Her eyes were growing heavy.

------◆◆◆------

Erickson's body started to shake; she was beside herself with dread. Yet again, the image of her brother zoomed through her brain. Back in the months following his death, she had wanted to believe that their real-life bond had transcended death, that he had become her guardian angel. Was this his attempt at warning her?

But before long, two recent memories forced a more logical conclusion. The image of her dead brother occurred *only* when the woman with the two backpacks had come close. *Why?* Erickson could think of no reason.

------◆◆◆------

When it happened, Kipling could not believe it. Erickson turned in Kipling's direction, eyes boring into hers, accompanied by a fear that blanched all color from her face. Immediately, Erickson unbelted her seatbelt and snapped to her feet. In one swift motion, she reached overhead, grabbed her bag, and started running toward the front of the plane, against traffic, forcing startled passengers to step aside.

Kipling was dumbfounded. *There's no way in hell that she knows me or has ever seen me!* Kipling wracked her brain, searching for any reason to explain why Erickson might perceive her as different from any other passenger on the airplane. *Could it be that...?* She lowered her head and sniffed. *Son-of-a-bitch!*

# — 23 —

## OUTFOXED YOU, DIDN'T I, BITCH?

*San Francisco International Airport (SFO), Gate 65*
*San Francisco, California, U.S.A.*
*39° 37' 9"N Latitude, 122° 23' 3"W Longitude*
*Saturday, March 31, 2018, 3:09 PM (PDT)*

Kipling's realization that her clothing reeked of combustion products *did* make her different. But, so what? Nowhere in Kipling's calculation could she imagine that Erickson would think that she had been near her house when it exploded. *There's more to it than that!*

As she undid her seatbelt, stood, and retrieved her backpacks, Kipling placed a hurried call to Henderson. "No time to talk. Situation's changed. Do NOT, I repeat, do not leave for Pittsburgh! Hold position until further notice."

"Understand. You should know that Dr. Brody, the neurosurgeon, says that the CAT scan was negative, revealing nothing that would require surgery. He wants—."

Seeing the aisle fill up in front of her, Kipling cut him off. "Listen. Sorry. That's fantastic news. I must go. Will be in touch."

Repeating Erickson's unexpected departure, Kipling aggressively made her way to the front of the aircraft, eliciting more than one irritated response. "Sorry! It's an emergency!" she repeated over and over.

In the Jetway, Kipling slowed to catch her breath and take stock. She imagined what she would do if she were Erickson. *I'd be questioning my decision to leave the plane. I'd desperately want to believe that whatever fear had overcome me was misplaced. How could I prove that? By waiting outside the Jetway. If the woman who sat behind me takes off with the plane, that would be proof that she never posed me any threat.*

With that hypothesis in place, Kipling stayed put, walking no farther than where the Jetway took a jog and made a straight line into the terminal. After showing her ID and reassuring airline personnel she meant no harm, Kipling opened her laptop and activated the app for the FC19D.

———◆——

At first, Erickson thought it best to find a convenient hiding place that would give her a clear view of the Jetway entrance. *Why?* She had finally pieced together the origin of her fears.

Erickson considered it astounding that she still remembered the overpowering scent from the explosion that had destroyed her home in Afghanistan, killing her parents and brother all those years ago. *That someone boarding the plane just happened to carry a similar odor is irrelevant. It has nothing to do with me!*

Her confidence restored, Erickson chose to roll the dice. Instead of hiding, she returned to the gate and picked a seat mere feet away from the entrance to the Jetway. If the two-backpacker came out, they would come face to face. *But that's not going to happen, is it?* Erickson thought to herself. *I'd be willing to bet the entire wad of cash that I'm carrying. In the meantime, I'll look for another flight to Pittsburgh.*

*I'll arrive later than expected, but there'll be no harm done!* Besides, it wasn't until she arrived in Pittsburgh that she intended to activate the third and most devastating component of her hacking triad. *A delay of an hour or two won't matter at all.*

———————◆———————

The FC19D was a miracle of modern science and miniaturization. In practice, it was no different than a tracker card one might purchase from Amazon. This one had a few more bells and whistles that made it very special—making it worth more than ten times its weight in gold, at $18,000 a copy. It was another of the success stories emanating from the Mensa Branch, a group of CIA brainiacs whose charter was to invent innovative methods and devices to improve spying. Imagine Q, who developed nifty gadgets for James Bond.

The FC19D was small, no bigger than the top half of a large blueberry cut in half horizontally. It came mounted on a special "applicator," which Kipling had positioned between her fingers earlier. As the downward motion of her hand impacted the rear of Erickson's coat, the "bug" took hold of the underlying surface.

To enable attachment to any medium, the bug utilized two independent systems. The first consisted of tiny "hairs" that worked like Velcro, to grab onto any substrate with texture. Alternatively, if the underlayment was smooth, a form of superglue, encapsulated in tiny orbs, broke upon impact and dried instantly.

One extraordinary feature spotlighted the genius of the FC19D. Before impact, the bug appeared to be clear or translucent. But upon contact, a special electronic circuit mimicked the chemical process by which a certain octopus changed its color to blend with the underlying surface. The tracker became next to invisible.

Now sitting on the floor adjacent to the bend in the Jetway, Kipling fired up the bug's tracking software on her laptop. Seconds later, it showed up—and only seventy-five feet away!

*I bet you she's waiting to see if I get off the plane! One hundred to one, she'll be on the move once the door closes.*

Meanwhile, in case Erickson chose to access the Internet with her computer, Kipling activated her computer's search mode. This algorithm was, without a doubt, Mensa's most useful creation. Within a range of one hundred feet, Kipling could monitor every keystroke typed on *any* computer. Scanning inputs for the keyword, *Pittsburgh,* it wasn't long before she identified Erickson's laptop.

Twelve minutes later, Kipling heard the Jetway door slam closed. It didn't take long before the tracker was on the move.

*Outfoxed you, didn't I, bitch?*

Kipling was handed a surprise as she followed Erickson's keystrokes. Straight away, Kipling called the FCDE to advise them of this development. After activating another version of the tracker software on her cell phone, Kipling found someone to unlock the Jetway door. She headed back to the street, making sure to remain clear of Erickson.

Kipling's Uber would arrive in ten minutes, she read from her screen.

———◆◆◆———

Erickson stood tall as she proceeded confidently away from Gate 65. It felt as if the weight of the world had lifted from her shoulders. The cash she had used to place the bet with herself remained secure inside her bag. The woman whom she had been so fearful of was just an ordinary passenger. *Nothing more!*

While waiting at the gate for her imaginary foe, Erickson had used her laptop to search for an alternate flight to Pittsburgh. Unfortunately, there were no more direct flights that day. For that reason, Erickson had just confirmed what waited for her behind Door Number Two. What point was there in carrying cash at the ready if she wasn't prepared to spend it?

# – 24 –

## PLAN B

*Joint Base Andrews*
*Prince George County, Maryland*
*38° 48' 40"N Latitude, 76° 52' 40"W Longitude*
*Saturday, March 31, 2018, 6:40 PM (EDT)*

Silverstein had been on the ground at Joint Base Andrews for almost two hours. The military compound he had known for most of his life as Andrews Air Force Base changed its name in 2009 when the Air Force and Navy took joint custody. The base was mostly famous for being the home of two copies of the military version of the Boeing 747—otherwise known as a Boeing VC-25—and called Air Force One when the president was aboard.

Refreshed and ready to face the devil personified, Silverstein gave himself a pep talk. What he envisioned for tonight might represent the most mentally consuming encounter he'd ever faced in his professional career. To match wits with a domestic terrorist—one who had set out to destroy the very tools with which his profession made its living—would be a challenge.

"Here! Memorize this face. It's Brickman," Lopez ordered, as he handed over a photograph.

Silverstein did a double take. Anyone looking at the photograph for the first time would have done so, wondering what it was that drew their eye. A looker he was not.

Lopez stepped up to Silverstein. "Brickman's going to be suspicious. He'll probably frisk you."

"I have nothing to hide."

"We're going to change that. Take off your belt."

"Why?"

"Because I asked you to, that's why. And because I can't in good conscience send you in there completely defenseless." Lopez handed over a replacement.

Silverstein looked it over. "Nice quality."

Lopez gloated. "Didn't notice, did you? That belt is, in fact, a battery."

Silverstein responded honestly. "I am impressed. But I've got to tell you, charging my cell phone isn't going to be a high priority, Hector."

"Cute!" Lopez pointed. "Now cinch the belt tight."

Silverstein complied.

"Good! Now, I know you're right-handed. Without looking, I want you to take your left hand and rest it gently on the buckle. You'll feel a small nipple."

"Got it."

"Okay. Memorize that location so that you can find it quickly."

"Now what?"

Lopez opened a small rectangular box and removed what looked like a pen. "This, my friend, is the SP150. Take a close look. It looks like an ordinary pen, but it has a unique feature."

Silverstein chose not to interrupt.

"Now, look at the button at the end, the one you'd normally push to extend the ballpoint."

"I see it."

"When you choose to activate this weapon—."

"Weapon?" Silverstein gave Lopez a sly smile.

Lopez, not appearing to appreciate the humor of the moment, continued. "*As I was going to say*, when you choose to activate this weapon, you will do three things in rapid succession. Our tests indicate that you should be able to get off a shot in less than four seconds. First, instead of pushing the end button, you will remove and toss it. Do it now!"

Silverstein did so.

"See what's left? The now exposed end is concave, and it fits perfectly onto the nipple on the belt buckle. I will now demonstrate what you need to do. Pay attention."

After reinstalling the end cap and putting the pen in his pocket, Lopez turned to face a cardboard cutout of a man some ten feet away. "Without taking a shot, I will go through the motions. With my right hand, I take the pen from my pocket. Second, I remove the end cap with my left. Third, with my right hand, I guide the pen to the nipple on the belt." Lopez looked Silverstein in the eye. "This is easier than it sounds because once you get close, powerful magnets will guide it into place.

"Fourth, again with my right hand, I pull the body of the pen away from the belt. As the belt and the pen separate, they'll stay connected through two insulated wires that I will be pulling out of the belt.

"Now comes the fun part. You aim the pen at your target and fire. Extend your right arm and sight along the pen. You have a practical range of some ten feet." Lopez demonstrated.

"You say *fire*. How do I do that?"

"Just squeeze the clip on the side of the pen." Lopez extended his arm and pretended to shoot.

"Okay. I understand. What happens then?"

"When you do that, you want to hold the pen steady and tight because there is a tiny kick."

*Seriously?*

"Once you press the clip, the battery pack in your belt energizes and activates a compressed air cartridge. That cartridge propels two darts toward the target."

Silverstein smiled. He finally understood. "This pen is a Taser!"

"We prefer to use the term, electroshock weapon. The electro-probes embed themselves into the target. Upon contact, 100,000 volts of electricity flow from your belt to the pen and then to the target, resulting in your enemy convulsing on the floor." Lopez handed the pen back to Silverstein. "Okay, I want you to do everything like I just told you."

"For real?"

Lopez pointed to the cardboard target. "Yes, for real. Don't go for speed. Put it in your pocket and start from scratch. We can only afford one practice shot."

Silverstein replicated the initial sequence. He then aimed and pressed the clip. A high-pitched whishing sound—almost a whistle—accompanied the action.

"Damn!" Lopez exclaimed. "Not bad for a rookie. Luckily, Flat Stanley doesn't have a girlfriend. Aim a little higher next time, okay?"

Lopez handed Silverstein a fresh pen. "Remember! You have only one shot. Questions?"

"None that I can think of."

Lopez seemed pleased. He held out his hand. "Take these, too. In the right situation, they could prove useful."

Silverstein took what looked to be two large marbles, each about three-quarters of an inch in diameter. "What are these?"

"Flash bangs."

Silverstein understood the concept of a flash bang, essentially a stun-grenade type weapon that produced smoke, noise, and light, but was not lethal.

Lopez proudly explained. "These tiny miracles each put out about half the force of the larger conventional versions. Plus, they roll. Notice the small protrusion on each. Push that in, and you have about nine seconds. When you go inside Brickman's house, use an old magician's trick and hide one in each palm. If he frisks you, he'll never think to check your hands. You can then stash them in your pocket. Okay?"

Silverstein nodded.

Lopez hesitated before speaking. "Listen! Are you sure I can't convince you to wear a wire? They're small these days, you know. He'll never see it. That way, Marc and I will be able to hear everything."

"Hector, I can't take the chance. If I had my way, there wouldn't be another agent within five miles of his house."

"You've said that a couple of times." Lopez lowered his voice. "I'd rather not lose a friend, you know. Things may not go the way you think."

"Aren't you listening? Unless we can convince Brickman to undo the destruction sequences, we'll have nothing to show for our efforts. Our weather satellites will be toast."

"Okay! You win. No wire. But I must insist on one precaution. This one is nonnegotiable!" He handed over a finger ring. "This one is from your memorable days at the Naval Academy."

"I never attended the Academy!"

Lopez's eyes rolled toward the ceiling. "You're a spy, for God's sake! If I say you attended the Naval Academy, you attended the Naval Academy."

Silverstein tried it on. "It even fits. So what's the point?"

"The point is that this ring is your version of a safeword—a panic button if you like. Just press hard on the red stone, and we'll come running." Lopez was serious. "Okay?"

"If it'll make you happy, sure."

Lopez gave Silverstein the once-over. "You look pretty sharp. The dark suit certainly makes you look the part: the consummate Fed, down to the sunglasses, white shirt, and tie."

"Thanks a lot, I guess." Silverstein managed a weak smile as he contemplated when to discuss Plan B, his fallback position. He would need Lopez's full cooperation but decided to wait until the last minute to bring it up—lest Lopez go ballistic with an expletive and a curt, "Like hell, you will!"

# ~ 25 ~

## WHO ARE YOU?

*Silver Spring, Maryland*
*39° 3' 42"N Latitude, 76° 59' 38"W Longitude*
*Saturday, March 31, 2018, 7:45 PM (EDT)*

Twenty minutes earlier, before departing Joint Base Andrews, Silverstein had rattled off his final requirement to a stunned Lopez. "If everything goes to hell, I'm going for it, Hector! It won't be pretty, but I've got to do it." Of necessity, because Lopez would play a critical part in Plan B, Silverstein had to brief him on his role. "When and if I call you, you need to play along, Hector. And when I say *play along*, I don't want to hear any hesitation. Okay?"

To Silverstein's surprise, Lopez offered no resistance. "That's a good idea, but don't you think I could be a bit more persuasive if I texted you a picture?"

*A picture?* Silverstein surmised Lopez's thought process. "You have enough time to pull that off?"

"So happens I have an agent in the area. I'll call her right now."

———◆———

Silverstein had driven himself and arrived at the address of one Raymond Charles Brickman III, in Silver Spring, Maryland. His nondescript government sedan drew no attention.

The CIA had, in record time, provided much-needed intelligence to facilitate the operation. President Trump, never one to ignore the political credit he might receive for rolling a hand grenade across the deck, jumped at the chance to participate in a covert CIA operation. Fortunately, he happened to be in town to make it happen.

Over the past several hours, in vehicles, on foot, and back at the CIA, operatives had been busy. While bugging Brickman's phone, they intercepted a telephone conversation between him and his wife earlier in the day, as she was in her car driving south. Using the cell's signal, they followed her to Charlotte, North Carolina, where the FCDE confirmed an address belonging to her sister. Once the operation began, Lopez took control of Brickman's home phone and cell, blocking all incoming calls.

CIA operators determined that Brickman used his in-house Wi-Fi to access the Internet. This discovery was key to the operation's success because technicians outside the house could monitor Brickman's keystrokes. Marc Miller's assignment that afternoon had been to locate one NSOF employee who knew the satellite code inside and out. He did, and his name was Jeremy Bryan, or JB as he was known at work. Bryan welcomed the opportunity to participate in a secret operation to get back their satellites.

Bryan said confidently that, by observing Brickman's keystrokes, he would be able to identify the backdoor Brickman had created to do his dirty work. During the operation soon to unfold, JB would monitor all activity coming from Brickman's computer.

*It's showtime,* Silverstein thought to himself. *But I'm not going to take any chances. As Alexander Hamilton said in Lin-Manuel Miranda's play,* Hamilton: *"I'm not stupid!"* Why? Because he wondered if Lopez had been completely honest. And if not, might Brickman be prepared to sniff out an electronic bug? So before he exited his vehicle, Silverstein made a minor tweak to one detail that he and Lopez had agreed to earlier.

On the street, he glanced about, casually searching for potential CIA operatives. Silverstein knew that most of the surveillance was coming from a house in clear view, across the street diagonally. Earlier negotiations by telephone had offered the residents $20,000 rent in exchange for one day's use of their home.

Unexpectedly, Silverstein's thoughts returned to his usual partner, Linda Kipling; typically, they worked hand in glove. He wondered how she was doing and whether she and Smirnov were making any progress at their end. If she could see him in his getup, he imagined her joking: "You look gorgeous, you handsome devil."

As Silverstein turned from the street sidewalk onto the inlaid brick walkway, he took in what he saw: a respectable two-story residence in a typical middle-class neighborhood. In this area, chances were good that every other house belonged to either a government employee or a contractor who relied on government funding.

Silverstein felt perspiration forming beneath his collar. A harrowing thought came to mind: His entire reputation could come tumbling down if Brickman had nothing to do with the terrorist they were searching for. But Silverstein could not bring himself to believe that he could be wrong. Too many clues pointed to him as their likely suspect.

Silverstein climbed the single step to the stoop. He pressed the doorbell button and smiled inwardly when he heard the recorded chime: *When Johnny Comes Marching Home.* When the door opened, Silverstein came face to face with someone who looked even more sinister than the person Lopez had shown him in the photograph. His disheveled appearance, together with unkempt hair and several days' growth of facial whiskers, made him look the part of a homeless man. Brickman appeared more surprised than startled and did not seem pleased. It was clear to Silverstein that a tall African American male was the last thing he expected to see when he opened the door.

The tone of Brickman's greeting lacked cordiality but was consistent with his appearance and demeanor. "Who the fuck are you?"

"My name is Calvin Emmett Jackson." Being careful to secure the flash bang in his right palm, Silverstein handed Brickman his business card and watched as he studied it.

"You're with the government?"

"Yes, sir," Silverstein replied.

"What do you want?"

"I'm here to answer your demands."

"Really?"

"Yes! The government knows what you've been up to and wants to resolve the situation before there's further damage. I'm here at the specific direction of President Donald J. Trump. He is sympathetic to your demands. May I come in?"

# — 26 —

## SAID THE SPIDER TO THE FLY

*Silver Spring, Maryland*
*39° 3' 42"N Latitude, 76° 59' 38"W Longitude*
*Saturday, March 31, 2018, 7:52 PM (EDT)*

Lopez and his long-serving assistant, Marc Miller, had earlier decided that the master bedroom on the second floor—opposite Brinkman's house—provided the best location for surveillance. It had a clear view of Brickman's residence.

The sun had set at seven-thirty. There was still enough light to make out objects on the street. They watched as Silverstein pressed the doorbell, and Brickman answered. The two engaged in conversation.

"I'm not picking up anything," Miller remarked.

Lopez's head snapped in Miller's direction. "What do you mean you're not picking up anything?" He knew that the microphone embedded in the Academy ring was as sensitive as they come.

"There's nothing!"

"Do a scan on the transmitter. It's impossible to switch off."

Miller switched on his laptop and activated the search feature. "The ring is transmitting, sir."

Lopez was getting flustered. "Let me see!"

Before he had time to check the screen, Miller had it figured out. "The signal is coming from that direction." He pointed. "But Dr. Silverstein's position is about eighty degrees to the right."

Although both agents came up with the explanation simultaneously, it was Lopez who put the discovery into words. "That son-of-a-bitch! He left the ring in the car!"

Lopez expressed his anger in words that caught Miller by surprise. "If Brickman doesn't kill him inside the house, I'll shoot him myself when he comes out the door!"

———◆◆◆———

Silverstein tried to judge Brickman's reaction to his request. What he saw was confusion that morphed into skepticism, which then transitioned into apprehension. Brickman stepped out into the open and looked to both sides.

"If you're looking for my backup, there isn't any. That's my car sitting there." He gestured. "As I said, I'm here at the personal direction of President Trump."

Brickman's eyes drilled into Silverstein's, his facial expression suggesting intense concentration.

Silverstein added some intensity to his request by making a show of checking his watch. "I think you want to hear what the President is proposing. I ask you again. Can I please come in?"

———◆◆◆———

Brickman's mind was churning. *How the hell did they find me?* he wondered yet again. *And if what he says is true, why would Trump choose a damn nigger as his liaison? It must be a trick.*

Brickman couldn't bring himself to say yes or no. This Jackson fellow had forced him into a corner, and Brickman despised corners. Still, unless he said yes, he'd know nothing of Trump's offer.

———◆◆◆———

Brickman's facial expression gave Silverstein nothing to read. It was a blank sheet, a poker face. Without so much as a nod in response to Silverstein's request, Brickman stood back and opened the door completely.

As Silverstein approached the threshold, he knew that his die was cast. Most of what would happen in the next twenty minutes, he had scripted himself. At least initially, there was little reason for things not to go smoothly. However, after that, a significant Achilles heel to the plan design would likely surface. Silverstein's wits would be challenged indeed if confronted with that sinkhole.

The beginning of Mary Howitt's famous poem passed fleetingly through Silverstein's mind:

*"Will you walk into my parlour?" said the Spider to the Fly,*
*"'tis the prettiest little parlour that ever you did spy."*

# ~ 27 ~

## A CERTAIN AMOUNT OF PRIDE

*Silver Spring, Maryland*
*39° 3' 42"N Latitude, 76° 59' 38"W Longitude*
*Saturday, March 31, 2018, 8:01 PM (EDT)*

No sooner had Brickman stood to the side than he changed his mind, blocking entry.

"What's wrong?" asked Silverstein, stopping abruptly.

"Prove to me that you're not carrying!"

"You think that I have a weapon? I'm here at the direction of the President of the United States, for God's sake." Silverstein held his arms to the side. "Check for yourself!"

From his days with the Military Police in the Army, Brickman knew the procedure. "How about a wire?"

"You're one suspicious son-of-a-bitch, you know that? You'll find my cell, my wallet, and my car keys."

Brickman took his time and did a thorough job.

"Are you happy now?"

Brickman acquiesced, and Silverstein entered the house.

Lopez and Miller watched with trepidation as Brickman went through his antics. They felt relieved when he finally allowed Silverstein to proceed. As Lopez had predicted, Brickman took no note of Silverstein's hands.

Lopez checked the time: two minutes after eight. Unless new information told them to abort, they'd proceed as planned. At fifteen past the hour, they'd issue the signal to begin transmitting. There'd *be* no new information because, by ditching the ring, Silverstein had made sure of that.

Lopez's cell dinged. He took a quick look, pleased that Agent Julie Hermosa had come through.

———◆———

Brickman didn't know whether to believe Jackson's story. Still, it was difficult to ignore his pronouncement that the government "knows exactly what you've been up to." He motioned Jackson a few feet forward and went straight to the point. "What is it that you *think* I'm doing?"

"You're sabotaging our weather satellites." Silverstein glanced at his watch. "In the newspaper, you said you could stop the sequences you've set up. My job, and the President's, is to convince you to do that before ten this evening. GOES-14? Ring a bell?"

*Cocky mother!* Brickman concentrated on keeping a neutral face. "What if I told you that I don't know what the hell you're talking about?"

"I'd say that you're a liar." He quickly raised a finger. "But it's not my job to say that or to make war. I'm just the messenger. What you have going for you is President Trump." Silverstein changed the subject. "You *are* aware that we're close to a nuclear war with Russia, aren't you?"

"I watch the news." Brickman cursed the providence that had interfered with his long-planned act of retribution.

"Then you understand that your timing was lousy. You couldn't have picked a worse time to make your demands." Silverstein shook his head, feigning disgust. "I can also tell you that your timing couldn't be better. Turns out, it's to your advantage that your story has fallen to back-page news. Do you understand what I'm saying?"

"Not really." Brickman didn't know what to think. That someone had even identified him was incredible; he had been so careful. There was little point in denying it further. Might this president be sympathetic to his demands for the South? Although supportive by omission, Trump's decision not to single out the patriots involved in the *Unite the Right* movement in Charlottesville was evidence that his head was in the right place. "I think there is blame on both sides," Trump had cleverly equivocated.

Brickman reconsidered his reply. "Strike that. I do understand."

———————◆◆◆———————

Silverstein was having trouble controlling his anxiety; the idea of sharing the same room with a terrorist was stressful. At the front door, it had taken every bit of his concentration to calmly hold his hands to the side while Brickman patted him down. Once inside, he had surreptitiously dropped the marbles into his pants pockets. Brickman was clearly on edge, and despite his statements suggesting his innocence, his body language betrayed him. *No matter what happens, I will at least go down knowing that I did identify the right man!*

Silverstein checked the time yet again. Five minutes! Lopez had strict orders to begin transmission at eight-fifteen.

———————◆◆◆———————

Despite Jackson's nonthreatening manner, Brickman was beginning to regret having let the nigger into his house. He was reminded of the timeless words of the universal skeptic: *Things are never what they seem to be.* He paused to remember where he had stashed his nearest weapon.

*Case in point.* "Why do you keep checking the time?" Brickman asked.

———————◆◆◆———————

Silverstein recognized that he needed to give some ground, appear deferential, an important component of negotiation, he knew. "You're an observant man, Mr. Brickman. Obviously, very intelligent. To answer your question, President Trump is willing to give you the benefit of the doubt and has decided to make the first move as a gesture of goodwill. He is taking a big chance politically and is counting on you to respond positively."

Silverstein checked his watch yet again. Three minutes! He spoke firmly. "Mr. Brickman, do you have a TV? Can you get FOX?"

"Of course!" he said.

"Listen to me carefully. You demanded a nationwide address by the President. In less than three minutes, you're getting what you want. Wherever your TV is, I suggest that you turn it on."

———————◆◆◆———————

*President Trump, addressing my demands?* The last thing Brickman had expected was for the government to back down to his requests.

He led the way into the adjacent family room, where he and his wife normally watched TV.

"Only two more minutes," he heard from his rear. "You don't want to miss this. It's your five minutes in the spotlight."

Brickman hurried to his controls, two hands nervously switching on the remotes for his big-screen Sony and his Dish TV.

———————◆◆◆———————

Lopez and Miller looked down on the van sitting by the curb. Having no communication or surveillance from inside Brickman's house, they were flying blind. Once they gave the signal, the powerful transmission through the van's directional antenna would overwhelm that from Dish's satellite.

———————•◆•———————

Brickman turned on his TV. Silverstein noticed that there had been no need to switch the channel. FOX's regular programming was airing. From his wristwatch, Silverstein counted down and was pleased to witness the seamless video transition, accompanied by curt broadcast words: "We have breaking news. The President has asked to address the nation. We are going directly to the White House."

Silverstein watched as the video feed switched to a wide-angle view of the Oval Office, followed by a transition to a close-up of the President at his desk. Trump looked every bit the image of a president, no different, no less than what he had projected during his inauguration in 2017.

*Good evening, my fellow Americans!*

*As you know, our country is currently facing two existential threats, one from inside and one from outside our shores. I am here to address only the first, the threat to our meteorological satellites, which are crucial to our national security. NOAA-20 has already been rendered inoperative, and as I understand it, GOES-14 may meet the same fate tonight.*

*I am personally reaching out to the individual who is holding our satellites hostage. Know this! I am not without sympathy to your cause and your demands. Accordingly, I want to meet you in the middle, to find common ground for negotiation.*

*With that in mind, I have just signed an executive order to return and restore all Confederate statues and other Southern displays relevant to the Civil War to their original places.* [President holds up a sheet of paper; camera zooms onto signature.] *I am aware that you have made additional demands, but I cannot, on my own, follow through with these requests without the concurrence of Congress. That will take time.*

*Please consider this Executive Order* [President again holds up paper.] *to be a good-faith response to your requests.*

*Accordingly, in conjunction with the sincerity that comes with my words, I ask that you respond, also in good faith. Please cancel the destruct orders that you have programmed for the remainder of our weather satellites.*

[President pauses and looks stern.] *I know that you have me at a disadvantage, not a position I'm comfortable with. I am trusting that your word and actions will be every bit as honorable as mine.*

*May God bless the United States of America.*

Following the President's words, the screen faded back to regular programming, and Silverstein knew that the next few seconds were crucial.

Silverstein, still standing and to the left rear of Brickman, had been watching his reaction. The speech was written to sound conciliatory, yet exude a measure of practicality—key to its believability. Hence, the President's admission that there were limitations to what he could do quickly and by himself.

Whatever happened in the minutes to follow, Silverstein felt a sense of pride in what had just transpired. And for a good reason: Every word that President Trump had just said was verbatim what Silverstein had texted to Lopez while flying over Kansas just hours earlier.

# — 28 —

## AN OFFER TO DIE FOR

*Silver Spring, Maryland*
*39° 3' 42"N Latitude, 76° 59' 38"W Longitude*
*Saturday, March 31, 2018, 8:21 PM (EDT)*

Silverstein reacted instantly, not waiting for Brickman to notice that the regular programming to which the broadcast returned would make no mention of President Trump's just-concluded address to the nation. "Look at me, Mr. Brickman! Our president has gone out on a limb for you, and he is counting on you to respond."

To Silverstein's relief, Brickman muted the TV, turned away from the screen, and faced Silverstein.

———◆◆———

Brickman considered his options. The broadcast certainly seemed legit. He knew Trump to be unconventional in his approach to solving problems. Once Trump issued an executive order, his Republican base would support his actions no matter the political consequences. Although he had not issued the apology to the South Brickman had requested—or any guarantee that funds would be paid in restitution—if anyone had told Brickman that he'd realize what he had just achieved, he wouldn't have believed them.

He thought it necessary to drill down into the details of the truce that Trump had offered. He could do what the President asked, but at what cost? "For argument's sake, if I agree, what happens to me afterward?"

"Nothing."

"What do you mean, *nothing*?"

"I mean *nothing*. If you were paying attention to the broadcast, you noticed that there was no mention of your name or where you lived. Look outside, and you will see nothing different from before. The press has no idea who you are. I was there, and President Trump was rather specific about that. You know him. He's not one to accept insubordination."

Brickman turned toward the window and looked out at the street, noting that the streetlights were beginning to turn on.

———◆◆———

Silverstein realized immediately that he shouldn't have said it. The TV screen might remind Brickman of the broadcast he had just seen. Luckily, Brickman's rotation toward the window had him facing away from the screen.

Silverstein needed to keep Brickman on topic. "So, Mr. Brickman, sir, do we have a deal? From my position as an unbiased observer, I see a win-win; the government gets back its satellites, and you get more than you ever expected to get. I've got to tell you, in all the years I've worked for Donald Trump, I've never seen anyone pull off what you just did. If we weren't so close to a nuclear war with Russia, I guess you know this would never have happened."

———◆◆———

Brickman stared back at Silverstein, analyzing his words. *Really? How could it be this easy?* "As a hypothetical, what happens if I say no?"

Silverstein had hoped that it wouldn't be necessary to fabricate even more lies. On the plane ride across the country, he had considered every possible ploy to induce Brickman to accept the logic behind Plan A. Now, to convince Brickman of Trump's sincerity, Silverstein would have to gild the lily of incredulity, to add even more bluster.

"Mr. Brickman, why would you be so stupid? My advice to you, sir, is that you withdraw that question. I could tell you that President Trump would simply out your name to the press and let you deal with the consequences. Within hours, you'd be in handcuffs. I can tell you from personal experience, that's not the President's style. My orders are of a different sort."

<hr />

*Stupid?* Brickman took what he heard as both an insult and a threat. And this proud Southerner didn't take well to threats. Coming from a damn nigger, to boot! In the old days, such demeaning talk to a white man would have provided more than enough justification to give this old boy a good ass-whooping.

"Talk is cheap, Mr. Jackson. I doubt you'd act so confidently if it was just you and I alone somewhere, out in the boondocks, all by ourselves."

Brickman was pushing back just a bit too hard, and Silverstein couldn't help himself. "First, you and I *are* alone—in case you haven't noticed. And second, I think you meant to say, ...if it *were* just you and I alone somewhere."

"What the fuck?" Brickman was incredulous.

Silverstein drove the point home. "You meant to use the subjunctive: 'if it were,' not 'if it was.'"

"Are you making fun of me? In my own home?"

"Not at all. In fact, I'm complimenting you. The next time you send an anonymous letter to the newspaper, you might consider adding a few grammatical errors. Your sentences were too perfect. That's part of how we found you. Do you know that you were the only employee at NSOF to have a Bachelor's Degree in English?"

Silverstein waved his hand dismissively, almost as a taunt. "That's why I'm surprised that you missed the subjunctive."

Brickman's face blazed with anger.

———————◆———————

Silverstein knew that he shouldn't have allowed his emotions to take over. As an older, mature male, he had become more mellow and forgiving. Kipling might have disagreed, but it was so. As anger had built up inside him in confronting this racist terrorist, Silverstein had reverted to his younger mentality when he arrogantly believed that he was always the smartest person in the room.

Brickman asked again. "One more time. What happens if I don't agree?"

*Here goes nothing.* "Fair enough. I promise to answer your question if you answer mine first. Why wouldn't you take the deal? Seems like an easy decision to me."

Brickman replied sarcastically. "Oh, I don't know. Let me think for a second." Brickman's lips curled into a smirk. "For openers, might this broadcast be some sort of trick?"

*Trick? Imagine that!* Silverstein laughed aloud. "You think that the President would go to all this trouble, to include the entire nation in on a scheme to dupe you into doing something. Use your brain, man? Don't you think that if he intended to do that, there might be a simpler way to pull that off? Like have me deliver his message via a signed letter—instead of broadcasting his intent to some *three hundred million* Americans?"

Brickman offered a concession. "I'll give you this. You're not as stupid as you look. Let's say that the President has done this just to get back his satellites, knowing full well that the public backlash will be so intense that he'll have to rescind his order to restore our statues."

Brickman stopped talking, seemingly to respond to a new idea going off in his head. "Come to think of it, it sure wouldn't hurt to see how my fellow citizenry are responding."

*Shit!* The Achilles heel of the entire operation was about to snap. If Brickman concluded that the broadcast was a hoax, Silverstein's leverage would evaporate. Accordingly, he had to answer Brickman's question.

Brickman had turned toward the TV and was about to unmute the sound.

"Wait!" Silverstein said. "To further this process along, I'm going to answer your question. I'm going to level with you."

Brickman turned back from the precipitous edge of this game-playing abyss. "Yeah?" he said.

"What I'm going to do now is not in the playbook. You were honest with me, and I'll return the favor. Except for the broadcast you've just seen, I haven't been entirely truthful with you. Look at the business card that I gave you. I can tell you that the ink is barely dry because it was printed only this afternoon."

Brickman took the card from his pocket and gave it a glance. It was clear that he had no idea where this was going. "So, you don't work for Trump?"

"I didn't say that. I've worked for Donald Trump for some twenty-five years. I'm part of his—how should I put it?—independent inner circle. He asks me to do the special, sometimes unpleasant, jobs that need doing. It's only been in the past fifteen months that his title has changed. My role in his life and business has not. Do I need to spell it out?"

"What?"

"Let's see if you can connect the dots. As Donald Trump's private employee, I get to do things that others within the government would never do."

Although the temperature in the room was cool, Silverstein suspected that he was finally getting through when he noticed beads of sweat form on Brickman's forehead. "Will you stop fucking with me? What are you saying?" Brickman asked.

Silverstein walked up close, choosing to invade Brickman's personal space, knowing that his six-foot-two stature could be intimidating to a shorter man. "As you know, the President is a brilliant politician and can wrap nearly anyone around his finger to achieve his ends. Everyone knows this. And he values loyalty above all. What you don't know is that he's also a man with a mean, vindictive streak. Although our weather satellites are invaluable to the nation, they mean absolutely nothing to him if he thinks he's been wronged. I've personally seen him throw away some ten million dollars of his personal wealth to get his revenge. Which brings us to you and me, right here and now.

"Mr. Trump has made what he considers a fair offer. You get some of what you want, he gets back his satellites, looks wonderful in the press, and you receive a get-out-of-jail card." Silverstein hesitated before making his final point. "Here's the thing, Brickman. If you say no to his offer, our relationship will enter a new phase. So before you choose to go in that direction, please consider one statistic that's relevant here. Over my career with Donald Trump, I've had to do nine special jobs for him. If you decline his kind and generous offer, you will give me no choice but to make it an even ten. I'll leave it to your imagination as to what those jobs entailed."

Silverstein backed up to give Brickman some space and allow him time to think. "With all of this in mind, may I respectfully suggest that we dispense with all of this back and forth bullshit and go fix us some satellites?"

Silverstein recoiled as he said the words, as he recalled that the cold, calculating eyes staring back at him represented more than the face of a terrorist seeking retribution for a perceived injustice from years ago. He was also a remorseless killer. Steve Hancock, the boss at NSOF and a respected member of the meteorological community, was murdered for no reason other than having been a descendant of a Union soldier. That fact gnawed at Silverstein's conscience—so much so that he wondered if, under the right circumstances, he himself might be capable of exercising the ultimate form of revenge.

# – 29 –

## TWENTY-FIRST CENTURY'S
## MAIN EVENT

*Somewhere over Central Utah*
*39° 1' 18"N Latitude, 111° 50' 32"W Longitude*
*Saturday, March 31, 2018, 6:27 PM (MDT)*

"Do you think he'll be okay, Dr. Brody?" Kipling asked.

Kipling had asked a similar question earlier but wanted to know more. On her return to San Jose from SFO, their dial-up neurosurgeon had briefed her by phone. In person, he came across as so young that she had to bite her lip not to poke fun: *Will your mother give you permission to fly all by yourself?*

Dr. Eli Brody, on temporary loan from the Stanford University School of Medicine, replied. "We'll just have to wait and see. As I told you, the CAT scan we took back at the airport revealed no bleeding. That eliminated our worst-case scenario. Most concussions don't cause bleeding unless you're dealing with an elderly patient when the odds are higher."

Brody provided additional background. "After I arrived at the airport, I gave Mr. Smirnov a complete neurological examination. We talked some, and I asked him if he remembered what happened. He told me that most of that memory was a blank. Although he said he had a headache, the good news was that he had no vision or balance problems. Your friend suffered a serious blow to the head. I've seen this hundreds of times. Although I'd be foolhardy to make a definitive prognosis, I see no reason for pessimism."

*Hundreds? You've been around that long?*

"Dr. Brody, I apologize. I'm exhausted. Please tell me again what you said about the extent of his concussion." Because Kipling had no current symptoms, she chose not to reveal that she too had probably suffered a concussion.

"From what you told me earlier, that he was unconscious for less than a minute, one commonly used classification system says that he's had a Grade 3 concussion. Three out of four, with four the worst."

"Back at the hangar, before I left for San Francisco, his conversation was returning," Kipling said.

Brody nodded. "That's a good sign, but every case is different. Don't forget the effects that can follow a concussion." Brody counted on his fingers. "Amnesia, ringing in the ears, dizziness, confusion, among others. So far, he hasn't exhibited any vision or balance issues. We're just going to have to wait and see. Typically, for Grades 3 and 4, you'd expect at least a couple of weeks' recovery."

*A couple of weeks?* Kipling knew that her expression gave her away. Once they caught up with Erickson, Smirnov's participation could prove crucial.

Brody clicked his tongue. "I know I shouldn't be asking this, but are you a spy?

"Why would you think that?"

"Because it's not every day that my boss gets a call from the CIA."

"All I can say is that I work for the government and that your patient here, right now, is a very important person. The sooner he can function, the better. *I need him.*"

"I heard him speaking to the captain earlier. It sounded to me like Russian."

"No, it didn't!"

Brody took offense. "It certainly did. I was standing only a few—."

Kipling interrupted by giving him the evil eye.

192

Brody was no dummy and came to his senses quickly. "My mistake. Sorry." He paused. "I don't suppose you'd like to tell me how your friend got his concussion either."

"You suppose correctly." Kipling chose to provide some intrigue. "Even if I told you, you'd never believe it."

Kipling turned toward Smirnov. "So what's going on now, Dr. Brody? Is he sleeping, in a coma, or what?" Henderson told her earlier that Smirnov had conked out after Brody gave him some sort of injection.

Following the initial scan, CIA technicians had removed a row of seats, making room for a gurney that served as a makeshift bed. MacDonald, the co-pilot, reported that he expected their flight to be smooth, eliminating concern that Smirnov might suffer another concussion from being tossed about the cabin by turbulence.

Brody was extremely cooperative, and Kipling appreciated his patience, if not his curiosity. Her initial assessment of the young doctor had been overly harsh.

He continued. "With no definitive bleeding, the only recommended treatment is rest, both physical and mental. In fact, the usual advice is to keep a patient awake, to observe any changes that might indicate spontaneous bleeding. In your case, Captain Henderson suggested that I take a *wider* view, to do everything I could to give my patient the best chance at being alert when we arrived in Pittsburgh. And so, I gave Mr. Smirnov a powerful sedative that put him into a deep sleep. You say when, and I'll make sure he does his best Lazarus imitation for you," Brody teased.

*Lazarus? Clever.* "What was it you used to make him sleep?"

Brody smiled mysteriously. "Why don't we let that be my little secret, a magic potion I happened to have on me? What I used would not have gotten the seal of approval from the FDA."

Kipling felt her strength fading, fatigue ravaging her body. "Touché. Fair enough." *Hmm. I wonder.* "We have at least three more hours of flight time left. I don't suppose that you have any more of that magic potion on you?"

Brody nodded. "Do you want some?"

"I just might. Give me a few minutes, please."

———◆———

Kipling retreated to the rear of the aircraft, pausing to observe Smirnov sleeping peacefully.

Back at the San Jose airport, using information that she had supplied, Henderson had worked with NCDE to corroborate what Kipling had concluded: Erickson had hired a private aircraft to fly to Pittsburgh. Kipling had tracked her to a company called PSA, Platinum Star Aviation, a private FBO (fixed-based operator) operating out of SFO. Kipling knew that the tracker she had placed on Erickson's body would be useless once she took to the air. But after she landed, it would prove functional again.

With that information, the sleuths at NCDE had all they needed to both verify her identity and track her aircraft. They confirmed that a woman had paid cash for a flight to Pittsburgh. Further, the FAA reported that a flight plan had been filed to that same city. Not wasting any time, Henderson had the CIA plane in the air five minutes following the departure of the PSA aircraft. He reported that they would arrive in Pittsburgh some thirty minutes ahead of Erickson's slower plane.

Kipling fell into the last seat in the aisle. Cupping her face in both hands, and with exhaustion turning all thoughts into gibberish, she concentrated on what needed to be done. She briefly reflected on Silverstein, who had to be facing his own set of challenges in dealing with Brickman.

As Kipling envisioned it, once Erickson landed in Pittsburgh, they'd follow her, primarily to see if she was meeting someone. If nothing proved obvious, they'd take her down. Kipling needed Smirnov alongside during this aspect of the operation. As one who spoke her native tongue and knew her history, he might gain insights into the puzzle that was Kathy Erickson—and most importantly, to determine if she had been behind the two hacking events that had spawned the crisis between the United States and Russia.

Unless Erickson had plans to attack yet another aspect of either nation's infrastructure, such confirmation would be enough to convince both countries to back off their saber-rattling. Smirnov would forward this information to Putin by way of Popov, and Kipling to Trump by Lopez. The crisis would be over.

Kipling checked the time. *Damn!* It had been hours since she last spoke to Popov, and she had promised to keep him up to date on their progress. Five thirty-one PM West Coast time meant three thirty-one in the morning Moscow time.

*Could he be sleeping? No matter. He'd want to know.* Kipling removed Smirnov's satellite phone from her bag and dialed.

"Linda! Thank God. Are you in Pittsburgh?"

"Oleg, we've had a minor setback, but we're back on track." Kipling detailed most of what had happened with Erickson since they last talked. She also described Smirnov's condition and expressed confidence that he would participate in the chase.

Popov's voice registered frustration. "And so, you lost her! And then you found her again?"

"Don't worry! Our plan is still the same. Once we're convinced that she's acting alone, we'll grab her and trust that Dmitri can get through to her. We're only about two hours behind the schedule we'd planned before. As I speak, we're in the air and will land ahead of Viktoriya in Pittsburgh."

The line turned quiet. "Oleg. Is this making sense to you?"

"I'm here. We've already concluded that my niece is a clever woman. Do you think she knows that you are following her?"

"I can't see how." Kipling chose not to go into the strange things that had happened aboard the United aircraft.

"You've lost her once. What if you lose her again in Pittsburgh?" Popov cleared his throat and spoke more forcefully. "You should have grabbed her at the airport like I told you to."

"Listen to me, Oleg! That is not going to happen! I installed a tracker on her coat. We're not going to lose her! You need to trust me on this!"

"Wait! You saw Viktoriya in the flesh?"

"I did, Oleg. I stood right next to her."

———◆——

Kipling commanded her body to return to the front of the plane. Any adrenaline that had propelled her movements earlier had long since dissipated. She passed Smirnov and noticed no change. Brody was reading a magazine.

"Dr. Brody. I'd like to take you up on your offer. Unless I get some serious shut-eye, I'm going to be worthless. I want you to put me out and wake me five minutes before we land. Could you do that, *please*?"

Brody reached for his black leather bag. "Just point to the vein you'd like me to use."

———◆——

In her chartered PSA aircraft, Erickson sat proudly, congratulating herself on her ingenuity that resolved the glitch at SFO. But deep within her subconscious, a gnawing doubt began to shake itself loose. Murphy's Law could not be ignored: *Whatever can go wrong will go wrong.*

*That woman with the two backpacks*: She was Erickson's concern. Could there be more to it than a random occurrence? And, if so, would it not be wise to take additional precautions?

What form could any insurance take? Although Erickson felt physically secure in her aircraft, winging her way to her secret hideaway in West Virginia, she would soon be on the ground—and more vulnerable. *For argument's sake, let's assume that someone has found you out and is chasing you.* Erickson knew from her lifelong experience as a computer scientist that random events can wreak havoc.

If so, she thought, would it not be wise to introduce a bit of chaos into her future? For example, if the two-backpacker knew that Erickson was flying to Pittsburgh, would it not be wise to make a subtle change to that plan? Further, wouldn't it be shrewd to make such a modification at the last possible moment?

With that in mind, Erickson recognized exactly how to eliminate that potential threat. On the approach to the Pittsburgh airport, she would notify her pilot that she had changed her mind. Turns out, Morgantown, West Virginia, would be preferable, she would casually explain. In truth, it would also shave off some thirty miles worth of driving.

But there was more! As brilliant as Erickson knew she was, she wanted—no, needed—to prepare for the absolute worst: the possibility that nothing in her arsenal of tricks might prevent her from being caught before she initiated her final coup de grâce. And so, she chose to institute one final failsafe, one that would operate in her absence even if she were dead.

Back at SFO, Erickson had planned to wait until she arrived in Pittsburgh before initiating round three of her hacking trilogy. But with what had happened, and the availability of her aircraft's onboard Wi-Fi, she decided to accelerate her game. Accordingly, she wrote fifteen new lines of code. That code involved a first script that would initiate a second script in a far-off server. That second script would execute in seven hours, at three-thirty in the morning, Eastern Time, giving her enough time to reach her refuge hide-a-way.

Erickson paused to appreciate the enormity of what she was about to do. While the first two assaults on the United States and Russia were noteworthy, both would pale compared to Erickson's final act of devastation.

The complete destruction of her native country was within sight for one Viktoriya Ratimirovna Popova. Retribution for her family would be coming soon, even if she did not live through what historians—those who survived—would undoubtedly call the twenty-first century's main event.

# — 30 —

## FLYING BLIND

*Silver Spring, Maryland*
*39° 3' 42"N Latitude, 76° 59' 38"W Longitude*
*Saturday, March 31, 2018, 8:33 PM (EDT)*

Brickman's nerves had frayed, leading him to the edge of betraying the image he was trying to project. *I'll be damned if I let this wannabe honky intimidate me in my own home.* That was his initial thought. *Still, I've got to keep my cool. I need to think!*

For the first time since Jackson had entered his home, Brickman commanded himself to ignore the man's skin color. Whoever this Jackson fellow was, he was suggesting that he was a private hitman for Donald Trump, the President of these here United States. *Lord have mercy!* Brickman knew that Trump was unconventional—hell, everyone in the country knew that. Bringing with him from the private sector his personal persuader was hard to imagine.

*What if that were true*, he wondered, as he recognized that he had used the subjunctive tense correctly.

"So what's it going to be?" Jackson asked. "Don't be stupid, okay? Let's get this over with."

The more Brickman thought about it, the more impressed he became. Who would ever suspect that this nigger was part of Trump's inner circle? *Genius! Sheer genius!*

---

To Silverstein's surprise, Brickman's defensiveness appeared to soften. *Hallelujah!* There'd be no need to resort to Plan B. He couldn't wait to tell Kipling—on the bench under the tree, of course—about the ruse he was about to pull off.

Brickman accepted Silverstein's assessment grudgingly. "You win. First, assure me again that I'll be in the clear."

"You can take that to the bank. If I'm lying, then I don't work for President Trump. And I'm pretty sure that I've done a good job of convincing you that I do." Silverstein wondered if Brickman took note of his negative speak.

---

*What did he say? I hate this coon. No matter. I saw with my own two eyes the President of the United States make a promise to the entire nation.*

"Okay, then," Brickman said. "I suppose you want to see me remove the Sword of Damocles hanging over your precious satellites."

"Damn straight. My orders are to stay here until I get a call that tells me that GOES-14 is in the clear."

"Follow me," Brickman ordered.

---

Silverstein followed Brickman, making their way through the house. Carpeted flooring transitioned to hardwood as they exited the living room and proceeded down a short hallway that fronted the kitchen and dining room. Significantly, Silverstein noticed a computer laptop sitting on the kitchen table, one that complemented another he had seen earlier by the TV. Nothing appeared out of the ordinary, a feminine touch evident in many of the styling details. Lopez had provided details about Brickman's wife, including that she was out-of-town.

To the right, Brickman opened a door and flipped a switch. He pointed down to what Silverstein recognized as a stairway, probably to a basement, as he noted the unfinished, wooden steps.

"This way," Brickman pointed.

As Silverstein stepped down into the unknown, his composure began to wane, knowing that he was placing himself at risk. As he stepped onto the flat-gray concrete floor, what he observed next was not typical of most home basements. Instead, it resembled the sparse, bare-bones office of many government nerds. In the middle of the room sat an old government-issue, battleship-gray, metal desk with papers strewn about haphazardly. On the walls were dozens of shelves holding books and computer binders. On the desk was an old-fashioned push-button black telephone and a keyboard that faced a large flat-screen computer monitor. Surrounding the desk's perimeter were numerous knickknacks, most of which were Civil War figurines of Confederate soldiers.

Silverstein felt some relief as Brickman passed him by and headed straight for the chair in front of the monitor. *So far, so good.* Silverstein considered it essential to maintain a dialogue to divert Brickman's attention away from any inconsistencies that might yet alert him to the bogus nature of Silverstein's plan. "I'm anxious to get home to my wife for dinner. Can you do what you need to do from your computer here?"

Brickman, sitting, looked back at Silverstein standing. "How come you don't wear a wedding ring?"

*Shit! I've got to be more careful!* "SOP, I'm sorry to say. Mr. Trump doesn't allow it for any of his private employees. He pays us a lot and expects complete dedication—which means that my family always takes a backseat. That's the reason most of his *special* employees never marry. I know! It sounds strange." Silverstein was making it up as he went.

Brickman seemed to accept the explanation. "Yes, *of course*. You think that I did all this from my office? How stupid do you think I am?"

Silverstein casually walked over to look over Brickman's shoulder. His photographic memory would allow him to reproduce what Brickman typed—in case Lopez's whiz-bang surveillance hardware crapped out on him.

Brickman looked up warily. "Back off! Go sit on that chair over there." He pointed.

---

Brickman was about to begin typing when he stopped cold; all this commotion had made him forget the time. *Judy should have called by now!*

Worried that something might have happened to his wife, Brickman reached for the phone.

---

Silverstein recognized trouble. *What?! What's going on?* "Who are you calling?" he asked.

Brickman waved his hand in dismissal.

---

Lopez and Miller reacted instantly, rushing over to their laptop that had just started beeping. Brickman was making a phone call from his house phone. Some twenty-five minutes earlier, they had intercepted two calls *to* Brickman, one to the house phone and one to his cell. Both had come from Brickman's wife's cell. CIA software had diverted both calls to Brickman's voicemail, which was temporarily unavailable to the user.

"He's calling his wife!" Miller said aloud.

Lopez did the mental calculations. If he let the call go through, there was the chance that Brickman would ask his wife if she saw Trump's address on television. That would prove instantaneously disastrous. On the other hand, how likely was it that he had even confided in her about his scheme? Still, could they take the chance and possibly blow the operation? Lopez decided he could not and hit F1 on his keyboard, activating a recording from the telephone company: *We are sorry. All circuits are busy in the area to which you are calling. We apologize for the technical issues we are having. Could you please try your call later?*

Lopez watched Miller shake his head. They both knew that the second ball was about to drop. Brickman would try again using his cell. He did, and Lopez diverted that call in the same way he had done the first.

Lopez again expressed his frustration. "If that son-of-a-bitch hadn't ditched his ring, you and I would have *some* clue about what's going on inside that house." As he stood and stared out into the blackness of the night, Lopez accepted the fact that they were flying blind. Whatever was happening across the street was a mystery.

# ~ 31 ~

## BLIND SIDED

*Silver Spring, Maryland*
*39° 3' 42"N Latitude, 76° 59' 38"W Longitude*
*Saturday, March 31, 2018, 8:47 PM (EDT)*

"What's wrong?" asked Silverstein, his heart nearly flat-lining after Brickman unexpectedly picked up his landline phone and started dialing. He then repeated the procedure with his cell. *Does he suspect something?* To Silverstein's relief, Brickman's demeanor remained unchanged.

"My wife, Judy, left this morning to visit her sister. I just realized that I hadn't heard from her. A recording says that they are having telephone problems where she is."

What just happened was the epitome of the definition of the word *random* and an example of the fickleness of Murphy's Law. This sort of unexpected occurrence could ruin even the most carefully planned operation. Obviously, Lopez had diverted the calls to a recording.

"Call her later. Plenty of time to talk after we're done," Silverstein volunteered.

Brickman gave Silverstein the eye. "Fuck you!"

Silverstein recognized that this was one problem he could solve on the fly. "Any chance your wife's in the North Carolina area?" Lopez had provided details regarding Mrs. Brickman's trip.

"How the fuck did you know that?"

"On the way over, the radio said there'd been some sort of software glitch that's taken out all telephone service there, both landline and cell. Made national news."

"You shittin' me?"

"That's what I heard. I'm sure your wife is fine." Silverstein did his best to hide his impatience. "So what do you say we get this show on the road?"

---

Brickman felt relieved to know there was a logical reason for not reaching his wife—and vice versa. *On the other hand! Is there no end to the list of bizarre events occurring this evening?* And wasn't it interesting that Jackson had the convenient answers? With his skepticism and suspicions rising again, he took a hard look at Jackson, having recognized that the worm had turned. With Jackson off to the side, Brickman could type anything and say that he was working on the doomsday clock. In the meantime, he'd search the Internet. President Trump's message to the nation, as well as the Charlotte phone outage, seemed particularly relevant.

"You win. I'll stop the count-down clocks right now," Brickman said as he began typing.

---

Brickman's keystrokes appeared simultaneously on Lopez's computer screen across the street—and on Jeremy Bryan's at CIA headquarters. It wasn't long before Bryan was on the phone telling Lopez what he already knew: that Brickman's typing had nothing to do with weather satellites. He was searching the Internet for responses to the President's address and, for some unknown reason, a telephone outage in the Charlotte area.

Lopez knew that everything would soon come crashing down. Should he and Miller storm the house? No! Silverstein had ordered him to swear on a virtual stack of Bibles not to interfere.

———◆———

The wheels were coming off the wagon, and Silverstein knew that Plan B was in the offing. Brickman's body language told him so. He was doing what Silverstein would have done in a similar situation: search the web for public reaction to Trump's announcement. Violence was imminent because Silverstein now had no choice but to take physical control of his adversary. Recognizing that Lopez's flash bangs might be of use, Silverstein surreptitiously removed one from his pants pocket, activated its timer, casually lowered his left hand to be in line with Brickman's position, and let it roll. Brickman had similar ideas. He opened his left desk drawer, removed a handgun, swiveled in his chair, and pointed it at Silverstein.

Brickman was fuming. "I don't know how you did it, but I now know that it was all smoke and mirrors, you goddamn fuck!" He hadn't picked up on Silverstein's movements but did seem to notice something rolling toward him.

Silverstein chose to divert Brickman's attention by using his remaining seven seconds to flatter him. "Congratulations! I knew you were too smart to fall for this. It doesn't matter, you know. You're still going to save our satellites."

"Like hell, I am! I'm not afraid to die."

The stun power of the flash bang at such close range was astonishing. Silverstein had never experienced anything like it and had the good sense—as he dived to the floor to the right of the desk—to squeeze both eyes shut and plug his ears with his fingers. To his advantage, the heavy desk provided some physical separation from the detonation. All said and done, his brain continued to function in real-time.

Before Brickman came to his senses and realized that he was the one with the gun, Silverstein needed to overwhelm him. Silverstein crawled frantically around the back of the desk in a flanking motion, hoping to surprise his adversary from the rear. Lying flat on the floor, he peeked around the side through the subsiding smoke. Brickman was not there.

# – 32 –

## JUDY IN DISGUISE, WITH GLASSES

*Silver Spring, Maryland*
*39° 3' 42"N Latitude, 76° 59' 38"W Longitude*
*Saturday, March 31, 2018, 8:52 PM (EDT)*

Although Brickman had not anticipated the ensuing blast, the fact that he was still alive told him that what had exploded was not a grenade. From his military training—and having seen his share of YouTube videos—he surmised that what he had experienced was a flash bang. *Where the hell did that come from? And if Jackson had a flash bang, might he have another weapon?*

Reeling from the blast, having fallen onto the floor in front of his desk, Brickman took stock. He'd had the good sense to maintain his grip on the Ruger LCP in his right hand, its six-round clip ready for action. Brickman swore—on his Confederate brothers' graves—that one of those rounds would find its way into Jackson's black nigger heart.

The only problem: Brickman's vision had suffered following the brilliant flash of light; just as bad, a high-pitched whine had replaced his normal hearing. With his body still functional and his Ruger at the ready, he flipped himself onto his butt and pushed backward against the front of the desk. Silverstein was likely hiding to the rear, on the opposite side of the desk.

———————◆◆◆◆———————

Silverstein willed his visual and aural senses to maximum sensitivity. Although neither was in great condition, both were functional and probably better off than Brickman's. Silverstein surmised that his adversary was hiding in front of the desk, gun drawn, waiting. Both adversaries were counting on the protection offered by a sturdy example of government-issue furniture.

Considering the upcoming demise of GOES-14, a stalemate wasn't acceptable. Silverstein needed to find a way to alter the balance. If he had any hope of jumping Brickman, he needed an element of surprise. Remembering the figurines populating the back perimeter of Brickman's desk, he inched his fingers upward and grabbed four.

The quiet that had followed the explosion ran its course. "I know you're back there, you motherfucker," came Brickman's challenge.

Silverstein decided that it wasn't to his advantage to reply. Recalling his days as a guard in high school basketball, he remembered the effectiveness of his lobs. In addition to the four figurines, he had one remaining flash bang.

———————◆◆◆◆———————

"You're not going to say anything, are you? Shows how much of a coward you are! Well, I'm waiting for you."

Other than talking trash, Brickman had little going for him. His hearing had somewhat returned, but not so his vision. On the positive side, he felt confident that he could defend the area in front of the desk. Brickman's trigger finger twitched as his ears strained to detect movement, his arm outstretched, ready to fire.

And fire he did, as he responded to a noise a few feet to the left in front of him. And again to his right. Unfortunately, there was no evidence that either shot had hit anything. "Show me your face, you coward!"

Instead, two more thuds repeated themselves in other nearby positions. This time he withheld fire. "Fool me once, but not twice, you bald, black-skinned motherfucker!" he yelled.

Silence returned—until he heard what sounded like a metal ball rolling toward him across the top of his desk! As it became airborne over the front edge—and before it landed in his lap—Brickman saw up close what looked like a gumball. *Fuck!* It looked remarkably like the one that had rolled toward him on the floor. Brickman reacted instinctively, thrusting his hips upward to dislodge the ball and, simultaneously, raising his arm to protect his eyes.

———————◆◆◆———————

Even though the building's structure muffled the sounds of the blasts, they were easily identifiable to the CIA professionals.

"What do we do?" asked Miller.

"We do nothing."

Miller tried to make the most of their present impotence. "At least he made use of our flash bangs."

———————◆◆◆———————

In preparation for the explosion, Silverstein had curled himself into a fetal position, ears plugged, eyes shut. Consequently, he survived the second flash bang with little effect. From the screaming that ensued from the front of the desk, he suspected that Brickman hadn't fared as well.

———————◆◆◆———————

Brickman's hearing, which had been making some progress toward improvement, suffered a relapse. But the reason for his scream had nothing to do with his head. Searing pain was coming from his upper left thigh. Although his vision had improved, the most he could make out was what looked like a missing pant leg. He touched the area with his left hand, and it came away wet.

It was time to make a significant move—before a third flash bang did even more damage! *Where the fuck did Jackson hide them?* Brickman suddenly recognized some hope, that the odds had tilted in his favor. The second flash bang had taken out the overhead lights. Only a faint glow from the computer monitor was visible.

It was time to act proactively! Fighting the agony coming from his leg, he raised himself to his knees, turned ever so slightly, and put a bullet through the monitor. The world inside his basement office turned into the blackness of hell.

"What do you think of that, you son-of-a-bitch? Isn't what you expected, was it? Now you're as blind as I am!"

---

*Touché!* Considering his options in what was becoming a fight to the death, Silverstein chose to remain silent.

---

Brickman lifted himself higher on his knees and struggled to detect any sound. *Say something, you fuck!*

*On the other hand, two can play this game*, he thought. *I can play possum too.*

---

From Silverstein's glance at Brickman's weapon as he had earlier dived to the floor, he felt confident that what he saw was a small semi-automatic, probably with a six-shot clip. Although Silverstein could continue to play games with his adversary, trying to trick him into shoot wildly, wasting his shots, there were two downsides. One, Silverstein's run of good luck might end. Worse, with every passing minute, they were approaching the demise of GOES-14. For Plan B to have any chance of success, Silverstein needed time for the sequence to unfold.

Silverstein chose to go for broke. From the scream he heard from the opposite side of the desk, he felt confident of Brickman's position. What he was about to do could be termed unconventional. One advantage of his six-foot-two frame and the fact that he was reasonably fit, Silverstein was stronger than most men, a fact that he decided to use to his advantage. He estimated the metal desk to weigh between one hundred and fifty and two hundred pounds.

With that decision made, Silverstein removed his cell phone and activated its built-in flashlight, covering the bulb before placing it face down inside his pants pocket. He then stood as quietly as possible, reached down to place both hands on the lower metal perimeter of the desk, counted to three, and gave a mighty heave-ho.

Perhaps the result of a larger than anticipated rush of adrenaline, the entire desk became temporarily airborne. When it landed, the resulting blood-curdling shriek gave proof that Silverstein's strategy had paid off. He removed the phone from his pocket and walked to the opposite side. Its small beam of light showed Brickman's shooting hand pinned to the floor.

Realizing that Brickman was no longer a physical threat, Silverstein lifted the desk from Brickman's body and flipped it to the side. He aimed the light from his cell phone at Brickman, whose left hand rose to his eyes' defense. He was a sorry sight indeed: blood oozing from his left upper thigh, right wrist useless. Worse, Brickman was struggling to breathe, which momentarily worried Silverstein until he realized what had happened.

Silverstein almost felt sorry for him. "My, my, it seems to me that you've gotten the wind knocked out of you. Give it a minute, and you'll be back to normal. It's a terrible feeling, I know. Probably makes you wonder if it mightn't have been better to go along with our earlier agreement. You think?"

Gradually, Brickman regained his wind, after which one expletive followed another. Silverstein checked his phone for the time. "Listen, I'd love to talk, but we don't have much time. I happened to notice a couple of laptops sitting around upstairs." Silverstein bent down to help Brickman to his feet.

With his good left arm, Brickman rebuffed the help. "What gives you the god-damned gall to think that I'm going to help you? You're a fraud."

"It's true that I set you up, that the Trump broadcast was a fake. He's going to be pissed, our President; he was so proud of his performance. He loves to act, you know. But I've got to tell you, the part about me working for him is still true. And I've been authorized to do what it takes."

"That's just fine with me," Brickman spat out his response. "Go ahead and shoot me. I think there's a bullet or two left." He gestured toward his gun.

"As much as you'd like me to do that, you're the only one who can save our satellites."

"I've got nothing left to lose. Let's get this over with."

Silverstein brought his face close to Brickman's and shook his head. "Now that's not quite true, is it Raymond? You don't mind if I call you by your first name?"

"Fuck you talking about?"

Silverstein accelerated the pace. "Raymond, I've tried to be nice to you, but things are going to start happening very quickly now. You've been calling me names ever since I arrived at your front door. Well, now it's my turn. Listen to me, you miserable, racist, god-forsaken, worthless piece of shit! You have a wife, right? Her name's Judy.

"Do you love your wife, Raymond? Do you?! If you don't, none of what happens in the next twenty minutes will make any difference to you. If you do, and you don't disable the kill code for our satellites, you're going to spend the remaining days of your sorry, hateful life in jail, realizing that you could have saved Judy's life—and didn't!"

# — 33 —

## MASTER CHARADE

*Silver Spring, Maryland*
*39° 3' 42"N Latitude, 76° 59' 38"W Longitude*
*Saturday, March 31, 2018, 9:08 PM (EDT)*

"You're bluffing!" Brickman repeated, as Silverstein dragged him up the stairs into the kitchen.

It was now dark outside. Fortunately, the upstairs lights were still functional. Recalling the laptop sitting on the kitchen table, Silverstein guided Brickman to the nearest chair and shoved him down. Brickman winced in pain.

Silverstein needed to make his point. "This time, I'm not bluffing, Raymond." He opened the laptop and gestured for Brickman to do something. "At last count, you still have five functional fingers. I suggest you make use of them."

His right hand hanging limply from his wrist, Brickman made a defiant, unsuccessful attempt at folding his arms. His facial expression, together with sweat streaming down his face, mirrored the pain he was under. The crushed right wrist, the bloody left hip, and whatever other damage that came by way of Silverstein's desk grenade did nothing to assuage his anger. He continued with further profanities—including several clever variations of his earlier epithets.

"I don't fucking believe you! Nothing you've told me so far has been true."

Silverstein appreciated Brickman's skepticism and girded himself for what would occur over the next several minutes. He hoped to God that Lopez was up to the challenge as well.

"Don't believe me, huh?" On the plane across the continent, Silverstein had developed his screenplay. "Any chance you follow the news? Does the name Joaquin Guzman ring a bell?"

"What the fuck you talking about? El Chapo? The drug kingpin that got himself extradited to the U.S? What the fuck does he have to do with the price of rice in China?"

"How about the name, Juan Francisco Gomez, more commonly known by Mexican drug cartels as JFG, or *La máquina de matar*?"

"Never heard of him."

"I don't suppose you would have. You should know that Gomez was Guzman's most trusted enforcer, his primary hitman. Do you speak Spanish? In case you don't, *La máquina de matar* translates directly into *The Killing Machine*. And, as it happened, when El Chapo left Mexico, Gomez found himself out of a job. I don't suppose you can guess who he works for now?"

"Don't know and don't care." Brickman hissed his response.

"Actually, I think you might." Silverstein took out his cell and dialed.

———◆◆◆———

"Finally!" *Hallelujah!* "It's Victor calling." Lopez raised his arms in triumph.

———◆◆◆———

A heavily accented voice answered. "Gomez." Silverstein turned his head to the side and stared at Brickman. "I'm not going to give up on you, Raymond. I know that you love your wife."

Brickman tried to laugh but found it difficult as he grabbed his ribs with his good hand. Between shallow breaths, he continued. "Now I get it. Like I said before, you can fool me once. You'd like me to believe that this supposed killer of yours stands ready to murder my wife? Do you really think I'm going to fall for that?"

Silverstein spoke resolutely into the phone. "Gomez, I'm here with someone who has something we very much need. The future of our weather satellites hangs in the balance. As I told you earlier, I asked you to go to Charlotte to give me some leverage if I needed it. I'm going to put you on speakerphone."

Brickman took the conversation in stride, still belligerent. "I've got to hand it to you! For a darkie, you're damn clever. So you know that my wife went to Charlotte. Big fucking deal! You're going to have to do better than that, you mother-fucking liar."

"Did you catch that, Gomez?"

"Si, Senor. This one has no respect, *sin respeto*, as we say back home. When I'm done with business here, I'll come back and do this one just for you. Three for the price of two. No extra charge for you, *Amigo*."

Silverstein offered his version of the good cop. "I'm hoping that won't be necessary, Juan. For the benefit of our doubter here, do you mind telling me where you are standing at this very moment?"

In broken English for which Silverstein had to stifle a smile, Lopez answered. "Yo amigo, you know full well where I gone. You want I should take out the bitch who lives here at 326 Cedar Street. And the blondie from up north? She wears big red glasses. You want I should tell you about the house?"

*Praise to God!* Lopez's last statement was proof that his agent in Charlotte had visited Brickman's sister-in-law's address and had communicated that description.

"Light blue, white trim, two-car garage, end of a cul-de-sac. Green Jap Honda sitting in the drive. Blondie's car, maybe. Garage door open, white Gringo Chevy inside. All the drapes in the house open. Got an okay picture of both marks in the living room. You want me text you it? Might convince your friend you're no mother-fucking liar. Him calling you that really pisses me off!"

Silverstein marveled at the efficiency with which the CIA's Charlotte agent had worked. "Si, por favor."

Twenty seconds later, Silverstein's iPhone dinged. Although window glass reflections marred the clarity of the image, the faces of both women were identifiable, as well as the red glasses on Brickman's wife. As he viewed the image, Brickman's bluster deflated in an instant.

Although Silverstein figured that the tide had turned in his relationship with Brickman, he didn't want to take any chances. To seal the deal, he felt he needed to up the ante. "Are you still there, Juan?" Silverstein asked into the phone.

"Si, Senor, standing by, waiting for your command. Can't come too soon!"

"Juan, what do you mean by that?"

"Amigo, I'm a man who likes to keep busy. My parents were good, God-fearing people. They gave me solid work ethic. In Mexico, El Chapo had lots of work for me. On average, a job a week. I been here four months, and there's been nothing. Not that I'm complaining, mind you; I'm paid *mucho dinero*. But Jorge and I are ready for some action."

To Silverstein's mind, Lopez deserved a supporting actor nomination. "Who's Jorge, Juan?"

"Jorge? My assistant? He's a little weak in the mind but completely reliable." Gomez paused. "By the way, *surely* you know me famous for my special kills?"

"I've heard that you like to take chances. Now is not the time, Juan. Get in and out! This isn't Mexico, you know."

"I hear you, amigo. Safety first. I take pride in my work. It's true that Jorge prefers the usual two taps to the head. But me, I like keep my creative juices flowing. For this one, Jorge and I have decided to send RPGs through the two front windows. No one inside could survive that. We'll be out of here in forty to fifty seconds, I'd say. Leaves a mess, but I'm proud to say it's one of my signature kills."

Silverstein watched Brickman's reaction as Lopez described the process. "So, Raymond, what's it going to be? We're twenty-five minutes away from ten. And at this point, Raymond, I'm so pissed off at you that I don't even care what you do."

It was now or never.

———◆———

Brickman was beaten, and he knew it. As much as he wanted to believe that this could all, somehow, be another charade, he couldn't take the chance. It wasn't just his wife. He had to think about his son.

There was one thing he had to know for sure. "If I do what you want, how do I know that your man will back off? Will you swear on your mother's grave?"

"As long as you clear all of our satellites—not just GOES-14— you have my word. Besides, you must know that if I gave Gomez the go-ahead after you cooperated in good faith, I'd be sentencing myself to my own death. There's nowhere I could hide that President Trump wouldn't find me."

"Give me the laptop," Brickman said.

Brickman was heartbroken. He'd spent his entire adult life devoted to one cause, and he had failed. To save his wife, he had no choice but to do what Jackson asked. But that didn't mean that all was lost. By taking out one nigger, he could proudly hold his head high for one brief moment. After all, he did have one more arrow left in his quiver.

———◆———

At CIA headquarters, Jeremy Bryan's eyes were burning from what seemed like an eternity of waiting for something, anything, to show up on his computer monitor. Then it happened!

Slowly—very slowly—letters, numbers, and symbols began to appear on the screen. And, this time, he recognized immediately what he was seeing. Whoever was typing at the other end was accessing the computer code stored on GOES-14. Compared to the earlier, effortless surfing of the web, this time it was a slow hunt and peck sort of operation.

Bryan watched as the user accessed each of the remaining satellites that the terrorist had targeted. It was no longer a secret where Brickman had hidden his kill sequences. As he watched each succeeding satellite addressed, he realized that Brickman had used the same procedure for each.

Bryan knew that the crisis was over. Notably, he was confident that he could also reverse the damage done to NOAA-20. He couldn't wait to tell Lopez the good news.

———————◆———————

"There! Are you happy?" Brickman barked at Silverstein. "I gave you exactly what you wanted. Your satellites are safe. Now do what you promised and call off your dogs."

With the speakerphone turned off, Silverstein had gotten confirmation from Lopez that what Brickman said was true. He and Miller were on their way over. For Brickman's benefit, Silverstein spoke into the dead phone. "Juan, you can go home. Leave the folks alone."

Silverstein turned to Brickman and spoke sincerely. "You did the right thing, Raymond. And now I think it's time we get you to a hospital."

At once, Silverstein's neck hairs stood on end: Brickman's behavior had changed. "Hey asshole, you don't mind if I get a glass of water, do ya?"

Before Silverstein could react, Brickman was on his feet and headed toward the sink. As he watched Brickman open one of the kitchen drawers, Silverstein knew that he was in trouble.

# – 34 –

## WHEN PUSH COMES TO SHOVE

*Silver Spring, Maryland*
*39° 3' 42"N Latitude, 76° 59' 38"W Longitude*
*Saturday, March 31, 2018, 9:42 PM (EDT)*

Brickman knew that he finally had the upper hand over the black Satan. Not once had Jackson displayed a weapon. Nor could he have! Brickman was convinced that his frisk would have identified one. How Jackson had gotten the flash bangs past the front door was a mystery. Nonetheless, if a third one existed, it would have little consequence against his Ruger LCP. Judy had repeatedly made fun of his weapon stashes. This one had finally proved its worth.

Brickman assessed his physical condition and felt confident that his banged-up physique was up to the task. With his adrenals flooding painkillers through his body, pain was nonexistent. The burned skin on his upper thigh had no impact on his legs, as he had realized climbing the basement steps earlier. To be sure, his right hand was useless, which meant that his left-handed aim might be a little off. But with a full, six-round clip, together with close-in action, he felt confident he'd be the last one standing.

Silverstein had no idea what was coming. Any karma generated from his earlier interactions with Brickman suggested that it would not be good. Why else was he moving so quickly, spanning the short distance toward the sink? Why was he opening a kitchen drawer? The only available weapon would be a knife, likely a big one. Still, unless Brickman had trained as a left-handed knife-thrower, Silverstein wasn't worried. Further, his two-man cavalry was only seconds away.

As Brickman rotated sharply, the sight of a second handgun caused no less consternation to Silverstein than had the one downstairs. *Who keeps a gun in the kitchen?*

Only seconds elapsed before two bullets came flying, sending Silverstein diving to the floor underneath the table. Both shots missed their target.

"I've got you now, you son-of-a-bitch! You're one dead nigger! I've got four shots left, and one of them is going to put you out of your misery."

---

"Why are we hearing gunshots?" Miller asked.

"Doesn't make any sense."

As he bolted through the bedroom door, Miller yelled to Lopez to the rear. "We might need the kit,"

"Right!" responded Lopez.

They then bounded down the steps two at a time.

---

Unless a forthcoming stroke of luck bore Silverstein's initials, he feared that Brickman's prediction would come true. The only advantage he had was that Brickman was shooting left-handed. Silverstein recalled kicking away the weapon from Brickman's right hand during their downstairs struggle. *What was I thinking? Why didn't I pick up the gun for myself?*

The smallish, four-foot-long, rectangular table under which Silverstein had dived was his only available protection. Instinctively, he pushed one end of the table upward, grabbed the center support, and held the table sideways to act as a shield.

Unfortunately, what Silverstein was doing was not working. The table weighed a ton, and its maneuverability as a makeshift battering ram was negligible. He decided the best thing he could do was to back himself into the hallway, ditch the table, and make a run for it.

It wasn't to be. After tossing the table back into the kitchen, and just as he cleared the hallway adjacent to the living room, Silverstein heard two more shots. His luck had spoiled. The first round hit him somewhere on his left torso. The second turned out to be worse as it struck the rear of his upper right thigh, and he fell forward onto the carpet.

Knowing that he would never reach the front door, he instead crawled left into the living room, using one good leg and two good arms.

------------◆◆◆------------

Lopez and Miller were halfway across the street when they heard the third and fourth shots. They arrived at the front door and found it locked.

------------◆◆◆------------

Silverstein crawled as quickly as pain and an uncooperative right leg permitted. He got as far as the television when he remembered that he had one more card to play. He maneuvered himself sideways so that he could lean against the wall.

Quickly, Silverstein jerked the pen from his pocket, ripped off the end cap, and guided it toward the nipple on his belt. With his right hand pulsing with fear, he couldn't find the nipple at first. Finally, the magnets nudged it into position. As Silverstein executed the final move, pulling the pen away from his belt, Brickman came around the corner, his left outstretched hand and handgun leading the way. Silverstein rested his hand on his lap, hardly an ideal location from which to aim.

"Well, well! What do we have here?" Brickman chided.

To Silverstein's relief, Brickman did not fire on sight but began with conversation. *If only I can entice him nearer.*

Brickman edged closer. "Do you want to die fast or slow?"

"Fast, if you don't mind."

Uncharacteristically, Brickman displayed a measure of compassion. "As much as I hate you, and as much as you don't deserve it, I'll do that for you."

"I appreciate that. And in response to your kindness, I'm going to do one for you," Silverstein said.

"What could you possibly do for me?"

Knowing that Lopez and Miller would soon charge through the door, Silverstein needed to buy time. Imagining himself in Brickman's position, he decided to answer the one question he himself would have asked. "I bet it's driving you crazy how I got those two flash bangs into your house. You are a pretty good frisker, I've got to admit."

Brickman inched closer, now about six feet distant. Silverstein figured he had no more than a fifty-fifty chance of hitting his target if he shot from his hip.

"That's exactly what I've wondered."

"Come closer, and I'll tell you."

"Fuck you! I'd prefer to stay just where I am," Brickman said. In the process of making that statement, he unconsciously edged to his right, the Ruger in his left hand aimed squarely at Silverstein. Worse, that hand was shaking, making Silverstein worry that the firearm might go off accidentally. "Go ahead, tell me!" Brickman said.

Despite Brickman's jumpiness, Silverstein held fire. He estimated that his chances of hitting Brickman had risen to only seventy percent. And he had only one shot. Without a distraction of some sort, Brickman would undoubtedly react to any movement and fire first.

*Lopez! Miller! Where are you?* At the least, Silverstein felt that he had bought himself several priceless seconds, that Brickman would wait until he had the answer. "Do you remember when I handed you my business card outside your door?"

"Yeah."

"What you didn't notice was that I carried the flash bang in that same hand. It's a common human reaction. Our minds think that if a hand is holding one thing, it couldn't possibly hold anything else. Close-up magicians use this principle all the time. Similarly, you never suspected that I had another one in my left hand."

———◆◆◆———

Lopez noticed that Miller seemed a little concerned.

"Don't you think that you're using maybe a tad more explosive than is necessary?" Miller asked.

"I'm not taking any chances! If we don't blow the door on our first try, we might be too late."

Lopez set the electronic fuse to six seconds, and both men ran for cover around the corner of the house.

———◆◆◆———

From Silverstein's position on the floor in the living room, facing obliquely to the house's front door, he knew he would later swear that he saw the front door flying sideways down the hall, well before he even heard the explosion. The blast was so powerful that he imagined the entire house imploding and burying them both.

When the blast occurred, Brickman flinched and instinctively turned toward the door. And with that movement, his weapon changed position.

Silverstein's opportunity had come. He raised his right arm, extended it fully, aligned his eyes along the pen's length, and pressed the release. He knew that, until the day he died, he'd remember the tiny kick and *whoosh* that would save his life. The connecting wires extended in an instant, the sharp probes easily penetrating the skin behind Brickman's shirt.

Brickman never saw it coming! Silverstein watched as three things happened in rapid succession. One: Brickman fired twice as his left hand spasmed. Both bullets found their way into the wall to Silverstein's left. Two: Brickman could have become a poster child on YouTube for anyone wanting to witness the effects of a Taser on a human being. Brickman's body resembled a bowl of spilled Jell-O that quivered uncontrollably as it made its way to the floor. Three: Silverstein saw his two CIA compadres rush in from the door, guns drawn, ready for action.

As it turned out, no further defensive or offensive actions were necessary.

# ~ 35 ~

## TOUCH AND GO

*On approach to Pittsburgh International Airport (PIT)*
*Pittsburgh, Pennsylvania*
*40° 30' 24"N Latitude, 80° 25' 14"W Longitude*
*Saturday, March 31, 2018, 1135 PM (EDT)*

"Linda, can you hear me?" Smirnov said, his eyes lingering over the sleeping form of his colleague.

Dr. Brody had just administered the counteragent to the sedative Kipling had requested. Some fifteen minutes earlier, he had given that same drug to Smirnov. Upon waking, Smirnov found himself searching frantically through fragmented memories that flashed in and out of focus. He raised himself onto his elbows and looked about, soon concluding that he was aboard an aircraft. "Where am I? Who are *you*?" he said to the young man sitting nearby.

"My name is Eli Brody. I am a neurosurgeon who works, at this moment, for Dr. Kipling. She's sleeping in the seat behind you. You are on an aircraft flying from San Jose, California, to Pittsburgh, Pennsylvania. You suffered a blow to the head and were unconscious for a while. The good news is that our CAT scan back in San Jose revealed no permanent damage to your brain. I don't know what's going on between you two, but Dr. Kipling seems to think it's

225

important for you to be fit for action. You've been sleeping since we left California." Brody stood and casually put his hands in his pockets. "Do you mind if I run a few tests? To see how you're doing?"

Smirnov tried to make sense of what this stranger was saying. "Dr. Brody? I know who I am and why I am with Linda. For the life of me, though, there is a piece missing that I cannot identify. The last thing I remember is running toward a truck and jumping in."

Brody responded. "What you are describing is not unusual. You have what's called anterograde amnesia. Your brain was temporarily damaged and unable to store new memories. But that doesn't mean that those memories won't come back," added Brody optimistically. "Probably when you least expect them."

"How long ago did this happen?"

Brody checked his phone. "From what I understand, I'd say it's been some nine to ten hours. But you've spent the last four sleeping."

"Sure. Go ahead and run your tests, doctor." Smirnov cooperated while Brody asked questions and had him following his finger here and there.

Smirnov concluded that his mental capacity for deduction remained intact. Ten minus four meant that six hours of his life had gone missing. What could have happened in those six hours? *An explosion?* At once, a fleeting recollection of a terrifying sound rammed through his consciousness. *Yes, there was an explosion!* He recalled Kipling's order to run from the house.

Memories from before the explosion came flooding back: Popov's suspicions regarding his niece; their drive north to the San Jose airport to drop off Silverstein; and, finally, their arrival at Viktoriya's San Jose address.

An announcement came from the cockpit: "Touchdown in twelve minutes."

——◆◆◆——

Kipling slowly regained consciousness, trying to hold on to the satisfaction that came from a deep sleep. She recognized Smirnov's voice and opened her eyes. There he was as she had hoped, his eyes clear, steady, and focused, attributes absent in the hours following the explosion.

Smirnov persisted. "Can you hear me, Linda? How are you?"

The veil of fatigue that had earlier overwhelmed Kipling had lifted. "The more important question is *How are you?* We've been worried, you know."

Smirnov shrugged. "Dr. Brody told me what he thinks happened. Temporary amnesia. I remember everything that happened before the explosion. That's what it was, right? An explosion? We were running toward the truck, weren't we?"

"What were we doing right before that, Dmitri?" Kipling wanted more confirmation that his mind was still functional.

"I had just picked the deadbolt to Erickson's house when you yelled for me to run."

"Correct. What you don't know is what I saw when I looked through the windows at the top of the door. There was a lit candle sitting on the top rung of a stepladder. Do you remember—?"

Smirnov cut her off. "Propane tank! There was a propane tank to the left of the house! Everyone knows that propane is heavier than air. You saved our lives, Linda. Erickson wanted to burn up any evidence of her existence in that house. No?"

Kipling's anxiety drained away. Smirnov's mind was working just fine, thank you very much. She straightened up and motioned for him to sit in the adjacent seat.

On the ground, as they taxied, Kipling brought him up to date on all that had occurred during his mental sabbatical.

Smirnov seemed impressed. "You actually spoke to my boss, Oleg Popov?"

"Your phone rang, and you were unresponsive. What else was I to do? You'll be pleased to know that we got along just fine. Without his pictures, one from the car and the other from your age-generating software, we would not have found Erickson at the airport. That was key. And that's when I attached the tracker to her coat."

"Wait a minute! You came face to face with Erickson, and you didn't arrest her?"

Kipling shook her head in disbelief. "You and your boss think alike. As I told *him*, there was nothing to gain. If she really is the person behind what's going on, and we grabbed her, she'd clam up, and we'd have nothing. By following her instead, we can confirm whether she's working alone. Maybe we can monitor her computer and latch onto some other clue that might implicate her. Or maybe tell us what she's up to next."

"So, I'm confused. Was she flying commercial? And if you were there with her at the airport, why didn't you just fly along with her?"

"Good question." Kipling explained the entire absurdity, with Erickson running from the plane and then contracting a private jet.

"She was on to you? What did you do to give yourself away?"

Kipling bristled, resenting any suggestion that she had somehow made a foolish mistake. "I didn't do anything! But the tracker is in place, and we know right where she is. She's headed right here to Pittsburgh. Henderson told me she'll land about fifteen minutes after us. Since we don't know where she's headed after she gets here, it's better to be ahead of her than behind. Gives us time to follow."

They had been taxiing for some minutes when the plane came to an unexpected standstill. Kipling looked out both sides of the aircraft. They seemed to have stopped just beyond the taxiway, shy of any building. Seconds later, Henderson appeared from the cockpit, concern evident in his face. "Houston, we have a problem!"

Kipling cringed. "What now?"

"Erickson's plane has been behind us for the past four hours. But NCDE just reported that while she was on approach to Pittsburgh, she called an audible. She changed her flight plan to Morgantown, West Virginia."

Kipling's mind reeled with the implications. "Dammit! Did she do that on purpose? I can't believe she's on to me!" She refocused her thoughts. "Morgantown's not that far, is it? Can you change our route?"

"I figured that's what you'd want. Skip's changing our flight plan as I speak. We'll be there in about a half-hour."

As Henderson returned to the cockpit, the engines spooled up. Kipling's plane was on the move again. "What's she up to now, Dmitri?" she asked Smirnov.

———◆——

Twenty minutes earlier, Erickson's pilot had seemed confused by the last-minute request. Nonetheless, it was her dime they were flying on, and they'd do what she asked.

She checked the time. With luck, she'd be on the road not long after midnight. After making the decision to divert, Erickson immediately called to arrange a rental car in Morgantown. About a two-hour drive to Berkeley Springs, she hoped to arrive around two in the morning.

There, in the privacy of her secure, remote little hideaway, she'd watch television and switch between news channels to witness how the world would come to grips with its own mortality. She might even pop some corn in celebration of the culmination of decades of preparation. Erickson had primed the pump; all was in readiness for her *coup de grâce*.

As she'd watch the world approach its Armageddon, she'd hold tight to her chest the only physical memory she'd chosen to take with her when she departed Moscow for that last time, half a lifetime ago: a photograph of her, her parents, and her baby brother, Alexei—back when they were a smiling, happy family.

# ～ 36 ～

## THE VANISHING ELEPHANT
## IN THE ROOM

*I-68 East, leaving Morgantown, West Virginia*
*39° 39 30.8"N Latitude, 79° 50' 15.1"W Longitude*
*Sunday, April 1, 2018, 12:20 AM (EDT)*

Erickson had given considerable thought to creating the perfect storm required to make nuclear war inevitable between the two nuclear powers. A casual observer might have concluded that she had chosen at random the timing and sequence of events that had preceded this moment: from the incapacitation of air traffic control systems; to the sabotage of hydroelectric power generation facilities; and now moving toward the final step. That casual observer would have been wrong.

Erickson's blueprint for the sequence had been mentored by a little-remembered book published in 1968 by Wilmington-Harrington Press, a book publisher long since forgotten. That one hundred and forty-nine-page exposition, penned by Dutch psychologist Lucas Van Dijk, had an appropriate title: *How and Why Human Beings React to Threats.* Fewer than five hundred copies of the English-language version sold.

To those who took the time to appreciate Van Dijk's dissection of the complexities of human interaction, its message was clear. Specifically, that Homo sapiens—and society in general—can take a lot of inflammatory abuse, but tolerance to those assaults is proportional to the length of time between assaults and inversely proportional to the magnitude of the injustice. In other words, infrequent bickering at a tolerably low level can continue for decades, as often happens in unhappy marriages or international relationships. Even then, limits can be breached, leading to a breakdown in relationships, resulting in separation or even violence.

At the opposite end of the spectrum were escalations that occur so quickly that the human capacity to accept and adapt is limited, sometimes resulting in a "shoot first, ask questions later" response. A good example was the immediate declaration of war by the U.S. following the Japanese bombing of Pearl Harbor.

Van Dijk's analysis seemed particularly relevant to Erickson's goals. Although she recognized that his theory was nothing more than common sense, by letting it guide her actions, she felt that she had the best chance of success. One final argument in Van Dijk's treatise would prove crucial to her design: *perceived* injustices can be as significant or powerful as real ones.

For her grand scheme, Erickson had chosen not one, not two, but three distinct and sequential terrorist acts. Numbers one and two would escalate tensions to a fever pitch, perhaps resulting in nuclear war by themselves. Still, Erickson knew that they might not be enough—that cooler heads on both sides would argue for restraint. For that reason, she had originally decided that if her initial efforts failed, she would push the nuclear button herself, launching a missile or two to get things going. She'd do that by way of one of the components of the nuclear triad: land-based missiles, submarine-based missiles, or bombers. And why not? She had hacked into the most secure of industrial computer systems. But it didn't take long to eliminate the latter two as candidates: Without a coconspirator inside, it *was* impossible.

After several frustrating years of effort, Erickson also realized that, even with her considerable Internet skills, it was impossible to hack into either country's ground-based Intercontinental Ballistic Missile (ICBM) systems. In the case of the Americans, they had done a commendable job of creating air gaps that prevented either direct or indirect connection to the Internet for anything related to the launch itself. For the Russian ICBMs, air gaps were unnecessary because the launch control system was hard-wired to the land-based missiles, with no Internet reliance. Critics might call this system primitive; adherents would call it brilliant. Accordingly, Russia's ICBMs were also unhackable.

Of necessity, then, Erickson came up with an alternate approach. Although it was impossible to breach the firewalls that stood guard over the U.S. and Russian land-based nuclear missiles, Van Dijk's fundamental treatise made clear that such a breach wasn't necessary. There was lower hanging fruit. After all, in politics or life itself, it wasn't always reality that swayed votes or opinions; it was the appearance of reality. President Donald Trump had turned that concept into an art form.

An illusion, as all magicians knew, was easier to pull off than the real thing. Making an elephant vanish in front of an audience's eyes is impossible—but not so the *illusion* of that same elephant disappearing. And there was no better example of the impact a perceived reality can cause than what had occurred three months earlier in Hawaii when a false missile alert broadcast to the public. When time is at a premium, perception becomes reality. In that example, panic ensued until a retraction came out some thirty-eight minutes later.

In the case of nuclear weapons, Erickson understood that the prevailing viewpoint underlying both the U.S. and Russian launch philosophy came made to order. It was called Launch on Warning (LOW). Once one side verified that missiles had launched from enemy territory, LOW required immediate nuclear retaliation. More than one concerned general had explained the absurdity of this tactic. An accident, mistake, or incorrect assessment of the enemy's nuclear status could start a war. The Hawaii incident represented a convincing example.

Understanding that inherent weakness, various U.S. presidents had proclaimed that LOW was unacceptable and that, instead, retaliation would occur only after detonation on home soil. However, launch on detonation had a serious flaw. The first strike by incoming missiles could be so severe as to eliminate any hope of a successful retaliation. Hence, both the United States and Russia had reverted to LOW. That weakness was to Erickson's obvious advantage.

One other reality played into Erickson's hand. Once nuclear missiles launched, they could *not* be recalled or destroyed en route. Erickson would wager that most American citizenry assumed the opposite, mainly because of their previous observation of NASA launches blown up on purpose when something went wrong with the launch. Contrarily, ICBMs did *not* have kill switches. The Air Force had long ago vetoed that addition—fearing that the enemy could manipulate the software and render the entire U.S. nuclear arsenal impotent.

Erickson pushed away any thoughts of sleep, noting the time on the digital clock in her rented Jeep: thirty minutes after midnight. Some three hours would pass before she would create the *illusion* that nuclear missiles had launched. That had come about through her crowning achievement, her hack of the Russian equivalent to America's Nuclear Command and Control System (NCCS), a system designed to monitor nuclear threats. Russia's version had turned out to be easier to penetrate.

At that point, as Van Dijk had so eloquently written, both sides would find themselves stranded in their proverbial corners, with nowhere to turn. Fight or flight? *Fight* would win by default. With minds compromised by lack of sleep and nerves stretched on tenterhooks, and only minutes left in which to parlay, one side or the other would react and launch their missiles in retaliation. The other would follow suit, and Erickson's retribution would be complete.

# ~ 37 ~

## FULL THROTTLE

*I-68 East, leaving Morgantown, West Virginia*
*39° 39' 30.8"N Latitude, 79° 50' 15.1"W Longitude*
*Sunday, April 1, 2018, 12:50 AM (EDT)*

Smirnov was once again riding shotgun—this time in a luxury car, a Lincoln Continental, the only rental vehicle that Hertz had available at that time of night. He noticed yet again, this time deciding to say something. "Do you think that I'm that pleasant to look at, or are you still checking to make sure I haven't gone catatonic—is that the word—on you?"

Since departing their aircraft in Morgantown, this was the first time they had discussed his condition. "I'm sorry, Dmitri," Kipling said. "You gave me quite a scare back there—."

He interrupted. "When the house blew up?"

Kipling flicked a glance in his direction. "Yes. I was at my wit's end! You were out of it, and I thought you might have serious brain damage. And I knew I needed you to help chase down Erickson. Popov's call obviously spooked her, and that is why she left town."

Kipling chuckled. "She probably thought that Russian agents were on their way to her house that very moment."

———————◆◆◆———————

Kipling's satellite phone interrupted the conversation. It was Lopez. It had been some nine hours since they had spoken back in San Jose.

"Hi, Hector. Dmitri and I are in your neck of the woods, heading east from Morgantown on sixty-eight."

"Dmitri's with you? Thank God! How is he? Was Dr. Brody of help?"

Kipling turned and caught Dmitri's eye. "We were very fortunate. If he's not 100%, he's close to it. Brody was great."

Lopez came back quickly. "Wait! Morgantown? I thought you were going to Pittsburgh."

"Yeah, about that. We did land there but had to take off again. Erickson changed her flight plan at the last minute."

"So, where are you headed now?"

"You tell me. The good news is that our tracker is working just fine. We left Morgantown, and I'd say we're about four miles behind her on sixty-eight. Listen, can I put you on speakerphone?"

Kipling handed the phone to Smirnov and made the introductions: "Hector, Dmitri Smirnov; Dmitri, Hector Lopez."

Lopez spoke first. "I know this is awkward, Mr. Smirnov. But even in as short a time as it's been, from what Victor's told me, I can trust you. May I call you Dmitri? You can call me Hector."

Kipling was impressed with Smirnov's reply. "Of course, you can call me Dmitri, but I would never call you by your first name, sir. You are on the same level as my boss, Mr. Popov. And by the way, he sends you his greetings."

Kipling was anxious to learn about Victor. "All right, already. Enough with the pleasantries." She noticed Smirnov wince as she said the words.

Lopez laughed. "Dmitri, you'll have to forgive Linda for her irreverence."

Smirnov turned serious. "Mr. Lopez! In case I never get the chance, I want you to know that Linda saved my life back at the house. She pulled me from a burning truck and practically carried me away from the fires."

By now, Kipling had had enough. "Oh, for God's sake, Dmitri! Don't make it out to be more than it was."

Smirnov held the phone close to his mouth. "Mr. Lopez, what I'm telling you is true."

A noticeable silence preceded Lopez's sincere reply. "I hear you, Dmitri, and I believe what you say."

Kipling wanted to get things back on track. "Hector—Mr. Lopez, I guess I should say—what the hell happened with Victor?"

The pace of the conversation picked up. "I have some good news there. Victor was right. Brickman *was* our guy!" Lopez gave a nutshell description of the operation and its successful conclusion. "That's the good news. Our satellites are safe. The bad news is that Brickman shot Victor twice; he just came out of surgery."

Kipling, hyperventilating, whispered the words. "Hector, how bad is it?"

"Not to worry. The good news is that the two bullets couldn't have found a safer place to enter: one in the thigh that missed the femoral artery and a through and through on his shoulder. The surgeon says he was *very* fortunate."

"Thank God!" Kipling could breathe again.

Lopez continued. "Now back to the elephant in the room. It's bad, and I'm as scared as you. We've moved to DEFCON 2, and Russia has reciprocated. Nothing this serious has happened since the Cuban missile crisis. Nothing makes sense. Dmitri, we know that we did not hack into any of your air traffic or hydroelectric systems."

Kipling jumped in. "Mr. Popov told me the same thing. Our two countries are being played, Hector. It has to be!"

"That may be so, but how, for God's sake? The hotline has been useless. Nothing but threats coming back from Russia. Everybody's yelling at each other at the UN. And we have a president who has taken a sudden interest in our nuclear football, tweeting up a storm, saying that he's not going to take much more of this. It won't be long before missiles start flying. I can't believe I'm saying this. You two may be onto the only lead we have."

Smirnov was next. "Linda's been in touch with my boss, but I have not, for some twelve hours now. I need to talk to him."

"Don't hang up yet," Lopez said. "Linda, what's your plan with Erickson?"

"Plan? All I can say is that thank God I have Dmitri here with me. He's from her native country, knows her background, and speaks her language."

"Okay, let's leave it at that. Let me know if you learn or need ANYTHING."

———————◦◆◦———————

*SVR Headquarters, Moscow, Russia*
*55° 35' 2"N Latitude, 37° 31' 1"E Longitude*
*Sunday, April 1, 2018, 7:55 AM (MSK)*

Oleg Popov was still at work. He hadn't been home since he first learned there had been an attack on America's air traffic control systems some twenty-eight hours earlier. The last he had spoken to Kipling was more than four hours previously. She and Smirnov should have landed in Pittsburgh by now.

Popov was about to make the call when he stopped to think. What would he say? What if Kipling answered and told him that Smirnov was still out of action, that she would have to go it alone? What if she said that they had lost all contact with Viktoriya? *Stupid woman! She should have grabbed her when she had the chance.* Still, Kipling's rationale seemed logical, and she felt confident that her tracking device would not fail. Should he just tell her that it had been nice knowing her but that both should prepare themselves to meet their maker?

Popov appreciated the irony that the calendar date read April 1, or April Fool's day. Russians could get caught up in the same silliness as Western countries. Some historians said that Peter the Great initiated the day's celebration in Russia some three centuries earlier.

Popov dialed and felt almost faint when he recognized Smirnov's voice. "Dmitri, is that you? Are you well?" he asked in Russian.

"Comrade Popov, I was just about to call you. I will speak to you in English because Linda and I are together here in our car. Yes, I am fine. Linda and her team have taken good care of me. Let me give you a summary of what's happened." Smirnov provided a detailed status report, including the reason they had flown to another city, Morgantown, after being tricked into flying to Pittsburgh.

Popov mulled over these details. "Could you put me on speakerphone, please? I need to talk to both of you."

"Hello, Mr. Popov. Linda, here. We were very fortunate with Dmitri. It worked out much better than I had hoped it would."

Popov understood that Kipling was responding more formally, probably in deference to Smirnov. "Linda, I want you to know that we will never forget what you have done for Dmitri."

"You're being kind, sir. I am the thankful one. When we confront your niece, Dmitri will be doing the talking."

"I understand. What's your plan?"

"I don't rightly know sir, but I swear to you that before the sun comes up this morning, we're going to be asking your niece some serious questions. You should know that I have assurances from my government that we had nothing to do with either your air traffic control or hydroelectric plant problems. When we talked yesterday, you said the same thing to me. Mr. Popov, the only rational conclusion is that someone wants to start a war."

Popov had to remind himself how late it was back in America. "Linda, Dmitri, listen to me. I agree with you, and I have tried to make that point to my colleagues. I made the mistake of doing what you told me not to, Linda. I told them that my niece might be behind it all. As you predicted, that did not go well."

Kipling offered a kind rebuttal. "Assuming she's innocent, do you have any other leads? Anything?"

Popov cursed his reply. Russia's intelligence gathering was world-class. "No, we don't! And the worst of it is that logic is taking a back seat to the war hawks. It is happening back in your country too, Linda. Did you know that your military has gone to DEFCON 1? Naturally, we've had to reciprocate."

Popov waited for a response. It came from Kipling. "No, sir, I did not."

Smirnov followed up. "Sir, I need to know from you what authority I have concerning Viktoriya."

Popov knew what he had to say. "The fate of our civilization hangs in the balance. You and Linda have my complete authority to do what you think necessary."

———◆———

The solemnity of Popov's final words caused all conversation to cease for minutes. Kipling was especially troubled to hear that the U.S. military had progressed to DEFCON 1, the highest degree of readiness, as close as you can get to a full-on nuclear war. Only minutes earlier, Lopez had reported they were at DEFCON 2. *Things are moving way too fast!*

By then, they had traveled another six miles. Driving more than eighty miles per hour, Kipling had closed the gap from four to three miles. She had been watching the onboard navigation map; Erickson had already passed the next major town along the freeway, Frostburg, Maryland. Next up was Cumberland.

At once, a third phone in the car came to life. Kipling's heart leaped as she recognized Victor's ring tone on her cell. "Victor!?"

"Listen, Linda! There's no time for chit-chat. For your information, I'm fine. That's enough said about that. Hector has brought me up to date on everything that's happened. I've given this a lot of thought. Someone is setting us up, and they're doing a brilliant job. If their strategy is what I think it is, the hammer is coming down very soon.

If you think that Erickson has anything to do with this, I would make extreme haste. Listen, I must go. I had to browbeat the surgeon into letting me make this call. Goodbye."

"What'd he say, Linda?" Smirnov asked.

"My boss, Victor, is a brilliant man. He says that he sees a pattern, that whoever is doing this is going to do something else real soon, something big that will finally push our countries over the edge."

Kipling watched as Smirnov covered his face with his hands. "God, Linda. I am an atheist, as you probably suspect. But right now, I am praying to whatever God might be out there in the universe to save our sorry souls."

With worry about Silverstein on her mind, Kipling flattened the accelerator pedal. Fortunately, traffic was light at this time of night. The Lincoln leaped forward in acknowledgment. Undeterred by the beginnings of a rain shower that pelted bullets against the windshield, she leveled off at one hundred and ten miles per hour. The sooner they had Erickson in their sights, the better.

# ~ 38 ~

## JAIL BREAK

*Walter Reed National Military Medical Center*
*Bethesda, Maryland*
*39° 00' 02"N Latitude, 77° 5' 38"W Longitude*
*Sunday, April 1, 2018, 1:20 AM (EDT)*

Silverstein knew how lucky he had been. Whether true or not, the old adage, *It's better to be lucky than good,* seemed apropos. No sooner had Lopez and Miller blasted their way through the door than an ambulance was on its way. By the time it arrived, Brickman had recovered enough from his electro-shock therapy to continue his profanities, centered upon some outlandish idea that Silverstein was a hitman for President Trump. His rantings amused ambulance personnel as they attended to Silverstein's injuries and carted him off on a stretcher.

After ambulance personnel had assessed Silverstein's injuries to be non-life-threatening, Lopez chose to transport him to the Walter Reed National Military Medical Center in Bethesda, only thirty miles away. Only ten miles from CIA headquarters, its location would make it convenient, he said. Lopez promised to drop by after the surgery. As the ambulance had sped away, Silverstein noted the time.

———————◆◆◆———————

"All right, already! I'm finished!" Silverstein yelled out in frustration, having wanted to talk to Kipling a bit longer. He and the surgeon had been going at it from the moment they had made each other's acquaintance in the operating room before surgery. He made a show of pressing a button on his cell to convince the surgeon, Colonel Mylene Manchester, that he had finished the conversation. Manchester came across as a take-no-prisoners Army colonel who, Silverstein suspected, had no doubt encountered other egotistical, know-it-all wise guys who thought they knew better than she did. Silverstein had met his match.

"What are you? A pumped-up teenager with testosterone poisoning? Just because you think you've cheated death doesn't mean that you can just go around and ignore everything I've been telling you the past half hour. I've patched up your sorry butt the best I can, but you can't leave the hospital until I say so. You need to rest to give your body a chance to recover." Manchester glared at Silverstein. "Do I make myself clear! You may be a hot-shot Navy scientist out there in the big world…" She made a big encompassing gesture. "… but here on my turf, your ass is mine!"

From the moment he had left the scene of the Brickman fracas, and again after he awoke from surgery, Silverstein had been hell-bent on understanding the unfolding international debacle. He had no intention of sitting on the sidelines. Nor could he! *Where the hell is Lopez?*

Manchester prepared to leave the room. "Get some rest! I've given you some intravenous pain medication that should hold you for a couple hours. When that wears off, call the nurse! If you need to go to the bathroom, don't try to limp there yourself. Call the nurse! Do you have any questions?" The cadence of Manchester's words reminded Silverstein of a drill sergeant.

Silverstein noticed the door opening slowly. It was Hector! *Thank God!*

"Dr. Manchester, it's good to see you again." To Silverstein's ear, Lopez's greeting fell short of 100% sincerity.

Manchester claimed the opposite. "Can't say that I agree, Mr. Lopez." Then, as if a light bulb had gone off in her head, she deadpanned. "Oh, don't tell me! Don't tell me you know this know-it-all son-of-a-bitch, who wanted to check himself out of the hospital as soon as he woke up from the anesthesia?"

"I'm afraid I do, ma'am."

Manchester shook her head as she approached the door and then turned to make one further observation. "Should have known. I bet you he's also from your funny farm down the street. Am I right?"

"Yes, ma'am, he is," Lopez conceded.

As the door closed behind her, Silverstein couldn't hold back. "You *know* this woman?"

"Yes. While you were in the ambulance, I called here to request her specifically."

"Why?"

"Oh, I don't know," Lopez said. "Maybe it's because I wanted my friend to have the best damn surgeon within a three-state radius of the District of Columbia. That and the fact that, even though she could retire and name her price, she's stayed in the United States Army. She can be a trifle edgy at times. That's just her nature."

Lopez pulled up a chair and looked concerned. "You didn't say anything to upset her, did you?"

Silverstein thought about the most diplomatic way to put it. In the end, he decided that the most honest thing to do was lie. "No. Of course not!"

———◆———

Lopez brought Silverstein up to date on what had happened since they last spoke. After some drama in Pittsburgh, Kipling and Smirnov were hot on Erickson's trail, just to the west of them in

Maryland. Silverstein was pleased to hear that Dmitri seemed to be none the worse off from the explosion.

"So, what do you think, Hector? Talk to me."

"It sounds like a con job to me, by some outside entity, say a North Korea or a China. It boggles my mind to think that both we and Russia could be duped into thinking that the other is responsible."

"Why aren't the embassies helping? That's their job."

"You'd think so, wouldn't you? We've called in their ambassador in Washington, and they've called in ours in Moscow. Both sides have stood up before the United Nations and proclaimed their innocence. Neither side believes the other! And get this! The hotline? Created expressly to resolve tense situations like this? It's not helping! The vitriol coming through that communication link is making things worse. What they're saying on the hotline is one hundred and eighty degrees away from what their diplomats are telling us in person. Worse, after we make a hotline transmission, it can be hours before they respond."

Silverstein continued logically. "Which brings us back to the only lead we have. Erickson. Everything she's done points to her involvement. And the fact that she happens to be Popov's niece is incredible."

"Linda and Smirnov are closing in. We have that going for us."

"Good. You and I need to be there when it happens."

Lopez reacted in disbelief. "What do you mean, *we*? Before I entered the room, I heard some yelling. It seemed to me that Dr. Manchester believes you aren't going anywhere."

"See that wheelchair. See that closet over there. You're going to help get me dressed, and then you're going to bust me out of here. If you have to, show them your badge."

"Show them my badge? Show them my badge!?" Lopez responded condescendingly. "Did I just hear those words come out of your mouth?"

Lopez played along but came back with only shoes and socks.

Silverstein remembered. "Dammit! I forgot. In the emergency room, they cut everything off. Wait! That was your fancy suit. Don't you still have my clothes back at Andrews? Andrews isn't far."

With Lopez's help, Silverstein put on his shoes and socks and slid slowly from the bed onto the wheelchair. "So far, so good," he informed Lopez. "Let's go. Let's make a run for it."

Their improvised scheme ended abruptly when the door opened, and Dr. Manchester saw them face-to-face. Lopez accepted the fact that their *deer in the headlights* expressions might be worthy of a YouTube video.

Silverstein took responsibility. "Colonel. Dr. Manchester. I wouldn't be doing this if I didn't have to. You've no doubt been listening to the news. *Please*," he pleaded.

The reaction on Manchester's face and the tone of her voice were not what either of them had expected. "Both of you! Stay right where you are until I get back. Promise?"

Silverstein nodded vigorously. "Swear to God, hope to die."

Lopez noticed the beginnings of a smile form on her lips.

Manchester followed up with an obvious question. "Were you planning to take the IV drip with you as well?"

Two minutes later, Manchester returned with crutches, a paper bag, and to Lopez's surprise, a hanger with pants and shirt. "Put these on," she said. "We have a closet full of odds and ends, and I think these will fit. And inside this bag are replacement bandages and painkillers, both pill and injection. Unless you do something stupid, my sutures should hold. Just be careful. Okay?" She then removed the IV needle from his arm.

To Lopez's surprise, Silverstein's aggressive disposition softened. His words seemed sincere. "Thank you, Dr. Manchester. Thank you!"

Before she left the room, Manchester's demeanor reverted to her normal combative nature. "Lopez!" She turned to face him directly. "If anything happens to this man, I'm going to hold you personally responsible. Do you understand me?"

From his earlier dealings with her, Lopez knew precisely what to say. "Yes, ma'am. Yes, Colonel."

———◆◆———

As Lopez pushed him out the door and down the corridor, Silverstein thought of something. "Hector, can you get your hands on an LD500?"

"Shouldn't be a problem," Lopez said. After a moment, he recognized the significance of the request. "I see where you're going with this."

Silverstein recognized that his obligation—and ultimate contribution—to humanity might come down to this very moment. He had to leave the hospital, no matter the risk to himself personally. That commitment revolved around a single word, chosen eight years earlier by a foreign adversary on the opposite side of the planet. If nuclear missiles launched because of an accident, some misunderstanding, or worse, outright trickery by a third party, there were only a handful of people who knew its significance. Silverstein was one of them. That word was *Athena*.

# — 39 —

## ONCE BITTEN, TWICE SHY

*Route 522, Berkeley Springs, West Virginia*
*39° 35' 33.4"N Latitude, 78° 14' 45.5"W Longitude*
*Sunday, April 1, 2018, 2:05 AM (EDT)*

Erickson hadn't visited her West Virginia hideaway in over fourteen months. With her strategic blueprint coming together over the past year, she had neglected that segment of her plan.

She had never really expected that her West Virginia refuge would prove necessary. But considering what had happened over the past twelve hours, she now considered herself fortunate to have created this emergency safe house. Erickson wanted to be alone when the missiles flew; she wanted nothing to interfere with her sense of fulfillment as she enacted this ultimate revenge for her deceased brother and parents.

To ensure that no one threatened or disturbed her there, she had chosen her property well, having taken precautions that anyone with normal insecurities would have considered paranoiac. Situated a mile off State Route 522, outside Berkeley Springs, the property consisted of an eighty-five-year-old, one-level, stone cabin located well inside thirty acres of forested land enclosed by sixty-two hundred feet of chain-link fence. On top of the fence was barbed wire facing outward.

If that physical barrier wasn't enough to persuade trespassers that they weren't welcome, the "Stay Out" signs posted every one hundred feet made the point more succinctly.

As Erickson approached the dirt road that connected her house to the highway, she was pleased to see that the entrance had overgrown with weeds and brush. That vegetation was now mostly dead following the winter's freeze, concealing the fact that a road even existed there or that some one-hundred feet deeper into the undergrowth was a gate. The only clue that the property might be habitable was an old rusted mailbox. The four-wheel-drive Jeep left waiting for her at the rental car agency would have little difficulty traversing the route, despite the heavy downpour that had begun fifteen minutes earlier. It had since abated.

Erickson stepped slowly from her vehicle, stood silently, and took in the sounds of nature. The air radiated freshness. Except for a slight breeze that allowed dead leaves remaining on the trees to whimper themselves to sleep, there was absolute quiet. She checked the mailbox, more out of habit than necessity; nothing important was ever there. What was there, she'd check later.

With the Jeep's headlights lighting the way, she stepped forward through the wet vegetation to unlock the three combination locks that kept the gate in place, pleased to note no evidence of tampering. During her visits over the years, the congeniality and honesty of the locals had impressed her.

Erickson drove her vehicle across the divide and relocked the gate, realizing as she did so that she might never again see the world outside of her private conclave. Russian missiles would certainly target Washington, DC, a scant two-hour drive away. She'd be too far away to die from the blast itself, although radiation could be an issue. No matter. If she couldn't escape using her car, once convinced that mother Russia had been driven back into the Stone Age, she'd call it quits with a bullet to the brain.

As Erickson made her way through the wet overgrowth and arrived at the house, she wasn't expecting any surprises. Ten exterior cameras with motion sensor alerts, all connected to the Internet, had allowed her to monitor her property from afar. The only alarms issued by the sensors had come from several nonhuman species of the four-legged variety.

Erickson checked the time: 2:16 AM. Only seventy-four minutes remaining. She hurried into the house. A few last-minute details required attention, especially the hotline transmissions. The main event would start soon.

*SVR Headquarters, Moscow, Russia*
*55° 35' 2"N Latitude, 37° 31' 1"E Longitude*
*Sunday, April 1, 2018, 9:25 AM (MSK)*

Oleg Popov caught himself in time not to appear startled, acknowledging the smartly dressed uniformed officer who had drawn his attention. With the country's military standing at DEFCON 1, all essential military and civilian personnel were moving to the National Defense Management Center (NDMC), a facility arguably comparable to the National Military Command Center (NMCC) located in the Pentagon in the United States. As head of Directorate X in the SVR, Popov was one of those essential personnel.

Earlier, Popov had debated whether to call his wife. But what would he say? What *could* he tell her that would make any difference? Why not let her go in peace, free from the knowledge of the fiery inferno that would consume them both? But he did call, lying yet again about some demanding project that had been monopolizing his time. He told her he loved her, hoping that his voice did not betray the reality of what he knew.

NDMC sat two and a half kilometers south of the Kremlin, and Popov would transfer there by car. For those farther away, the center featured three helicopter pads. Russia's new state-of-the-art command center brought together critical intelligence during sensitive or crucial situations involving the nation's military. Putin had decided in 2013 that this aspect of Russia's command and control needed modernization. Erected in record time and built on the grounds of an existing defense complex on the Moscow River, the facility had numerous underground tunnels that connected three separate and impressively large auditoriums.

Shown to the press not long after construction, this structural nerve center was far more grandiose than necessary, Popov thought. The large rooms could hold many more people than would be required during those dire situations for which the facility had been designed. *What was Putin thinking? When missiles start raining down, does he think there will be time for a vote?*

Although Popov knew that America's intelligence-gathering capability was ridiculously bloated and expensive, with far too many government agencies providing their spin, the American government had had the good sense to create one additional central facility. That one was situated in a lower level of the White House and called the White House Situation Room. To which, in a fast-driven emergency, the President and a small contingent of advisors could abscond within minutes.

Rumor was that the room was President John F. Kennedy's idea. Disappointed over the lack of coordinated intelligence available to him following the catastrophic Bay of Pigs invasion in 1961, he ordered its creation. It was there, Popov imagined, that President Trump had already hunkered down. The seriousness of DEFCON 1 would demand no less.

Popov's head hung dejectedly as he walked toward the elevator. He felt as if the weight of the world was on his shoulders. What if his own flesh and blood were at the root of what was happening? As Linda had predicted, Popov's colleagues ridiculed such "nonsense." If true, Popov blamed himself for not recognizing his niece's mental condition when she had returned to Moscow. Popov believed in neither heaven nor hell but now imagined that he would certainly head toward the latter if there were such.

As he exited the building with his driver, Boris, Popov realized there'd be few opportunities to make a call once he arrived at the NDMC. It had been an hour since he had spoken to Smirnov. "Дай мне минутку, пожалуйста," he yelled ahead. The driver understood, walked a distance to the side, and took out his smokes.

The satellite call to Smirnov went through swiftly, but the conversation didn't last long. Popov told Smirnov where he was going, and Smirnov reported that they were getting very close to Viktoriya. He'd call back when he knew more.

Before motioning to Boris, Popov took stock. His hopes now rested with one of his own, a capable Russian spy—together with an American having a similar job description, whom he had never met and, worse, had known for less than twenty-four hours. No thriller writer could have concocted such an outlandish set of circumstances. Popov cursed the nonexistent God who had positioned him nearly five thousand miles away from the potential solution to this crisis, his niece, Viktoriya. He had no choice. He had to trust his two surrogates.

*Exit 82B from I-68 East: I-70 East/US-40 East*
*39° 42' 35"N Latitude, 78° 11' 11.5"W Longitude*
*Sunday, April 1, 2018, 2:27 AM (EDT)*

"Anything new?" Kipling asked. Smirnov had been speaking in Russian.

"Yes. President Putin has called together his staff, intelligence officials, and military commanders to his new command center just outside Moscow. I think you have something comparable. That is not good, Linda! If my government decides to fire off missiles, that is where they will make the decision. I told him that we were getting close to Viktoriya."

The heavy rainfall that had begun minutes earlier had forced Kipling to slow down. Erickson had slowed as well, finally leaving the Interstate and heading southwest on US-522. As Kipling drove, Smirnov had been reporting her movements from Kipling's laptop.

Kipling wanted instant gratification. "Talk to me," she demanded.

"Okay. She is on the move again." He had already reported that she had pulled off the road and stopped, just outside Berkeley Springs on 522. "She's now moving perpendicular to 522, more or less westward, really slowly."

"How far are we away from her right now, would you say?"

"Not far. I'd guess less than ten kilo—." Smirnov interrupted himself. "She's stopped again."

"Six miles," Kipling added. "We'll be there soon. First, I need you to memorize the exact latitude and longitude of where she is right now. Okay? Then, search the Internet. See if you can see what's there. A hotel, maybe? Makes sense. She checked in and then drove to her room. Maybe we're finally catching a break."

Kipling waited anxiously as she watched Smirnov use mapping services to locate commercial establishments on the outskirts of Berkeley Springs. "Well?"

"There's nothing there!" he replied.

"What do you mean there's nothing there!?" The stress of the situation was having its effect. She backed off. "I'm sorry, Dmitri. I didn't mean to snap at you."

"We're both under a lot of pressure, Linda."

"Okay, here's Plan B," Kipling said. "Have you ever used Google Earth?"

"Is that a trick question? I've probably used it more than you have."

"Why am I not surprised?" Kipling sniggered. "Well, then. Type in her GPS location and see the hell where she is." The rain was getting heavier, and Kipling had to concentrate on the road. Still, she was fixated on the typewriter keys clicking to her right.

"It's a house in the middle of a forest, about a kilometer and a half from the main road," Smirnov finally came back. "Looks like some kind of unfinished road in between."

Kipling pondered the implications of what Smirnov was saying.

Smirnov brought the screen close to his face. "I now know why she stopped by the roadside before going in. Looks to me like there's a fence and…a gate."

Kipling briefly locked eyes with Smirnov. No words were necessary. They both understood the implication: still another piece of damning evidence pointing to a woman with secrets to hide.

*On the other hand*, thought Kipling, *if Erickson's at the center of the unfolding international crisis, where better could Dmitri and I be than here? You almost killed us once, Viktoriya. On top of that, you tricked me twice on our trip across the country. Dmitri and I are coming for you.*

# ~ 40 ~

## ALEXEI'S GHOST

*Route 522, Berkeley Springs, West Virginia*
*39° 35' 33.4"N Latitude, 78° 14' 45.5"W Longitude*
*Sunday, April 1, 2018, 2:32 AM (EDT)*

Kipling and Smirnov arrived at the spot where Erickson had turned off Route 522, freshly beaten down vegetation the evidence. Smirnov took stock of his physical condition and convinced himself that, despite his recent travails, he was in reasonable shape and ready for the upcoming challenge. Crucially, his mind felt clear. He couldn't quite wrap his head around the fact that all that had transpired between him, Silverstein, and Kipling had begun only two days earlier!

Smirnov stole yet another glance at his peacetime rival, now fully vested as fifty percent of a two-person team brought together possibly to save the world. While Washington and Moscow were shouting at each other and contemplating each other's nuclear annihilation, here the two of them sat, jointly fixated on a common objective. The idea that one of his own was behind what was happening made Smirnov nauseous. Was Erickson a traitor to Russia or, worse, to all inhabitants of Planet Earth?

Kipling pulled up to the gate and turned off the engine. The rain had abated. Smirnov knew what to do next. "You don't happen to have a pair of wire cutters on you, do you?"

————◆◆◆————

Kipling had better ideas. "Do you remember when we got off the plane, and Henderson handed me what he called a Goody Bag?"

"Are you still checking to see if my brain is functioning? Of *course,* I remember! That's where you keep the wire cutters. No?"

"Let's not jump the gun, Dmitri. Before we worry about the gate, I think we need more timely intelligence. That photo you saw on Google Earth could be years old. If we are going to rush this house, I'd like to know the lay of the land."

Smirnov shook his head. "Have you looked up recently? I don't think that even your fancy spy satellites can see through these clouds."

The two exited the car. She opened the trunk, removed the backpack Henderson had provided, walked around the front of the car, and set it on the hood. The backlight from the headlights of the car provided illumination. She opened the pack and removed the PD13.

Smirnov strained to see what he was seeing. "Is that a drone?"

"You're sharper than most," Kipling teased. "Standard issue. We call it the PD13. I decided early on that if I ever had my own copy, I'd call her *Betsy.* That was my Mom's name."

"I like it, Linda. *Betsy.* She flies at night? No?"

"You bet. Night certified. Infrared and all that other technological wizardry."

Smirnov whistled audibly. "I am impressed. How do you control it?"

"From the same laptop you've been using to follow Erickson. Could you get it, please?"

Kipling proceeded to unfold the $150,000 technological marvel. What she had told Henderson back in California had been correct-- she *had* been properly trained. Of her class of twelve at CIA school,

255

Kipling had been the best pilot—and the only woman! She had read once that even though women comprise 10% of Army helicopter pilots, they were responsible for only 3% of accidents.

By the time Smirnov returned, Kipling had the drone positioned on a bare spot on the ground, ready to fly. "Only one more thing we need to do," she said.

Although the laptop looked normal in all respects, a careful inspection revealed that the keyboard's middle section, including the touchpad, was physically separate from the right and left portions. Kipling grabbed the laptop in her left hand, unsnapped the center section, and pivoted it backward for removal. She then took the replacement from her backpack and clicked it into place.

"What the hell?" Smirnov exclaimed.

What Kipling had done was to instantly reconfigure her laptop with controls typical for an off-the-shelf civilian drone—with a few extra bells, whistles, and digital displays. The computer screen came alive and displayed a picture of what the drone saw from its position on the ground: Smirnov's shoe.

"Pretty neat, huh?" Kipling gloated. "Okay. Now, if you'll please give me the coordinates I asked you to memorize."

Kipling typed in Erickson's latitude and longitude and gave Smirnov a thumbs-up signal. "I think we're good to go. From now on, I'll be controlling Betsy from our computer here."

Kipling turned around and used her backpack to support the laptop on the car's hood, a reasonable substitute for a stand-up desk. She gently added power, and the drone lifted off to an eye-level position to their rear. She proceeded to test all controls, and once satisfied that the device was operating correctly, added more power to lift it into the sky. It wasn't long before it disappeared into the blackness.

"How high do you think these trees are, would you say?" Kipling asked.

Smirnov glanced about. "I think you'd be safe at forty meters."

"Kipling watched as the digital height increased on her screen. "Okay, we're there, Dmitri. Now watch this!"

She rotated the forward infrared camera downward. Before long, after the autofocus had kicked in, the laptop screen showed two individuals standing in front of a car. To show off, Kipling raised her right hand, dangled the car keys, and zoomed in. Visible on the hi-definition screen was the rectangular Lincoln logo on the back of the key fob.

"Pretty slick, huh. I'm sure your military-grade drones have similar capabilities," Kipling said seriously. In fact, she was telling the truth. The Russians had *accidentally* lost one of theirs, and the CIA had rescued it. Compared to the PD13, it was no better and no worse; each had its positives. One of the standout features of the PD13 was its five onboard cameras: two in the front, one in the back, one left, one right. Except for the two forward cameras, one dedicated to visible and one to infrared, the other three were switchable.

Kipling noticed Smirnov shaking his head in amazement. "How fast can Betsy go?" he asked.

"She tops out at somewhere over sixty miles per hour." Kipling had altered the truth because that information was classified. The PD13 had been clocked at more than one hundred and ten. In field tests, the Russian drone could go even faster. "In case you don't know, max speeds are less important than you might think. In terms of the things you can do with a small drone, twenty miles per hour is the more practical upper limit."

Smirnov did the math. "Erickson's about a mile in. Twenty miles per hour means about a third of a mile in a minute. So, three minutes to get there." He looked for confirmation.

"Sounds right." With that decided, Kipling engaged the autopilot and pushed the throttle to 60% power.

Smirnov expressed concern. "Maybe I should have said fifty meters just to be safe."

Kipling knew that wasn't a problem. "I think we'll be okay. I'll keep an eye out." Again, Kipling chose not to reveal to Smirnov the real reason why the drone would not likely fly into anything. Betsy had onboard radar that swept back and forth as she flew, with the capability of stopping on a dime and changing routes.

Kipling adjusted the forward infrared camera to wide-angle, and they watched as trees flew by underneath. Before long, the trees disappeared, and a house came into view. Kipling throttled back and took over manual control.

"There it is," she said. "First, I'll position us directly over the house so that we can evaluate the clearing. It's certainly a lot bigger than I expected. You could add a couple tennis courts or have a really big garden."

"There's her car in the back," Smirnov added. "No garage. This shows pretty much what I saw on Google Earth. No surprises that I can see. Any chance you can switch to visible so we can see if she has lights on in the house?"

Kipling backed the drone to the edge of the clearing and added the visible camera's display to complement the infrared. "Whoa! Looks to me like she's turned on every light in the house," Kipling remarked.

Smirnov mirrored Kipling's surprise. "Either she doesn't care about the electric bill, or she's paranoid as hell."

"I'd guess the latter," Kipling chuckled. "She's probably still wondering if someone was chasing her back in San Francisco. Interesting. It looks to me like she doesn't have any curtains on the windows, either. And no outside lights!"

Smirnov came up with the idea first. "What would you say to going down and looking inside one of her windows. You saw her back in San Francisco. You could confirm that we have the right person. No? And I could see her for the first time."

"Excellent idea, Dmitri. It's dark outside. She'll never see us."

"How about that picture window to the left?"

Kipling, already on manual control, swooped down in the direction Smirnov had suggested. When Betsy came within twenty feet of the window, Kipling transitioned to hover mode and took control of the visible camera, zooming in to see what looked like a living room. Sure enough, sitting on a sofa was Erickson, wearing the same outfit Kipling remembered. "That's her, Dmitri. She's working on her laptop. First, I'll zoom in to give us a better look. And then..."

Kipling manipulated the controls. "...I'll move just a smidge to the right to give us a better view."

"Whoopsy-Daisy!!" Kipling knew they were in trouble when an exterior spotlight to the right of the window suddenly oversaturated the visible image.

"Woopsy what?"

Kipling's training took over. Her right index finger darted to the EEM button on the keyboard. EEM stood for Emergency Escape Mode, basic shorthand for *Let's Get the Hell Out of Dodge*! With this command, all cameras on the drone instantly rotated inward so that no reflective surface remained visible. Simultaneously, all four fan motors revved to 110% power. Within seconds, the drone was at one hundred feet and climbing rapidly. Kipling halted Betsy's climb at two hundred and moved her sideways to the edge of the clearing, descending slowly to a position inside the forest canopy.

"She won't see us here," Kipling stated calmly.

"When Betsy moved sideways, she triggered an infrared sensor that activated the light," Smirnov said.

"I'm sure that's what happened," Kipling agreed. "But did you happen to notice Erickson's reaction the instant the light came on?"

"She jumped up and almost dropped her laptop."

"That's right. What else?"

Smirnov shoved his hands in his pockets. "I see where you're going with this. There was no delay. From her angle sitting on the sofa, she would not have seen the outdoor light."

"Precisely! Which means that there was an alarm inside the house that she reacted to." Kipling turned to make the point eye to eye.

At once, Smirnov pointed to the screen. "There she comes, around the left side of the house, hunched down, carrying something." Erickson had come into view on the infrared image.

"Let me zoom in."

Erickson was sporting some sort of rifle. After walking back and forth for some minutes, Erickson's posture seemed more relaxed, and she returned to the house. Before long, all exterior lights shut off, including additional ones she had triggered.

"Well, that was certainly interesting," Smirnov responded matter-of-factly. "We now know pretty much what we're up against. I say we get out your wire cutters and head on in."

Kipling couldn't help feeling mischievous. "Dmitri, are you familiar with the phrase, *jerking someone's chain?*"

"Yes. We have a comparable Russian saying. It means to tease or harass someone. No?"

"Before we bring Betsy home, I have a request. Because she's one of yours, I respectfully ask your permission to jerk Erickson's chain." Kipling smiled widely.

Smirnov seemed to understand what Kipling was getting at. He began to laugh, which he had trouble stifling. Soon they were in it together and accidentally bumped into each other as they nearly fell to the ground trying to suppress their cackling.

Smirnov regained his composure and tried to respond seriously but had difficulty saying it straight-faced. "To make sure that I understand, do you think that Erickson may have even more of those sensor lights we saw?"

"I am," Kipling responded through a snort.

"Well then, on behalf of Oleg Popov, President Putin, and the entire Russian Federation, I give you official permission to jerk Erickson's chain," Smirnov said in an exaggerated official tone.

Kipling returned to her controls and prepared to use the skills she had learned in school. The first step was to press the CM key. CM stood for *Combat Mode*, which activated all onboard sensors and collision avoidance systems. She then slowly lifted Betsy out of the forest foliage, ready for action.

"Okay, Dmitri, here we go!"

In a dive from two hundred feet, mostly to show off, Kipling briefly spiked the throttle to full power, which fleetingly brought Betsy's airspeed to forty-four miles per hour. As Betsy slowed and leveled out at six feet above the ground, Kipling aimed for the right side of Erickson's house to begin her flight around the structure. With nerves of steel, she flew as close as possible to the sides of the building, pleased to see the sensors activating. For good measure, she made a second circular pass, triggering one she had missed the first time. Upon completion, she pressed EEM to avoid any detection by Erickson.

As they looked back from their two-hundred-foot perch, they observed the entire exterior of Erickson's house flooded by spotlights.

"Linda, she won't be getting away from us this time. From the Google Earth image, it looked to me like the fence extends all around her property; there are no roads other than the one we found. And we have that one blocked. We've got her trapped."

Kipling nodded, her emotion held in check. To complete the mission, she pressed the CH button, which stood for *Come Home*. Her duties as a pilot were complete. Betsy would retrace her outgoing route and find herself on the same spot on the ground where she had been minutes earlier.

Smirnov's looked thoughtfully at Kipling, his face revealing appreciation and respect. "Well done, Linda! WELL DONE!"

"Thank you, Dmitri." Without warning, Kipling came to grips with a heat that had enveloped her body, a sensation that she had not experienced in some time. Without considering the ramifications, Kipling chose to do something she knew was inappropriate. With the state of the world the way it was and tomorrow no more than a mirage, she didn't care.

Kipling faced Smirnov, took his head firmly in her hands, and pulled him down toward her. "Listen to me, Dmitri. What I am going to say now is important. If I die tonight, I want you to know what my last thoughts were before my heart stopped beating. They were of the two of us having a *damn* good laugh together...and this kiss!"

Kipling's lips enveloped those of her fellow spy. Whatever was to happen in the next few hours, she'd have no regrets.

———◆◆———

*Berkeley Springs, West Virginia*
*39° 35' 58"N Latitude, 78° 15' 50"W Longitude*

Her rifle still at the ready, Kathy Ann Erickson had bolted out the back door even faster the second time around. The individual sensor alarms that had gone off in sequence had driven her to panic. "What the hell is going on?" she muttered to herself. Having monitored those same sensors from California for years, such an occurrence as this had never happened before.

She walked the perimeter of the house twice but saw nothing suspicious. The only possibility she could think of was that a wild animal, possibly an owl, had inadvertently activated one spotlight, becoming so frightened that it flew in circles around the house, triggering the others. Erickson had ordered herself to calm down when she realized something relevant. None of the sensors that bordered the outside perimeter of her property had activated. That fact was proof that no one had come in from the highway.

Bothered by this inexplicable occurrence, Erickson's mind stumbled upon another possibility. Less than twelve hours earlier, on an airplane in San Francisco, a similar warning had come from out of nowhere. That one manifested itself as a scent, a distinctive odor from that fateful day back in Afghanistan. Erickson had interpreted it as an admonition from Alexei, and that was the reason she had bolted from the airplane.

Erickson chose to believe that Alexei was once again warning her from the grave. *There's danger in the air, he's telling me!*

# — 41 —

## PAVE HAWK UP

*Route 522, Berkeley Springs, West Virginia*
*39° 35' 33.4"N Latitude, 78° 14' 45.5"W Longitude*
*Sunday, April 1, 2018, 2:52 AM (EDT)*

The proverbial feather could have knocked him over. Weak-kneed, Smirnov nearly stumbled to the ground after Kipling released her grip. It had been a while since he had kissed a woman. Before he had time to respond—and as if what had just transpired had occurred weeks earlier—she returned straightaway to the task at hand.

"I'm sorry, Dmitri. Even if I had wire cutters for the fence, I have no desire to hike through a mile's worth of wet grass and mud. I'd rather drive. You still have your wallet, don't you? Could you please give your lock-picking skills a try?"

Smirnov regained his composure enough to realize that Kipling's suggestion made no sense. "Sorry, Linda. I would have done that already if it were possible. You probably didn't notice that all three locks are combination locks."

Kipling winced, obviously embarrassed that she had not noticed that critical detail. *Maybe I'm not the only one who hasn't been kissed in a while*, thought Smirnov.

"Sorry. In that case, I have something even better than wire-cutters."

Kipling returned to her backpack and removed a bar of material wrapped in plastic film. "Have you ever used C-4?"

"Can't say I have."

Kipling smiled as if she had finally gotten one over on her partner. Mocking his earlier comment back in San Jose regarding her lock-picking skills, she retaliated. "What kind of spy are you if you don't know how to use explosives?"

Smirnov hated to burst her bubble. "Explosives? Why didn't you say so? Of course I know explosives, but only those with Russian names. Can I assume that your C-4 is like the British PE-4? If so, I know that it is a plastic explosive, very malleable. We can wrap some around each lock. Do you have three detonators?"

"No, but I do have one that can service three leads. Wait! You'll need this too." From her backpack, she produced a small LED flashlight. "While you do this, I'll back the car out to the side of the road. By the way, the detonator has a timer; you'll figure it out. I'd give yourself at least twenty seconds to run back to me. Okay?"

About to enter her vehicle, Kipling yelled out. "Dmitri! If you hear me talking out on the road, it's me calling Lopez to give him Erickson's coordinates."

As he ran back to the gate, Smirnov raised his right hand in acknowledgment. Holding the flashlight in his mouth, he wrapped each lock with the malleable explosive. He knew what he was doing and soon inserted the three leads into the detonator. After setting the timer, he pushed the red start button.

Smirnov sprinted to the road and angled left, all the while counting down in his head the seconds. When Kipling saw him running at full speed toward her, she ducked behind the rear driver's side of the car and motioned for him to join her. She had the satellite phone to her ear.

*Joint Base Andrews*
*Prince George County, Maryland*
*38° 48' 40"N Latitude, 76° 52' 40"W Longitude*
*Sunday, April 1, 2018, 2:57 AM (EDT)*

On the tarmac at Andrews, Lopez and Silverstein had been waiting for an update from Kipling. From Lopez's prior conversation with Kipling, he knew that Erickson was headed in their direction and within chopper range.

Lopez was glad to get the call. Kipling provided Erickson's position coordinates, apparently a private residence.

"Berkeley Springs? I spent a weekend there once with my wife." Over the phone, Lopez heard what sounded like an explosion. "What was *that*?" he asked.

"Not to worry. Dmitri just blew the gate. Turns out that Erickson's house is a mile back from the highway. It's all woods, and catch this: a chain-link fence with barbed wire at the top surrounds the entire compound."

"Sounds like you made use of the PD13."

"First time I've used it for real. Good bird's-eye view. Got a good perspective of what to expect when we go in. Quite a bit of cleared area around the house."

"Room to land a helo?"

"As a matter of fact, yes. Are you telling me you're coming *here*?"

"It's not my idea, Linda."

"Then who?"

Lopez knew this would be awkward. "It's Victor's."

"What do you mean? Victor just had surgery and is in the hospital."

"About that…" Lopez hesitated. "Victor insisted I break him out. He's climbing onto a sixty as I speak."

"You've got to be fucking kidding me? He told me he'd been shot twice."

"He was. Trust me; he'll be okay. From what you've told him, he agrees with you and Dmitri that Erickson is playing an active role in what's going on. He says he has a *bad feeling* about her. And I've got to tell you, the way rhetoric is heating up between both sides, I'll grab at any straw that might be attached to anything."

"Understood. Dmitri and I are going in now. Can you hold off landing until I give you the all-clear?"

"Roger. We'll be out of here soon. You're not that far away."

———◆◆◆———

With help from the loadmaster, Silverstein climbed aboard the Air Force MH-60G Pave Hawk helicopter. A derivative of the Army's UH-60 Black Hawk, the G designation indicated a machine designed to insert and recover Special Operations personnel. Together with the Air Force pilot, Major Rick Hammer; co-pilot, Captain Henry Smith; and loadmaster, Tech Sergeant Albert Jimenez, Lopez and Silverstein filled out the passenger list of two. Silverstein's photographic memory reminded him that the Pave Hawk's cruise speed was 150 knots, which meant 172.5 miles per hour.

"How many miles to Berkeley Springs, Major Hammer?" Silverstein inquired of the pilot.

"Ninety-two miles as the crow flies, sir. We'll have you there in—

Silverstein cut him off. "Thirty-two minutes."

The pilot responded, grinning ear to ear. "Very good, sir. If you want, we'll get you there two minutes early if you authorize me to haul ass."

Silverstein glanced at Lopez, who nodded his approval. "Captain, you have authorization."

———◆◆◆———

*Berkeley Springs, West Virginia*
*39° 35' 58"N Latitude, 78° 15' 50"W Longitude*
*Sunday, April 1, 2018, 2:58 AM (EDT)*

It was two minutes before the hour when Erickson heard what sounded like an explosion. She only briefly considered the unlikely possibility that war had started early. She rushed for her remote and turned the TV to CNN. The main event would begin soon. While she waited, she flipped through her mail.

# ~ 42 ~

## BUT YOU'RE TOO LATE!

*Route 522, Berkeley Springs, West Virginia*
*39° 35' 33.4"N Latitude, 78° 14' 45.5"W Longitude*
*Sunday, April 1, 2018, 2:58 AM (EDT)*

Following the blast, Kipling informed Smirnov that Silverstein and Lopez were on their way. Smirnov jogged back to the gate, pleased to see that the C-4 had blown off all three locks. The gate now swung freely on its hinges. As he pushed the gate inward, Kipling's Lincoln rounded the corner from the road, and he hopped in. The dirt road, although moist and overgrown with vegetation, was drivable. Kipling proceeded slowly, following the tracks from Erickson's earlier path.

"Well I'll be damned," Kipling exclaimed.

"What?"

"You don't see it?" Kipling rolled the car to a stop and doused the headlights.

As Smirnov's eyes adapted to the dark, he saw what she was talking about. The clouds had parted, allowing moonshine to bathe the forest in soft, fragile light. It looked to be a full moon. "This will make it easier for us to sneak up on the house. We just need to avoid the light sensors this time. No?"

"We'll be through the forest soon," Kipling said.

"Don't you think we should walk in the last hundred feet or so?"

"I agree."

Smirnov remembered an item of some significance. "Please tell me that you didn't forget our Glocks back at the airport."

Kipling motioned to the back seat. "They're in my backpack."

Smirnov retrieved the guns and checked the clips.

———————◆————————

Kipling considered their options. "Dmitri, I'm not sure what good our Glocks are going to do us. We *must* take her alive. She dies, and we have nothing."

"I agree."

"Follow my thinking here. Erickson knows what I look like. On the other hand, she's never met you and has no idea who you are."

"I've thought about that, too."

"Then you should be the one to approach her. You can speak to her in Russian, make her feel comfortable."

"But what do I say, Linda? *So sorry about blowing up your gate. I'm an old friend of your uncle's and happened to be in your neighborhood. Thought maybe we'd have coffee.*"

Kipling chuckled. "If you put it like that, you're deader than a doornail. That's another Americanism you can add to your list."

Smirnov turned somber. "If that is what it takes, Linda, I don't mind dying. You need to do whatever is necessary to determine if she is behind the hacking. If you do that, you can instantly diffuse the international situation. You did say that Victor is on his way, no? Lopez too?"

The Lincoln came to a stop, lights doused. They discussed their strategy and what Smirnov might say. "And in case she decides to shoot you anyway, you need protection," Kipling said.

"A bulletproof vest would be nice," said Smirnov, laughing nervously. "Too bad neither of us thought to bring one."

Kipling responded. "Speak for yourself."

"What?"

"Please hand me the backpack."

Smirnov offered his advice. "There's nothing in it. I couldn't help myself but to feel around."

"Take off your shirt," Kipling ordered.

Smirnov reacted nervously. "Why?"

"I think that by now, you can trust me. Don't you think?"

Smirnov started to undo his buttons. Kipling noticed that he was not wearing an undershirt, and she had some difficulty averting her eyes. *Now is not the time, Linda!* She refocused her efforts and began to reconfigure the backpack, another clever invention from the Mensa group.

The CIA had created "Mensa" back in the early 1990s, to develop novel technology for the CIA, primarily for use in the field. Their success in 2007 with the tracking transmitter embedded in the scalp of the terrorist Ghali had the Mensa crowd crowing. However, it wasn't just because all Mensas had genius mentalities (which they did) or because they were all scientists of one form or another (which they were). It was also because one of their resumes included the words, *professional magician.* He had been the one to invent this trick backpack.

Kipling proceeded to undo buckles, unzip hidden zippers, and invert the inside to create the new outside. Within thirty seconds, the backpack had converted into what looked like an oversized, mid-length-sleeved, pullover shirt.

"Ты меня разыгрываешь!" Smirnov exclaimed in Russian.

"Here! Put this on. Your shirt should fit over the top," she said.

With Smirnov now clad in his protective garb, both spies exited the vehicle. Kipling grabbed Betsy from the back seat and proceeded to the trunk where she set up shop. "I'll be keeping an eye on you. If necessary, I'll intercede."

"Intercede?" Smirnov asked.

"Betsy's mainly an observational tool, but she has one little offensive trick up her sleeve. Have you ever heard of Propofol?"

"Doctors use it for minor surgeries. No? Didn't your Michael Jackson die from using it for insomnia?"

"You are well-read, Dmitri. Our Betsy here can shoot a dart loaded with the chemical. Normally, doctors inject it into a vein, but our Mensa chemists developed a version that will work anywhere on the body." Kipling brought up the targeting screen and explained how it worked.

"How long would she be out?"

"Not long. That's the downside. Five to ten minutes, give or take." Kipling hesitated, trying to decide if she should tell him. "There is one problem, though. The dart will not penetrate clothing. What that means is that I have to aim for either the face or neck. And for me to have a decent chance of success, both the target and Betsy need to be stationary. It's next to impossible if either is moving. So what I plan to do is come in behind her while you two are talking. Make sense?"

They reviewed their strategy one more time before Smirnov started walking toward the edge of the clearing. Before long, Betsy flew past him and out into the open, taking a position midway between the house and the clearing's edge at an altitude of two hundred feet.

———————◆◆◆———————

*Sunday, April 1, 2018, 3:12 AM (EDT)*

Erickson had been watching CNN, counting down the minutes when, *yet again*, came an alert from one of her infrared sensors. This time it wasn't one of the spotlight sensors surrounding the house. This one came from the edge of the forest, to the left of the incoming road. Moonlight provided enough light to see where the road disappeared into the forest. She saw no movement. *Probably an animal*, she thought. But then she did a double take. Walking out of the woods was a man, hands held high, approaching the house.

For the third time tonight, Erickson grabbed her rifle and headed out the rear door, leaving it open in case she needed to beat a quick retreat. She ran around the house and came to a stop. "Stop where you are, or I'll shoot."

The man cooperated, body posture and hands implying that he was no threat. *Probably a trick!* she thought.

"What are you doing here? You're trespassing on private property, you know," Erickson yelled out.

To her utter bewilderment, the stranger replied in Russian. "My name is Dmitri Smirnov, and I work for your uncle, Oleg Popov. When he found out that you live in America, he asked me to find you and tell you that all is forgiven. No matter what you have done, Viktoriya, he still loves you. He wants you back."

*I'm sure he does, the son-of-a-bitch, but that ship has long since sailed. And right now, I've got more important fish to fry.* With that thought pushing aside everything in her mind, Erickson raised her rifle, aimed, and fired. Smirnov fell to the ground.

———◆◆◆———

*Sunday, April 1, 2018, 3:16 AM (EDT)*

Monitoring the action from aloft, Kipling felt as if she'd been sucker-punched. Popov's niece was evil embodied. Reeling from what had just occurred, Kipling weighed her alternatives—now that everything had turned to shit. Trying to confront Erickson head-on would not be easy. In school, Kipling had achieved only a modest twenty-five percent success rate with a moving target.

At once, Kipling became aware of a second possibility. Because Betsy had been on station when Erickson exited the house, Kipling knew that she had again come from the rear—and had left the door open! Kipling put Betsy into a sharp dive to get there before Erickson.

———◆◆◆———

*Sunday, April 1, 2018, 3:21 AM (EDT)*

Erickson felt a twinge of regret for having killed a man. That remorse didn't last long. What was one life compared to the millions about to lose theirs? She retook her spot on the sofa.

———————◆◆◆———————

*Sunday, April 1, 2018, 3:22 AM (EDT)*

Kipling tucked her laptop under her arm and took off sprinting. The quickness with which Erickson had shown up following Smirnov's earlier entry implied that he had set off another tripwire. No matter! If Erickson returned, Kipling decided that this time, she would fight back with her Glock and aim for Erickson's legs where a bullet wound would likely not prove fatal.

Kipling headed straight to the spot where she had last seen Smirnov. But he was gone! At once, she heard a strange clicking noise to her left. As she cautiously moved in that direction, a pair of waving arms became visible.

"Get down, Linda. Get down," he whispered loudly.

Kipling dropped to all fours and crawled. The vegetation there was deep enough to hide in. "Thank God, you're alive. Where were you hit?" she asked, as she tried to assess his condition in the moonlight.

As she reached for her cell phone flashlight, Smirnov grabbed her hand. "We can't give ourselves away. Erickson's too good a shot; she hit me right in the middle of the chest. It knocked the wind out of me, but I'll be okay."

Kipling bowed her head in thanks and struggled to fight back tears. If ever in her life she had had a more stressful twenty-four hours, she had forgotten when. Smirnov took her hands in his, his face coming close to hers. "Linda, we're both alive, and we're not finished. It's too bad that Betsy wasn't able to bring her down." At that instant, he noticed that Kipling was still carrying the laptop. "Where *is* Betsy?"

Kipling opened her computer. "You want to know where Betsy is? See for yourself."

As Smirnov's face drew close to the screen, she could make out a smile. "Where *exactly* is she?" he asked.

"On an open shelf near the ceiling. Watching television with Erickson."

———◆———

*Sunday, April 1, 2018, 3:29 AM (EDT)*

Erickson was ecstatic. In seconds, her algorithm would take control of the computer at the Main Centre for Missile Attack Warning on Moscow's outskirts, setting in motion the sequence of events she had so carefully orchestrated. Simultaneously, her code would disable the Moscow-Washington hotline.

Leaning forward on the edge of her seat, listening to the TV, hanging onto every word, Erickson noticed a humming sound. Assuming interference from the TV, she reached for the remote to increase the volume. As she did so, she caught a sense of motion to her left. Suddenly frightened by what appeared to be a giant flying insect staring into her face, she leaped to her feet.

Waiting for her mind to process the absurdity of what she was seeing, Erickson froze in place.

———◆———

*Sunday, April 1, 2018, 3:30 AM (EDT)*

Having moved Betsy hastily into position, Kipling lined up the crosshairs. Firing from point-blank range, both spies watched as Erickson's right hand instinctively shot to her neck. Before long, she slumped to the floor.

Kipling tossed the ball into Smirnov's court. "Assuming that she's locked the door, you get another chance to make use of your legendary lock-picking skills."

Acting like a man possessed, Smirnov took to his feet and ran, Kipling not far behind with computer in hand. As the motion sensor lights kicked on, it was easy to locate the rear entry. Checking to make sure that the door wasn't already unlocked, he then used his knuckle to test the door. "It's a wood door, and hollow at that. Stand back!"

Concerned over his choice of technique, Kipling watched as Smirnov ran full speed toward the door. At the moment before impact, he turned his body sideways and lowered his shoulder. Had the seven-second sequence been preserved on high-speed film, Kipling would have been surprised to see the door offer any resistance. Instead, it exploded into pieces.

With that problem solved, Smirnov and Kipling raced into the living room. Erickson lay quietly on the floor, while Betsy had returned to her last position near the ceiling. Kipling's cell phone broke the evening's silence, with Silverstein's familiar baritone music to her ears. "We're about two minutes out. Do we have permission to land?"

"Roger that," Kipling replied. "Subject has been neutralized. Repeat! Subject has been neutralized."

Smirnov's adrenaline seemed to be running a tad high. He grabbed a chair from the kitchen, and as if her weight was no more than that of a rag doll, hoisted Erickson up and slammed her down. "Linda, can you look around and see if there's anything we can use to tie her hands and feet?"

Kipling didn't have far to look. Erickson was wearing tennis shoes with long laces. Kipling removed the shoes and jerked them out, handing one to Smirnov and using the other to tie Erickson's feet. Smirnov did the same with Erickson's hands around the back of the chair.

With that accomplished, they had time to assess their surroundings: an unexceptional, nondescript bungalow. But a mystery presented itself. Having just arrived from her cross-country flight, why was this woman watching CNN in the middle of the night?

As Erickson began to come around, Kipling suggested that they continue their charade. She'd remain out of sight to the rear, allowing Smirnov the opportunity to question Erickson as originally planned.

Facing both the television and Smirnov on the sofa, Erickson's first words—as the drug's effects wore off—were, perhaps, expected. "I thought I killed you," she said in English.

Smirnov responded. "You almost did. And this was the second time."

Erickson continued, her voice strong and resolute. "I know why you're here, you know. But you're too late!"

# — 43 —

## THREE TWO ONE

*Main Centre for Missile Attack Warning,*
*Timonovo, Russian Federation*
*56° 14' 28"N Latitude, 37° 00' 48"E Longitude*
*Sunday, April 1, 2018, 10:30 AM (MSK)*

Army Major Yuri Orlov recognized that his position at the Main Centre for Missile Attack Warning was both prestigious and vital. After all, his assignment within the Russian military was one step removed from the pointy end of the nuclear spear that protected Mother Russia from foreign adversaries. All high school students came to understand that much of Russia's history, dating back to the Mongol invasion of 1237, had been turbulent and dangerous. The average Russian who had spent even a modicum of time studying Russia's past could be forgiven for being paranoid.

Russia's long and complicated history had made its citizens perpetually distrustful of nearly everyone—both from within and beyond Russia's geographic boundaries. Whether it was an inside job, like Stalin's 1934 purge of some twenty million Russians, or World War II, when Hitler's invasion cost the country another twenty-seven million military and civilian citizens, each episode led to pain, hardship, *and* fear. And both events had occurred within the past one hundred years. To further dampen the spirits of patriotic Russians, the Soviet Union collapsed in 1991. In 2005, President Putin characterized that event as the major geopolitical disaster of the 20th Century. For all those reasons, every Russian considered a strong defense crucial to the country's survival.

In the modern age, defense of the homeland involved more than positioning troops at critical border entry points. These days, the most frightening and devastating peril would rain down from the heavens. The mechanism for such potential devastation was the ICBM, the Inter-Continental Ballistic Missile, carrying a nuclear warhead. Of course, there were other delivery systems for nuclear weapons, namely aircraft and submarines. Still, it was the ICBM with its hefty payload that would be called upon first. Augmented by a technology called MIRV, standing for Multiple Independently Targetable Reentry Vehicle, each ICBM could strike multiple targets simultaneously.

Warnings for such a launch originally came from radar that could peer beyond a nation's borders. However, that World War II invention had serious geographic limitations. Also using radar initially, the Americans had what they called NORAD, the North American Air Defense Command. That name changed in 1981 to the North American Aerospace Defense Command. Technology had advanced to the point that satellite detection of missile launches was technologically feasible.

Russia had similar technology. Compared to radar, satellites had no geographic limitations. They could fly anywhere over the globe, constantly searching for the signature of a missile launch. Sophisticated software then deduced the missile's likely path and probable target.

Normally, Orlov had the weekends off. To accommodate a colleague who had a wedding to attend, he had traded shifts. Upon entering the secure facility, his first task was to receive an update from the previous watch commander—followed by a quick visit to the galley for a cup of strong coffee. Notwithstanding the incredible importance of his job, there was no denying that it was boring. Coffee was his go-to pick-me-up to survive the twelve-hour shift.

That said, Orlov also knew that the previous twenty-four hours had been extraordinary. The hacking of Russia's air traffic control system and hydroelectric power facilities—all supposedly concocted by Russia's nemesis, the United States of America—had suddenly brought decades-old Cold War tensions back to the fore. State television had been following every move, and citizenry were jittery.

Orlov didn't know what to believe. Conversations between himself and his fellow officers came in hushed tones. It was hardly a secret that Putin felt disdain over the free flow of information and ideas endemic to the Western world. Putin did his best to shield the public from outside propaganda that might criticize or question his enlightened viewpoint. Still, bootlegged reports from American media claimed that the U.S. had nothing to do with what was happening in Russia. Worse, and even more confusing, U.S. officials said it was Russia who had instigated the whole affair, that America's air traffic control and hydroelectric plants had been targeted first.

Bolstered by coffee fortified with three teaspoons of sugar, Orlov took his station, facing six huge monitors covering the entire Northern Hemisphere. Geostationary and orbiting satellites, supplemented by radar, continually fed information into one large computer system. The system architecture, revolving around that single computer, had been a source of concern for more than one of its developers, who vehemently argued that the design left them vulnerable to hacking. In the end, political and cost considerations mandated this design and the computer's location, some twenty meters down the hallway.

Using sophisticated software imbued with artificial intelligence, their computer's job was to assess any suspicious "brightening" observed within a satellite's field of vision. In plain language, brightening meant a very bright flash of light.

The only normal, natural source of brightening was lightning, and it occurred frequently, with estimates on the order of forty-five times a second around the globe. Brightening caused by lightning was easy to dismiss because the flash dissipated instantly. Further, once gone, it rarely repeated itself in the same location. Even an "anvil crawler," a form of lightning that lasted long enough for an observer to follow it with the naked eye, traveled horizontally, thus eliminating itself as a potential missile launch. On occasion, a meteor could trigger the software but was easily dismissed for the same reasons.

A ground-launched missile or rocket launch was different. Not only would brightening continue over seconds or even minutes, but its consistent movement also confirmed that it was a man-made object. Direction and trajectory were calculable. That information, combined with the geographic source, would determine whether a threat existed—and that determination came about within seconds following detection.

Because Russian intelligence knew the exact location of every land-based American ICBM launch facility, it didn't take a rocket scientist—as the in-house joke went—to deduce that trouble was on its way should brightening originate from the Great Plains of America. Because of previous treaties that had limited the number of launch facilities for both sides, Russian intelligence knew that there were four hundred so-called Minuteman III missiles, all pointed in Russia's direction.

Because lightning was so easy to dismiss, very little of significance ever appeared on the massive computer displays, contributing mightily to the perpetual boredom. The only opportunity for excitement came from other routine space launches, whether they be Russia's own Soyuz delivering supplies and personnel to the International Space Station, or various scientific and commercial launches conducted around the world. Russia knew that there were eleven countries capable of such launches. It was the job of their foreign intelligence to keep track of such capabilities.

With that degree of tedium inherent in his job description, Orlov occasionally found himself hoping for a bit of excitement to come his way. North Korea's recent test launches had provided that. Known for his unpredictable behavior, North Korea's leader, Kim Jong Un, had recently fired off several test missiles without telling anybody. Trajectory software quickly determined that there was no threat to

Russia. To be sure, the episode had been unnerving. A curt phone call to North Korea made clear that Russia was not pleased.

And so, it happened when least expected: Orlov was speaking to his second-in-command when he heard a noticeable gasp permeate the room. Rotating quickly toward his screens, Orlov did a double take, his face turning instantly ashen. Dozens of red dots appeared over the central U.S., almost as if there were a spreading grass fire. Over the next tens of seconds, the computer count of those dots, displayed in the upper right-hand corner of the screen, rose exponentially, finally leveling off at three hundred and eighty-five.

Typically, the circular dots would appear first as red in color, soon turning white, indicating that detection software had deemed the launches benign. As Orlov watched these markers head northward toward the Poles, he prayed for a retraction of his earlier foolhardy request. His plea came back unanswered. The dots were red and staying that way.

Prompted by the visual display, a loud klaxon made itself known, advising anyone who hadn't been paying attention that something was amiss. His body now visibly shaking, Orlov reached for the red phone that he alone was authorized to use. *Pull yourself together, man! Now is not the time to fall apart.*

# – 44 –

## NO APOLOGY NECESSARY

*National Defense Management Center*
*Moscow, Russian Federation*
*55° 43' 40"N Latitude, 37° 35' 23"E Longitude*
*Sunday, April 1, 2018, 10:32 AM (MSK)*

Oleg Popov reacted differently from the others when the Main Centre's results appeared on the huge monitor at the NDMC. The display showed that an armada of U.S. ICBMs had launched from Middle America and was on its way toward the Russian Federation.

Most Politburo members and other high-ranking government officials, including Vladimir Putin himself, stood frozen in disbelief, likely accompanied by a feeling of utter helplessness. Several of the delegates ran toward the bathrooms, not sure whether they would make it in time. Others took to their cell phones to call loved ones to offer their goodbyes. And still others remained seated, head in hand, begging their creator to forgive their earthly sins.

A few, like Popov, who had served in the military and understood his responsibilities, forced those emotions to the side and addressed the practicalities of what could be done. For certain, he realized that he would die soon. Before that happened, his training would dictate his actions. He would defend the motherland and save as many of his compatriots as possible.

His position within the military nuclear defense establishment—a decade before he attained his position within the SVR—where he had participated in more war games than he cared to remember, had prepared him for this situation. For that reason and one other, he jumped to his feet and ran toward the stage. Because Putin and other members of the defense staff knew his qualifications, they would welcome his participation. The second reason was his alone.

Popov understood that the other military leaders would also know that their first response would be to activate the A-135 anti-ballistic missile system, known cynically as *Last Chance Joe*, an unflattering reference to Joseph Stalin. The A-135 was a collection of defensive missiles armed with nuclear warheads designed to intercept incoming ICBMs. The optimists in the room would only half-heartedly cheer its success because they knew that its purpose was to protect only the city of Moscow. Worse, MIRV technology meant that the A-135 would take out only a fraction of incoming missiles.

Thirty! That was the number now emblazoned on everyone's cerebrum, the length of time in minutes that they could count on to remain among the living! There was a second significant number: twenty-five. That one represented how many minutes remained for Putin to launch a counterstrike—before incoming missiles eliminated any chance for retaliation. The Launch on Warning philosophy dictated that he do so. And once that action took effect, nearly a third of the world's population would be dead or dying within the hour.

---

*Berkeley Springs, West Virginia*
*39° 35' 58"N Latitude, 78° 15' 50"W Longitude*
*Sunday, April 1, 2018, 3:33 AM (EDT)*

As Kipling watched Erickson from behind, the thumping of helicopter blades broke the night's silence. Unfortunately, Smirnov was getting nowhere. He had switched to Russian in his interrogation. Kipling couldn't tell what he was saying, but it didn't matter because Erickson was not cooperating. Their goal was straightforward, to determine if she was responsible for the back and forth hacking scenario.

While Smirnov continued his desperate struggle to penetrate Erickson's veneer of silence, Kipling slipped out the back door to meet Lopez and Silverstein. They had already landed and were exiting the chopper, the area ablaze from the MH-60G's high-intensity lighting.

Kipling couldn't help herself. She ran to Silverstein and nearly hugged him before she pulled up short, realizing that he was struggling, pain contorting his face, and barely able to stay vertical even using crutches. "Thank God you're alive, Victor!"

"Thanks to Hector here," he replied, seemingly taken aback by Kipling's enthusiasm. "And a good surgeon."

"So why are *you* here, Victor. You should have stayed in the hospital."

"Because I *have* to be here, Linda! Let's just leave it at that!" he snapped.

To Kipling, Silverstein's response came across as cold and self-centered—qualities not unknown for her colleague to exhibit, but in light of the situation? She shot a glance toward Lopez who responded with a *Why is it you think I know more than you do?* look.

Introductions followed, Kipling shaking hands with the flight crew.

Consistent with his usual MO, Silverstein took charge and wanted to know what was going on.

Kipling complied. "Erickson's inside the house. Dmitri's questioning her and making no progress. But you need to know this: She did say one thing after we tied her up. 'I know why you're here, but you're too late.'"

Silverstein's dark skin often camouflaged emotions more easily seen on a Caucasian. Still, Kipling believed she could see a noticeable pall.

Silverstein turned to face Lopez. "Hector, please tell me that you didn't forget the LD500."

"I told you *earlier* that I had it. It's right here in my hands, Victor."

Silverstein stormed off toward the house, making slow progress on his crutches. Kipling and Lopez walked slowly by his side. The three-man helicopter crew, not knowing what else to do, brought up the rear. Silverstein made it about twenty feet when his right crutch gave way, and he tumbled to the ground. "Goddammit!" he screamed in agony.

Lopez and Kipling knelt by his side.

Silverstein grabbed Lopez by the collar. "You have the bag that Manchester gave us, right?"

"It's back in the chopper."

Tech Sergeant Jimenez, from the helicopter crew, overheard the conversation and took off running.

Sweat rolled off Silverstein's face. "Hector, all of the pain medications have worn off. I need you to give me a hit in my leg and my shoulder."

Kipling, alarmed at Silverstein's request, noticed blood oozing down his pant leg. "Hector, he's bleeding. Is that where he was shot?"

"I have bandages," he added quickly.

Silverstein simultaneously turned belligerent and sarcastic. "Hector, my long-time friend. You need to listen to me. FORGET THE FUCKING BANDAGES! I need you to inject me now!!"

Kipling watched as Lopez weighed the request. "I'll make you a deal, Victor. I'll do as you say if you let two of these big strong men here substitute for your crutches. They'll get you where you want to go." He pointed to Hammer and Smith.

The compromise seemed to make sense to Silverstein. "Agreed." As he said this, Jimenez, the service member introduced earlier as the Loadmaster, returned with the bag.

The negotiation complete, Lopez removed two syringes. Silverstein pointed, and Lopez jammed both needles to the hilt and depressed the plungers.

Kipling watched as the pilot and co-pilot—big men, who Kipling decided would have been strong enough to transport the helicopter if necessary—one under each arm, hoisted Silverstein upright. Even though they performed their task as gently as possible, Silverstein's face twisted with pain. Kipling, who rarely allowed emotion to interfere with logic, was beside herself with concern over her dear friend.

With Silverstein's transportation issue resolved, the group of six arrived at the back door, Kipling in the lead. She stepped inside the house and watched as the Silverstein trio turned sideways to negotiate the narrow door.

———————◆———————

Smirnov sprang to his feet from the sofa, not believing what he was seeing: his old friend being carried into the room by two hefty men in military uniforms. Outfitted in odd, ill-fitting clothing, drenched in sweat, face distorted in pain, and with blood running down his leg, Silverstein looked ghastly. Smirnov gestured toward the sofa behind him.

"What happened to you?" Smirnov asked. "And before you answer that, in your condition, why are you here?"

Silverstein responded with a weak smile. "Remember that little weather satellite problem we had?"

"Yeah."

"Well, it's not a problem anymore."

"Brickman?"

"Yep. I'd like to tell you that as bad off as I am, he's in worse shape. But that would be a lie."

At once, Silverstein noticed Erickson sitting opposite, tied to a chair. His strength seemed to return. "Well, well. What do we have here? Is this the elusive Kathy Erickson, or would you prefer that I address you by your given name, Viktoriya? From what I'm told, you've been a tough one to chase down."

For the first time since Erickson's first comment earlier, she responded. "You can go to hell!"

"That might happen eventually, but not right now," replied Silverstein. "Until then, whether you want to or not, you're going to cooperate with me. More to the point, you're going to tell me if you're responsible for the computer hacking that has brought the Russians and us to the brink of war."

"I'm not going to tell you anything, whoever the hell you are. You can torture me all you want."

"Sorry. I've forgotten my manners. Let me introduce myself. My name is Victor Mark Silverstein. I'm an American and happen to be a good friend of Dmitri Smirnov, a former compatriot of yours." He gestured in Smirnov's direction. "My other good friend here, Linda Kipling, has told me a lot about you. From what I understand, she's had a rough time keeping up with you."

With the mention of her name, Kipling exposed herself, walking around the chair to Erickson's front. She leaned forward, her face inches from Erickson's. "I don't suppose that you remember me."

At once, Erickson's demeanor changed, as if transformed into a schizophrenic alter ego. Her face flashed scarlet, anger shooting off in daggers toward the face opposite. As if all the frustration in her body had transferred into her head, her skull twisted and contorted itself. "Yooouuu! Yooouuu! You're the bitch I saw back in San Francisco! Well, fuck you!!"

Kipling saw it coming but responded too slowly. The first wad of spit hit her square to the left of her nose. The second volley landed on the right side.

Everyone in the room, especially the military, went on alert, ready to pounce to save a comrade. Kipling calmly raised her left hand to indicate that she wanted none of that. Simultaneously, she drew back her right hand and let it fly. The crack of her hand against the left side of Erickson's face was so loud that Smirnov swore that he heard an echo reverberate back from the kitchen. Several of those standing had flinched.

Kipling rotated to face Smirnov and meekly mouthed the word, "Sorry."

To which Smirnov voiced loud enough for all to hear. "No apology necessary!"

# — 45 —

## CALL FORWARD

*National Defense Management Center*
*Moscow, Russian Federation*
*55° 43' 40"N Latitude, 37° 35' 23"E Longitude*
*Sunday, April 1, 2018, 10:42 AM (MSK)*

Confusion combined with dread reigned at the NDMC. Those who could fathom the reality of what they were witnessing on the television screens, that U.S. missiles had already traversed the North Pole, knew that only minutes remained before mushroom clouds populated the landscape of the Russian Federation.

Beyond the reality of what the computer-generated output indicated, war game protocol dictated that there be confirmation before retaliation commenced. After all, no one wanted a war started by accident. No one in the auditorium, save Popov, imagined that anyone could have compromised Russia's sophisticated nuclear launch detection system.

Nonetheless, set-in-stone procedures demanded validation. Therein lurked a snag from the get-go. Dedicated telephone lines between the NDMC and the Main Centre became inexplicably blocked. Supporting data that would have originated from the Space Command of the Russian Aerospace Defense Forces, higher up on the hierarchical chain, were unavailable. It was there that radar and satellite feeds responsible for launch detection originated. In this bleakest of situations, safeguard number one proved useless.

Safeguard number two was the Moscow-Washington hotline, explicitly created for situations like this. That line had gone dead as well. Had the Americans sabotaged it on purpose? If so, was that part of their strategy to help guarantee the success of a sneak attack?

One phone call that did go through was to the American embassy in Moscow. With Popov listening in and seconds ticking away, Russia's Prime Minister, Olexi Kandronich, second in command to Vladimir Putin, demanded an explanation from the American ambassador, Robert Newhower.

"An explanation for what?" Newhower responded. "How many times do we have to tell you that we've had nothing to do with your air traffic control system *or* your dams?"

Kandronich became incensed. "I'm not talking about our *fucking* airplanes or our *fucking* hydroelectric plants. I'm talking about *your* ICBMs that you just launched."

"What ICBMs? Are you mad? If missiles were flying, don't you think I'd know about it and already be running for the hills?"

With that reply, Kandronich abruptly hung up the phone. He understood that if the United States had planned a surprise attack on the Russian Federation, the last person they'd keep in the loop would be Moscow's American ambassador.

Kandronich checked the time. Desperate now for any form of communication before Putin activated the Russian version of the nuclear football, he next called the Russian ambassador to the U.S., Alexander Mutinoff, located in Washington D.C. This call also went through quickly. At three forty-five in the morning, it took a few seconds for Mutinoff to process the urgency of the Russian voice he was hearing.

"What? The Americans have launched their ICBMs? I'll call you back," Mutinoff responded, also in Russian.

As had most of the senior military staff surrounding Putin, Oleg Popov had listened in on the last two conversations. He knew that their president would soon be making the most important decision of his life. It was time for Popov to make his own telephone call.

———◆———

*Berkeley Springs, West Virginia*
*39° 35' 58"N Latitude, 78° 15' 50"W Longitude*
*Sunday, April 1, 2018, 3:43 AM (EDT)*

Dmitri Smirnov imagined that he would have done the same had he been in Kipling's situation, perhaps with more than an open hand. He had to stifle a smile, first from watching the other men in the room react to this violent confrontation between two women, and second from Kipling's subtle confession that she felt sorry for her violent behavior.

If blame was to be had, it was his. He had failed! Erickson's wall of silence had been impervious to his attempts at breaking through, whether he spoke in English or Russian. Still, her silence spoke volumes. Plus, her visceral reaction to Kipling only added to the obvious, that they were onto something important.

Following the spit/slap episode, Silverstein introduced Lopez and the helicopter crew to Smirnov. He then motioned for Smirnov to step close. Silverstein explained that he had brought along a lie detector machine that he felt could get the information they needed.

As Smirnov observed the interaction inside the room, it became clear to him that Silverstein was the one in charge, even though his boss was standing nearby. In addition to knowing Silverstein personally, Smirnov had heard stories of this man's mental capabilities. Hell, back in California, Smirnov had listened to Silverstein's brilliant dissection of the list of parties who could have been complicit in the weather satellite debacle.

With everyone in the room seeming to understand this hierarchy, besides Lopez, no one dared to inform Silverstein that he was bleeding to death. His color, especially for a dark-complected African American, looked abnormal. Lopez finally convinced him to allow a tourniquet, adapted from a belt found in Erickson's closet, above the wound on his leg. That did seem to slow the flow of blood somewhat.

———◆———

Silverstein was weak and getting weaker but had to keep going.

"Ms. Erickson, we think you are involved in what's going on between us and Russia right now. Because you won't talk, you give us no choice. We'll have to use another method to get the information out of you. I suspect you've heard of a lie detector. This one," he pointed, "is what we call the LD500. I don't want to brag, but it's state-of-the-art. This man here, Hector Lopez, is my boss. He's going to hook you up, and then I'm going to ask you questions. If you lie to me, I will know."

As Silverstein completed his explanation to Erickson, an uncommon ring tone invaded the room. From his earlier memory back in Monterey, Silverstein recognized Smirnov's satellite phone.

Smirnov checked his phone, looked at Silverstein, held up his left index finger, and darted toward the door.

———◆———

Knowing that satellite phones worked best with an open view of the sky, Smirnov waited until he was clear of the house before answering the call.

Dispensing with the usual cordialities, Smirnov couldn't help himself. Speaking in Russian, he summarized quickly. "We've got her, sir. We're interrogating her now. I tried to talk to her, but she wouldn't say a thing. Everything is pointing towards her. I'd lay odds at ten to one that she's behind the computer hacking. Silverstein is connecting her to a lie detector machine as I speak. We'll have answers soon, sir! We'll be able to put all of this behind us."

The ensuing silence made Smirnov wonder if they'd lost the satellite connection. "Comrade Popov. Did you hear what I just said?"

———◆◆◆———

*National Defense Management Center*
*Moscow, Russian Federation*
*55° 43' 40"N Latitude, 37° 35' 23"E Longitude*
*Sunday, April 1, 2018, 10:44 AM (MSK)*

Contending with the crescendo of voices coming from the auditorium, Popov had plugged one ear with his finger and listened with the other. The last time he and Smirnov had spoken, the topic of concern was the apprehension of his niece, Viktoriya. The launch of the ICBMs had happened since. Smirnov knew nothing of this latest crisis.

"Dmitri, I'm here," Popov finally replied. "Listen to me very carefully. First, tell me who is there with you."

"Linda and I were here alone with Viktoriya until Victor Silverstein and Hector Lopez arrived by helicopter. The helicopter has a crew of three. That's it."

Popov knew the name. *Hector Rodriguez Lopez.* Hispanic. His parents had emigrated from Mexico a generation earlier. A significant player in counterintelligence at the CIA, he was on a level roughly equivalent to that of himself. His SRV file suggested a man of high intelligence—and a personality of someone unafraid to operate outside of the box. Russian operatives had picked up rumors of his involvement in defusing more than one terrorist event over the past decade.

"Dmitri! As fast as you can move, I want you to put Lopez on the phone. Now!!"

———◆◆◆———

*Berkeley Springs, West Virginia*
*39° 35' 58"N Latitude, 78° 15' 50"W Longitude*
*Sunday, April 1, 2018, 3:44 AM (EDT)*

Lopez had just completed attaching the last of the electronic sensors to Erickson's body. They measured everything from pulse rate to blood pressure, to body temperature, to respiration rate. Polygraphs worked because they made use of involuntary bodily responses to stimuli. The problem with using this technology was that some individuals could control involuntary physical reactions. Overall, polygraph results were only about seventy-five percent accurate.

It was for that reason that CIA scientists had added a fifth sensor to the gamut. Attached to Erickson's forehead was a device capable of measuring blood flow that occurred during brain activity. Previous studies using functional Magnetic Resonance Imaging (fMRI) had demonstrated a correlation between lying and blood flow in certain regions of the brain. No small feat was the development of a miniaturized brain scan device that performed similarly to that of a complex MRI machine. Together with the traditional polygraph sensors, the accuracy of this improved polygraph rose to ninety percent.

Lopez was about to hand Silverstein the laptop control for the polygraph system when Smirnov came sprinting back into the room. Except for Erickson, who had her back toward him, everyone took notice.

Smirnov, hyperventilating, skidded to a stop and stared at Lopez. "My boss, Oleg Popov, wants to talk to you *now*! *Please* follow me outside!"

Lopez couldn't have been more surprised if Smirnov had told him that Jesus Christ himself was calling for a consultation. *Oleg Popov, who reports to the Director of the SVR RF, the Foreign Intelligence Service of the Russian Federation, wants to talk to me?*

# — 46 —

## SLIPPERY SLOPE

*Embassy of the United States*
*Moscow, Russian Federation*
*55° 45' 20"N Latitude, 37° 34' 59"E Longitude*
*Sunday, April 1, 2018, 10:45 AM (MSK)*

The call from the Russian prime minister was unexpected, especially on a Sunday morning. The American ambassador to the Russian Federation, Robert Newhower, had been catching up on paperwork—in particular, a high-priority visa request from a Russian dissident. Olexi Kandronich changed Newhower's priorities in a hurry.

"I'm not talking about our fucking airplanes or our fucking hydroelectric plants! I'm talking about the ICBMs you just launched," he had said.

It was an understatement to say that the concern in Kandronich's voice caught Newhower by surprise. *ICBMs?* The international tensions that had arisen over the previous forty-eight hours had put both nations on high alert, but had it come to this? Had the United States been the first to attack?

After taking a few seconds to check the time and subtract seven hours, Newhower couldn't get to his personal version of the Washington hotline fast enough. The call went through instantly.

"Patch me through to the Secretary of Defense," he ordered.

"Sir, do you know what time it is here? It's four in the morning," came the reply from the graveyard shift at the Pentagon.

By now, Newhower's fury boiled over. "*Whoever* you are, sir, you are speaking to Robert Newhower, the America ambassador to Russia. I need you to get me the Secretary of Defense on the phone! *And I mean now!*"

◆

*Russian Ambassador's Residence in Washington, D.C.*
*1125 16th Street NW, Washington, D.C.*
*38° 54' 16"N Latitude, 77° 2' 9"W Longitude*
*Sunday, April 1, 2018, 3:46 AM (EDT)*

Alexander Mutinoff had barely enough time to rub the sleep from his eyes when he hung up the phone. The urgency expressed in his prime minister's phone call made clear that there was no time to make the twenty-minute drive to the Russian Embassy, three miles distant from his residence. He'd have to make do with his downstairs telephone line.

"ICBMs?" his wife, Ingrid, mumbled through a sleep-induced daze.

"It's nothing," he lied, knowing that she also knew that the guard downstairs would not have transferred the call to their bedroom had it not been important.

"Go back to sleep," he whispered as he grabbed for his robe while searching for his house slippers with his feet.

On the way down the stairs, Mutinoff's mind leafed through his mental Rolodex. Who would he call—who *should* he call—particularly at this time of night? From his list of contacts and acquaintances that had come together during his two-year assignment, one person's name rose to the top of the list. He was someone with whom Mutinoff had hit it off, a government official who had even invited him to his house for a backyard cookout celebrating his daughter's twelfth birthday.

That person's name was John Baxter, Chairman of the Joint Chiefs of Staff. Mutinoff had his private home telephone number. If anything were going on militarily, he'd know, thought Mutinoff.

———◆———

*Berkeley Springs, West Virginia*
*39° 35' 58"N Latitude, 78° 15' 50"W*
*Sunday, April 1, 2018, 3:47 AM (EDT)*

Hector Rodriguez Lopez had recognized the alarm evident in the face of an experienced spy. He snapped to his feet and took off running, not far behind the fleet-footed Smirnov, who didn't stop until he was well clear of the house.

"There's a good signal here," said Smirnov, breathless, as he handed over the satellite phone. "My boss speaks English, in case you didn't know."

Lopez did know and took a moment to decide how to best converse with a fellow spy from a country whose very essence revolved around undermining western democracy: Ukraine and the 2016 American election, recent examples, coming to mind.

"This is Hector Lopez," he said. Considering the urgency, he chose to use as few words as possible. "May I help you?"

No sooner had Lopez spoken than he heard and felt his government-issued cell in his pocket. Yet again, CIA agents across the country were receiving the same Codex signal, further confirmation that more trouble was afoot.

———◆———

*George Bush Center for Intelligence, McLean, Virginia, U.S.A.*
*38° 57' 7"N Latitude, 77° 08' 46"W Longitude*
*Sunday, April 1, 2018, 3:48 AM (EDT)*

Even though he was sitting in his office within the very building from which the Codex signal had originated, Marc Miller, Hector Lopez's assistant, had received no warning that it would be coming. Before Silverstein's helicopter lifted off from Andrews on its way to Berkeley Springs, Lopez had ordered Miller back to headquarters to be available if needed. The last Miller had heard from him was when they had landed. He briefly considered calling but realized that Lopez would then ask *him* about the latest Codex, and Miller knew nothing.

Coincident with that thought came the sound of incoming helicopter blades beating the air. *What the hell?* Only the director of the CIA would be flying to this location at this time of night. Miller flew to his keyboard to see if their internal network gave any clue to what was happening.

---

*Berkeley Springs, West Virginia*
*39° 35' 58"N Latitude, 78° 15' 50"W*
*Sunday, April 1, 2018, 3:49 AM (EDT)*

Popov's voice sounded authoritative, as Lopez expected. "Mr. Lopez. I know you, and I'm sure you know me. There is no time for pleasantries."

Lopez was professional as well. "Understood."

"I need you to confirm, *right now,* that your country has launched your land-based ICBMs at us. As I speak, our satellites are following them as they cross the North Pole. We have less than six minutes before we will have no choice but to order a retaliatory launch of our own." A brief pause. "Do you understand my question, *sir?*"

"Sir, I know of no such attack!"

"How am I to believe you?"

"Sir, my agent Kipling and your man Smirnov have been chasing your niece, Viktoriya, across our country for the past twelve hours. Well, we've caught her. We believe that she was responsible for the computer hacking that has put our countries at odds over the past two days. None of us here know anything about what you are saying. As I speak, we're giving her a polygraph test. Give me two minutes!"

Lopez returned the phone to Smirnov. "Follow me!" he ordered as they took off running back to the house.

"Wait!" Lopez said as he came to a quick halt after noticing a tree stump to his left. "Leave the phone here on this stump. We can't take the chance of losing the satellite connection."

———————◆————————

*Sunday, April 1, 2018, 3:50 AM (EDT)*

In the minutes that had elapsed since Lopez went rushing from the house, Silverstein had come to one conclusion. He was positive that Erickson was responsible for the hacking episodes. From previous training during spy school, he had learned the sequence of questions to ask to enable the lie detector software to do its job.

Erickson's refusal to articulate yes or no answers to Silverstein's questions didn't matter. Ten questions that anyone would know the answers to, such as *On a beautiful day at the beach, is the sky usually blue?* formed the baseline. From those questions alone, the software that monitored the inputs had come to the remarkable conclusion that Erickson was ninety-eight percent transparent when it came to revealing the truth.

With that determination affirmed—and under the scrutiny of four other people captivated by the ongoing mystery—Silverstein moved on to the questions of interest. Did Erickson hack the American and Russian air traffic control and hydroelectric power plant systems? Did she do it alone? Was it her purpose to make the U.S. and Russia go to war?

With Kipling by his side, Silverstein asked the questions rapidly, rephrasing them continually to create both positive and negative replies. The results were consistent, and he smiled at his colleagues. Not only did Erickson confirm her involvement, but she also told them that she alone was responsible.

Silverstein was hoping that some color had returned to his face. He smiled and addressed the group. "I can assure you all that I know now, with nearly one hundred percent certainty, that Ms. Erickson here was the one who created the situation we've experienced over the past days. Our crisis with Russia is over!"

Kipling and the three members of the helicopter crew clapped their hands. Tension in the room evaporated by the second.

It was then that Lopez and Smirnov reappeared, bounding into the room. *What now?*

Lopez ran to Silverstein and Kipling and whispered so that only they could hear. "Oleg Popov says that American ICBMs are flying over the North Pole this very minute."

———◆———

*Sunday, April 1, 2018, 3:51 AM (EDT)*

Kathy Erickson was not stupid. Eyeing the black man's reaction at the end of her interrogation, she knew that her lie detector results confirmed what they had suspected. His statement to the group corroborated it. But as the saying goes, *It ain't over till the fat lady sings.*

And from what she had observed before the interrogation began, the fat lady was already singing. Why else would a Russian, this Smirnov fellow, request that the man called Lopez speak to her Uncle Popov, a prominent Russian official? And just now, Lopez had returned, obviously disturbed, whispering something to Silverstein and the San Francisco bitch.

She knew that Putin had to be within minutes of launching a counterstrike, falling prey to the artificial reality that she had created.

With that in mind, Erickson expected a few more questions. But this time, she vowed to give them nothing. A stunt she had pulled during her childhood would prove useful just now.

———◆◆◆———

*Sunday, April 1, 2018, 3:52 AM (EDT)*

*Really?* U.S. missiles are traversing the poles? Silverstein had already concluded that Erickson's goal was to start a war. But had the U.S. actually done so and launched its missiles—or had Erickson somehow tricked the Russians into thinking that had happened.

Silverstein thought it through. There had to be a reason why Popov had called. *Was he also considering the possibility that Erickson had staged a sham?*

Silverstein knew what he had to do next—and fast. "Ms. Erickson, I have a few more questions for you."

But he knew instantly that something was wrong. He jumped to his feet, cringing from the pain in his leg. "Goddammit!"

"What going on, Victor?" yelled Smirnov.

Silverstein spoke to the group. "Hector just talked to Popov. The Russians think we've launched our ICBMs as a first strike. Because Erickson's already confirmed to us that she's behind the earlier hackings, it's hardly a stretch to think she's also hacked into their launch system to make them think that's so. Dammit!"

As Silverstein watched Erickson's face mirror her body's stress, he explained to the group what was happening. "She's holding her breath. She knows that we can't get meaningful results from anyone experiencing such extreme pain."

Everyone in the room watched as Erickson did exactly what Silverstein predicted. Her face and neck color transitioned from light red to beet red, and then on to scarlet. At the same time, she closed her eyes, her torso moving back and forth, accompanied by a sickening moan. Silverstein heard a siren-like sound and looked down at his computer. Erickson's heart rate had exceeded one hundred and eighty-five beats per minute.

Silverstein knew that there was a reason why holding your breath was not a reliable method of committing suicide. Erickson passed out, her head slumping to her chest. Before long, her body's involuntary response system took over, and she started to breathe again.

Erickson opened her eyes and slowly became aware of her surroundings. She lifted her head, found her inquisitor, and locked eyes.

What happened next sent a chill down Silverstein's spine. She smiled sweetly, took two deep breaths, and held the second one as before. What was different this time was that she never lost eye contact—or the smile—until she once again lost consciousness.

All the while, Silverstein was questioning what had just happened, and he realized that his earlier negative outburst had been premature. Erickson had just made a serious mistake in logic. *If* U.S. missiles were indeed on their way to Moscow, it would be a *fait accompli*, and she'd be prone to brag about it. Instead, by suggesting that she had something to hide, Erickson had inadvertently provided proof of the opposite. To wit, *the U.S. missile launch was a fantasy.*

———————◆◆◆———————

*Sunday, April 1, 2018, 3:55 AM (EDT)*

Kipling had witnessed the entire sequence of Erickson's strategy to thwart the lie detector and wondered why Silverstein was now smiling. "What?" she asked.

Lopez and Smirnov leaned in their direction to hear what was going on.

Silverstein stated his conclusion. "The U.S. launch is a fake. Erickson just *proved* it by trying to hide it from us."

Kipling understood the implication of his statement—and so did Silverstein. "Go!! yelled Silverstein.

"Where's the phone?" Kipling screamed.

"Follow me!" With Smirnov in the lead, Lopez and Kipling raced out the back door.

With adrenaline pumping, Kipling won the race back to the stump and snatched the phone a second ahead of Smirnov. "Oleg, this is Linda Kipling! Do *not* fire your missiles! We are being fooled yet again. Not only did she hack the airplanes and dams, but she is also making you think we have launched our missiles. Victor has confirmed it's all a trick staged by Viktoriya!"

Kipling's heart thumped wildly. Too long a pause! Had they lost connection? "Oleg, do you hear me!? Oleg!" she shrieked into the phone.

Popov's voice was somber. "I'm sorry, Linda. If we had waited any longer, we would have lost our retaliatory capability. All of our land-based missiles are in the air."

# – 47 –

## INCOMING/OUTGOING

*National Defense Management Center*
*Moscow, Russian Federation*
*55° 43' 40"N Latitude, 37° 35' 23"E Longitude*
*Sunday, April 1, 2018, 10:55 AM (MSK)*

Oleg Popov had nothing more to say and hung up the phone. He believed what Kipling said, that Viktoriya had orchestrated the hacking episodes. By themselves, the air traffic control and hydroelectric incidents had been enough to drive two nations to the brink of war! Popov damned the timing. If he had received that information only an hour earlier, he would have begged his superiors to once again reach out to the Americans who, like the Russians, had been innocent of any wrongdoing!

Now, Popov had to wrap his mind around a second, even more grotesque possibility. Could Viktoriya have been clever enough to deliver the coup de grâce? Was what they were seeing on their TV screens the fictitious elephant in the room, the most horrid of all conclusions possible? Kipling had said, "Oleg, this is Linda Kipling! Do *not* fire your missiles! We are being fooled yet again. Not only did she hack the airplanes and dams, but she is also making you think that we have launched our missiles. Victor has confirmed it's all a trick staged by Viktoriya!"

Burdened with the horror of the consequences should Kipling prove correct, Popov had to relegate such thinking to lunacy. Understanding America's current political situation—where a sitting president happily ruled with a *shoot first, ask questions later* philosophy—wasn't it more likely that Trump had decided to order a first strike? To provide himself with a better argument with which he might later negotiate leniency in the hereafter, Popov hoped that was what had happened.

Popov knew that one of two scenarios would soon play out: Moscow's incineration within minutes—*or* a sixty-minute reprieve. If the former, he would go to his hereafter knowing that his country had responded appropriately to America's sneak attack. If the latter, then *God help me!* Once American satellites picked up incoming Russian ICBMs, politicians there would have no choice but to also launch on warning.

At best, then, Popov figured that he had five remaining minutes to breathe Russian air and to contemplate this ending to his life.

Popov returned to the auditorium of the NDMC. The excited, shrill, fearful voices that had earlier made it difficult for him to use his satellite phone were gone. As if everyone were watching a Hollywood blockbuster, all eyes fixated on the red dots converging on Mother Russia. He joined the others in prayer—to the Supreme Being that Communism had tried to convince the country was only a philosophical artifact manufactured from human frailty.

———◆◆◆———

*Berkeley Springs, West Virginia*
*39° 35' 58"N Latitude, 78° 15' 50"W*
*Sunday, April 1, 2018, 3:55 AM (EDT)*

Kipling dropped the phone to her side and stared first at Smirnov—who had been standing close enough to listen in on the conversation—and then at Lopez. "We're too late. Russian missiles are on their way," she said.

"What should we do now, Hector?" she followed up, immediately recognizing the futility of anything he could add.

A beyond-somber expression now etched in his face, Lopez pulled his agency cell from his pocket and dialed.

———◆◆◆———

*George Bush Center for Intelligence, McLean, Virginia, U.S.A.*
*38° 57' 7"N Latitude, 77° 08' 46"W Longitude*
*Sunday, April 1, 2018, 3:55 AM (EDT)*

The CIA took pride in having instant access to every piece of intelligence data generated by any U.S. intelligence agency. Accordingly, Marc Miller, having logged into the agency's in-house computer system, was among the first in the nation to learn that America's spy satellites had picked up ominous signals emanating from Russia proper. Computer software identified those signals as recently launched ICBMs.

"That CANNOT be!" Miller said aloud.

As he was reaching for his phone to call his boss, Lopez beat him to the punch.

Lopez couched his words in hope. "Please tell me that our satellites *cannot* confirm what Oleg Popov told us happened in Russia just minutes ago."

Allowing his mind the time to process the improbable, it took a moment for Miller to reply. "I assume that you're asking me if Russia has just taken the first step in starting World War III. They have. Russian ICBMs lifted off from Russian soil just minutes ago."

In the background, Miller noticed the sound yet again, only eight minutes later. This time the helicopter was heading out. Under the circumstances, he could imagine only one relevant passenger and one destination: The White House Situation Room.

# ~ 48 ~

## BLOOD FLOW INTERRUPTUS

*Berkeley Springs, West Virginia*
*39° 35' 58"N Latitude, 78° 15' 50"W*
*Sunday, April 1, 2018, 3:58 AM (EDT)*

Silverstein was going crazy. Waiting for a response from the outside, he and Erickson were biding their time staring each other down. The helicopter crew had grown tired of standing around and had taken seats. Suddenly, Silverstein noticed that Erickson's expression had changed and that she was looking past him. Remembering a TV sitting behind him, with muted sound, Silverstein turned to look. Displayed in larger than normal lettering were the words *BREAKING NEWS*. The nighttime broadcaster's facial expression seemed especially serious.

Silverstein gestured towards Jimenez. "Sergeant Jimenez, could you please turn the sound back on?" By then, the two pilots noticed Silverstein's concern.

The television volume returned mid-sentence. Silverstein recognized Susan Cadillac, long-time veteran CNN journalist and broadcaster who had made her name back during the Iraqi war:

*...not sure of what to make of this. Our correspondents are reporting sudden and unusual activity at both the Pentagon and the White House. Traffic cams are reporting bumper-to-bumper traffic heading toward both the Pentagon and the CIA. And all of this at four o'clock in the morning Eastern time!*

Cadillac paused, hand to her ear. "Dan Wilson, our Pentagon reporter, is on the line." A photograph of Wilson appeared in the upper right corner of the screen.

"Dan, can you shed some light on all the activity? What's happening?" Cadillac asked.

"Susan, all but one of my contacts have gone silent on me. I *have* learned something. Our spy satellites have picked up some unusual activity coming from some fifteen Russian locations."

Cadillac remained professional. "Let's be clear here before we go further. When you say *unusual activity,* what is it you are saying?"

Cadillac waited for a response, her voice projecting concern. "Dan, are you still there? Please tell our listeners what you mean by *unusual activity?*"

"What I am being told is that our satellites are picking up flare signatures, unusual light displays typical of ground-launched missiles."

"Dan, you mentioned something rather specific: some fifteen locations. Why is that significant?"

"The reason it's important is that these locations are where Russia has stationed nearly all of its ICBMs."

———————◆◆◆———————

*Sunday, April 1, 2018, 3:59 AM (EDT)*

Silverstein had heard enough! The worst thing imaginable had happened. If the reporting he had just heard was not enough to confirm what Erickson had done, the broad smile on her face was the ultimate validation. He stood as quickly as his mangled leg would permit. "Samson! Smith! I need you to get me back outside. Fast!"

The two pilots, visibly shaken by what they had heard on the TV, nonetheless reacted like the professionals they were. As they carried him from the room, Silverstein turned and issued one more order: "Jimenez, your job is to keep an eye on Erickson here!"

---

*Sunday, April 1, 2018, 3:59 AM (EDT)*

Kathy Ann Erickson was ecstatic beyond words. What she'd just heard was confirmation that her plan had worked to perfection. To be sure, once Russia's ICBMs came within range of the U.S., President Trump would launch a counterstrike. With that final stroke, her task would be complete. *Oh, to be a fly on the wall.* Erickson had chosen something special for the Russian government to see—a memorable conclusion to their day.

Before the apocalypse came down on everyone, Erickson still had cards to play. If she could escape and head west, she might outrun the effects of the nuclear blasts on Washington, DC—and survive! She'd then head south to Mexico and vanish.

Erickson took stock of Jimenez, the enlisted man standing to her side and watching TV. Unbeknownst to others in the room, Erickson had been working the shoelaces behind her back, taking advantage of the sweat generated during her interrogation. Never in her imagination had she thought that cutting off one of her little fingers would prove to be an advantage later in life. The loss of that single appendage had given her just enough space to free herself from the shoelace. She eyed the small table nearby where she had earlier opened her mail.

"Sergeant Jimenez," Erickson said in as nonthreatening a voice as possible. "I don't suppose that you could get me a glass of water?"

Jimenez, riveted to the CNN broadcast, looked over.

She gestured with her head towards the kitchen. "The glasses are in the cabinet to the right of the sink."

Jimenez seemed conflicted, perhaps thinking he should wait for approval by a superior.

"Please," Erickson said sweetly.

"Ok. I guess there's no harm in that."

"Thank you so much. Like I said, the cabinet just to the right of the sink."

Erickson watched as Jimenez made his way to the kitchen. She knew that the sink was out of sight from where she sat. As he made the left-hand turn, she quickly brought both hands in front of her, hopped the few feet to the end table where she had been opening the mail, hopped back, and returned her hands to the rear of the chair. Jimenez soon appeared with the water.

"I'm afraid, in my situation, you're going to have to hold the glass for me," Erickson said, as she smiled widely.

"No problem. Here, I'll help you out. I'm experienced," he said. "I do this for my grandmother, who lives in a nursing home and needs help sometimes."

*How nice you are to me, dear boy. Well, get ready to meet her in hell!* As Jimenez bent down with the glass, Erickson calculated the trajectory her hand would take. Briefly looking Jimenez in the eye to divert his attention, she willed all her strength into her right hand.

Before the Air Force sergeant had any idea about what was happening, the stiletto-like letter opener made its way deep into the left side of his neck. Instinctively bolting upright, left hand reaching for his throat, he staggered back into the sofa and fell. For upwards of a minute, he flopped around, eventually immobilized on the floor.

Erickson tuned out the unpleasant gurgling noises, untied her feet, and raced toward the back bedroom, where she kept her stash of weaponry underneath the floorboard. She grabbed two grenades, together with a much heavier automatic firearm. These should be enough, she thought, to take out the remaining obstacles standing in the way of her escape to Mexico.

With that accomplished, Erickson commanded herself to slow down, to take a moment to reflect. There was a decision to be made here. Would it be better to confront the group outside—or ambush them on their inevitable return to the house?

# — 49 —

## FAT MAN RUNNING

*National Defense Management Center*
*Moscow, Russian Federation*
*55° 43' 40"N Latitude, 37° 35' 23"E Longitude*
*Sunday, April 1, 2018, 10:59 AM (MSK)*

As the seconds evaporated, and with most in the room having made peace with their maker, all eyes converged on the electronic display. The American ICBMs were close. In the back of the large auditorium, behind the politically important members of the ministries and executive branch, Popov took in the scene.

Perhaps not surprisingly, his mind reverted to the real world in which he'd trained. How soon would their electronic display go dark? How many seconds or fractions thereof would the nation's electrical infrastructure survive the first nuclear electronic pulse, that ring of electromagnetic radiation that spread concentrically away from the blast. Not long, he knew. None of these details mattered: Everyone in the room would be dead or dying within seconds.

The red dots, each representing a single ICBM, were nearing the lower portion of the screen. And then, it happened! Each red dot morphed into what appeared to be a tiny electrified explosion, reminding one of a pinwheel sparkler. The screen faded to black.

Every mouth in the auditorium fell open, each person frantically searching for an update from the giant TV. Most observers, including Popov, presumed that the first strike had knocked out the electronics. For that reason, everyone braced themselves for the explosions that would soon reach their location. Popov imagined that their impressive building would disintegrate around him.

But none came!!

Seconds later, Russian words appeared in large letters, filling the screen: Счастливый день дурачков в апреле.

Whether translated into English or interpreted from the native Russian, the implication of "Happy April Fools' Day" meant only one thing: *They'd been had!* And Oleg Popov knew that his niece, Viktoriya Ratimirovna Popova, had masterminded the single greatest act of terrorism ever, dooming much of the life on Planet Earth for the foreseeable future. *May God damn her to hell!*

Popov had never experienced such quiet. Had the proverbial pin fallen to the floor, even those who were hard of hearing would have heard its echo against the auditorium walls.

Until that moment, there had been few uncertainties about what was happening. Everyone in the Russian government had confidently cast their vote: The Americans were guilty as charged. Now that all cards lay exposed on the table, everyone knew the converse: Their geopolitical adversaries were innocent.

Popov knew what he had to do and recognized that there was little time to do it. He jumped to his feet and took off running—in the way only a fat man runs—down the aisle, toward the stage, feet slapping the floor left and right, arms pumping at his side, necktie sailing in the breeze behind him. Everyone in the auditorium, especially those sitting near the rostrum, cast their eyes on the rotund figure with the red face and the unruly hair making his way toward the stage.

Popov knew that of the five Russians initially involved in Project Athena back in 2010, only he and one other person remained within the government. Of the three others, one had left his position, one had retired, and one had died. Ironically, the person whose idea it had been to create Athena should have been sitting on the stage next to

President Putin: Prime Minister Dmitry Medvedev. He would have come to the same conclusion as had Popov. But as chance would have it, he was out of the country on a tour of the Middle East. With only minutes with which to work, Popov needed to make his case by himself.

Popov clamored to the stage, breathless. Hours earlier, he had failed to convince his colleagues. And so, he repeated his claim. "It is my niece, Viktoriya, who's responsible for both the computer hackings and the electronic farce we've just experienced!" He had proof, he told them.

That was the bad news, he said. The good news was that there was a solution to their problem. A combination of horror and surprise could best describe the looks on the faces of those sitting on the stage—especially President Vladimir Vladimirovich Putin.

# — 50 —

## TEN DIGITS, ALL ZEROES

*Berkeley Springs, West Virginia*
*39° 35' 58"N Latitude, 78° 15' 50"W*
*Sunday, April 1, 2018, 4:01 AM (EDT)*

With every physical movement shooting waves of pain through his body, Silverstein did the math. It didn't take a genius to compute how much time they had. Five minutes earlier, Russian ICBMs left Russian soil. If the Joint Chiefs of Staff, along with the Secretaries of Defense and State, among others—no doubt huddled with Trump in the Situation Room—waited no longer than fifteen more minutes before approving a massive retaliation, those fifteen minutes were all that remained between normalcy and a cataclysm.

With the considerable assistance of the two Air Force pilots, Silverstein made his way through the cool night air toward the solitary Russian and two Americans. Knowing what they knew, he understood why there was no reason to celebrate his unexpected appearance.

"Victor, you're burning up," Kipling noted, obviously concerned over the copious amounts of sweat pouring from his face.

Silverstein ignored the comment and spoke forcefully to Smirnov. "Dmitri, I need to speak to your boss. Could you please reach him for me?"

Smirnov nodded and stepped aside.

Lopez frowned at the verbal interchange. "Don't tell me that you too know Oleg Popov personally?"

"You might say that," Silverstein answered dryly.

A sudden surge of nausea overwhelmed Silverstein, and he wretched violently. Crescendos of pain from his shoulder and leg were starting to affect his mind. He briefly considered asking Lopez for more injections but decided against it, fearing that additional medication might affect his thinking.

Silverstein's physical condition was weakening by the moment. As Smirnov approached, outstretched hand holding the phone, Silverstein recognized that he had to make a split-second decision. Only a handful of people in the world knew about what he and Popov were about to discuss. Although the current circumstances might soon render that concern moot, protocol demanded that, for the moment, he and Popov speak in private.

"Major Samson, Captain Smith, could you please set me down on that stump?" They obliged, after which he shifted his body around to find a position where the pain was bearable. Alas, there was no such position.

To try to clear his head, Silverstein took a couple of deep breaths before addressing the group. "I'm sorry to do this to you. Could you please step aside while I speak to Mr. Popov privately?"

---

Lopez, Kipling, and the others, confused by this mysterious request, did as Silverstein asked.

Kipling nudged Lopez. "Do you know what's going on here? I talked to Popov just yesterday after the explosion put Dmitri out of commission. I know for a fact that at no time did Victor have access to Dmitri's phone."

Lopez shook his head.

---

*National Defense Management Center*
*Moscow, Russian Federation*
*55° 43' 40"N Latitude, 37° 35' 23"E Longitude*
*Sunday, April 1, 2018, 11:03 AM (MSK)*

Oleg Popov had made his case to Putin and was waiting for his authorization to activate Project Athena. Inputting a simple ten-digit code into Russia's version of the nuclear football gave Putin the power to deactivate all nuclear warheads on each of the Russian ICBMs making their way across the North Pole. Both Popov and Putin knew that deactivating the nuclear portion of the warhead would have no effect on a missile's trajectory. It would continue its course and arrive at the spot initially targeted. When it finally slammed into the earth, the impact would be horrendous, destroying and killing everything within a block or two radius. To be sure, distributed nuclear material would create a radiation hazard. But that concern was insignificant compared to the consequences of a nuclear blast.

When Popov answered his phone, Smirnov told him that it was Silverstein who wanted to talk. Popov recognized the voice from some eight years previous. "Oleg, this is Victor Silverstein. I hope you remember who I am? We need to talk."

"I remember you, Victor, and I know why you're calling. I've just spoken to President Putin about Athena."

Popov heard what he interpreted as a sigh of relief on the other end. "That's wonderful, Oleg!" Silverstein said. "Activate the code, and this nuclear nightmare that your niece created will be over!"

"Give me a second, Victor. Please." To Popov's dismay, it was not at all clear that the leader of his country was as relieved as he was to learn that there was a solution to their problem.

———◆◆———

*Berkeley Springs, West Virginia*
*39° 35' 58"N Latitude, 78° 15' 50"W*
*Sunday, April 1, 2018, 4:03 AM (MSK)*

By now, Silverstein's colleagues had migrated back to him. With their expected upcoming demise, they saw no reason to follow orders. Silverstein understood, and considering his worsening condition, recognized that everyone, *especially* Lopez, needed to be in on both sides of the conversation. He beckoned to Smirnov, who showed him how to put the Russian satellite phone on speaker.

Silverstein couldn't imagine what was going on. It was an obvious easy decision for Russia's leaders to neutralize the impending disaster that they had created. The beauty of Athena's design was that both the U.S. and Russian control systems incorporated one identical component, each specific to that country's missiles—and unhackable. A multi-digit code fed into the nuclear football would spawn an electronic command to the same group of observational satellites whose job it had been to recognize an enemy launch in the first place. That command would initiate another transmission that sped its way down to the missiles themselves.

After a long moment, in which seconds ticked by like minutes, Popov came back. "Victor. We have a problem."

With what little blood remained in his body, Silverstein's blood pressure was petering out, and he made his point using willpower alone. "Problem! What problem? Have you forgotten the goddamn code? Let me help you out! Ten digits, all zeroes." He remembered that those involved in its design had agreed on simplicity itself.

Following this outburst, Silverstein's colleagues inched even closer, forming a tight circle around the stump.

Popov explained. "President Putin says that if we destroy our missiles, we will be at your mercy for decades to come. He said that Russia would rather die than be under the thumb of Yankee imperialism."

"For Christ's sake, Oleg! What is it you want? Surely you don't want us to fire off our missiles too?" Silverstein's spontaneous exclamation came before he even had time to think through the implications.

Popov replied gravely. "That's precisely what he wants you to do."

# ~ 51 ~

## OVER AND OUT

*Berkeley Springs, West Virginia*
*39° 35' 58"N Latitude, 78° 15' 50"W*
*Sunday, April 1, 2018, 4:05 AM (EDT)*

Silverstein was incredulous. "You can't be serious, Oleg! You and I have only minutes left to stop World War III. What if one of our missiles doesn't receive the signal? Do you want to take that chance?"

"You and I know that won't happen. The beauty of the override was in its simplicity. And don't forget what else we did to confirm that the activation code had been successful. After each missile receives its deactivation signal, that same missile broadcasts back, on international emergency radio frequency, 16.23 megacycles, a coded digital confirmation. That information is then automatically inserted into each country's ballistic missile tracking software."

Silverstein recalled the months of design and discussion and knew that what Popov was saying was true. Both sides would want, and need, automatic confirmation that neutralization had occurred. "Oleg, you do appreciate the fact that you are blackmailing us into launching a nuclear strike against your own country?"

"I recognize the irony. You will neutralize your missiles, just as we will do the same to ours. You remember, Victor, President Obama and President Medvedev took a considerable risk to create this agreement back in 2010. Do you think there would be any hesitancy on their parts?"

"Oleg, I do understand what—" Silverstein wasn't quick enough to cover the telephone before he yelled out and doubled over in agonizing pain.

"Victor! What's going on?"

Silverstein knew that he was fading fast. He gathered what was left of his mental acuity to create a firewall against the physical agony. "I'm sorry, Oleg…it's not been a good day for me." He tried again. "There…there…may be a bigger problem. Does either of us trust our politicians to do the right thing?"

"I get your point. Once everyone's missiles are in the air, who is going to want to go first to deactivate theirs?"

"Yup, that's what I'm saying."

*It's come down to this,* thought Silverstein. *A matter of trust.*

Victor Mark Silverstein had made his reputation within the Navy as a problem solver. Most of those problems had been technical, far different, and usually easier to unravel than those involving complex psychological interactions between fellow Homo sapiens.

"Oleg, this could be a problem. I think that you and I together are the solution."

"We're moments away from oblivion, Victor. I'm listening."

"Oleg, the nature of our jobs is different from those of most people. You and I worked together for months, and I can honestly say that I trust you. Do you trust me?"

"Absolutely!"

"Then, our future will be determined by that trust."

Silverstein, now fading in and out of consciousness, hoped that Lopez had been absorbing every word said.

———◆◆◆———

*National Defense Management Center*
*Moscow, Russian Federation*
*55° 43' 40"N Latitude, 37° 35' 23"E Longitude*
*Sunday, April 1, 2018, 11:06 AM (MSK)*

Oleg Popov hung up his cell, accepting Silverstein's assertion that the trust between two spies on opposite corners of the planet was critical to the world's survival. He explained aloud to Putin what they had discussed, together with Silverstein's concern. To his considerable relief, the President of the Russian Federation reacted favorably. Popov looked around to assess the reactions from others who had been listening in. Troubling was that the body language of several high-ranking military officials did not appear to be as conciliatory.

With that part accomplished, there was nothing more for Popov to do but wait. Russian missiles were in the air, ready to obliterate their geopolitical foe. Whether a catastrophe of Biblical proportions happened was now in the hands of their arch-rivals. For everything to work as they agreed, the first thing the Americans had to do was light off their own version of fire and brimstone. *May God help us all!*

---

*Berkeley Springs, West Virginia*
*39° 35' 58"N Latitude, 78° 15' 50"W*
*Sunday, April 1, 2018, 4:07 AM (EDT)*

Hector Rodriguez Lopez was nothing if not a quick study. From listening to Silverstein's side of the conversation, he had ferreted out the essence. Sometime in the distant past, Silverstein and Popov participated in a secret deal to install on both countries' ICBMs a mechanism that would allow for their deactivation once launched.

And now that the Russians had launched their missiles for real—tricked by Erickson to think that the Americans had already started the war—they didn't want to neutralize their ICBM armada without the Americans reciprocating. Not an unreasonable request, thought

Lopez. Still, Silverstein was afraid that politicians, on both sides, might try to game the interchange.

Lopez understood that Silverstein would not remain conscious much longer. He had lost so much blood that his very survival might be at stake. Hammer and Smith stood on either side of him, trying to keep him upright. The balls that Silverstein had been secretly juggling by himself had found their way into Lopez's hands.

Lopez *had* to know if his assessment of their dire situation was correct. With Kipling and Smirnov hanging on every word, he began. "Victor, you need to tell me if what I'm about to say is what you know? The Russians have launched their missiles..." Lopez highlighted the key points, including the ten-digit code of all zeroes and, importantly, that each side would receive instantaneous confirmation of each missile's deactivation.

Silverstein was having trouble keeping his eyes open. He was losing control and on the verge of passing out. With one final surge of energy, he opened his eyes, focused on Lopez, and managed to nod his head up and down—twice.

Lopez glanced at his watch: ten minutes after the hour. He needed to establish communication with the White House Situation Room—and fast! Of those in the government whom he knew personally, only one person had the stature, position, and ability to pass this information to President Trump.

# ─ 52 ─

## IN MEMORIAM?

*White House Grounds*
*1600 Pennsylvania Avenue NW, Washington, D.C.*
*38° 53' 50"N Latitude, 77° 02' 14.7"W Longitude*
*Sunday, April 1, 2018, 4:11 AM (EDT)*

When her company cell rang, Dr. Alexandria Jane McFadden, Director of the Central Intelligence Agency, was on a dead run from her helicopter to the White House Situation Room, located in the basement of the White House's West Wing. Her trio of personal security was by her side. Considering the ongoing international crisis, President Trump and the NSA had requested her presence. Earlier, she had received calls from both the Secretary of Defense and the Chairman of the Joint Chiefs of Staff.

"Hello!" said McFadden, breathless. She knew that the call was legitimate; the CIA's encrypted lines were impervious to hackers.

"Director McFadden, this is Hector Lopez. We need to talk."

McFadden slowed to a stop.

"Hector? You know this isn't a good time, right?"

"Ma'am, I wouldn't be calling if I didn't have to."

"I'll give you ninety seconds, Hector. Talk fast."

Walking around in tight circles as her security detail set up a three-legged protective perimeter, McFadden digested Lopez's words and then replied. "Let me get this straight. First, you're telling me that a former Russian citizen, now called Kathy Erickson, is behind all the hacking episodes that have brought us to World War III. Second, that after being tricked into firing off their ICBMs by this same woman no less, the Russians are now asking that we respond in kind?"

"Yes, ma'am. Doesn't matter though. We'd do it anyway. Their missiles will be here in twenty minutes."

McFadden's brain worked much faster than those of most mortals, powered by a one hundred and seventy-five IQ. "But, third, you're also telling me that we can deactivate those missiles already in the air? That there was this secret Athena Project that Obama and Medvedev created back in 2010. And—make sure I get this straight—the Russians don't want to be the only ones to sacrifice their nuclear umbrella?"

"Correct. Back then, an employee of the Naval Research Laboratory worked out the details with Oleg Popov, who now heads Directorate X of the SVR. His name was Victor Mark Silverstein. In recent years, he's also worked with us.

Lopez quickly explained Athena, as well as Silverstein's description of the use of the international emergency frequency to verify the missile deactivations. He also provided Popov's personal phone number.

"I know of Popov, and I've heard the name Silverstein."

McFadden recognized a slight hesitation before Lopez spoke. "I have to tell you that I've learned all of this in just the past thirty minutes. Most of this information is secondhand from Victor."

"Shit! Then why isn't he doing the talking instead of you?"

"Ma'am, I'd trust this man with my life. The reason is that right now, as I stand in the middle of a grass field in West Virginia, he's here right next to me, unconscious and nearly dead from loss of blood."

*Berkeley Springs, West Virginia*
*39° 35' 58"N Latitude, 78° 15' 50"W*
*Sunday, April 1, 2018, 4:12 AM (EDT)*

Lopez's conversation with McFadden ended. He felt confident that he had gotten across all key information, including the ten-digit code. There was nothing more that he could think to say.

As the senior representative of five other disparate government personnel, Lopez knew that he needed to take charge. The ball that Silverstein had passed to him was now in the capable hands of Director McFadden.

Lopez eyed his group. "I know that each of us here is scared. *All* of you now know as much as I do, and from what we've all heard, there *is* hope. I say that we act like the professionals we all are. That means that we get Victor to a hospital, stat! That's priority one."

Major Hammer seemed to answer for the group. "Yes, sir. I say we get this sixty in the air now!"

Lopez considered the bigger picture. "Folks, I can't do much from here. I need to get back to Washington. We need to move quickly. Major Hammer, do you mind if I substitute myself for Sergeant Jimenez?"

"Sir, you're senior here. Who am I to argue?"

Lopez next addressed Kipling and Smirnov. "You two stay here with Jimenez and babysit Erickson. Okay?"

With that plan of action understood and accepted by all, the two pilots lifted Silverstein using a two-man carry whereby, with interlocking arms, they essentially created a "seat." They then took off at a jogger's pace toward the chopper, a hundred feet farther from the house. Lopez and Smirnov brought up the rear. Kipling led the way, zigzagging back and forth, searching for tripping hazards, all the while offering verbal encouragement to the friend with whom she had worked for decades.

Before long, Hammer was in the cockpit and had the twin-turboshaft engine revving up. Looking back to confirm that Silverstein and Lopez were fastened in, he smoothly pulled back on the collective to gather lift.

It was at that moment that all hell broke loose.

In all the years that Dmitri Smirnov had served at the pleasure of the Russian Federation, he had never come under fire. That did not mean that he didn't recognize what sounded like a light, semi-automatic machine gun. *What? Has Erickson escaped? Did she have reinforcements that came in behind them?* Answers to those questions would have to wait.

Smirnov also understood rifle mechanics enough to explain the accompanying sequencing of sounds. The average person was unaware that rifle bullets flew supersonically. For that reason, before he heard gunfire, he heard the pings of the bullets striking the metal housing of the helicopter.

Instinctively diving to the ground, Smirnov looked up to recognize three distinct situations. First, the pilot had recognized the attack and was desperately rotating the chopper counterclockwise to shield the cockpit. Simultaneously, he was adding full power to lift themselves out of range of the gunfire. Second, Smirnov saw Lopez lunging to close the side door of the helicopter.

It was what Smirnov saw next that nearly gave him heart failure. There was Kipling, standing tall as could be, Glock ready to fire, scanning the horizon from which the shots were coming—and evidently thinking that she was wearing some sort of Harry Potter cloak of invisibility.

As a trained operative, Smirnov accepted the responsibilities he had to his comrades. He needed to save Kipling from the barrage of automatic gunfire, and at the same time, lay down a protective shield to allow Lopez and company time to escape.

With these two requirements utmost in his mind, Smirnov did two things concurrently. As he lunged at Kipling, knocking her off her feet, he reached behind his back to remove the Glock 23 with its thirteen-round clip. He immediately bounded to his feet, facing the direction he thought fire was coming from.

Aided by the lights from the house, he spotted Erickson crouched down behind what looked to be a bipod. Owing to the limitations of a handgun at that distance, Smirnov knew that he had scant chance of hitting anything. Nevertheless, mentally adjusting for the drop-off for that distance and the slight breeze coming from the right, he let fly a half-dozen rounds.

Whether accurate or not, Smirnov's fusillade had its intended effect. Erickson took off, running toward the rear of the house. At the same time, Smirnov was pleased to hear the helicopter fading into the distance, hopefully escaping without serious damage.

Closer to home, Kipling wasn't any too happy. "What the fuck? Did you really have to hit me like an NFL linebacker?"

"You're welcome, Linda." A pause. "What's an NFL linebacker?"

———————◆◆◆———————

Seconds later, Kipling responded to the ring of her cell. It was Lopez. "Please tell me you two are okay."

"We're fine, Hector. What's the condition of your sixty?"

"Major Hammer seems to think that nothing vital's been hit. We're hauling ass back to D.C. After I hang up from you, I'm calling the hospital to let them know we're coming."

Lopez's words suddenly slowed. "Hey, listen, Linda. Can I assume that it was Erickson doing the shooting?"

"Correct. I got a visual."

"You know what that might mean, don't you? Captain Smith just told me that he's never lost one of his own."

Kipling did know and was getting more upset by the moment. Erickson's rap sheet from just the past twelve hours alone was damn impressive. It now included the possibility that she had killed Sergeant Jimenez.

"I do, Hector. And it also means something else! Whether or not there's a nuclear holocaust in our future, I'm going to take down this bitch if it's the last thing I do in this lifetime."

# ～ 53 ～

## IF I SHOULD DIE BEFORE I WAKE...

*White House Situation Room*
*1600 Pennsylvania Avenue NW, Washington, D.C.*
*38° 53' 51"N Latitude, 77° 02' 15.4"W Longitude*
*Sunday, April 1, 2018, 4:13 AM (EDT)*

Accompanied by her bodyguards, CIA Director McFadden burst into the Situation Room. Secretary of Defense Jim Robinson was laying out the realities of the moment to a group of ashen-faced men and women: *specifically*, that they couldn't wait much longer to fire off the nation's ICBMs. A large video display depicted the incoming Russian missiles, having just overflown Canada's northern reaches.

All heads turned in McFadden's direction. Everyone in the room, save for one high-level official in the Executive Branch, acknowledged that the smartest person within the upper reaches of the U.S. government had just walked in. Most had interacted with her during her first year on the job and recognized her abilities.

McFadden was on a mission. "Ladies and gentlemen, we have ten minutes at most before we and Planet Earth are FUCKED! I have just learned how to make that NOT happen, but it requires precise actions. Can ANYONE here put me in immediate contact with Barack Obama? And I mean NOW!"

"I *can*, ma'am." A voice came from the back.

"What's your name?"

"Major Frederick Wilkinson, ma'am."

"Then do it, Major Wilkinson!"

In the seconds that ticked by, McFadden described the nuclear missile debacle created by one Kathy Erickson. Help was at hand, she told them, in a secret project called Athena, but before the Russians would commit to destroying their ICBMs, they insisted on the U.S. doing so first.

The NSA staffer dashed to the podium and handed her a cordless phone.

"Mr. President. My name is Alexandria Jane McFadden, Director of the CIA. As you know, we have a situation. I need to ask you two questions, and I need you to answer quickly."

Ex-president Obama's reply was measured, calm, and reassuring. "I understand."

"Can you confirm that in the year 2010, you and President Medvedev put into operation a secret project called Athena? And that it had a secret code?"

"Yes, Ma'am," he said.

McFadden willed herself to breathe. Eight seconds later, Obama confirmed both Athena's existence and the numerical code.

McFadden knew exactly what she needed to do. With everyone now staring at her as if she had become the second messiah, she yelled out again.

"Major Wilkinson!" As she rushed down the aisle toward him, she simultaneously reached into her pocket.

"Yes, ma'am!" he said as they met up.

"Major Wilkinson, I need you to dial this number," she said as she handed him a strip of paper. "This is the direct line to an official in the Russian government, Oleg Popov."

"Yes, ma'am," Wilkinson replied.

With that accomplished, McFadden made the announcement that was necessary to make this all work. "Mr. President, please! I need you to launch our entire arsenal of land-based ICBMs. Not in a minute! Not in thirty seconds! I mean NOW!"

———————◆—————

*National Defense Management Center*
*Moscow, Russian Federation*
*55° 43' 40"N Latitude, 37° 35' 23"E Longitude*
*Sunday, April 1, 2018, 11:13 PM (MSK)*

Oleg Popov stared at his cell, making sure it was receiving a signal. *Why is it not ringing?* He and everyone else in the auditorium, including President Vladimir Putin, understood the surreal position they found themselves in. The earlier bogus visual display of incoming missiles that had convinced them of their imminent demise was replaced by Russian missiles headed in the opposite direction.

Since that reprieve, Popov had given Putin the expanded summary of how this diabolical situation had come about, including the entire Viktoriya saga, as well as his association with an American agent named Silverstein. He also explained that one of his agents, Dmitri Smirnov, currently in America, had helped chase Viktoriya down with help from another CIA spy named Kipling.

Fully accepting the possibility that what he was saying might be the final nail in his coffin, Popov also admitted to Putin that he had been complicit in the development of Project Athena. With the consummate poker face of any seasoned espionage agent, Putin did not indicate either acceptance or displeasure.

To Popov's surprise, Putin excused himself and left the room. "I'll be back," he told Popov.

The audience remained in a suspicious and paranoid state of mind. The reason was obvious. Each was aware that it would be only minutes before the Americans sent their own ICBMs flying, this time for real. The rumor that there might be a way to disable the missiles—on both sides—led to quiet rumblings that moved through the auditorium like a wave at a sporting event.

At the center of their concern lay the inalterable fact that there was little time to play with. Popov had earlier communicated to Silverstein Putin's demand that Russia would not neutralize its missiles unless America did the same. According to computer projections, Russian missiles were eight minutes away from touchdown. *Why were the Americans holding back? If the launch of the outgoing American missiles left no time for Putin to call off his, both countries would be screwed. Or, might Putin roll the dice and neutralize the Russian missiles at the last second and hope that the Americans did the same?*

———————◆◆◆———————

*Somewhere in the vicinity of Martinsburg, West Virginia*
*at 9500 feet altitude*
*39° 27' 22"N Latitude, 77° 57' 50"W Longitude*
*Sunday, April 1, 2018, 4:15 AM (EDT)*

Once in the air, realizing that they'd averted serious damage to the helicopter, Lopez gave his full attention to Silverstein. Bright lights inside the chopper gave him his first clear view of the damage. Blood continued to ooze from his upper back, but his left thigh was worse, the fabric of his pants below the wound soaked with blood.

After some observation, Lopez came to realize that Silverstein was not unconscious. He was trying to talk. Thinking that it might help, Lopez yelled encouragement into Silverstein's ear, above the racket of the helicopter's engine and whirling blades.

Before long, Lopez looked up to see Captain Smith, the copilot, coming back to assist, accompanied by a small bag. "Can I help? Back in my civilian life in Cleveland, I was an EMT."

"Please!"

Smith removed a penlight from his bag and conducted a cursory physical exam. He then forced open one of Silverstein's eyes and shined the light inward.

"What's that tell you?" asked Lopez.

Smith cupped his hands and yelled. "His pupil constricted when I shined the light. That's good. It means that his brain is still functioning."

Smith then took out a cuff, wrapped it around Silverstein's right arm, and pumped up the pressure bulb. "His blood pressure's way down."

"How bad is that?"

"It's not good. Any loss beyond one-third of a body's blood supply is extremely serious. Right now, he has all the symptoms of hemorrhagic shock, which means that his blood isn't carrying enough oxygen to his organs."

"Anything we can do?"

"We need to stop any further bleeding. The first thing is to redo this tourniquet on this leg. Second, replace the bandages and apply pressure to that back wound."

Smith removed from his kit what looked like a one-inch rubber band to replace the belt they had used in the house. He wrapped it around Silverstein's thigh, cinching it tightly above the leg wound. "Listen, I need to get back. Can you handle the bandages?"

"Of course. I'm supposed to let up on the tourniquet every fifteen minutes or so, right?"

Smith shook his head vigorously. "No! We learned during Iraq not to do that. We lost too many soldiers because we let the bleeding restart. Besides, we'll be there soon."

Smith excused himself and returned to the cockpit. Lopez rolled Silverstein onto his side and proceeded to replace the bandages, pleased to see less bleeding from his thigh.

With that done, Lopez steeled himself and made the call. Fearing the imminent wrath of Dr. Mylene Manchester, he tried to remain calm while explaining to her that her patient, from only hours earlier, was close to death from loss of blood. He inquired if she might be available to assist him in another twenty minutes or so.

Knowing what was coming, Lopez grabbed hold of a nearby tie-down on the floor and braced himself.

"Lopez, I swear to God that the first chance I get, I'm going to kill you! And I want you to know, right now, that it will be a horrible, *horrible* death. Do you understand me, Lopez?"

"Yes, ma'am."

---

*Berkeley Springs, West Virginia*
*39° 35' 58"N Latitude, 78° 15' 50"W*
*Sunday, April 1, 2018, 4:15 AM (EDT)*

Kathy Ann Erickson couldn't believe that she had taken a bullet from some peashooter twit of a handgun from fully one hundred and fifty feet distant. She hadn't felt anything until she stepped inside her house from the rear door; her mind had done its job of ignoring the pain. The bullet had blown right through her right shoulder, directly above the collarbone. She stuffed the wound with bandages, taped them all down, and changed shirts.

Erickson had decided to come out firing for two reasons. First, she knew that she had finally accomplished what she had set out to do. Second, however, for her to have any chance of escaping her compound and heading south, it was to her advantage to reduce the number of adversaries, which she had counted as six men and one woman. Of course, she had cleverly reduced that number by one: The sergeant lying on the floor had bled out big time and was no longer a concern.

It wasn't until she had begun firing her AK-47 that she realized that preventing the helicopter from leaving was counterproductive to her goal. That said, no harm done. The chopper *had* gotten away. According to her logic, that left behind a minimum of one person, up to a maximum of four, assuming that it took at least two to fly the helicopter. Knowing that she had enough armament and ammunition to outfit a squad of soldiers, Erickson wasn't worried.

Having reset all outdoor sensors, Erickson knew she'd have ample warning if someone approached the house. In the meantime, she'd return to her TV. It wouldn't be much longer before the Russian ICBMs arrived. The Americans would have no choice but to retaliate.

———————————

*Sunday, April 1, 2018, 4:15 AM (EDT)*

From their positions, prone on the grass, not far from where the helicopter had taken off, Kipling and Smirnov watched all outdoor lighting surrounding the house go dark, leaving only the moon for illumination. That came and went as scattered clouds passed overhead. They understood that their assault on the house best coincided with the movement of those clouds.

Dmitri stated what Kipling was thinking. "Poor Sergeant Jimenez. I fear for his life."

"She somehow got loose from the shoelaces. The fact that she shot you earlier, almost as fast as you identified yourself, tells me that she'll do whatever it takes to survive."

After a moment, Kipling continued, as she thought about her own mortality. She could see his face in the moonlight. "Dmitri, what do you think our chances are?"

"We both heard what Victor said, that this Athena project that Obama and Medvedev agreed to may still save us." Smirnov's voice changed tone. "With that in mind, I say we wait a bit before we attack. If we're all dead, what difference will it make? No?"

"I agree." Kipling raised herself slightly above the ground and stared into Smirnov's eyes. *He might reject me,* she knew.

The emotion of the moment forced her to clear her throat. "Dmitri. Until all of this is decided, would you mind holding me in your arms? Right now, if I'm going to die, that's where I think I'd like to be when it happens."

# – 54 –

## CALL 911

*National Defense Management Center*
*Moscow, Russian Federation*
*55° 43' 40"N Latitude, 37° 35' 23"E Longitude*
*Sunday, April 1, 2018, 11:15 AM (MSK)*

*Ring, dammit! Ring!* Popov begged his cell phone. And to his relief, it did! His concentration consumed by the call, he ignored the collective gasp from everyone else in the auditorium. He had assumed that he would be listening to the voice of either Victor Silverstein or Hector Lopez. Instead, the caller identified herself as Alexandria McFadden, director of America's Central Intelligence Agency.

"You aren't who I expected, Director McFadden," Popov said honestly.

"Sorry about that. I'm all you've got. I'm here with President Trump and other security personnel."

Popov checked his watch yet again, and his pulse continued to elevate. "Why haven't you launched your missiles, ma'am?"

"We have! Thirty seconds ago. You should be picking up their heat signatures by now."

Popov realized that the earlier reaction inside the room had been from their sudden appearance. He stared up at the screen and confirmed what McFadden said. The humongous video display had switched to split-screen to show Russian and American missiles separately.

*Thank God!* "I see them. You need to activate Project Athena NOW! Do you know the code? We don't have much time."

"Yes." McFadden elaborated. "Victor Silverstein told Hector Lopez that we can trust you. Is that so?"

"Ma'am—and with all due respect—there's no time left for pleasantries! Yes, goddammit, you can trust me! Neutralize your damned missiles!"

"Sir! Please stay on the line!" McFadden replied.

------◆-◆-◆------

*White House Situation Room*
*1600 Pennsylvania Avenue NW, Washington, D.C.*
*38° 53' 51"N Latitude, 77° 02' 15.4"W Longitude*
*Sunday, April 1, 2018, 4:18 AM (EDT)*

The procedure had been more complicated and took longer than McFadden had expected, but the nation's force of land-based ICBMs was finally in the air. The video screen showed hundreds of digital arrows, red ones progressing south across Canada and blue ones heading north, having just crossed the northern boundary of the continental United States. At that moment, both sets were intersecting each other's path.

McFadden knew that haste was essential. "President Trump, I need you to activate Athena to neutralize all outgoing U.S. missiles. The Russians have agreed to do the same. Please! NOW, Mr. President."

"What if..." Trump began.

McFadden remained calm. She had read secret CIA analyses of President Trump's mental status. While he claimed to possess high intelligence, which was probably so the analysts admitted, he appeared to have one glaring weakness—a remarkably short attention span. Consequently, his thinking process was, at best, two dimensional, lacking the ability to process large quantities of disparate data in complex situations.

In terms of human capabilities, IQ wasn't everything, McFadden knew. Many factors contributed to overall intelligence. Common sense played a role. In Trump's case, specialists also deduced that his personal feeling of superiority, together with a background in which intimidation and deception had given him success in the business world, made him into the controversial, charismatic individual that Americans had elected President.

McFadden knew she had to act fast. Over the years, she'd been told that she had an unusual ability, to mesmerize people with whom she had contact. *If there's ever a time to take advantage of that ability, it's now, Alexandria.*

She made her case using simple words, mostly those with one syllable. "Mr. President, there is no time! Do you see the Russian missiles on that screen?" She pointed. "If they are not deactivated, in five minutes we will all be dead. And for the Russians to deactivate their missiles, they insist we deactivate our first. SIR! PLEASE give me your approval!!"

"Do what you have to do, Director," Trump said. Her message had gotten through.

With that authority given, McFadden turned her head in the direction of the Colonel holding the nuclear football. "Colonel, please enter a sequence of ten zeroes into the digital keyboard. That entry will trigger software that will deactivate each of our missiles. Once that happens, each missile will broadcast a signal on international emergency radio frequency, 16.23 megacycles, confirming to the Russians and us that the missile has been rendered inert."

McFadden put the phone to her ear. "Mr. Popov! Did you hear all that?"

*National Defense Management Center*
*Moscow, Russian Federation*
*55° 43' 40"N Latitude, 37° 35' 23"E Longitude*
*Sunday, April 1, 2018, 11:23 PM (MSK)*

Even though the auditorium was a comfortable twenty-one degrees Celsius, Oleg Popov was dripping with sweat. When he heard over the phone that the Americans were finally implementing Athena, he leaped into the air. "President Trump has authorized the destruction of America's ICBMs," he yelled out to the entire audience.

As he did so, all eyes turned toward the split-screen, to the side representing the American ICBMs. As they watched, the arrows colored blue began transitioning to white, signifying that the neutralization procedure was working. In less than thirty seconds, all three hundred and eighty-five missiles had gone non-nuclear. Gasps of relief careened against the curtain of doom that had existed only minutes earlier.

———◆◆◆———

*White House Situation Room*
*1600 Pennsylvania Avenue NW, Washington, D.C.*
*38° 53' 51"N Latitude, 77° 02' 15.4"W Longitude*
*Sunday, April 1, 2018, 4:25 AM (EDT)*

McFadden had done her part. The United States had spared Russia from a nuclear disaster. She listened over her phone to the exuberant celebration and waited for Popov to come back on the line.

"Mr. Popov," she yelled into the microphone of her smartphone. "We have only three minutes!" McFadden had never felt so powerless. Everything she had just done had evolved from a remarkable trust between two adversaries, one Victor Silverstein and one Oleg Popov. Two world powers had rested their future—and their very existence—on this two-person relationship.

———◆◆◆———

*National Defense Management Center*
*Moscow, Russian Federation*
*55° 43' 40"N Latitude, 37° 35' 23"E Longitude*
*Sunday, April 1, 2018, 11:27 AM (MSK)*

Oleg Popov heard McFadden yelling on the phone but didn't have time to talk. His job was to input ten consecutive zeroes into the Russian nuclear control system. As he walked toward their version of the nuclear football, under the control of Putin's aide, President Putin nodded his approval, stood, and motioned for Popov to continue. He, like Popov, had glanced at the display screen, which told him that only one minute and fifteen seconds remained before each of Russia's missiles created its mushroom cloud.

Popov, a large man in his own right, was halfway to the control box when two burly men, whom he recognized as two of the more hawkish members of Putin's Ministry of Defense, blocked his path.

"Get the hell out of my way!" he roared in Russian, as he made his charge between the two. To Popov's dismay, they refused, resulting in a brawl among the three of them.

Struggling to free himself from their grip, Popov was apoplectic with rage. A glance at the screen showed only fifty seconds remaining. "Help me, anyone!" he shouted. "HELP!!"

To Popov's horror, everyone within his forward range of vision appeared to be catatonic, unsure of what was happening. Or worse, refusing to take sides!

———◆◆◆———

*White House Situation Room*
*1600 Pennsylvania Avenue NW, Washington, D.C.*
*38° 53' 51"N Latitude, 77° 02' 15.4"W Longitude*
*Sunday, April 1, 2018, 4:29 AM (EDT)*

McFadden understood the futility of trying to summon Popov. There was nothing she knew that he didn't. Instead, she had the phone pressed tightly against her ear, trying to gain a sense of what was happening. Russian voices were now screaming back and forth. The two Russian language courses she had taken were of little help. What little she could make out suggested that there were two schools of thought regarding what they should do.

With the countdown approaching forty seconds, McFadden came to grips with her own mortality, that her life and the lives of millions of U.S. citizens would soon be extinguished. Missile trajectories revealed that the Great Plains, where most U.S. ICBM siloes resided, would take their strikes some five seconds before the U.S. capitol.

McFadden looked about the room. She had never witnessed anything like it before. Of the thirty-odd personnel in attendance, roughly a third were on their knees, hands folded, heads bowed, reaching out to their God of choice. Contrarily, McFadden had long since made her peace with the Almighty and was not afraid of death. Her upbringing in the Deep South, where black folks' religion had remained the mainstay of their lives for centuries, had left her immune to any fear concerning her mortality. She truly believed and accepted God's plan for her life.

And then it happened! The resonance of what sounded like two explosions reverberated through the smartphone's speakers. Total silence followed. Not knowing what was happening, McFadden's attention went back to the screen, where the countdown was down to thirty seconds.

One by one, the color of the incoming missiles began changing from red to white. *Twenty seconds!* Although the color changing was proceeding apace, almost half of the missiles were still red.

*Ten seconds!* Six missiles were still active. Worse, two of them headed toward Washington, DC.

*Zero seconds!* All lights in the room went dark, perhaps a millisecond before a terrifying explosion. If McFadden had to relate to others what she had just experienced, she would say that she didn't have the words. In the total blackness, she listened as screaming bodies flew about the room, upward, downward, and sideways through the air, often colliding with each other. McFadden was transported obliquely into the podium, her head striking the wood surface so hard that she briefly lost consciousness.

With her hearing close to nonexistent, McFadden switched to her other senses. The putrid smell and bitter taste of dust made her cough. She ran her hand along the floor, trying to assess the physical space around her. She needed to know if the entire room had collapsed and if others were still alive.

It was her other surviving sense that gave her hope when none had existed previously. *Could it be?* Toward the back of the room, the direction from which they had entered the underground facility, McFadden saw a glimmer of light appear in an area where she remembered the entry door. Before long, she also saw multiple lights dancing about the room, creating tunnels of luminosity as the beams blasted their way through the dust.

McFadden realized that what she was seeing were flashlights. Together with those lights came weak shouts. A rescue team was on the scene.

# ~ 55 ~

## FINALE

Erickson paced in front of the TV, making a point of avoiding the pool of blood and not tracking up the house. Her state of mind had gone downhill, from ecstasy to mild worry, from mild worry to outright concern and, finally, from outright concern to apoplexy. Some forty-five minutes earlier, the CNN correspondent had reported that Russian missiles were in the air. The next thing that should have happened was an American retaliation. Further, long before America's nuclear payloads landed in Russia, the first of Russia's should have exploded here.

But based on news coverage, there was no confirmation that America had responded—or that any nuclear missiles had detonated on American soil. Listening to CNN, confusion reigned.

Kipling chose not to move, wanting to enjoy every second of the warmth and smell of one Russian spy, Dmitri Smirnov. Fifteen minutes earlier, she had buried her face in his chest—partially, naively, thinking that she might avoid the expected flash of blinding light coming their way. Truth be told, she did so because that was where she wanted to be, feeling comfort in hearing his thumping heart, steady and strong. Smirnov didn't seem to mind her actions. He had pulled her closer and, at one point, kissed her on her forehead.

Alone in her cocoon of half-consciousness and security, Kipling had no desire to go anywhere. The repetition of her name brought her back to reality, back from her Camelot of wishes and dreams. "Linda. Linda." Smirnov repeated.

"Are we dead yet?" she inquired.

"I don't think so."

"Why not?"

"Maybe this Athena thing that Victor talked about actually worked. I wish we had some news about what's happening."

Kipling's consciousness returned in full. "What time is it?"

"About ten minutes after when we thought we'd be dying of radiation poisoning."

Kipling reluctantly crawled from Smirnov's embrace and checked her cell, confirming Smirnov's time report. "Maybe you're right. That means that you and I have some unfinished business."

* * *

Dmitri Smirnov had had so little experience with women in recent years that Kipling's advances—even in the guise of a pleasant humanistic experience before death—had caught him off guard, as had the mouth-to-mouth kiss she had smothered him with earlier. Maybe he should have responded more positively. In his dreams back home, he would have made a much better showing for himself. In real life, the best he could come up with was a kiss to the forehead.

*But reality is now, not in some dream.* Even if Silverstein and Popov had somehow saved Planet Earth, the female Russian who had wreaked havoc on both their countries existed within a stone's throw of their current position.

"I agree," replied Smirnov. "You want to take her alive?"

Kipling replied diplomatically, but her demeanor suggested that she had already made her decision. "She's Russian. She's yours, Dmitri. Whatever you say goes. Did Popov say anything?"

"He told me that I had complete authority."

---

Kipling understood Smirnov's dilemma. "Then I say that we shoot her in the head and be done with it. Think of the court costs you'll save the Russian judicial system," she joked. "One appeal after another. Your country will go broke."

Her last statement was enough to break the tension. "Don't you know anything about Russia?" he asked. "I don't think that'll be a problem."

Kipling turned serious. "We could try to take her alive. But from what we already know of this woman, the chances of that happening are between slim and none. And slim has already left town."

"Huh?" Smirnov asked. "Who's Slim?"

---

Erickson had no idea what had gone wrong with the missile launches. But before long, her instinct for self-preservation kicked in. With everything that had happened, she knew she would soon become Public Enemy Number One. Her original plan to head south seemed to be her best choice. She still had contacts in Mexico.

She walked to the edge of the living room window and stared out. Between one and four people were out there waiting for her, and she needed to take them out—and soon, before that helicopter returned with reinforcements. *On the other hand, is that necessary?* Erickson returned to the kitchen and looked out the back window.

Her Jeep rental sat where she had left it. With that observation, her plan became apparent—and more straightforward.

In the bedroom, her suitcase remained open on the bed. To its contents, she stuffed the additional cash she had kept at the cabin.

Erickson gave further thought to an escape plan, damning her decision not to build an access road to the rear of the property. She continued to worry about how many people waited outside. Unexpectedly, an answer presented itself when she remembered what had happened after she had regained consciousness. Before the helicopter arrived and more men poured into the house, there had been only one male and one female. They had probably come together. Likely as not, that meant that only one vehicle blocked her access to the highway. The forest wasn't so dense that her four-wheel-drive Jeep couldn't maneuver around a parked car.

With the decision made to run for it, Erickson reviewed her offensive capabilities. She grabbed an AK-47 with one full standard thirty-round clip attached, along with a spare. She added two hand grenades and a large folding knife to the mix, stowing them all in a large cloth bag.

Erickson carried her suitcase and bag to the back door. Before leaving, she'd listen to the TV one more time, desperately searching for confirmation that her meticulous preparations had not been in vain. CNN was beginning to report various explosions around the Capitol and in a few Midwest states. But none of those descriptions sounded anything like a nuclear blast.

---

Smirnov understood Kipling's drive for justice, especially if Erickson had done anything to Jimenez.

Kipling's words slowed. "You know, don't you? I'm assuming that Sergeant Jimenez is still alive, that Erickson has some scrap of humanity remaining for an innocent bystander. I'm picturing him tied up in the corner of the living room."

"I hope that too, Linda."

"Okay, let's take stock. I still have all thirteen rounds for my Glock. How many did you waste trying to hit Erickson from over here?" she motioned.

Smirnov grimaced. "Waste? Waste? You're forgetting that I saved your life." He took out his clip and counted. "I have seven rounds left. Maybe we should switch."

Kipling ignored his request.

Smirnov thought ahead. "Trouble is, as soon as we get close to the house, the sensor lights will give us away. From what we've seen so far, we'll be outgunned. I wish we knew more about what's going on inside that house."

Kipling smiled. "You've forgotten, haven't you?"

"Forgotten what?"

"Stay right here. Don't move. I promise I'll be right back."

Crouched over, Kipling ran back toward the house. Smirnov was about to follow when she dropped to the ground, grabbed something, and ran back.

"You've already forgotten about Betsy, haven't you?" she teased.

"Of course not," Smirnov replied with less than total honesty. With everything that had happened since Erickson's interrogation, he *had* forgotten.

"After Betsy hit Erickson with the Propofol, I noticed a high shelf near the television, and that's where I parked her. She's dormant. Unless Erickson happened to look up and spot her, she should still be there."

Kipling opened the laptop. "Betsy can work in a silent mode, where her cameras and microphone still function."

With Betsy's systems ramping up, the first thing Smirnov noticed was sound. "That's probably the television."

Kipling went to work, jockeying the joystick for the left-most camera. Sure enough, on the first pivot, the television came into view. "That's the broadcast network, CNN. I wouldn't mind listening to that myself."

"Let's find Erickson! No?" Smirnov was anxious.

345

At once, Erickson came into view, sitting, facing the TV. It didn't take much more manipulation of the right-hand camera before they found what they had been hoping never to see.

Smirnov caught his breath. *Who would do that? And then be able to sit only feet from the body as if nothing had happened?*

Kipling responded differently. She carefully placed the laptop on the moist ground, turned to face opposite from Smirnov, and threw up!

Smirnov reprogrammed his thinking. "Remember our earlier discussion that we take her alive?" he asked. "Forget that we ever had that conversation."

They returned to watching Erickson. It wasn't long before they realized that she was up to something. She was planning to leave the house!

"I'm going over to the road to set up an ambush," said Smirnov, as he jumped to his feet.

Kipling grabbed his ankle. "Hold up for a second, Dmitri."

------◆◆◆------

Having checked the TV yet again and learning nothing more, Erickson revisited her escape plan, pacing about the cottage, wondering if she had forgotten anything. In preparation for her departure, she disabled all exterior sensors, especially those that triggered lights. No point in tripping over one's own tripwire.

Erickson approached the rear door and then turned back to look one more time. She was about to leave when she stopped mid-step. A fleeting memory returned. *Back before they tied me to a chair, I came face to face with a flying insect.* She recalled the painful sting as the dart struck her neck.

It didn't take Erickson long to scan the living room and locate what she now knew to be a drone. "You son-of-a-bitch!" she yelled.

At which point, she returned to the bedroom to retrieve one weapon she had chosen to leave behind.

———◦◆◦———

"Uh-oh!!" Kipling exclaimed. "She found Betsy!"

Until then, they had been watching Erickson dart about the house. A suitcase sitting near the back door reinforced their conclusion that she was leaving. Next to the suitcase was a large cloth bag that seemed to be on the heavy side.

Both spies understood that Betsy's existence was in danger. "Do something!" he demanded. "Betsy needs to hide." Kipling was impressed by Smirnov's concern for a flying robot.

Kipling manipulated Betsy's controls with a vengeance. With all systems, mechanical, electronic, and sensory, activated, Betsy's motors revved up, and she shot out into the open. Kipling desperately scanned all four video monitors, searching for somewhere to either escape or to hide. With nothing obvious, she flew Betsy to a location on the floor, out of sight, behind the sofa.

Kipling maxed out the sensitivity on all onboard microphones, trying to discern the direction of Erickson's movement, ready to transition Betsy into evasive combat mode to save her hide.

But, alas, Kipling's mind and fingers could not react quickly enough. Before Betsy's video picked up what appeared to be the barrel of a twelve-gauge shotgun had come the audio. "There you are, you little bastard!"

Betsy's video feeds turned blank. Her microphones, having been turned into electronic waste, proved unnecessary. Two blasts from a double-barreled shotgun were easy enough to identify from outside the house. Less identifiable was what Kipling and Smirnov heard a fraction of a second later.

———◦◆◦———

"Damn it all to hell," Erickson screamed in agony, nearly passing out from the pain ricocheting its way through her upper torso. In the frenzy of killing the drone, she had forgotten about the shoulder wound she had sustained while exchanging gunfire outside. If she had to do it over again, she vowed to reconsider the wisdom of pressing a twelve-gauge shotgun firmly against an open wound.

Teeth clenched, waiting for the pain to subside, Erickson's thoughts returned to the drone. It would have been expedient to imagine that the mechanical device she had just demolished was an entity unto itself. But she knew better. Someone outside the house was manipulating the controls. How else did it know to hide?

Erickson cautioned herself not to let emotion outpace reason. After all, her life was on the line. Practicalities first! *I need to know if there's a vehicle parked on the road, blocking my exit.* For still a third time, she ran back to her weapons stash, this time choosing a pair of infrared binoculars she had purchased to eavesdrop on nocturnal visits by deer and bears. If she could see the couple's vehicle, she'd know best where to enter the dirt road to return to the highway.

Erickson ran out the back door and to the right, to the far end of the house. There she discovered that she was lined up perfectly with the dirt road. It wasn't long before her glasses pinpointed a car sitting beyond the clearing, facing her. Infrared radiation from the hot engine stood out like a beacon.

It was time to vamoose. Erickson loaded the Jeep, the AK-47 within reach on the passenger seat, and the two hand grenades, each in its own cup holder. The folding knife she stuffed into her pants.

———◆———

In the quiet night air, there was nowhere for the sound of a gasoline engine to hide. Kipling and Smirnov snapped to their feet and made a run for two trees that bracketed the dirt road. The earlier moonlight that had worked in their favor was now a disadvantage. They would have preferred to be invisible.

To augment Smirnov's supply, Kipling decided to play fair and gave him three shells from her own thirteen-shot magazine. Now they each had ten.

———◆◆◆———

Erickson knew the terrain and vegetation surrounding her home. Except for one tree stump, the cleared area could be driven safely without damage to a vehicle. Importantly, she was certain that there was room to pass by on either side of the vehicle blocking the road.

Erickson worked the odds, appreciating another critical fact. Whoever had fired at her from the direction of the helicopter had nothing more than a handgun. Since her house was beyond handgun range, she decided to make a strategic maneuver to draw out her pursuers.

Erickson drove slowly toward the right rear of her house, exited its protection, and turned her vehicle to face the road that lay squarely ahead. She stared through the windshield, straining to sense motion, but saw nothing out of the ordinary in the moonlit landscape.

In a daring move, Erickson killed the engine, opened her door, and stepped into the open. A game of cat and mouse was in the offing. She'd like nothing better than for her adversaries to start shooting and give away their position.

———◆◆◆———

With the moon fully ablaze and few clouds, Smirnov had earlier made out Kipling's form crouching behind the tree to his left. She had no doubt also stolen a glimpse of the now silent vehicle sitting some one hundred and fifty feet away. Like him, she would question Erickson's strategy, standing motionless beside the driver's door.

Now was the time to be patient, thought Smirnov. They had the upper hand. *Let her come to us. That is the best option, no doubt!* Besides, having only twenty rounds between them was nothing to feel confident about.

When he looked over a second time, Kipling was gone. No, *not* gone! She was standing on the opposite side of the tree, out in the open, in a firing stance! To Smirnov's surprise, her Glock let loose a single round. A resounding ping followed, as the bullet struck the Jeep.

---

Erickson's plan was working. One less round from what appeared to be a woman. Abruptly, Erickson remembered the incident inside the house and the name, Linda Kipling. Erickson seethed with contempt yet again. *Who is this bitch witch of a woman? Is she a government agent? And then to pull off the improbable: to somehow match my movements, step by step, to arrive in an isolated field in West Virginia in the middle of the night?* Although this woman spoke American English, Erickson recognized that her partner was a Russian national, judging by his facility with the language.

With hate and revenge trumping other emotions, Erickson knew that she couldn't count on herself to react rationally. She grabbed the AK-47, ran to the front of her Jeep, and opened fire. She returned to her vehicle, replaced the spent clip, started the engine, and waited, considering her next course of action.

---

Although Kipling knew that her partner would not have approved of what she had done, she couldn't help but make it known that there'd be repercussions for Erickson's actions, most recently the brutal slaying of Sergeant Jimenez. This on top of everything else.

Kipling made it back to her tree before the salvo broke out. The melee of bullets whizzing by was frightening at best and terrifying at worst. When the shooting stopped, and Kipling heard the engine start, she chose to attack one more time.

---

Smirnov had no choice other than to try to fit into Kipling's on-the-fly operation. He had watched as she ran for cover from the automatic gunfire. As each of them outlasted the fusillade of terror, they looked across at each other. Yet again, Kipling walked into the open.

———◆◆◆———

Erickson acknowledged a worthy opponent. This time, firearm raised in the air—not unlike what one would expect from an eighteenth-century duel—Kipling walked smartly into the lot and stopped. She lowered her weapon and aimed.

Perfect, thought Erickson. *I'd much prefer to run you over anyway.*

Then, something happened that Erickson had least expected. As if someone had flipped the switch, a thick layer of clouds turned the lightly glowing scene into total darkness.

———◆◆◆———

Trained as a meteorologist, Kipling often found herself staring at the clouds. As she had earlier run for the trees, she continued to watch a dark formation moving in from the west. Her timing of that movement had been the reason for her initial foray into the field to taunt Erickson. Once Erickson's shooting ended, Kipling calculated that it would be less than thirty seconds before the main event arrived. As anticipated, winds picked up, and the first drops of rain started to fall.

Kipling knew that her accuracy at that distance was next to nil. Nonetheless, she aligned her sights along the barrel, made a mental calculation of the bullet's drop, and began to fire at the very moment of diminishing light. Figuring that a barrage of bullets had some chance of hitting something, she fired off all remaining nine rounds and then retreated to her tree, groping her way forward as she got closer.

————◆◆◆————

The incoming rounds of small arms fire shattered the windshield glass on the Jeep. Erickson opened her door and slid to the ground for protection.

Erickson needed to make a choice. Stay and fight or use this opportunity to make a run for it. The engine was still running, and although it was pitch-black, she figured that she still had the advantage. She knew the layout of the clearing and her precise position within it. If necessary, she could wait until the last second to turn on her headlights. She'd ride the odds and assume that at least one headlight had survived Kipling's fire.

Before gunning the engine and taking off, she switched the transmission into four-wheel drive, at the same time making sure that her AK-47 was ready with its second clip.

————◆◆◆————

Smirnov was in the literal dark, as were the other two players in this game of death. He could hear the idling engine and imagined, in his mind's eye, Erickson's position within the clearing. That didn't last long. The engine's speed accelerated, the source of the sound now moving. First, he sensed motion to his left, then back to the right. Then left, then right, twice more. Before long, the wind picked up, the heavens opened, and water saturated the air. Occasional lightning strikes became more intense. One that was particularly brilliant flashed the clearing with light, pinpointing Erickson's vehicle pointed directly toward him and the road.

Smirnov figured that Erickson's current opportunity to escape was as good as she'd get. Protected by the wall of darkness, he cautiously ventured a few feet into the clearing before muzzle flashes from a second round of automatic fire drove him back. *Trying to soften us up, Viktoriya, are you?*

That was exactly what Erickson was doing because within seconds, the Jeep's engine raced again, and he heard the vehicle speeding toward him. In the final moment, a single headlight appeared as the vehicle roared by to his left, spraying mud that hit him from the waist down.

Smirnov was ready. As Erickson tore by, he began firing. Concluding that he had little chance of hitting the driver, he concentrated instead on disabling the car. As he shot, he counted the rounds and stopped at nine.

Erickson swerved left to go around the Lincoln and, for a moment, got stuck in the thick brush. With the engine at full throttle and four wheels spinning, she made it through to the other side. She now had clear sailing to the highway.

Behind him, Smirnov heard Kipling screaming. "Get in the car, Dmitri! Get in the car!"

———————— ◆ ◆ ◆ ————————

Between lightning flashes, Kipling had kept track of Erickson's position. Although the second round of gunfire caught her by surprise, the trees were once again her protector. When she saw the car's single headlight, and it became clear that Erickson was making her escape, Kipling ran at full tilt toward the action.

Kipling jumped into the Lincoln an eyelid's blink ahead of Smirnov. With the wireless remote still in her pocket, the engine fired up instantly when she pressed the ignition button.

"Dmitri!" she yelled. "I need you to turn around and follow her taillights. We need to know which way she turns at the highway."

Smirnov did as he was told. "She's getting away. I can barely see her."

"Not for long, Dmitri. Not for long. Put on your seatbelt!"

———————— ◆ ◆ ◆ ————————

Smirnov lost sight of Erickson's vehicle. Not only had Erickson increased their separation, but the torrent of rain seriously diminished visibility.

He watched as Kipling worked the gears. Jamming the car into reverse, she floored the gas pedal. After a moment or two, as the tires gained traction, the force from the backward movement threw Smirnov forward against the dash. Skillfully, Kipling controlled the fishtailing in their backward movement.

"Did I or did I not tell you to put on your seatbelt?"

Smirnov couldn't help but sneak a peek at the instrument panel. Within ten seconds, their speed had shot to thirty-five miles per hour—*backward*!

Kipling repeated herself. "Look, Dmitri! Goddammit! Which way is she turning?"

"I see her! I can see her now! For some reason, she's slowed down. At the end of the road, she's turning to her right!"

"Get ready! I'm going to execute a ninety-degree drift."

"A ninety-degree what…"

If Smirnov had ever been as scared inside a motor vehicle, he couldn't remember when. One hundred feet from the highway entrance, Kipling hit the brakes while simultaneously jerking the steering wheel hard right. In a geyser of flying mud, the vehicle slid sideways to the road, pointed in the proper direction.

Kipling jammed the transmission into Drive and accelerated hard in Erickson's direction. Almost immediately, she backed off, rolling to a stop.

Both tried to make out what they saw through the driving rain, with windshield wipers flapping at high speed. "That's her," Smirnov said. "Why has she stopped?"

"She's moving again," noted Kipling. "I'll get closer."

———◆———

Kipling recognized that they had been fortunate that all of this was happening late at night. Accidentally killing an innocent motorist when they slid sideways onto the highway had been an obvious risk. Kipling crept up slowly on their adversary, coming within two hundred feet, hand on the gear shift, ready to reverse direction should Erickson again emerge with her AK-47.

"What do you think she's up to?" Smirnov wondered. "If she had any ammunition left, she would use it now. No?"

With that comment, the chase began anew, with Erickson accelerating slowly and Kipling reducing the gap to one hundred feet.

Kipling prepared for a repeat of Erickson's earlier performance with her automatic weapon. Instead, Erickson caught them by surprise when they saw her toss something back toward them from the driver's window.

"Grenade!!" yelled Smirnov.

Kipling didn't have to be told twice. She jammed on the brakes, rammed the transmission into reverse, and floored it. And none too soon! The din from the explosion itself complemented the cacophony of sounds produced by shards from the fragmentation grenade as it struck the Lincoln, fortunately bypassing both headlights.

"Can you fucking believe this?" Kipling yelled as she pounded her fists on the steering wheel.

Smirnov took a more analytical approach to their dilemma. "I know what's going on."

"What? What is it that's going on?"

"Take a closer look. See how the left side of the car is leaning. I bet you I hit her left rear tire. I mostly aimed for the tires. Otherwise, she would be way ahead of us. She's riding on the rim."

Until then, only the taillights identified the rear of Erickson's Jeep. That changed suddenly! "She's putting it in gear," said Kipling, as she saw brake lights adding to the mix. "She's on the move again."

What Kipling said was true, but not in the way she had expected. Following the brake lights came the back-up lights.

Smirnov braced himself. "Here she comes!!" he yelled.

Erickson caught them both by surprise. Although Kipling replicated Erickson's shift sequence, it was not quite fast enough. Erickson's Jeep came barreling toward them, hitting the Lincoln squarely. As scary and loud as was the crash created by one vehicle ramming into another at some twenty miles per hour, another explosion piggy-backed on the first—the activation of both forward airbags with their explosive charge. Even with both of Kipling's feet standing on the brake, Erickson's vehicle pushed them backward.

"Linda, are you okay?" Smirnov asked as he pushed aside the guts of the apparatus that had exploded in front of him. He and Kipling began to cough from what smelled like talcum powder.

Kipling's reply was more controlled than Smirnov's but sounded like she was speaking through clenched teeth. "I'm fine, Dmitri! I'm just fine!" As she said the words, the engine died, and the interior dash lights went out.

To add more drama to the situation, it felt as if their vehicle was moving forward. "Our bumpers must have locked up," Smirnov said.

As Erickson finally jerked away, Kipling engaged the starter, trying frantically to energize their mangled vehicle. "Turn over, you son-of-a-bitch," she ordered. It soon became apparent that it wasn't going to happen.

Smirnov was now monitoring Erickson's forward progress by following her sole functioning headlight. Her taillights had fallen victim to the collision.

Realizing that there was little advantage in staying where they were, Smirnov gave the order. "Linda, I think it is time to abandon ship."

Kipling, who had the better vantage point from which to judge the movement of Erickson's vehicle, expressed alarm. "Too late, Dmitri. Hold on! Here she comes again!"

Once more, the Jeep crashed into the Lincoln. Having learned from the first collision the proper way to brace themselves, they were better prepared this time. However, Smirnov noticed that the windshield and side windows were now gone, having disintegrated into thousands of glass shards that covered their torsos. Modern engineering had kept the passenger cabin intact, even though the engine compartment had shortened considerably, probably by half.

Yet again, Erickson pulled away.

"Will your door open?" Kipling asked. "Mine won't budge."

Smirnov pulled the handle and forced his legs and butt to the side. To his relief, the door gave way, spilling him onto the berm. He reached across the seats to drag Kipling outside with him.

All these actions happened in near-total darkness, the only available light coming from Erickson's single headlight pointed in the opposite direction. So, when Smirnov noticed Erickson walking in their direction, he hoped that he and Kipling had caught a break. Erickson was looking into near-total blackness and would have no idea they had crawled away from their car. The sound of her engine likewise camouflaged the noise of their movements.

As they hid in the darkness, Smirnov witnessed Erickson activate and throw one more hand grenade, this time through the windshield into the body of their car. As Erickson ran back toward her car, Smirnov and Kipling sprinted in the opposite direction. Whatever of value remained inside the Lincoln was reduced to salvage by Erickson's final assault.

———————•◆•———————

As they hunkered down in the driving rain behind her now-totaled rental, Kipling took stock of her physical condition—and Smirnov's.

"Are you hurt?" she asked.

"Don't think so. You?"

Content that neither of them had serious injuries, Kipling focused her attention on Erickson's vehicle, which began to drive noisily away.

"Dmitri! Soon, either Erickson or I will be dead. If I go down first, it'll be up to you."

Before Smirnov had time to react to Kipling's plan of action, she took off running. Heavy rain continued to fall. The Jeep had a two-hundred-foot lead; that gap did not appear to be widening.

As Kipling gained ground, she was continually wiping rainwater from her eyes. But as quickly as the downpour had started, it abated. More importantly, the clouds opened to reveal, once again, a full moon. There was nowhere for Erickson to hide, the entire roadway now awash in light. As Kipling approached the Jeep, she could see why it was in trouble. Smirnov had shot out both driver-side tires. The rims that were riding on the asphalt gave off a grinding, scraping sound.

Although Kipling had no more rounds for her Glock, she knew that Erickson had no way of knowing that. As she approached the driver's door, the Jeep now wholly immobile and the engine stalled, she pointed her weapon at the now-visible driver. The window was down.

"It's over, Viktoriya! It's over. Get out of the car."

To Kipling's surprise, Erickson stepped outside without drama or threat.

"Where's your Russian partner?" Erickson asked.

"You killed him with your second grenade," Kipling bluffed.

Then to Kipling's surprise, Erickson started a conversation. "I need to know something. After we saw each other at the airport in San Francisco, how did you know that I was coming here?"

Kipling saw no reason not to grant a dying woman her last wish. "On the airplane, I stuck an electronic tracker to your coat."

"And before that, how did you even know to follow me?"

"That was your uncle's doing. He's been looking for you for a long time. Your mistake was running that red-light camera in San Jose. He identified your photo."

"Just one more. Why have the nuclear missiles not exploded?"

"If we're lucky enough to have avoided World War III, it's because your President Medvedev and our President Barack Obama agreed a while back to a scheme for deactivating the missiles should there be an accident. It was a secret project called Athena."

Kipling maintained her charade with the useless gun. If this was a time for openness, why not get something in return? "Fair is fair, Viktoriya. I've answered your questions. Now answer me one. Why have you done all this? Why do you hate America so much?"

Erickson frowned and shook her head. "I don't hate America."

Kipling had not expected that reply. "It seems to me that you've been trying to start a war."

"That's true, but only as a means to an end. The American public needs to know that Russia is my enemy, not you."

"Let me restate my question then. Why do you hate Russia so?"

"Because they killed my little brother and my parents in Afghanistan."

Kipling was incredulous. "And for that, you're willing to destroy the lives of hundreds of millions of people?"

Erickson cocked her head. "Of course. For that, I'd be willing to kill the entire world. And because you stopped me, I'm now going to kill you.

*Uh-oh!* Erickson reached behind herself and unfolded what looked to be a large knife.

Kipling had not expected hand-to-hand combat. Erickson let loose a maniacal scream and closed the twelve-foot separation in no time, knocking Kipling to the ground, the Glock sent flying. Before she could react, Erickson jumped sideways to straddle her victim, pinning her to the ground, knife raised for a final assault.

Kipling grabbed frantically for Erickson's arm, trying to deflect the blade before it struck. Kipling's strategy paid off when her efforts forced the knife to miss, just inches from her left eyeball. Enraged, and now shrieking like a banshee, Erickson withdrew the blade and tried again, this time with both hands wrapped around the handle, applying double force to the downward thrust.

---

Erickson's sudden assault with a knife caught Smirnov off-guard as well. He had followed Kipling but chose to remain hidden behind

Erickson's Jeep, especially after he heard Kipling say that he was dead.

Smirnov knew that Kipling was bluffing with the gun. He had counted the shots, and she was out of ammunition. Surely, she was aware of this critical fact, he reassured himself. Was Erickson? Or did she even care?

Having listened to the ongoing conversation, Smirnov had learned nothing new. Erickson was a revengeful psychopath who lacked any sense of remorse or morality. Her options for escape were diminishing by the minute. And with Kipling's bald-faced admission that she had been the root cause of Erickson's failure, he could only imagine her intense hatred of this stranger. How long would it take before her frustration exploded into an uncontrollable rage?

It wasn't long at all! As Erickson rushed toward Kipling, Smirnov stepped into the open, dropped to one knee, raised his weapon to eye level, and aimed. Erickson had already managed one downward stab with her knife. With two hands, she was now going for the kill.

Smirnov prayed. *God! Please help me!*

As he squeezed off his final shot, he sensed all his mental and physical energy converging on the two hands holding the Glock 23.

# EPILOGUE NUMBER 1

## PUTTING ALL OF THE PIECES TOGETHER

From *The Washington Post,* Sunday, June 3, 2018

### Making sense of it all

Editorial Opinion
Jim Manheim
*The Washington Post*

**WASHINGTON**—*Somehow, ironically, beginning on April Fool's Day of this year, this nation and the world underwent a modern-day trauma that doomsayers have predicted for decades. Either because of sheer luck or divine intervention, what could have been a worldwide nuclear catastrophe did not happen. Even after two long months of scrutiny, certain details are still unknown to this reporter and the public. Government sources from the two dominant players, the United States and Russia, have been less than forthcoming in their interactions with the press. The ordinary citizen could be forgiven for thinking that they were hiding something. In case you have been in a coma for the past two months, I will summarize what has happened.*

*First, briefly, we need to close the book on another near-tragedy that presented itself as the opening act to the main event. At least in this case, the details are mostly known. It involved a disgruntled NOAA employee, Raymond Charles Brickman III, who worked for the National Satellite Operations Facility (NSOF) in Suitland, Maryland. Brickman not only murdered his boss, Steve Hancock, but also attempted to blackmail the U.S government into paying Civil War reparations to the South by threatening the destruction of critical U.S. weather satellites. Some details are sketchy. What we're told is that government operatives foiled the blackmail plot before irreparable damage could be achieved. Brickman was arraigned on federal charges last month and is awaiting trial.*

*Regarding the main event, I will now summarize what we know:*

***How did it all start?*** *Beginning on March 30, software systems controlling air traffic and hydroelectric power generation were hacked in both the United States and Russia. The air traffic control debacle led to a massive mid-air collision of two airliners over Colorado, killing hundreds. As tensions elevated between the two superpowers, each side blamed the other and denied any involvement.*

*After military escalation brought both countries to the edge of nuclear confrontation, on Sunday morning, this past April 1, Russia launched its entire fleet of land-based, nuclear-armed ICBM missiles, all targeted for the continental United States. Russia categorically denies that it did so on purpose, saying that it was an accident and that they contacted American authorities immediately.*

***If it was an accident, why did the United States respond in kind?*** *Here is where the two countries' official joint statement, although remarkable in detail, calls for speculation beyond the pale. That is because the joint statement reveals a secret that both countries, for political reasons, had chosen to hide for nearly a decade.*

*We're told that in 2010, President Barack Obama and President Dmitry Medvedev of Russia, fearing the possibility of an accidental nuclear launch, secretly agreed to install on each ICBM missile a kill switch, whereby its nuclear package could be disarmed in flight. This top-secret agreement came to be known as Project Athena. Once the Russian missiles had launched, President Putin took advantage of the situation by blackmailing the United States into launching and neutralizing its own missiles before the Russians would deactivate their own.*

*While Putin's logic is sound, believing that a one-sided denuclearization could prove suicidal to Russia, conspiracists point out that this explanation is too logical. One theory goes that Putin, knowing that his own nuclear defense capability was becoming costly and outdated, purposely authorized the launch, knowing that the subsequent destruction of all land-based ICBMs would be in Russia's favor.*

*However, not all conspiracy theories emanate from the dark web. President Trump, always on the lookout for political enemies to skewer, has stated via tweet that the Democratic Party orchestrated the debacle in an attempt to assassinate him and weaken American defenses. Remarkably, he has suggested that Hillary Clinton was behind it all and demands that she be brought before the Senate Intelligence Committee for questioning.*

***What happened to the ICBMs?*** *As most everyone now knows from continuous press coverage, even though the nuclear innards of each missile were deactivated, the track of each missile remained unaltered. All missiles continued to the same locations that each had been intended to fly. As a result, three hundred and eighty-five American and four hundred and fifteen Russian rockets rained down on unsuspecting citizens. To date, 15,285 Americans and 18,767 Russians have died, with many more injured and hospitalized. Missiles that landed within cities caused the most fatalities and damage.*

*The most significant missile strike in this country included the White House, which was completely destroyed. Fortunately, the president's wife and family had moved to a safe location.*

*President Trump, his staff, and other security personnel were monitoring the crisis from the Situation Room, a heavily fortified underground bunker located in the basement of the West Wing of the White House. President Trump and others survived unscathed, but more than half in that room sustained serious injuries.*

*Sadly, there was one fatality in the Situation Room, a rising star within the intelligence community, Dr. Alexandria Jane McFadden, the director of the CIA, who remained a hero to the end. After the explosion, Dr. McFadden took personal charge of the disaster, directing rescue personnel and attending to those with injuries. Sadly, while so engaged, she collapsed and died. An autopsy revealed a hemorrhagic stroke, commonly called a bleeding stroke, typically caused by a blow to the head.*

***What about the nuclear materials aboard the missiles?** Other than the considerable consequence of a multi-ton rocket impacting the ground at upwards of two thousand miles per hour, there is the issue of the radioactive material released upon impact. In essence, each missile, which started as a multi-million-dollar nuclear bomb delivery system, turned into a cheap dirty bomb. Accordingly, before the land is ever again safe for human use, fissile material must be cleaned up.*

*In an unusual measure of cooperation between the U.S. and Russia, negotiators came up with a unique solution to the problem. Each country volunteered to be responsible for cleaning up its own materials in the country hit. Of course, part of the enthusiasm for this action involved the fact that neither country wanted the other unearthing potential secrets regarding its weapons of mass destruction.*

*As of this date, Russian and U.S. military personnel guard and supervise each of the sites impacted by their own missiles. The irony and sheer implausibility of seeing Russian soldiers patrolling the former White House grounds is not lost on either Washington residents or tourists. Estimates for completing the entire cleanup range from two to three years.*

***Although we know a lot, we don't know it all.*** *Nowhere in the communiques and official statements from either country is there mention of who was behind the computer hackings that led to the nuclear standoff. Does that mean that neither country knows and is too embarrassed to say so? Or is there some deeper explanation that the United States and Russia choose to hide? Further, how did this accident, whereby all of Russia's missiles came to be launched at once, come to pass? That's the $64,000 question. But no one is talking.*

***So where do we go from here?*** *No matter the utter irrationality of how we got to this point within the guise of mutually assured destruction, many political leaders, learned academics, and philosophers have pointed out the fortuitous situation that we find ourselves in today.*

*Representatives from both countries appear to be taking heed, addressing what until now would have been considered unthinkable: eliminating nuclear weapons in totality. At the United Nations, negotiations have been proceeding apace, involving all world powers that possess missiles outfitted with nuclear payloads. The words of a former U.S. president were perhaps influential.*

*Once the secret of Project Athena was out, former President Barack Obama gave a national address, broadcast worldwide, recalling his meeting with Medvedev. He remembered the episode as if it were yesterday, he said. While Obama sat on a sofa, Medvedev paced back and forth, and with total, unbridled honesty, railed over the insanity of fielding a military weapon that could never be used by a rational human being. It was then that Project Athena was conceived and set into motion.*

*With clear, erudite reasoning, President Obama put the world's situation into stark perspective: "If global climate change isn't enough to destroy this home we call Planet Earth, then a full-scale nuclear exchange between the world's superpowers should do the trick."*

*This reporter prays that the world's citizenry—at this critical juncture in history—will choose wisdom and common sense over irrationality and insanity.*

# EPILOGUE NUMBER 2

## ONE REMAINING PIECE OF THE PUZZLE

*National Defense Management Center*
*Moscow, Russian Federation*
*55° 43' 40"N Latitude, 37° 35' 23"E Longitude*
*Friday, October 5, 2018, 11:05 AM (MSK)*

Outside the NDMC, Popov and Lopez shook hands and promised to stay in touch. Lopez had to fly back to Washington. Along with Silverstein and Kipling, he had come to Moscow three days earlier. Having never met before—and knowing that their positions within their adversarial agencies were roughly equivalent—he and Popov at first had been a bit reserved. That barrier melted away as they spent time together away from the Smirnov/Silverstein/Kipling triumvirate and realized that their views were more similar than different.

As the remaining four waved farewell to Lopez's taxi, Oleg Popov came to grips with the historical significance of what had just occurred. That the ceremony took place in the very auditorium where he and his comrades thought their lives had ended seemed appropriate. President Vladimir Putin himself presented the awards.

Popov felt a colossal measure of pride. Based partially on his endorsement, two foreigners had each received the nation's highest civilian award, Hero of the Russian Federation, to honor a heroic deed in the service of the state. That pride, sadly, stood in juxtaposition to the damning reality that Popov's niece had orchestrated the entire nuclear debacle.

That something positive involving international relations might take wing from this fiasco was the unseen benefit of a family shame that would haunt him to the grave. Should he or his wife have noticed the hatred brewing within the soul of their niece? If they should have, they hadn't.

As the principal players on the Russian side of the nuclear escapade, months earlier, Popov and Smirnov had briefed the entire SVR security staff on what had occurred. No stone had been left unturned by the determined inquisitors. In a related, rare instance of Russian/American cooperation, both sides agreed that it was in neither country's interest to release to the public the sordid details of what just one person, Viktoriya Popova, had been capable of doing on her own.

And so, after these briefings—including descriptions of the incredible feats involving Silverstein and Kipling—the personal accounts took on a life of their own, and it wasn't long before Russian government officials, Putin among them, decided that the two Americans should receive commendations. That those two had acted heroically to save Russia and the United States—and the world— from nuclear obliteration was undeniable.

Within the Russian intelligence agencies, the SVR spies wanted more. They demanded to know the intricate details. The testimony of Popov and Smirnov had made out the two Americans to be nothing short of superheroes. Fellow spies wanted to hear for themselves what had happened. And so, with Washington's approval, in conjunction with the award presentations, Silverstein and Kipling, together with Lopez, had flown secretly to Moscow to participate in a day's worth of closed-door briefings. Neither the American nor the Russian press was aware of the trip.

Sitting alongside Popov and Smirnov, Silverstein, Kipling, and Lopez answered every question imaginable: from Kipling's and Smirnov's death-defying escape from Viktoriya's exploding house; to Smirnov's close call with his concussion; to Kipling's cat-and-mouse cross-country chase tracking Viktoriya; to Silverstein's prior relationship with Popov, his participation in Project Athena, and his escape from a hospital after having been shot twice; to Kipling and Smirnov's assault on Viktoriya's compound; to Silverstein's lie detector interrogation of Viktoriya; to Silverstein's beyond heroic behavior, near death from loss of blood; to the roles played by Popov, Lopez, and the director of the American CIA; and finally, to Smirnov and Kipling's fight to the death with Viktoriya in the American state of West Virginia.

Although many within the SVR wanted a selfie with the two heroes, both the SVR and CIA had laid down the law: No one outside of their organizations would ever know these details.

Popov stared at the clear sky above, reminding himself how lucky he was to be alive. "Dmitri and I know Moscow as well as anyone. What is it you two would like to see or do? We should take advantage of this beautiful day." He had earlier invited Silverstein to a private dinner at his countryside dacha.

———————◆◆◆◆———————

After a whirlwind two days, compounded by jet lag, Victor Mark Silverstein needed some downtime. Yesterday's marathon session, albeit exhilarating and very special, had taken its toll. Although mostly recovered from his gunshot wounds, he'd readily admit that he wasn't yet 100%.

Popov's earlier offer that the two of them spend some private time together prompted Silverstein's suggestion. "Linda, Dmitri, would you two be offended if Oleg and I spent a little time alone? For my part, I'd like to reminisce a bit with my old friend."

In reality, Silverstein wanted this opportunity because he had a question for Popov. Spy to spy, he felt confident that Popov would tell him what he wanted to know.

———◆◆◆———

Linda Kipling was happy to hear Silverstein's recommendation. Any sightseeing would pale in comparison to what they had experienced. She and her boss had just received the highest civilian honor in the Russian Federation, for God's sake! So with everyone in agreement, Popov called for his official vehicle to take him and Silverstein back to Moscow proper.

Before departing, as Popov gave Kipling a made-in-Russia bear hug, he unexpectedly drew her close and whispered in her ear. Although her training had taught her to remain calm and to listen carefully, what he said caught her flabbergasted and flatfooted. He concluded by drawing back and creating a diversion, repeating aloud the suggestion he had made to her on the phone, back in San Francisco: "Just between you and me, you won't forget my offer, will you?"

Without missing a beat, Kipling regained her composure, kissed him smartly on the cheek, and nodded appreciatively. "Just between you and me, you can be sure that I won't."

As Popov and Silverstein drove away, Kipling and Smirnov stood respectfully, gazing in their direction. This visit would be a short one for her and Silverstein. They'd fly home at noon tomorrow and had agreed to meet at the airport.

"Do you mind us just sitting for a bit?" Kipling motioned toward a bench under a large shade tree. "If it's all the same to you, could we also spend a quiet day together, Dmitri? Yesterday took a lot out of me."

Smirnov voiced no objection. After a few moments, he was the first to speak. "You know, I need to thank you one more time, Linda. For all that you did for me."

"For what?"

"You *know* for what. For saving my life back in the explosion. No?"

"You're welcome. But you and I both know that if I'd let you die, Oleg would have been all over me. No doubt it would have caused an international incident," Kipling teased. "Besides, don't forget that you were completely out of it. You have no idea what I *did* or *didn't* do."

Smirnov laughed. "You are a very funny person, Linda. No? What you don't know is that over the past couple of months, most of what happened that day has come back to me. What you did was extraordinary: dragging me away from the fire; working with my boss over the telephone, with someone you had never met; arranging for a neurologist!"

"You forget that you repaid that debt many times over. I remember pretty clearly you taking out—with only one shot—the maniac who was determined to slice me in half."

"Oh, that?" Smirnov waved his hands in dismissal. "If you had counted my shots, you knew that I had saved one bullet, just in case. I knew you were out of ammunition, and I was ready. How is it, you say? I didn't have to be a rocket scientist to know that Viktoriya wasn't going to go down without a fight."

"One bullet? You nailed her in the right temple! Thank God you didn't miss."

"Highly unlikely," he responded matter-of-factly. "I probably never mentioned that I was number one in my class in pistol shooting."

As if spring-loaded, Kipling leaped from the bench and stomped her feet on the ground. "Damn you, Dmitri! Is there nothing in your spy class that you weren't number one in?"

Smirnov ignored the question. "I do have one thing I'd like to ask you, though."

"What's that?"

"Remember when we passed by that group of people as we walked away from the explosion? I was almost unconscious, and you were desperate that we not be caught."

"Yeah. Rings a bell."

"Did you really tell that couple that you were my sister and that our mother had dropped me on my head when I was a baby?"

Kipling cringed. "Yeah, I might have. In my defense, what would you have said? I certainly didn't want to explain that we were an American/Russian spy team intent on saving the planet from a nuclear catastrophe!"

———◆◆◆———

Victor Mark Silverstein was impressed. Because of his high-level position, Popov laid claim to a car and driver, 24/7. As they drove away, sitting together in the back seat, Popov insisted on being the gracious host, first by driving around Moscow pointing out various historical sites as well as new construction that, he insisted, rivaled anything in the West. "There's even talk of a Trump Tower," he bragged.

After stopping at a local restaurant for lunch, they hit the road again. "Unless you object, my wife, Natasha, has planned a special Russian dinner for you at our countryside dacha. It's only an hour's drive from our apartment. You'll stay the night. We'll pick Natasha up on the way." Popov lowered his voice. "Of course, she knows nothing. Our cover can be our meteorological connections."

"Sounds wonderful. But you didn't have to go to such trouble."

"Trouble? I've *never* met a Hero of the Russian Federation. I'd love to show you off to Natasha, although that's not possible, of course. It's just as bad for you, my friend. Linda's the only one you can talk to."

"I've thought about that. In a way, it's better. Heroes? From what I know, you were as much a hero as I was. Simple timing and a bit of luck allowed Linda and me to do what we did."

"You're too modest a man, my dear friend Victor. From what Dmitri told me, you lost so much blood that you were in shock and nearly dead by the time you explained Athena to Lopez."

"Dmitri may have exaggerated a bit."

———◆◆◆———

*Popov's In-Town Residence, Moscow*
*55° 44' 24"N Latitude, 37° 36' 18"E Longitude*
*Friday, October 5, 2018, 2:16 PM (MSK)*

The rest of the afternoon proceeded as Popov had proposed, with their first stop being Popov's town condominium, which he insisted Silverstein see. Guarded by an armed door attendant, the eighth-floor unit, opulent even by Western standards, overlooked the Moscow River and was located within a stretch of the city called the Golden Mile, exclusive and expensive. The waning sun provided a picture-perfect postcard of the river to the east.

From Silverstein's experience with wives of high-level career military officers, Popov's wife fit the mold. Perfect manners and dutiful support for her important husband were on constant display. Although she spoke a few words of English, Popov stood in as a translator.

———◆◆◆———

*Popov's Dacha, West of Moscow*
*55° 44' 37.1"N Latitude, 37° 15' 55.7"E Longitude*
*Friday, October 5, 2018, 3:55 PM (MSK)*

Before long, Silverstein and Popov were on the road to the dacha, Popov in the front seat and Silverstein and Mrs. Popov sharing the back. An hour later, they pulled up to the waterside dacha, little different from large lakeside homes back in the States. EXCEPT, this one had household staff who were waiting outside to greet this important official from the United States. With the setting sun nearly gone, everything visible appeared in shades of gray.

The Russian dinner was one for Silverstein to remember. A soup called Shshi, made from beef and white cabbage, provided the starter. The main course followed: stroganoff, a dish Silverstein admitted only to himself that he did not realize was Russian in origin. Thinly sliced beef smothered in a sauce heavy with mushrooms, sour cream, and "drop" noodles was exquisite. Dessert consisted of blini—not unlike his mother's blintzes—thinly sliced dough, fried, and filled with a blended mixture of ricotta cheese and dried apricots, the finished product topped with fresh apricots and flaked almonds. The Cabernet Sauvignon of Russian vintage was better than Silverstein had expected.

After a long dinner accompanied by polite general conversation, the evening began to peter out. Natasha went to bed, and the serving staff disappeared. What remained on the table was primo vodka, a Russian staple, which Popov drank like water. Silverstein tried to keep up but had to slow down as his head began to swim. He realized that if he was going to ask his question, he'd better do it soon.

"Oleg, I need to ask you something."

"Aha! My friend, Victor!" Popov laughed loudly. "I *knew* this was coming. I must tell you that President Putin himself told me to keep my mouth shut. He mentioned your name specifically. Since I want to keep my job, I must decline."

"How can you possibly know what I was going to ask?"

"*Victor*, you and I are seasoned professionals. Neither of us is a fool. I heard the testimony you gave about how your CIA director talked to me during those final moments. I guarantee that the answer I'd give you if I could would be the one you're looking for."

Popov continued. "Oh! By the way, my sincere condolences. Our file on Dr. McFadden implied that she was an exceptional leader."

◆

To Kipling's mind, the rest of her day with Smirnov reminded her of her late teens, back when the excitement of it all, infused with appropriate hormones, triggered a mental imbalance akin to that produced by narcotics. It came to a head after dinner at a good restaurant a short walk from Smirnov's apartment. As they sauntered back in the direction of his apartment Smirnov unexpectedly reached down for Kipling's hand. Kipling knew she would later swear that the electricity that flowed between them had nearly silenced her heart.

Ever the gentleman, Smirnov offered to call a taxi to take her back to the hotel.

"Don't you want to show me your apartment?" Kipling asked.

"By your standards, it's nothing special."

"Neither is mine! When I get back to Monterey and think of you, I'd like to picture where you live."

Smirnov seemed reluctant but agreed. His one-bedroom apartment, although modest, was fully furnished and neat. Its only window looked out on a parking lot.

Kipling was about ready to give up on any hope of a romantic adventure when Smirnov offered some encouragement. "You know, it's getting late, and I'd rather you not go back to the hotel on your own." He continued with his rationale. "We can pick up your things in the morning. I have an extra toothbrush, a pair of pajamas, and the sheets are clean. I don't mind sleeping on the couch."

Kipling walked up very close, eyes glistening with desire. Perhaps that was the inspiration that Smirnov needed because he then blurted it out. "Would you mind if I kiss you goodnight?"

"Dmitri! For God's sake! For someone who claims to be a super observant spy, you sure don't seem to pick up on some obvious clues. Do you remember back in West Virginia when I kissed you on the lips?"

"I remember that."

"Do you remember later that night when I grabbed onto you so hard, when we both thought we were going to die?"

"Of course."

"Didn't that tell you something? Yes, goddammit! You can kiss me goodnight! And not just on the forehead. As a trained spy working for the mighty Central Intelligence Agency of the United States of America, I hereby authorize you to imagine that I am playing the role of a honeypot. Do your country proud, Dmitri! Do your country proud!"

———◆◆◆———

The next morning, Silverstein arrived at the Moscow Domodedovo Airport, south of Moscow, courtesy of Popov's car. They had said their goodbyes back at the dacha. It being Saturday, Popov said he'd likely stay home for the day and wouldn't need transportation. Kipling arrived shortly after that. She and Smirnov had come by taxi and parted at the curb. It was evident to Silverstein that Kipling had feelings for Smirnov.

The trip back to the U.S. consisted of two flights: Moscow to Munich, and then nonstop to San Francisco. Conversation between the two was minimal. So much had happened in the recent past that nothing said could match the memories created by their experiences.

It was of some surprise to Silverstein, then, that before waiting in line for customs in San Francisco, Kipling pulled him to the side into a corner, away from the crowd. "I have something to tell you."

"Okaaay," he replied suspiciously.

Kipling reached for his head, pulled his face down to her level, cupped his ear in her hands, and whispered. "Popov told me that what I'm about to say is for your ears only, and I wasn't to tell you until we arrived on American soil. Repeat! *This is for your ears only*, and I quote:

"'During the final tense seconds, there were two high-level military officers who saw no reason to neutralize the missiles headed to America. President Putin calmly walked over and shot each one in the head. Point blank. He will never admit it, but President Vladimir Vladimirovich Putin saved the United States of America from total nuclear annihilation.'"

# GLOSSARY

AKA—another known alias

ARTCC— Air Route Traffic Control Centers; twenty-one geographic centers that control the movement of aircraft across the United States

ATCSCC—Air Traffic Control System Command Center (ATCSCC), the center to which all ARTCCs report

Audible—a term originating from the American game of football, a reference to a last-second decision when the quarterback changes the offensive play as the result of evolving defensive conditions

C-4—malleable plastic explosive

CIA—Central Intelligence Agency, a civilian foreign intelligence service of the United States of America

Collective—a hand control used by a helicopter pilot to regulate up and down movement

DEFCON—DEFense CONdition. From *Wikipedia*: The DEFCON system was developed by the Joint Chiefs of Staff and unified and specified combatant commands. It prescribes five graduated levels of readiness (or states of alert) for the U.S. military. It increases in severity from DEFCON 5 (least severe) to DEFCON 1 (most severe) to match varying military situations.

Directorate I—a division of the SVR specializing in Computer Science

Directorate X—a division of the SVR specializing in Science and Technology

DRA—Democratic Republic of Afghanistan (April 1978); Soviet-backed movement that promulgated atheism and various progressive ideas

FAA—Federal Aviation Administration

FBO—fixed base operator

FCDE—Federal Center for Data Examination, in Las Vegas, Nevada; commissioned one year after September 11, 2001

FC19D—CIA-developed (Mensa Group) wireless tracker

GOES—Geostationary Operational Environmental Satellite

GPS—Global Positioning System

Honeypot—in clandestine spy operations, an agent who uses sex as a means to blackmail or otherwise control an enemy agent or citizen

ICBM—InterContinental Ballistic Missile. From *Wikipedia*: An intercontinental ballistic missile is a guided ballistic missile with a minimum range of 5,500 kilometers (3400 miles), primarily designed for nuclear weapons delivery.

IFR—Instrument Flight Rules

JPSS—Joint Polar Satellite System

Lazarus—from the Biblical Gospel of John, the recipient of one of the miracles of Jesus, in which Jesus brings him back to life four days after he dies

LD500—CIA-developed lie detector; unique among its kind, it incorporates a device capable of monitoring blood flow within the brain

LOW—Launch On Warning, the concept that nuclear retaliation occurs as soon as the enemy's first strike missiles are launched

Main Centre for Missile Attack Warning—From *Wikipedia*: Russian early warning network against ballistic missile attack

Mensa Group—in-house CIA section whose mission is to develop advanced devices and techniques for field operations

MIRV—Multiple Independently Targetable Reentry Vehicle. From *Wikipedia*: An exoatmospheric ballistic missile payload containing several warheads, each capable of being aimed to hit a different target.

NCAR—National Center for Atmospheric Research, located in Boulder, Colorado

NCCS—Nuclear Command and Control System. From *Wikipedia*: The NCCS provides the President of the United States with the means to authorize the use of nuclear weapons in a crisis and to prevent unauthorized or accidental use.

NCDE—National Center for Data Examination, U.S. government data repository for both military and civilian use, located in Las Vegas, Nevada

NDMC—National Defense Management Center, Russia's military command center, built in 2013

NOAA—National Oceanic and Atmospheric Administration, under U.S. Department of Commerce

NPOESS—National Polar-orbiting Operational Environmental Satellite System

NRL Monterey—Marine Meteorology Division of the Washington DC-based Naval Research Laboratory, located in Monterey, California

NSA—National Security Agency, a national-level intelligence agency of the U.S. Department of Defense

NSOF—NOAA Satellite Operations Facility, located in Suitland, Maryland

PCR—Preemptive Computer Resolutions, software company; Erickson's employer

PD13—CIA-developed drone for use by field agents; follow-up to the pioneering and highly successful PD12

Project Athena—secret agreement by Presidents Barack Obama of the United States and Dmitry Medvedev of the Russian Federation, in 2010, to install a kill switch in all ICBM missiles, to counteract an accidental launch on either side

PSA—Platinum Star Aviation, the company from whom Erickson rents her plane

RPG—rocket-propelled grenade; shoulder-fired, anti-tank weapon

Ruger LCP II—lightweight, compact, automatic, .380 caliber with a six-round magazine, ideal for close-in action

Ruger GP100—357 Magnum revolver, heavier, ideal for outdoor duty and target practice

SCI—Sensitive Compartmented Information. From *Wikipedia*: Sensitive compartmented information (SCI) is a type of United

States classified information concerning or derived from sensitive intelligence sources, methods, or analytical processes.

SFO—San Francisco International Airport

SOP—Standard Operating Procedure

SORT— Strategic Offensive Reductions Treaty, also known as the Treaty of Moscow, follow-on to START

SP150—CIA-developed electroshock weapon hidden inside a pen

START—Strategic Arms Reduction Treaty

Stat—medical term meaning "at once" or "immediately"

SVR—foreign intelligence service of the Russian Federation

Sword of Damocles—in Greek mythology, Damocles was a courtier who, after making exaggerated claims about the happiness of Dionysius I, the ruler of Syracuse, found himself sitting beneath a sword held aloft by one single hair, to demonstrate to him how precarious that happiness could be

TCAS—Traffic Control Avoidance System, an automatic aircraft control system that alerts the pilot to an impending collision and tells him or her what actions to take

TRACON—Terminal Radar Approach CONtrol, an FAA facility that guides departing and approaching aircraft from/to airports outside 5 miles and 2500 feet using radar and radio

TSA—Transportation Security Administration, an agency beneath the U.S. Department of Homeland Security; created after the September 11 attacks to maintain security for America's traveling community

VFR—Visual Flight Rules

Printed in the United States
by Baker & Taylor Publisher Services